D0392541

FOLKLORN

FOLKLORN

Angela Mi Young Hur

This is a work of fiction. All of the characters, organizations, and events portrayed in this novel are either products of the author's imagination or are used fictitiously.

FOLKLORN

Edited by Sarah T. Guan

Erewhon Books
2 W. 29th Street, Suite 3S
New York, NY 10001
www.erewhonbooks.com

Erewhon books are available at special discounts when purchased in bulk for premiums and sales promotions as well as for fund-raising or educational use. Special editions or book excerpts can also be created to specification. For details, email specialmarkets@workman.com.

Library of Congress Control Number: 2020950734

ISBN 978-1-64566-016-3 (hardcover)
ISBN 978-1-64566-021-7 (ebook)

Cover design by Helen Crawford-White
Author photograph by Miki Anagrius
Watercolor feather line art by Shutterstock (Cat_arch_angel)

Printed in the United States of America

First US Edition: April 2021
10 9 8 7 6 5 4 3 2 1

for Henrik,
min älskling

Part I

The Icy Netherworlds: A Metaphysical Fairy Tale

Then

"Long ago—not in this land, but our own—the monks created giant bells so large they could only be rung by wooden beams made of tree trunks, suspended by rope and swung against the bronze like battering rams. These bells hung in temples in the mountains, looming over us all."

My mother always spoke Korean to me, but when telling her stories, she didn't sound like herself. No rich amber tones, weighted with regret—instead, her voice hollowed like a will-o'-the-wisp untethered. Still, I preferred this to her looped medley of sighs, lectures, and rebukes. And while story-telling, she wasn't so tense and bristled, expecting danger to burst through the door. Maybe not the commie or Yankee soldiers she feared in her childhood, but more likely a screaming husband raging over some slight or misstep. The back door wasn't secure either, not when thieves had broken in twice while we were sleeping and once while we were on a semi-triumphant emigrant's visit to Seoul. Tragedy could also intrude through the phone. Maybe my father had another accident at his auto body shop while wielding his blowtorch, or maybe he'd been assaulted again, not to survive this time. Or perhaps a relative we rarely heard from died across the Pacific, leaving my mother more alone than before.

But even in times of relative calm, my mother anticipated danger. With a childhood forged in war, her default mode was to always be on high alert. As an immigrant, she had to double down on her fight for survival. Thus, her anxiety had become a constant, vindicated and put to action in times of emergency. Never subsiding, even when the threat had been diminished.

My brother Chris said our parents were stuck in a war mentality. Hoarders and preppers, with cash and gold ready to smuggle across borders, and kitchen drawers stuffed with embossed napkins and ketchup packets from bounteous fast-food restaurants. It didn't help that most of my father's friends were also refugees like him from what was now North Korea. Some had even served together in the 502nd, a US military battalion. They were cooks, errand boys, and interpreters back then, working for the GIs. But in my childhood, these middle-aged men and their wives convened monthly as members of the 502 Club to dance and party, pooling their resources to help each other establish dry cleaners, liquor stores, and bodegas. So how could my parents accept the war was finally over when their immigrant village kept the specter of it alive in their drunken reminiscences, business dealings, and paranoia over hidden enemies—from both within and without—those foreign, and those resembling kin?

But when my mother spoke of ancient times—long before the squabbling between men and their maps and their new gods of ideology—when she revealed to me women of divine magic and elemental power, I could relax with my head in her lap, her fingers combing my hair. She wasn't really with me anyhow, wasn't even in her own body. She was warm and forgiving instead. With a stranger's voice she told stories, inevitable and unalterable, that had been retold by countless others before her. This kept her still long enough for me to simply be with her.

That is, until her stories became something else—half-remembered dreams and recovered memories, testimonies conveyed through her as vessel, maybe the voice of an ancestress demanding vengeance.

"These giant bells were rung as calls to prayer, as prayers in themselves. But one monk made a bell that would not sing. He asked the villagers for money to recast it. One woman joked she was so poor she had nothing to give except her daughter. 'Why not take her—I've got nothing else.' Later that night, the monk dreamt that the bell needed the voice of a little girl, so the next morning, he went back for the one who'd been offered.

"He melted the silent bell and tossed the girl into the vat of molten bronze, glowing like liquid fire. Screaming flesh bubbled and swirled with metal. The recast bell was struck again, and the sound released was so beautiful, everyone paused to hear it and weep. The echoes in the valley crested like waves through the villagers, their hearts shuddering with each passing vibration. Every time the bell was struck, it sang 'Eh-meh-leh, Eh-meh-leh.' And that was how the child called to her mother, to everyone's mother perhaps."

I asked why the girl was singing her own name because I thought "Emmileh" was "Emily" in a Korean accent. My mother sighed, her disappointment in me making her familiar once more. She explained that "Emmileh" meant "Mommy" in an old-fashioned dialect. Then she sang the bell's cry again, low and mournful, burrowing deep into my chest.

"Whenever I hear her sing," she said, "there's only sadness, but she must be holding back a terrible, fearsome anger."

"When did you hear the bell?"

"Long ago, before I came here, before I was married. On a school field trip, when I was just another teenage girl with a dead mother and dead sister, both lost to war. It's a national treasure, so nobody's allowed to strike it anymore. But I hear her voice—the girl in the bell—and sometimes I hear the others too." The softest smile caressed her lips. "But you'll never hear them—I've made sure of it."

1

Now

I've been awake for forty-fucking hours. Sure, it's easy when the sun lingers above for six months long, stretching time like taffy. Night won't come for another two. Before then, twilight will bruise the sky for several weeks. The sun will lap the horizon, circling until it drops, leaving those remaining with a half year of darkness. But *this* was never my intention, to jitter around all tweaked up and nerve-jangly, so painfully alert I can feel my brain crammed against my skull.

For most of my summer, I've adhered to my schedule—eating and sleeping the same time every twenty-four hours, regulating my circadian rhythms so I can carve days and nights out of the interminable brightness. Only the reckless and cocky forego their regimens, like the outdoorsy white boys from Colorado, who accessorize with carabiners and stay up seventy-two hours straight only to collapse into sun-drenched mania and get forcibly tranqued in sick bay.

But I'm on my third tour. I'm a postdoc physicist with a private berth inside the Amundsen-Scott South Pole Station. I know how to suppress giddiness while exploiting the everlight—like a fine dusting of cocaine in espresso, shot through the veins. With scientists committing to their shifts, the

Antarctic experiments can run round-the-clock, but we must remain disciplined to preserve our physical and mental health. I'm the one who lectures the rookies about this. But lately, I'm letting things slide—sneaking a second scotch nightcap, joyriding snowmobiles beyond our project perimeter.

Maybe I just want to soak up every minute of this geeky Shangri-la on planet Hoth before returning to Stockholm. Why else have I stayed awake the last two nights? Certainly not because of too-vivid dreams. Definitely not because I'll soon be leaving Jesper, my colleague and seasonal Swedish lover, who's staying behind all winter long.

So, with excess solar-charged energy to burn, I volunteer to help Jesper's team with their last task. They're on the graveyard shift, according to the New Zealand time zone we all follow. Strangers, bodies sharing the same space, but in seemingly different dimensions. Works for me though, Jesper crawling into my bed when I'm rested but drowsy, perfect for sex or whatever else before my allotted two-minute shower. After dinner, when I return, someone's picked my clothes off the floor, cleared my dirty dishes. The best phantom roommate ever.

But right now, I'm the interloper. Out of time and out of body—levitating with caffeine and boundless sunlight.

Neutrinos, one of the building blocks of all matter in the universe, are elemental particles, born from cataclysmic violence like supernova explosions, gamma ray bursts, supermassive black holes, and the Big Bang. Electrically neutral and practically massless, the neutrino doesn't deign to interact with much else. Trillions pass through the tips of our noses every second. From time's beginning, they've traveled the longest and farthest. Drifters across galaxies, survivors, they keep on keeping on, the lone wolves of particle physics.

Really, I'm not projecting.

But no one's ever *seen* these elusive neutrinos. They're called "ghost particles." Catchy, but dead wrong. Ghosts hang around; they loiter. Like uninvited guests, they crash on your couch and use up all your toilet paper. They stain you with their sorrows.

Jesper invites me to a team breakfast. I'd rather meet his students at the worksite, where I know my place and everyone else's in relation, so I lie, claiming I've scheduled a G-Chat with my brother. Truth is, I've postponed that as well. Chris will just bitch about Dad anyhow.

So, avoiding both the social meal and family catch-up, I head out onto the ice instead. Dressed in my US Antarctic Program "Extreme Cold Weather" gear—thermal underwear, fleece, snow pants, bright red parka with fur-lined hood—I push through the six-inch-thick door and step outside to greet the midnight sun—well, the 3:00 a.m. sun, to be precise.

No hills and valleys. No jagged mountains for visual relief or orientation. The land is so flat, stretching to the horizon in every direction, it induces vertigo. I fight the urge to tip over and cling to the surface. When the sky is clear, the expanse is crushing. We should be cowering, but there's nowhere to hide except in our meager temples to science.

A mile away from the station, we've got seventy-eight holes drilled into the ice, each hole two kilometers deep and embedded with detectors. A total of 5,000 detectors are spread out in a cubic kilometer of ice. The world's largest neutrino observatory, known as IceCube. I've been part of this international collaboration for the last five years, first at Princeton, now at Stockholm University. A quarter-billion-dollar endeavor involving hundreds of scientists from around the world and lifetimes of hours. The data we've collected already surpasses what humans know about neutrinos. When we're done, we'll have enough data to study for decades.

No wonder I get teary. When installation's complete, I'll no longer get to swagger around like the explorers of yore, commandeering teams to drill through the Antarctic. Instead, I'll be strapped to my laptop, peering across galaxies and back into time through algorithms, plots, and point source analyses. So here's to one last hurrah, standing on the edge of rabbit wormholes, before we close them up and bury our heads in cybersand instead.

Of course, I'll miss station life the most, surrounded by scientists, not having to justify or explain. Recently, my brother asked again, "You curing cancer, Elsa? Fixing climate change?"

"I told you, this is fundamental physics. There's no application, not yet. It's more about understanding our existence, unlocking the past, maybe even our future."

"With my tax dollars?"

"Since when have you paid taxes?

"Dad's money is my money. Should be anyhow."

I hitch a ride with a bearded engineer in his Sno-Cat, with its steel-belt tracks that can claw over the ice. We leave the station, built on hydraulic-jack columns that raise the building when the snowdrift gets too high. We pass the old retired station—a geodesic dome half-buried in snow like a postapocalyptic Epcot—now used for storage. But when we cut through "Summer Camp," where the grad students sleep, I can't help but shudder. Clustered here are authentic vintage Korean War–era Jamesways, half-cylinder army-green shelters that can house dozens with their radiators, cots, and canvas partitions.

My first two stints, I slept here, and hated that everyone had a pee bucket under the cot—easier than using the outhouses in the middle of sleep. But more pungent and pervasive were memories conjured by this historic period setting.

While others made jokes about M.A.S.H., I envisioned my father's old war stories—how he'd worked as a houseboy for the GIs and got bullied and beaten by them because the soldiers were bored, scared, and suspected him a thief; how he retaliated by pissing in the stew he cooked for them; how he actually *was* stealing their cigarettes and lighters to sell on the black market; how an old white man lieutenant colonel offered to adopt him and take him to Connecticut; how my father refused because he already had a rich father whom he was running from; how my mother interrupted his reveries with, "Connecticut's real fancy, where the rich white people live. You should've gone. Least then, I would've never married you."

Why didn't this merit a slap from my father, when he doled out punishment for much milder offenses and for no reason in particular? Probably because he was driving and she was seated in the back, though the only time he'd hit me was also from that position when my five-year-old self wouldn't stop wailing on an endless drive to the Grand Canyon. My brother always snorted when I brought this up, as it was the one time, nothing to crow about, nothing like what he and Mom got. Set apart in my own family, no wonder I'm used to being the outsider, why I prefer it.

"They're digging deeper this year," says the engineer. Takes me a moment to remember where and when I am. He points to snowplows in the distance, readying the site for the end-of-season festivities. "I only care about the music though. Preferably psych funk."

"Oh, the party," I say. "Never been."

"Never been to a party?"

"Never to that one. Don't enjoy water sports, especially when the water's warm."

He laughs. I wasn't trying to be funny.

Finally, we reach the tower—skeletal steel, three stories high. At the top, a giant reel unspools insulated hose, dangling its connected drill over the ice. Engineers blast boiling water through the hose at a hundred kilometers per hour to gouge two-kilometer-deep holes. Another tube siphons the melted ice back into the tank, with a holding capacity of 5,000 gallons, to be heated again and fed back through. Elegant and efficient.

But I'm struck by what's standing beside this tower—a person dressed like me, red against the snow. Her long, dark hair, escaped from her hood, wind-slashes across her face. Most unnerving—ice-frosted lashes and brows. How long has she been out here?

The engineer parks the Sno-Cat. "Looks like another one of yous is already here."

"What do you mean?" 'Cause she's also Asian?

"She's a beaker like you, right? Scientist? Or is that offensive, coming from a nailhead?"

"Right, a beaker like me."

She's still staring. Jesper's side piece? But he's not organized nor ambitious enough to juggle two women, let alone two Asian scientists, both likely smarter than he. But why am I even playing myself into this narrative when I know Jesper isn't like that? As if the assumptions of others—when seeing a white guy and Asian girl (or two!) together—can override what I know to be true. Am I letting others dictate my reality, or is racialized sexual jealousy a symptom of sleep deprivation?

No, this woman puts me on edge for other reasons than the usual when two of our kind exist in a white male setting, thus making us interchangeable or defined in relation to each other—who's the hot one, who's more Americanized, which one's the bitch? Beyond these banal socio-workplace considerations, the woman on the ice unsettles me because she's somehow familiar—intimately, but from a distance—as if from another lifetime.

The engineer lumbers off to the tower. Next to it is the deployment shelter, a refashioned metal shipping container. I was headed there, but instead I approach the woman. She's taller, with wide cheekbones and cinnamon eyes. Silk Road beauty? My brother once dreamily wondered if Kazakhstan was full of Phoebe Cates clones, the *Fast Times* Eurasian goddess of his youth. She blinks and snowflakes drift from her eyelashes. "Dr. Park," she says in an unplaceable accent. "I'm honored to be working with you."

So she's just an eager grad student. Not American. I'd feel more secure though if I knew which Asian pedigree—easier to handle when categorized. "Call me Elsa." I smile awkwardly because my gums sting from the chill. "How long you been out here?" I ask, squinting from the freeze and the brightness reflected off the ice all around.

She laughs, shedding more frost. "I am Mongolian. This feels like home."

I picture her with a bow and arrow on a horse, galloping across the steppes. Is this less racist of me to think this, since I'm not white?

"Your surname," she says, "you are originally from Korea? But you are Swedish now?"

"I'm doing a postdoc in Stockholm, but I'm from the US. My parents are from Korea."

"Ah, Korea was part of the Mongol Empire. A long time ago."

"Korea was a vassal state, but only for like eighty years. Who are you?"

"You may call me Sasha. Easier to pronounce. My English name and my professional name. Your paper on gamma rays and collapsing binary stars was excellent. I wonder—"

Jesper and his students arrive on snowmobiles. He looks like a snow-dusted faun, with Sailor Moon eyes of blue and a nut-brown beard. So sweet and fey, I can't take him seriously.

"Hey!" he shouts. "Been meaning to introduce you to each other!"

Undoubtedly, when the Vikings sailed off to pillage and plunder, his petite ancestors were the doe-eyed boys who stayed home, looking after the cattle and all the lonely women. (And thank you, Jesper, for dispelling the uncanny and rooting us safely in the mundane. Rivalry, whether sexual or academic, I could understand and deal with.)

"Is it true," I ask Sasha, "that the Mongols were afraid of the sea? I heard that during one invasion, Korea moved its entire royal court to an island off the coast. So the Mongols were, like, charging toward the ocean, but totally freaked out when the waves hit their toes. Makes sense, being a desert people and all."

Sasha looks bewildered and hurt. I wasn't trying to be mean.

Inside the deployment shelter, Jesper introduces me with: "Dr. Park will be leading installation while I monitor the computers . . ."

Sasha stands much too close. Bad enough we're all wearing the same "Big Red" parkas. There are three others, all white guys. I've only met one of them before—PhDick, who'd applied for the position I have now, who doesn't remember me from inter-prep-school science comps back in the day, and who wears a Deerfield lacrosse cap, even under his helmet. He's the only one who looks annoyed that I'm speaking, but I'm no longer the mute Asian scholarship kid who'd assumed invisibility, felt safer anonymous, sneaking to first place out of nowhere.

My fear of whites was near pathological then, but I wasn't just bussed in across city lines. Instead, at age fourteen, I'd been flown in cross-country to a New England boarding school. Before this, the only white people I'd seen in my neighborhood were teachers, cops, and my dad's business associates with whom he'd be ingratiating, tossing in an accented "bullshit!" with an impish grin to elicit their laughter and hearty shoulder pats. He might curse these same men in Korean if they crossed him, but I always cringed. Academia requires performance too, but since the arena is still mostly white, streaked with gold, the politics are more gendered.

My women physicist friends, for example, keep their voices calm and low during discussions lest they come across shrill, even if the men scream at the whiteboard. My voice is already husky and loud, but since only 20 percent of physics PhDs are women, I claim aural space for five. So for PhDick's benefit, when he tries to talk over me, I become a goddamn Greek chorus.

After sufficiently asserting dominance, I lead the students in prepping the Digital Optical Modules—DOMs, for short. Each DOM, the size and shape of a fortune-teller's crystal ball, contains a computer along with a photomultiplier tube and a recalibration LED flasher. Strong enough to withstand decades in the ice, sensitive enough to record subatomic interactions, time-stamped to the nanosecond. Into each of the previous holes, we've installed sixty DOMs, connected by a cable like a strand of giant pearls.

Meanwhile, the engineers drill into the ice. When they finish, they drive the 5,000-gallon water tank back to the camp for the party. That means go-time for us. We've got sixty DOMs to secure to the cable and lower one by one before the water freezes them in place.

But despite the time crunch, the costly consequences if we fail, and the ocean of coffee surging through my body, my tension melts away because I'm back in my element. *This* is why I sought refuge on the ice instead of lying helplessly awake in my berth. Achievement redeems me; excellence makes me whole. Moreover, the tactility and hardware manipulation of this specific work grounds me. It's why I became an experimental physicist instead of a theorist.

The general public doesn't even know that *we* do the heavy lifting in physics. They prefer reading about that other kind—those dreamers and speculators who scribble and spin implications that translate well to best-selling books, their lives transmuted on-screen as mad geniuses chatting with their hallucinations. But theorists don't have to consider *if* and *how* their theories are testable. We the experimentalists must understand the theory *and* create the experiment to test it. We do the real work—disproving theories to narrow uncertainty, ruling out possibilities, becoming a little less ignorant. We can never prove anything is true; we can only prove something is not true—for now at least. We are the real knowledge seekers, even if we come across as naysayers. Or, as Ernest Rutherford put it, "They play games with their symbols, but we turn out the real facts of Nature."

Besides, consider how fucking wondrous it is to stand at the edge of a hole wide enough to fall through, almost reaching bedrock! A tunnel of ice in jagged, luminous blue. Hypnotic and thrilling—the temptation of diving, becoming both footnote and fossil, preserved until the end.

However, for the first time in all my Antarctic summers, it occurs to me that I might be staring into the grooved gullet of an ancient frozen beast. This state of mind is distressing, as I haven't been whimsical since puberty. Then it happens again as I stare dumbly into the ice, wondering if some thawed creature has clawed its way out, leaving angry gashes in its wake.

Right now, I'm supposed to be sleeping. Maybe part of my brain is dreaming, wires crossing. Rather not join in on the conversation around me, but I welcome its insipid distraction.

"The NSF *does* know about the party," says PhDick. "No biggie. Lot worse been done round here. Who knows what the Chinese or Russians are up to at *their* stations?" He glances at Sasha and me. "No offense—you two are different. Like one of us."

I'd gotten this comment before by much less smarmy people, friends and strangers, who really did think they were being complimentary by making this distinction on my behalf, as if I could almost belong to them by virtue of not really belonging elsewhere.

"Under the Antarctic Treaty," says Florian the Bavarian, "anyone may visit and inspect the other stations. No colonies or national jurisdictions here."

"This station and McMurdo are American outposts," replies PhDick. "This thing that we're building, all our salaries—half-funded by American taxes."

"Typisch," mutters Florian. German, I'm guessing, meaning "typical," similar to its Swedish counterpart. I've gotten it a few times in Stockholm, once for laughing too loudly in a hipster bar. At least, the "typiskt" insult was for me being an obnoxious American, not for being Asian. Progressive in its own way.

"Even if the party is not officially sanctioned," says Sasha, quiet till now, "I would be grateful for the opportunity to say goodbye to friends before beginning work as a winter-over." Her gaze is focused on the task I've given her, far from me but close to Jesper, who's fixedly staring at his computer screen.

I try not to imagine things, but the facts are these: Jesper is also wintering over for the first time, along with Sasha and forty-eight others. They'll be stranded here, no planes coming and going, for almost eight months. No one else is surprised about Sasha. Jesper hadn't mentioned it, or maybe I wasn't paying attention until now.

In the darkness, could Jesper tell the difference between Sasha and me? Would she be the simulacrum or was I the seasonal lover instead? But then my jealousy shifts, and I envy that Jesper will spend the winter with her. Inexplicably, I feel like the black-haired woman on the ice belongs to me—or she would, if I'd only remember how we knew each other once, long ago.

"Like a colony in exile," Nils from Mankato says dreamily, "on a far-flung planet."

"Like a fucked up behavioral experiment. People go batshit crazy," says PhDick. "They all screw each other and become bi and shit, 'cause of the gender ratio."

"Twenty more DOMs to go," I say. "It'll be faster if we all shut up." I focus on the task at hand. I could've wintered over too and chose not to. My entire academic career was already built on exiling myself in increasingly white, frigid spaces—before the Antarctic was Sweden. Anyhow, the winter-over application was unnecessarily fussy, with far too many psych tests.

Ten hours later, we finish deployment in record time, and I'm finally about to crash.

But then Jesper says, "What the fök?" and stares at his screen in horror.

I wince. Who is this man I've been sleeping with who can't spit out a proper "fuck"? No matter how many TGIF sitcoms he'd grown up with, how much Seattle grunge he'd memorized, this Swede couldn't curse like an American. Mimicked, performed, making everything around us slightly off, as if we're a few degrees tilted from reality.

The others gather behind Jesper's computer. DOM 1, the topmost detector, is registering an unusually large energy reading. The visualizer conveys this as bright flashing bursts on-screen. But this is impossible, as the DOMs haven't been activated yet. Jesper enters a blur of keystrokes to terminate a glitching detector that the computer claims isn't even alive. I take a stab at it, but Jesper snaps, "I already did that." His curtness is out of character and further disorients me. He tries something else, muttering a Swedish curse with a native's authority. Roughly translated: "Devil in hell's damned shit." Here among the international scientists, I've never heard Jesper speak Swedish, not even to other Swedes. Yet somehow, I'm the one who feels foreign now.

Then it dawns on me, a beat too slow—this rogue DOM gone berserker is compromising the data as the surrounding detectors record its manic stutter. A truly massive fuckup all on my watch and possibly my fault. I can't show anybody I'm freaking out. Need to fix this instead. So I lunge for the covering over the hole and manage to shove it partly aside. The top DOM is a kilometer below. Even with my headlamp, I can't see anything. Maybe if I get closer though, lowered headfirst by rope—it's just a half mile.

"Recalibration flasher," says Jesper, explaining to the others. "Must be going off on its own, even with a dead connection. Like a zombie. Or a DOMbie." He chuckles, then groans, burying his face in his hands.

"My first time at the Pole ends in failure," says Nils.

"Mechanical failure, not human," says Florian.

"Actually, we could check the logs," says PhDick. "Who tested DOM 1?"

"Me," I answer, peering into the hole, tempted to dive in to hide from censure.

"Who was your secondary?"

"I don't need a secondary." I turn around, not expecting so many eyes. Jesper directs their attention to his screen instead. No more manic bursts. DOM 1 is finally activated and responsive, so Jesper kills its connection to the power feed and the rest of the working DOMs. He releases a slow, misty breath of relief. I'd forgotten how cold it was because I'm hot and itchy all over.

"The best outcome we could hope for. Deployment glitch," he says. "That's what I'll report. I'll disconnect, and we'll monitor. Kill one and save the rest. Recalibrate data as necessary."

Simple and swift, crisis averted. Yet I can't let it go.

I'm still apart from the others, staring into the tunneling depths, disappointed there's no need to risk life to investigate further. Then a low-pitched ringing emerges.

"Now what the fuck is that?" I cry out. A wild laugh erupts from my throat. "Is that a gong? A fucking gong in the ice?" Exhausted and unmoored by the absurdity, I throw my hands up and laugh, mystified and even delighted with the lunacy of it all. But nobody's laughing with me. Of course not—because I'm the only one who hears the sound. Deeper now, more resonant and somber, like a massive bell echoing down below.

Everyone's still staring at me. They're stunned, bewildered, disgusted. Jesper's face scares me the most—because he doesn't recognize me.

The bell is louder now, clarifying into three notes, a familiar musical phrase.

"Tinnitus," I whisper. "I get tinnitus when I'm stressed." Florian nods sympathetically. "Haven't been sleeping well lately," I add. Sasha remains unconvinced.

Jesper approaches. "Maybe you should—I'll take you, let me radio for replacement—"

"That'll take too long. I'll walk." I didn't trust myself on a snowmobile either.

Sasha says, "I can take you, Dr. Park."

I want to be alone, but I've been rude to her all day, so I agree.

"I'll come as soon as I'm done here," says Jesper, hugging me.

I pull away. "I don't need a babysitter. Just go to the party."

Jesper gives Sasha a look I can't interpret, so I imagine terrible things.

The ghost particle passes through nearly everything, but in extremely rare occasions, it collides with another particle and is deflected or transformed. The neutrino remains invisible, but the interaction emits a lovely blue streak of light, the Cherenkov radiation. Water provides an ideal medium for detecting these energy readings, and the Antarctic ice is the world's cleanest H_2O.

With this blue light, we can trace back to the neutrino's turning point and deduce its trajectory. Since neutrinos emerge from violent cosmic phenomena to drift across space, we can trace their origins—their point sources—and thereby map the universe. At least, the part within our observable sphere. After all, the universe is expanding more quickly than expected—so many galaxies speeding apart, whose light will never reach us. Neutrinos redefine what is within our reach, but we still can't know what lies beyond, as worlds spin faster and farther apart.

Once outside, no more ringing. I puff a cloud that crystallizes imperceptibly. So my lie was truth—temporary tinnitus caused by stress and sleep-dep along with postponed synesthesia, an auditory accompaniment to the throbbing on-screen light.

After all, flashing lights cause migraines in some, epileptic seizures for my brother.

"Look," I tell Sasha, pointing to the sky. On either side of the ever-hovering sun, the sun dogs shine. They cast halo arcs and flash like companion stars, split apart, yearning to be one again. Also known as "mock suns," they were considered omens back in the day. But there's nothing to fear because I know how these phantom suns are created.

Diamond dust—hexagonal, plate-shaped ice crystals—floats in the air. The crystals refract light and create this atmospheric phenomenon called parhelia. No need for embellishment, simply glorious. And that's what's truly beautiful, how we can elucidate physical reality, strip away its symbols and foretelling. Mystery is for the suckers of the world, its romantics and martyrs. My toes tingle in my boots. My breath frosts my lips. Sasha smiles, tilting her lovely face to the sun. These things are real.

While Sasha drives the snowmobile, I close my eyes and lean against this beautiful Mongol, who is not some mysterious figure from a forgotten past, but only a woman whose curved back is tucked underneath my body, our red parkas blurring into one. We gallop over the snowy steppes. Soon, we're flying over the frozen sea. But before I can give myself over and let her take us back to her world, we come to a sudden stop and I open my eyes to the void.

Sudden winds, shrouding us in snow. We're caught in a whiteout, blinded. They warned us about this in survival boot camp. If we wander, we can become disoriented and invisible. We're supposed to stay put, radio for help.

"Station," I mumble. "Go straight."

"We will wait here." She removes the keys, clenching them in her fist.

I slide off and trudge into the white. She tries to grab me, yelling in what I assume is Mongolian.

"You're not my khan anymore!" I shout back. "And it was only eighty fucking years!"

No reason to fear, just keep moving—the sea is solid and subdued. Sasha yells my name. I turn to shut her up, but can't see her anymore. Can't say anything either. I only hear that ringing bell again, at first smothered and distant, now clearer and closer.

Like a fissuring crack, I recall: At the South Pole, the ice moves 2.7 centimeters a day, ten meters per year, at different speeds, in different directions. In about 140,000 years, the ice I'm standing on will crawl to the edges of the continent, crumble and dive into the Weddell Sea to follow the currents, to feed into other oceans and embrace other shores. The tips of my ears and nose are numb, about to break off too. Along the Antarctic coastline—giant chunks of ice the size of small countries shuddering off the edges to crash into the ravenous sea.

Sasha shoves her face close, confronting me with my warped, fun house reflection in her mirrored goggles. She pulls down her mask. I stare at her pink tongue, flashing against so much white. She must be yelling, but I can't hear her. Don't know how much time passes, but she holds on to me throughout.

The winds finally cease, the whiteout clears, and the ringing fades. I hear her say my name and allow her to lead me back to the snowmobile, only a few steps away.

But when we reach the station, she's no longer my protector or even a colleague, only a witness to behavior I'd rather forget, a memory I'm already suppressing. Too bad I couldn't leave her in the whiteout too.

"Look, Jesper and I aren't serious," I say. "If you want to be my replacement, it's to be expected—upgrade with the younger, more culturally authentic model."

Her face hardens. I bite my tongue until it hurts. Sasha drives away at full speed.

I stand alone at the station entrance, at the bottom of the steps. Penitent, I want my body to freeze. But the doors open and Germans dressed in Hawaiian shirts heave their beer kegs down the stairs. A trio of Japanese women, wearing bikinis under open parkas, carry pitchers of bioluminescent Midori-green. Other revelers stumble out, gripping the necks of champagne bottles.

For the last few years, the austral season has ended with a hot tub party using the last of the water melted from the ice. It's not included in the reports, and the NSF and US military look the other way. Earlier today, engineers dug out of the snow a depression the size of a suburban pool, though only chest-deep, and lined it with heavy-duty tarp. The tank pumps in the water, keeping it a toasty 105 degrees Fahrenheit. Some people compete in building the best ice slide.

I've never joined before, but right now I need noise to drown out the false signal ringing in my ears. So I let the human tide take me. Up ahead, under the Antarctic sun, steam rises from a simmering lake in the icy desert.

But what if people ask how things went? I stop and the crowd moves on, leaving me exposed. A couple of naked Norwegians in Viking helmets charge toward me, then hoist me on their shoulders like a queen. Whooping, they fly me past everyone and deposit me on deck. Then, tucking their ice-chapped buttocks into cannonball formation, they jump into the water.

A few women have styled fleece blankets into sarongs. I shed everything except for my electric-blue thermal underwear. But I'm the only one without a helmet. Most are wearing the usual construction hard hats, but there're also baseball and football helmets, even a fireman's topper. I'd trashed all the emails but had overheard: as the party was technically near a drill site, everyone needed to dress for safety, but the definition had been expanded this year. Lacking festive headgear, I feel more vulnerable than I usually do at parties.

My Welsh friend Kate approaches, saucy in a constable's hat and a strappy black swimsuit. "You've finally joined us!" she says. "But where's your—?" She pats the top of my head.

I say I forgot, but really, I want to ask for a hug. I want Kate to reassure me that mistakes will be forgiven, that I'm still a good scientist and deserve to be here even if I don't play well with others, that I won't be sent back whence I came.

"No worries, luv," she says. "Plenty by the bar."

A specialist in primordial gravitational waves, Kate is one of the few to return for a winter-over. She tried to recruit Jesper and me, pitching it as a productive sabbatical from the world—three articles published and the most ripped she's ever been. This year, she'll also write a novel about a lusty time-traveling Rhiannon and the Welsh national rugby team.

"How about that one?" She gestures toward a samurai helmet.

"You know I'm not Japanese, right?"

"'Course not. And never call me English."

I point to an antique diving helmet between the rum and pineapple juice.

Kate knocks on the brass. "Weighs a ton, I bet."

"Ever heard of a helmet party?" I ask. "It's American English."

"I've recently been enlightened."

"Europeans don't really circumcise, I've noticed. Fits anyhow. Science parties are always sausage-fests."

"Yes, dear. Why don't we give this one a try?" Kate lowers the helmet onto my shoulders. I stagger under the weight. She opens the hinged window over my face and asks, "How is it?"

"Cozy!" I grin and shut myself in again. Through the ancient glass, Kate appears underwater. I feel safe, like a child in a closet or tucked in ice. Behind her, Jesper wavers through the crowd, searching. Must've followed me. How long was I trapped in the whiteout? Balancing the heavy dome on my head, I waddle toward the pool.

Around me, nailheads and beakers party together—how lovely. Nonscientists are always surprised by how much we can drink, but they don't know what the botanists grow in the station's hydroponic garden, what the chemists cook in their labs.

Clambering off the deck's edge, I ease my legs into the pool. Hot water seeps through my long underwear, pulling me into the steam. Inside my helmet, my hair frizzes and may suffocate me before anything else. This is the ice we melted, so I'm soaking in my failure—dead DOM, ringing bell.

Two women in matching red polka-dot halter tops and spiked pickelhaubes, like Prussian army pin-up girls, bounce a volleyball back and forth.

I push through water that was once on the surface, then buried incrementally over millennia. Time-traveling by wading pool? More like time-swirling. But we can never unswirl it because time's arrow is irreversible. I stick out my tongue—what does yesteryear taste like?

Ice, water, steam—solid, liquid, vapor. The glacial edges calve into the ocean, flow to warmer seas, evaporate, and fall again from the clouds. Along the coastline, the humid air blows snow into the center to become ice once more. All the water molecules cycle through. Nothing is fresh, not the seas we cross to escape from one life to another. Most of Earth and its people are made of water, so some of me now, as I sweat and exhale, is shape-shifting.

I see Sasha in the pool, moving deeper into the mist. I want to apologize for being such a shit. She's wearing a white slip dress. Looks familiar. Her long hair is braided down her back.

I open my helmet's window, but the steam's too thick. No worries, time will take care of this, along with the Second Law of Thermodynamics—the pool will lose its heat, then its people. Splash it up for now, all you beautiful nerds, before the universe comes to its chilling end.

A few waves away, a couple of redheads are making out, one guy's legs wrapped around the other guy's hips. Together, a ginger-topped octopus.

Jesper's calling my name. From his tone, I know he can't see me.

A centurion's head slices through the fog, then disappears. Wet-slick faces howl. Drunken ghosts, they're all laughing at me. High-pitched sobbing to my left. A woman holds her untied bikini top to her chest, strings dangling. Her wet hair straggles in blond clumps over her shoulders. She's crying and screaming, but I can't see who she's yelling at.

"Why's she crying?" I ask no one.

"She's crying 'cause she's lost her head." It's Percy, astrochemist from the Bronx, with icicle-tipped locs. He knocks his own football helmet, sprouting antlers. "Jesper's looking for you. He's real worried."

"Then why didn't he come after me himself?" I intended to sound defiant, but my voice breaks. Would've been less disturbing if people were in full costume, but these slight disfigurements unsettle because I can still see what's familiar lurking underneath.

There's Sasha again at the far end. Then I realize, more in wonder than confusion, it's not Sasha after all. I've been following someone else all this time, or maybe she's transformed before my very eyes. The elegant shape of her head with its long braid down her back, the thick rope of it hanging between delicate shoulder blades—something in me unbuckles.

At the pool's edge, she rises from the water. Knotted at the end of her braid—a red ribbon unfurls. Turning head over shoulder, she meets my gaze and smiles bittersweet. Her pale dress pulses with breath. Like a jellyfish, the hem flares and subsides, slow and rhythmic. Her beauty, sadness, and recognition of me strike to the core. The bell is inside me, and what starts as a trembling judders throughout my body to threaten tsunami waves, crashing over us all.

Then the ringing clarifies into three notes, three syllables—*eh-meh-leh.* This is what she mouths, looking at me. *Eh-meh-leh.*

But it's not her voice I hear. Someone else, not heard in sixteen years—my mother.

Trailing red ribbons that seem longer than before, she climbs out of the water and onto the ice. The Antarctic is a desert, so dry the wind blows the snow easily, sculpting the terrain into ripples and dunes. The air is still now, leaving dips and swells and cresting waves. She walks on top of this illusory tempest sea. Her dress is frozen in its billowing shape, but her red ribbons flutter, reaching for me. The rest of her fades into the white.

2

When I was nine, I had a friend nobody else could see.

Only once did I describe her to my brother: "She looks like a girl from those books Mom buys me in Koreatown, with English on one page and Korean on the other. This girl has a braid tied with red ribbon like the ones in the pictures, but she only wears her underdress, not a hanbok. Or maybe she crawled out of the TV from one of the Korean history dramas Dad likes to watch—but she left her silk dresses behind."

Chris called my friend imaginary, saying, "Aren't you a little too old for that?"

I didn't mention her to him again. I knew my friend wasn't real, but she was still somehow true. When the same old Korean voices screamed through the wall at night, she'd appear in my bed beside me, her finger to her lips. When all I saw were her eyes staring into mine, I couldn't hear the shouting or sobbing on the other side.

She was also my secret, which made her something that could easily disappear—like the girl across the street who had to suddenly move back to Korea because her parents "didn't have the right papers." Or as my dad said, "Was too stupid or too poor to buy the right ones." Or my neighbor Ricky who moved back to Mexico City because his dad couldn't be a doctor here.

My secret friend came and went as she pleased, but she was there when I needed her, so I didn't ask many questions. If you poke at something too much, it'll fall apart or get taken away by men in uniforms, who aren't even cops but act like they're so much more.

Not that anyone could grab my friend to drag her away, because even I couldn't touch her. And the only part of her that touched me was the ribbon. No bow, just a square knot and two long strips of red, how Korean girls wore their hair in olden times.

My mom often complained about my own wild, bushy hair, which no elastic could subdue. Having an aging beauty for a mother, especially one who still admired herself in photos and mirrors, was plenty annoying since I resembled my father more. Why bother trying to emulate her, when even my hair defied her ladylike expectations? That's why I both envied and pitied my friend's glossy-smooth hair—so lovely and compliant, with nary a single strand escaping its thick black rope, braided tight and rigid down her back.

One day, my friend and I argued about where to play. I wanted to stay in, she wanted to go out. But bad things happened to me out there, worse than what happened inside. There was the girl who spat on my face as she pedaled past, not bothering to speed away. The teenage boys who circled around me on the sidewalk and the man flashing his hairy, jiggly belly. All this on my block, in a town outside LA, and the only suitable weapon I had was a plastic shoehorn.

I worried she was getting bored of me, and that's why she wanted to leave. She looked like a kid, but also seemed older than my mom, who also had the same expression, like she wanted to "bust out of here," as my brother said. Mom grew up motherless because of the war, so she'd feel guilty leaving us behind, but I could still see the thought cross her face from time to time.

My father joked about it a lot too—her running away. Whenever I asked where she was, instead of telling me she went to the market or the bank, he'd claim she'd run back to Korea and I'd follow up with, "Oh, to be with her boyfriend?" It was our routine, similar to: "Where did I come from, Dad?" Then he'd say, "Oh, we found you left under a bridge," with the Korean words suggesting I'd been scavenged from trash.

Eventually, when talking to other Korean Americans, I discovered this was a common family joke. Gallows humor, my brother explained, in response to the war, how so many children were lost and orphaned. Also, Chris added, Koreans are assholes, especially to their own kids.

The joke hits too close to home though because our aunt *was* lost for a while during the mass exodus from North to South. This, too, Dad laughed about, how after three years missing, his kid sister had been found panhandling along the Han River with some other brats, who'd all been taken in by an old couple who made them beg on the streets in exchange for shelter.

This aunt later immigrated to New Jersey, opening a fancy store selling luxury handbags. Her daughter became a cheerleader, her son a quarterback. She even had them call her by her first name. "Does she think that'll make her white?" Chris wondered. She didn't teach her kids Korean, and my cousins still don't know their mom was a temporary war orphan. Nobody would've thought this stylish, witty woman had once been a street urchin, but Dad said that her cunning and stubborn will to survive are what got her through then, and what made her now into such a rich bitch in Jersey.

Another family classic, especially lethal from Mom: "Why are you crying? Did *your* mother die? What do you have to cry about then? Go blubber outside." Actually, for that one, I never had a comeback, so I wailed in the backyard, snotting against the sliding glass doors.

Years later, before I finally busted myself out to the other side of the country, Chris told me that Mom *did* almost run away before I was born. Dad had always been a jerk, more so then because he'd gone into debt building a business. He was younger, angrier, and stronger, with more to prove as a new immigrant. So when my brother was eight and Mom was six months pregnant—but not with me—she'd gone alone to Korea. Instead of returning after two weeks as planned though, she came back a few months later—without a baby.

"Stillborn," Chris said. "That's why Mom was so sick for a long while. That's why Dad was so pissed at her, never forgave her. That's why he was so happy when you were born, and you got the best of everything—then and now."

So maybe that's why Dad joked so much about Mom running away. The momentary panic I felt the first dozen times he told me this probably mirrored what he felt too when he couldn't easily reach her and pin her down. And when he made some crack about finding me under a bridge—was it about some other lost girl in his past or even the baby he didn't get a chance to say goodbye to, left behind in the country he'd abandoned?

And with all these constant jokes about runaway moms and missing children, no wonder I feared losing my red-ribboned friend as well. She couldn't hop on a plane like Mom did, but I worried she'd leave me in other ways, or that I'd finally outgrow her as Chris predicted, promised, threatened. No wonder I usually let her tell me what to do. But the day we'd been fighting about whether to play inside or venture out, I didn't back down. She even suggested we go to the park, a few dangerous blocks away. I stuck to my guns, demanding we stay put.

In response, she stared moodily at the grandfather clock my dad had imported from Korea. For a long while, she stood looking up at its brass face. I remember the pendulum swinging and me wishing her braid would echo—tick tock, tick tock. Beside the floor-to-ceiling clock was the large-screen TV that folded in and out of a cabinet like a Transformer. Behind this, a black grand piano that only I played. Barely enough space for two girls, and one of us wasn't even entirely real. Was this why she wanted out?

Our house was crammed with oversized stuff because the other Koreans had moved on to big houses in white neighborhoods, up in the hills or near the ocean, and my dad had to compensate somehow. He could've left too, but refused because he wanted to stay close to his auto body shop. As a concession, right before I was born—his first child in America—he bought a silver Cadillac and moved his family out of an apartment into a three-bedroom bungalow on the other side of the block. When the neighborhood got rougher, with drug deals and drive-bys and burglaries, he poured his money into expanding the shop, installing black gates around it. The family house got black bars too—decorative wrought iron over the windows.

I was just a baby when the other Koreans left, but I liked imagining how my brother had so many friends in the neighborhood, kids who looked like him who wouldn't tell him to "Go back to China!" or yell out "Chinito" or "gook" as he walked by. Though really, what a silly-sounding word—gook—but also surprisingly chilling when used by old white men. I pictured how Mom must've been less alone, how the other Korean wives were probably savvier at defusing the tempers of Korean husbands, especially if not their own. Or who could, at least, provide a hiding place until it was safe to emerge.

All this to say that I had a lonelier childhood than my brother and wondered how he simply biked around with friends or walked to someone's apartment after school when I was so scared to leave the house, which never grew bigger but shrunk instead. With my father's giant TV and the grand piano threatening me with my mother's Asian ambitions, along with all the shouting, slaps, and kicks that were also too big to contain—I felt like Alice in Wonderland—arms stuck through the windows, feet out the door, neck squeezed by a twisting staircase.

Finally, my friend turned away from the looming grandfather clock. Sighing, as if she'd given up, she said, "How about we find someplace new, right inside this house. You can hide there anytime. Even when I'm not here, it'll still be our secret place."

In the hallway, we held my mother's gold-framed mirror between us like a tray. We looked down into the glass where our feet should be and saw the ceiling instead. The floor of the other house in the other world, I realized. We shuffled down the smooth blank corridor that led to an open moon-field, gritty and pebbly. A gold fountain in the middle, with twist-tipped light bulbs screwed into the ground. Diamonds, strung along gold chains, looped over the lights. If I snuck through the mirror into this other world, would my friend be forced to live in mine?

But before I could ask, a car tore up the driveway. My father shouted for my mom. Usually, when I heard him clomping toward the door, I'd whisper, "Monster's back!" then run towards the towel cabinet or duck under the piano. Most often, I hid in my mother's closet behind the sliding mirrored doors. But this time, my father was the one who sounded frightened. What could the Monster be scared of?

Another car screeched up the driveway. A woman, not my mother, yelled out in perfect English: "Stop right there!"

Still gripping my mirror and looking through its glass, I swung the front door open. But before I could fall through the blue sky and into cotton-candy clouds, the woman demanded, "Is he your daddy?"

My father stood at the top of the driveway. Behind him, a pretty Black policewoman, hair smoothed into a neat bun and a gun in her hands. I blinked; the gun disappeared. She was only pointing her finger. I dropped the mirror; it broke into pieces. I held my hand out to my side. My friend put hers next to mine, and the red ribbon bound us together.

Dad barked at me to phone Mom at the shop. The policewoman told him to shut up.

"I couldn't see!" he cried in Korean. "Didn't hit anyone. She came after me anyway."

"Is he your daddy or ain't he? Can you speak English?"

My father's sweat-stained undershirt was tucked into his work pants, bunched tight around his middle with a cracked leather belt. The thin cotton shirt hung loose on his skinny body. I didn't want to claim him as mine.

"You sure look like him anyhow."

People were always saying this, Korean and not, and I hated it. I sucked in my bottom lip, making it less like his. His tanned-brown face was specked with burnt skin because he never used masks or goggles. I stepped back onto the broken mirror by accident. I cried out, my father moved toward me, the woman told him to stop. Across the street, people hooted and howled. Someone shouted, "Get that dirty chink's ass!"

"Sir, stay put like I told you." The policewoman nodded at me. "Honey, lemme see. Oh that's nothing, only a scratch, baby. Now you ask your daddy for me—"

"Explain to her I could not see! The sun was in my eyes. Tell her I am a US citizen."

"Quit that. I don't speak no Chinese, Japanese, or whatever." Shaking her head, she said, "Ask your daddy why he hit and run. That ain't right. Running away from me ain't right either."

I could've told her we didn't speak Chinese or Japanese either, but what I really wanted to say was that my father studied English in university in Korea, but the words clumped in his mouth, and he sounded angry when he was trying to be understood. He worked all day and night, beating his tools against metal, and he spoke his new language the same way. But I couldn't explain all this, so I only said, "I should call my mom."

On the phone, my mother told me to explain how my father was "strange in the head." "Tell her how his skull was cracked last year," she said, "by a Black man stealing from him. Tell her he was beaten senseless, left to die, that he's been different ever since."

I came back to the doorway and saw the policewoman patting my father's body. I was worried for her. Surely he'd lash back, as he did with strangers, customers, friends. Afterward, he'd have enough anger left over for his wife and son, but never for me. I'd be left alone to watch. Would my father strike this woman too, or was that something you only did to family? Would he call her that ugly Korean word for a Black person that not even my fearful mother would use, as it was so vulgar?

In a rush, I told the woman what my mother said, except for the thief being Black. It was all true, but telling it to a stranger made it feel not mine anymore, just some story I heard.

"If he ain't right in the head, he shouldn't be driving. Not if he's handicapped."

My father wasn't handicapped, but how could I explain when I didn't understand myself why he was considered different, even before the accident, even compared to others who'd also grown up during the war, who'd also been refugees and immigrants, as my mother often wondered in trying to understand what kind of man she'd married.

"Is she coming?" asked my father.

"He wants to know if my mom's coming, and she is," I offered the policewoman first. Then I added in Korean for my father, "She's coming now."

"Good, she can pick him up at the station," said the policewoman. When she handcuffed him, the neighbors cheered. She told me to get inside and lock up.

My father asked in slow, careful English, "My daughter, she come too?"

I saw myself cuffed to my dad, and my friend cuffed to me with red ribbons.

"Oh, so now you can talk English?" She guided my father into her car.

"Tell her I couldn't see," he said. "She can understand your words."

Red silk crawled up my friend's neck and slid over her mouth. So I kept mine shut too. The policewoman took my father away. The day I'd wished for had finally come.

I hid the mirror shards in a trash bag under my brother's bed.

Chris was the one who broke stuff anyway. He'd punched a hole in the plywood door after fighting with Dad, after he'd called Chris an idiot, retard, loser, piece of shit, or told him to drop dead. Mom covered the hole with a church calendar. Another time, Chris hurled a wrench at Dad's car, cracking the windshield. Mom lied, saying a Mexican kid had thrown a brick.

Another car in the driveway. Mom hollering for me. She'd say I hadn't explained things right. That it was my fault Dad got arrested. The door was locked, all three locks, so I had time. But where could I hide when my hiding places were also hers, when we often hid together?

I slid open the mirrored closet door in my parents' room and shoved aside clothes and blankets, uncovering the Korean wood-chest, discovered long ago while snooping. I already had the key in hand, discovered another time I'd been digging around in my mom's stuff. I unlocked the front-facing double doors of the wood-chest. Brass scrollwork and butterfly hinges. Silk hanbok gowns folded inside, wrapped in tissue.

When my mom found me, I was on hands and knees, my head inside the wood-chest, her hanbok gowns tossed all around me.

"What are you doing?" she asked in Korean.

"Nothing." I pushed my head farther in, closer to the mothballs.

She pulled me out by the hips, then pressed her palms tight against my cheeks. Her face was shoved close to mine, so I couldn't see anything but her wild, dark eyes. "What made you climb in?" she asked. "Was it a memory, a dream? Was it a voice?"

I pried her hands off me and scooted away. She crawled after me, demanding, "How did you know? Do you also remember?"

I was afraid of her crying-jag prayers, when she'd wrap her body around mine and try to speak in tongues, like that time she held me on the floor, sobbing in the church choir room. I stared at the carpet, waiting for it to pass, while she babbled some magic spell she couldn't get right. Then just as sudden, she'd push me away, frustrated how God—or any god really—couldn't or wouldn't hear her despite all her begging.

"Don't look at me like that!" I said. "I told the cop what you wanted me to say."

Kneeling before me, she closed her eyes and whispered, "Now's not the time. She's not ready."

"Mom! Stop being so weird!"

Her eyes snapped open. Standing, she smoothed her skirt. "Don't go rummaging through my things. Put everything back and keep the hanboks secret. You're coming with me to the station."

Of course, she needed a translator. She should've waited for my brother, but no one knew when he'd be home. At least, she didn't seem so mad at me anymore, so I took a chance to ask, "Mom, you've got so many hanboks. Why don't you wear any of them?"

She paused in the doorway. "Come to the living room after you change into something presentable."

After my mom left, I turned to my friend, the silent witness. Instead of consoling me, she held out the end of her braid, arm extended to lift the heavy rope off her neck. The red ribbon stretched and fluttered toward her lips. "I can't go with you to the police," she said in a breathless rush.

"Chris will fix things. And if Dad's in jail—" I didn't dare finish my thought.

"I always hope that he'll drive to the body shop first and lead the police there, instead of coming home where you can see him like that. But his shame would be greater at his place of work. And in the stories, it's the father who cannot see, who needs his daughter to—"

The red ribbons snapped against her mouth like whips. Wincing, she whispered, "I'm with you forever. I'll come to you again and again, but not right away." She couldn't hold her braid off any longer—the ribbons wrenched it free from her grip, then settled in silken grace down her back. My friend became as stiff as the rope tracing over her spine. I couldn't ask what all this meant though, because my mother was shouting for me.

In the living room, Mom held a knife and a leaf of barbed aloe, freshly sliced from her backyard garden. She stood beside the old Korean apothecary cabinet with its rows and rows of tiny drawers that held things like spare keys and shoelaces, my dead grandpa's tobacco pipes, and Mom's secret cigarettes. "Find me the ruler," she said.

A cruel carnival game—if I found the right drawer, I'd get punished right away, but the longer she had to wait, the worse the prize would be. She yanked one drawer, then another. They hung like fat, lolling tongues. "You rummage through everything. You know where it is."

I opened drawers in a row, then jerked them at random.

"Never mind." From an old-fashioned Korean vase nearby, she reached for her usual switch. The long grass—twigs painted sea green—were for decoration and not really Korean, except in how my mother used them.

In the hallway, my friend was gagged and blindfolded with ribbons. Taking the hint—I clamped my mouth and shut my eyes and gripped the edge of the chest. Mom whipped my calves. Each strike rattled the drawers and their brass handles, but the hurt took longer to bloom.

"This pain is real," she said. "Only real can save you. Feel the difference." Each time she hit me, I shut another drawer inside. "Anything not real, you must kill before it's too late."

Ribbons wrapped all around, covering every last bit of my friend's face.

My mother smeared the aloe against my burning skin. Juice dripped down my calves. Removing a comb from a drawer, she dragged it through my hair, its teeth sharp against my scalp. "Reject your instincts, purge your fantasies. Forget the old stories—I was wrong to share them. In this new plastic country, you will be safe from their designs." Then she murmured, her lips brushing against my ear, "You never listen, never obey. Perhaps your stubborn defiance will save you, keep you from succumbing." She whispered other things, but I couldn't see or hear her anymore. Invisible ribbons had wrapped around my head as well.

But I could still see my friend. Her ribbon had shrunk, small and pert, like the bows on my socks. Without waving goodbye, she walked out the front door, passing through like a ghost.

She didn't return that day or the next, though the voices continued to rage through the wall. She didn't appear during the many years after, maybe because I'd actually obeyed my mother for once, putting away storybooks and mirror worlds. I devoted myself to the real instead—numbers, formulae, facts—what Mom couldn't understand but fearfully respected. That's how I reached escape velocity, away from home into a life I'd determined for myself.

But my friend also made good on her promise. At the bottom of the world, in a seething lake carved from the ice, she'd found me again.

3

I'm alone in my station room, huddled in the closet with my laptop, while everyone else is at the hot tub party. Promised Jesper I'd sleep off whatever was wrong with me, but first I need to talk to my brother.

Chris answers my video call in bed, camera angled down. The padded grey tweed cubicle wall behind him serves as headboard and bedroom wall. So, he's sleeping in the loft space above our father's body shop again. "I'd rather live in a cubicle than work in one!" he'd say. He alternated between that and his childhood bedroom in our family house. His laptop's edge is propped on his chest, his preferred position for lying down and watching YouTube lectures about the recent global financial collapse and clips from his favorite 1930s screwball comedies. It's dark over there too, so his face glows spectral. His jowls hang heavy over his jawline. At least he's still got his handsome nose—high-bridged, straight with a refined tip. Our mother's nose, lucky bastard. I got her eyes though, he'd counter.

"You back in Stockholm?" he asks.

"Still at the pole, leaving tomorrow. Sorry I couldn't talk earlier."

"Thought you said we couldn't video chat."

"Not allowed for personal use. Limited bandwidth. Imagine all the porn torrents otherwise. But satellite's at the right angle, and I'm leaving soon anyhow."

He nods, blinks slowly. His medication makes him groggy, but something else is going on. How long has he been up? Must be around 4:00 a.m. in California.

When younger, my brother fancied himself a Byronic hero, but for the last decade, he's settled with: "Mad, fat, sad, and dangerous to know." His hair, the prettier version of my own, is longer now, but the shaggy ends are concealed by smooth waves. He's looking Oscar Wilde again out of laziness and vanity, except the white streak at his left temple gives him a Mister Fantastic vibe. Last time we spoke, he told me how he'd held the door open at a 7-Eleven for a Black woman in a gold pantsuit and leopard-print high heels. Giving him the once-over, she'd said, "Shōgun—you too old for that hair!" then sashayed past him. Chris howled with laughter recounting the story, saying, "Shōgun! When's the last time you heard a James Clavell reference?" But his eyes are bloodshot now, his voice thick. Could be sliding into another funk. Probably picking at the perma-scabs on his knuckles.

"Everything OK with Dad?" I ask, finally getting to it.

He chuckles. "Might be shitting his pants, but not for the usual reasons."

"You need to get him more fiber. He needs to exercise and you should—"

"Mom spoke. A few days ago."

I'm waiting for the punch line.

He scootches himself up in bed, angling the screen so he's looking down at me. "You hear what I said? She talked, Elsa. After all these fucking years—"

I correct my brother. "Mom can't talk." Our mother has been institutionalized for the last sixteen years, ever since the Spa Accident. Catatonic and mute, exhibiting what the medical community calls "waxy flexibility." She can be posed in a chair. She can chew and swallow, even be put on a toilet.

Her body responds with muscle memory. But she hasn't said anything since I was fourteen, hasn't looked at me with recognition, not even in accusation.

"A nurse swears she heard her," says Chris. "Doc called me right away."

"What'd she say?" I ask, skeptical but curious.

"The trippiest thing. She said, 'Where is the other girl?'—in English!"

A lullaby refrain—something about a bell? Those strange tales from childhood—mistranslated, misremembered. My mother's intentions—slippery, shape-shifting. But what my brother claimed was highly improbable. For one, her English was never that good, not enough to form a grammatically correct sentence, never mind the sixteen years of catatonia.

"In all likelihood," I explain, "the nurse mistook some nonsensical mumbling for—still, mumbling's a good sign. Though maybe just reflexes of the vocal muscles. Does Dad know?"

Chris laughs. "I keep taunting him, 'Hey, old man, your wife is coming back! Whatchu gonna do?' He ignores me. Freakin' hilarious. Crazy wife comes back from the dead—"

"She was never dead."

"Right. Dead people don't rack up bills. Hey, what if she could talk all this time and was just faking it? And what the hell—'The other girl, where'd she go?'"

"That's not what you said before. What were her exact words?"

"The other girl, where's she now?"

"My God, Chris! Why can't you get things right?"

"You come here then, deal with this shit! *You* deal with Dad. *You* pay for Mom's bills."

"I *have* been paying them, ever since—"

"Forget it." He puffs his cheeks, then blows out a long, wet raspberry. He's on the verge of both crying and laughing. He wants me—his younger sister by ten years—to tell him everything will be all right. But what is it that we're hoping for—or afraid of?

"The satellite will be out of reach soon," I say. "Gotta go." I hinge my brother's face into the keyboard, but I remain crouched in the dark for a good while longer.

Hours later, I wake up in bed with a parched throat and no memory of having left the closet. Jesper is sleeping beside me. Even after guzzling from my water bottle, my body feels desiccated. So I slip out of my room and into the station hallways. Eerily quiet, except for some plastic cups and stray pieces of clothing. Everyone else must be passed out drunk.

I keep myself steady with my hand against the walls. Turning the corner, my palm slides over cushioned rubber tiles that form a checkered pattern in baby blue and mint green, colors that soothe and sedate. I stumble by the gym where we're supposed to exorcise our cabin fever and other demons. I pass the music room, decked out with drums, guitars, and tambourines. There's even a weekly painting club that meets near the observation deck. How could I not have noticed before? My life at the station is run on a strict schedule with regular discussion groups and check-ins with our supervisors, and I spend the bulk of my time alone in my room thinking about the invisible and primordial.

Then there's Chris, living in a padded cubicle in our father's body shop, behind cement brick and tinted windows. So no matter how far we run, we all end up like our mothers.

The hallway rolls forward and back, sways side to side. The glacial ice under us shifts ten meters a year, and the ice moves in different directions. Thus, the connecting walkway between the modules was made flexible and extendible to keep the station from being pulled apart. But this doesn't explain why it feels like I'm walking down the plank of a storm-tossed ship.

Finally, the right door. On the other side, tropical humidity engulfs me. I bypass the lounge, step through the yellow-glass inner doors into the heart of the hydroponic growth chamber. During the summer, vegetables are flown in from New Zealand, but in the winter, this is the only source for fresh greens. Our oasis in the icy desert. Massive grow lamps hang from the ceiling. The air is sultry, smelling of herbs, fungi, and microbial fecundity. A space-age Eden the size of a living room, this is NASA's prototype and practice lab so that astronauts can someday grow salads on Mars.

Sometimes, the doctor prescribes therapeutic sessions here for the light and humidity. Because the Antarctic is bone-dry, at orientation we're instructed to "always be chugging—at all times your pee should be copious and clear." But being here drains more than just water from us. During the winter, many come to this garden to rehydrate—then weep.

I brush my fingers along leaves and flowers that will soon give way to fruits and vegetables. Lush lettuce beds float in terraced trays of nutrient-dense water. All around me—red and orange nasturtium blooms, hanging globes of watermelon, and bushes of dark green chard.

After the last plane takes off, these will be the only living things at the pole, besides the fifty stranded humans. This flora is non-native, like everything else here. We're all foreigners, no matter how many flags are stuck in the snow. Like these plants, living here is an act of defiance, thriving in a place not meant for us.

I pluck a cherry tomato and bite through its skin. Next, I gnaw on a ghost chili pepper. The pepper's capsaicin makes me feel like my tongue is on fire, but the sensation is chemically induced, receptors in my nerve cells mistranslating to my brain. I chew in order to localize and rationalize—the burning clears my mind, focusing all its pain and confusion within my mouth.

A childish part of me wants my mother to come back when I can provide a better reality for her than the one she left behind—her own apartment that my father doesn't know about, no wifely or maternal responsibilities. Maybe I'd set her up in another city, a relocation protection program, close to a Korean church, a library, mall, and some nature. But a truer part of me wants her to sleep forever, because her reality would destroy the one I've carefully cultivated for myself.

I bow my head over a blossom of butter lettuce and nibble on a leaf. On tiptoe, I kiss a sunflower, my lips brushing against its cluster of florets. How mathematically sensual—its alignment of interconnected spirals maximizing its seed-packing, the number of left and right spirals adhering to successive Fibonacci numbers—

Someone says my name.

I run up and down the aisles between snap bean trellises, looming walls of woven green. I dart around corners and peek through leaves. But I'm the only one here.

"Ehll-ssah," I hear again.

Sounds like my mom. After sixteen years, I thought I'd forgotten her voice, how she said my name with her accent, extending the vowels and stressing the consonants. Sometimes she'd say it like a caress, sometimes a slap. When she searched for me throughout the house, yelling louder when she couldn't find me, her panic stretched out the last syllable as she went through each room, each closet, and I knew it wouldn't be funny anymore, she'd only be angry when she eventually found me, so I'd wedge myself deeper into hiding, willing myself invisible.

"El-sah," I hear again. Sounds like me this time. As a kid, I'd pick up the ringing phone and answer "Hello?" in English, and Korean voices would unleash their gossip, grief, fury, or bitchery until I interrupted and asked in their language, "Pardon me, perhaps you are wishing to speak to my mother?" They invariably replied with: "Oh, is this Elsa? You sound just like her!"

I rub my eyes, spreading pollen across my face. I'm not allergic, but my eyes water. Then, in a voice definitely not mine nor my mother's, I hear: "Soon, we'll be together again."

More than her face or red ribbons, her voice hurtles me back into my child's body—always tense and alert, bracing for the next outburst, the next rush to the hospital, the next robbery or financial disaster that Mom and Chris would never let Dad forget. My friend was my comfort, but she couldn't dispel everything. Hearing her again, it's the same tumble of emotion. I recall the wonder and relief of being graced with secret magic, but looming before me now is the fear I'm still the same girl despite all my running to the ends of the earth.

I spit out everything and trip over pumpkin vines, the tendrils curling around my ankles. I focus on the doors, but along the way, flowers bloom and vegetables swell. The giant swaying fronds of kale seem near-Triassic. I close my eyes and breathe deeply.

Ghost chili peppers can make you hallucinate. Nutmeg too. Everything can make you go crazy, given the right dose.

A moment later, I open my eyes. The cucumbers are shriveled. Wilting lettuce dangle their roots in fetid water.

Back in my station room, it only takes me a few hours to find several rational explanations, but I keep coming back to the Ganzfeld effect.

Miners submerged in dark caves or polar explorers lost in the white sometimes experience hallucinations. Immersed in a uniform environment, the brain compensates for the lack of input and visual stimuli by projecting visions and sounds onto the blank screen of our surroundings. Neural noise—what we typically suppress except during dreams or bad acid trips—can froth and spill over into our waking conscious moments, as the mind may be desperate to fill the void. Also known as "the prisoner's cinema."

This all veers toward parapsychology rather than real science. There's even an Instructables webpage for how to replicate the sensory deprivation with headphones delivering white noise and a ping-pong ball, cut in half and taped over the eyes. Still, it's plausible enough for me to banish the bogeywoman—for now, at least.

Curled beside Jesper, who doesn't seem to notice that I left and returned more shaken than before, I recite the Ganzfeld rationalization over and over like a Hail Mary, Buddhist mantra, and AA prayer all rolled into one. But despite my incantations, memories still surface.

4

Dad's old joke about a runaway mom resulted in a prophetic punchline when she ended up institutionalized with a mind long gone. But when she was still with us, Mom warned me that it was the women in our family whose utterances could summon the old stories, whose voices could invoke an ancestress. So I can't help wondering if it's her fault that my brother turned out the way he is when she commanded him to be "*im-po-tent.*" In her heavily accented English, with her finger jabbing into his chest, she told him that for all she's done for him, Chris was duty-bound to be "*im-po-tent,*" especially as this was a "stranger's land," she added in Korean. We laughed, cruel and mocking, and her confusion made us giggle even more; but familial wishes, like curses, enjoy their own trickster sense of humor.

Mom's demands on my brother as a Korean son simply required him to be rich and successful, enough to redeem her suffering. Doctor or lawyer would do. Chris's secret ambitions then were also equally nebulous. He justified to Mom that the path to law school required studies in philosophy, literature, and human nature. Even as a kid, I knew this was cover-up. I had a simpler goal—get out. But my brother—despite teachers who slipped him brochures for gifted magnet programs and scholarship applications for private schools—never took a chance. When I asked him why, he said, "You're a girl. You can come back home a failure. Just don't get knocked up till you marry a rich Korean. But me—well, who's gonna watch out for Mom?"

"If that's all I gotta do, not get pregnant, then why'd she push all those piano and art lessons on me? How come she hustles Dad for money to pay for all my science camps?"

That threw him off, but only for a moment. "Sure, she wants you to be cultured and refined, but all for the end goal of nabbing the right husband. She even wanted to find you a finishing school to fix the way you walk."

"What's wrong with the way I—"

"I told her there aren't any charm schools in America, not anymore. She'd have to send you back to Korea. That's basically what her own college was like. Just you wait—all this, all your future degrees, won't mean a thing if you end up a childless spinster. You can take the Korean mom out of the old country, but . . ."

When Chris finally did leave home for college, a few years after high school, his escape didn't last long because he was saddled with more than just cliché immigrant-parent expectations. Ostensibly, my brother's roommates ejected him because of his epilepsy. They'd skipped the techno dance clubs and all-night video game binges, but stress triggered Chris's insomnia, which led to seizures. And the real reason for his banishment were his dreams afterward because he believed them to be holy visions. His roommate confided to Mom, and she asked me if I knew. She had her own prophetic dreams, but she believed hers were culturally authentic and divinatory, while my brother's were mongrelized and therefore blasphemous.

Chris moved back into his childhood bedroom and refocused his academic energies onto me. Mom would yell at him to quit hiding at home, playing professor. But when Chris showed her the four boarding schools he'd chosen, crying out, "I'm doing what you should've done for me!" she left the room without a further word.

My brother oversaw my applications and rewrote my essay, which was about how I idolized him, my intellectual rather than biological father. He even played the admissions offices of two rival schools against each other, thereby securing me a full scholarship at the academy he deemed more "cosmopolitan."

The biggest obstacle, however, was my father, who couldn't understand why a place 3,000 miles away wanted his little girl. For what purpose would they offer a "yearly grant" of over twenty thousand dollars? What kind of school would give housing and meals and not expect her to earn it? Chris had to convince him it wasn't an orphanage or trafficking scheme. Dad rebutted how after the war, plenty of Korean brats were stolen off the streets and sold to white countries, "our most profitable export." He added that "those Jap bastards recruited poor Korean girls from the countryside with fake jobs or scholarships and ended up using them as sex slaves." Dad didn't really think I was being lured in as a comfort woman, said Chris, but his "medieval mind" couldn't understand the concepts of diversity recruitment, need-blind admissions, and top one percent on standardized tests.

All this sounded suspiciously generous, however, especially to a man whose own university admission was probably bought by his wealthy father. Really, how could a fourteen-year-old girl, however clever, be worth all this? But eventually he agreed, impressed by the promo video, glossy catalog, and especially the white alumnus who interviewed me at our house. A district court judge, he politely removed his shoes without us needing to ask. His hulking size took up most of the couch as my mother served him a fruit platter. He politely took an apple slice, then told me how he'd grown up blue-collar nearby. Instead of interrogating me, he talked up how the boarding school gave him a scholarship and changed his life's trajectory. My father listened and for once was quiet.

Also, who knows what else my brother promised or threatened during his five hours of repeated explanations and arguments with visual aids, just him and Dad behind a closed door?

Once I got permission, I was too nervous to feel guilty about abandoning the others. I had a "cold soul" by nature, my mother noted, adding it was good to be selfish. "You'll get further this way." But in the weeks before my departure, as I shipped boxes east, Mom grew agitated, buying me more socks than necessary. Then a week before Dad, Chris, and I were supposed to fly out for orientation, my mother woke me at dawn, saying, "I'm taking you myself by car."

I figured this was her desperate attempt to seal some bond before I left home. Her side-stepping my father was risky though—I assumed she knew how to avoid blowback. Anyhow, it was the least I could do—a farewell cross-country road trip with my mother.

By late morning, we were speeding into the desert, past sun-bleached motels crouching along the highway, toward mountains coolly unreachable. Soon, we were surrounded by rust-colored plateaus, stone piles, and squat towers—sculptures made by toddler giants. The scattered trees, coated in beige fur, also dreamt up by some weirdo child-god. They sprouted green only at the ends of their stubby branches, thrusting spike-leafed pom-poms to the sky.

Farther down, the road seemingly dipped into a lake, resurfacing on the opposite shore. But no, only an optical illusion, simple refraction. Light waves passed between the hot air at the asphalt's surface and the dense, cooler air above to bend and cast a mirage. Not a lake, just a slice of blue sky reflected by a burning highway.

The last few years, I'd replaced fairy tales with textbooks, subjected my Barbies to chemistry experiments, and won science competitions, beating out all the other Asians. Their parents were doctors and professors, but I was the true devotee because science was my survival, the language my mother couldn't understand—how I disproved and refuted her.

But how was it hot enough for this illusion unless I'd lost count of the hours? Maybe Mom did have tricks up her sleeve, pleating time like a closed paper fan. And even after her occasional drinking binges and Old Testament histrionics, she could cast a glamour, so all we saw the morning after were beer bottles lined up serpentine, sprouting rolled pieces of ink-scribbled paper.

After driving along a lonely road, we approached a concrete building, a grey box squatting in the desert. "We'll stay here for the night," she said, even though it was only 2:00 p.m.

Through the double doors, we entered a corridor. Sheets of water poured along concrete walls on either side, disappearing along the edges of the slate walkway. While my mother checked us in, I examined the courtyard, walled off with glass and empty except for a single bare-branched tree rooted in smooth concrete. Its sprawling branches cast tangled shadows on the ground. "The courtyard is closed during the day," said a man in a grey suit. "But you may visit after sunset." Before I could ask why, my mother took me away.

Once inside our room, I threw myself onto a downy white bed. The air-conditioning dried the sweat on my face and chest into a tight second skin. Taking her suitcase into the bathroom, Mom told me to get lunch by myself. I wondered if driving me to school was a ruse, using me to plot her own escape. But I was too hungry to interrogate. No matter what, I had a new home waiting for me with a meal plan, stipend, and full tuition. If Mom wanted to be my secret roommate, so be it. No one was going to pull me out, not even an abandoned father tearing the house apart for clues about his runaway wife.

I ate in the dining hall, surrounded by robed women nibbling fruit. Afterward, I wandered, trying to find the courtyard entrance. I asked a man in a grey suit when sunset would be. "7:15 p.m. Clear skies," he said. "Bet you'll see all the way to the heavens."

It was only four o'clock. I returned to check on my mother. She answered through the bathroom door: "I'm busy."

"What if I need the toilet?"

"Go to the lobby."

Pressing my ear against the door, I heard the frantic scratch of pen against paper. On the coffee table were a bucket of melting ice and a single tumbler. On the sofa, her open suitcase. Like a freshly dug grave, a rectangle had been hollowed out among her clothes—the shape and size fitting the cardboard box of her favorite whiskey.

It'd been a while since my mother last warned me about a dream. She often transcribed them in her journals and consulted her notes at a later date. Though she was a devout Christian most of the time, she also covered her bases. She noted dates murmured by ancestors, and after an earthquake, burglary, mugging, the LA Riots, or one of Chris's more upsetting episodes, she'd consult this almanac of predetermined disaster and cluck her tongue. I asked her why she didn't take extra care on those days if she knew something was going to happen. She explained, "We can't live in fear, waiting for tragedy. I write these dates not to warn myself, but to console myself after the fact, that there was nothing I could do to prevent it."

Though she'd wanted me to stop playing make-believe and acting out the stories in my head, she often grabbed my palm to read it again and again, as if my fate had been carved anew. She even stretched the skin taut, painfully so, erasing my destiny. She swung from God to whatever would allay her fears for a moment. I avoided her when she got too Christian, with her prayer hugs and babble of tongues, and especially when she got mystical and Cali-Korean gothic.

In the middle of the night, I went to the lobby bathroom to pee. Robed guests wandered in the courtyard, like a herd of animals in a glass exhibit. They tilted their faces to the moonlight.

Back in our room, I was tempted to call Chris to get his take on Mom's impulsive road trip, find out if he knew or suspected beforehand. And if things got too weird and sad, if Mom indulged in her annual drinking binge at the hotel, would he come get me? Instead, I climbed into bed and fell asleep to the sound of scribbling, pouring, whispers.

Waiting for family to emerge after seclusion wasn't new. My brother slept all day when depressed. After seizures he'd pass out for hours. Some of his slumbers were caused by his meds. On his nightstand, he'd line up his amber bottles with anticonvulsants, antidepressants, and capsules that dulled his senses, dampening impulses. But his mind kept talking during his dreams, and he often returned with newfound conviction, a secret gleaned from another realm.

The seizures also took my brother from me, transforming him into a synaptic storm that gave off its own force field. I'd creep away while my parents restrained him. When Chris was sick, I didn't recognize him. I didn't recognize my father either, not his tenderness. While Chris shouted about being the "true son of the true father," Dad murmured unexpectedly in English as if to break through to Chris. "You are *my* boy. *My* son." When Chris sobbed, not bothering to wipe his snot, our father held him like a baby. I only witnessed this through a crack in the door. Always, I couldn't look at their faces afterward.

The next morning, I woke with Mom hovering over me. "It's time," she said. The desert sun shone, lighting her permed hair like a glowing nimbus. Her smile was unnerving—serene, beatific, assured. Her calmness worried me, more than the impromptu road trip, more than her locking herself in the bathroom. It was as if all her nervous energy scribbling the night away had dissipated into the pages, and all that was left of her was this lovely husk of a woman sheathed in a lacy white nightgown.

Skipping breakfast, she led me to the underground spa, set close to the thermal hot springs. It extended two floors below and was larger than the hotel above ground, since it also used the space under the courtyard. In the locker room, we changed into our robes. I was the only non-adult, the only one shy about being naked. Others walked around baring droopy breasts and heavy, slapping thighs.

The caverns were dark except for small golden lights that lit up the steam. The floor, covered in slick stone tiles. The moisture made everything shiny, especially the permed black hair favored by the middle-aged clientele. The mist lent grace to all these old bodies, but still they looked alien. I couldn't understand how my flesh would turn into theirs, but I was the most self-conscious, only opening my robe when facing the wall.

Choosing the darkest, emptiest corner, I draped a small towel over the wooden stool and filled the bucket beside it with water. The faucets jutted from a stony ledge, molded like a natural rock spring, but the metal knobs ruined the illusion.

Instead of using the wooden stools, the women around me squatted, their butts hovering above the tiles, knees raised to their shoulders. It was the "kimchi-squat," used for hand-washing laundry in the backyard and, of course, for making kimchi—massaging red pepper into lettuce heads in a plastic tub on the ground. On family vacations to Seoul, I'd seen old women in this crouch, smoking cigarettes in alleys. Mom said they weren't ladylike to do so in public, that it was illegal for women to smoke outdoors, but they were clearly in charge of their domain, just like the women here. In this powerful hunched pose, they poured over their heads, making waterfalls down their backs. But before I could pour too, my mother pointed me to a new door.

In another room, we met a trio of sturdy bikini-clad women. Mom approached the sumo wrestler of the bunch, whose outfit included well-placed daisies, telling her I hadn't had a proper exfoliation in years. Leaving me with the daisy pasties, she told me to "come to our sauna when you're clean." So I lay naked on a table while the woman sloughed my body, scraping my flesh raw. I tried not to grimace, knowing she'd only smile. Shreds of tough skin, rolled into grey maggots, gathered at the end of each drag she took along my arms, belly and thighs.

"This stinging pain means you're finally getting clean," she said in what sounded like dialect, what I'd only heard in movies set in the Korean Jeolla-do countryside. "I shudder thinking about all the filthy Americans who only use their slimy soap, then slather themselves in lotion." While she flayed me, I asked her why people weren't allowed in the courtyard during daytime. She replied, "The baths are right under the courtyard. We can't have people walking so close above old Koreans while they're bathing."

"Why?"

"Because you only walk over the heads of the dead. You think that's good for business? These women worried about who's prancing above them?"

"It's a three-story hotel. Lots of people are walking over our heads."

"Different. The courtyard is a single layer separating the bathers from heaven."

"What about sunset?"

"All-you-can-eat dinner buffet—these old bitches never miss a single minute." She tossed a bucket of cold water over me, revealing pink skin, shining bright and insulted. Never realized how much dead flesh we could carry on our bodies.

In our private sauna, my mother lay naked on a towel on the highest bench. The cedar walls smelled of burnt spice. Coals sizzled in the corner. Yellow lights glowed between the bench slats. I took shallow breaths, worried about cooking my lungs. She swung her legs off her perch. Whiskey sweated from her body, suffusing the dank air around me.

"Elsa, listen carefully to what I'm about to tell you. It's time you knew."

Of course, this was it. Mom brought me to this desert spa so she could impart confessions and dire warnings. That way I'd be inspired to redeem her suffering and be too scared to let a boy touch me and ruin my life. But Chris had already told me about her tragedies because he was tired of being the only one burdened with secrets and believed I was old enough to finally share in the sadness. So I knew about the baby she'd removed, the doctor who advised another pregnancy to heal her body, how I was that child. I'd cried when my brother told me, because it meant Mom hadn't wanted me, hadn't wanted the previous one either. The doctor made it sound like her body was punishing her for not wanting the other child, so she had to have me just to keep living. But Chris said I was the one who saved her.

"It's okay, Mom." I pushed my sweaty bangs off my forehead. "Chris told me."

"You think you know everything about me because of your brother?" She ladled water over the coals. They hissed and steamed. "Here's something I never told him. I should've never gotten pregnant. Then I wouldn't have had any daughters." I shifted away from her and the coals.

"Did your brother tell you I spurned my first proposal as well as my second? That all I wanted was to sleep in my childhood bed and dream of my dead mother and sister? But I was getting older, and Stepmother and Father found me a husband, forced me out of the house. By then, I'd learned it wasn't the war that took them—Mother died from poisoning herself to rid an unwanted baby, Sister died because—if they'd lived, they would've warned me about the man who'd tempt me with dresses from New York and Paris.

"And what I tell you now, Chris has no idea." She smiled with her perfect veneered teeth. "Despite not having my mother and sister, I figured it out for myself. I saw the patterns, read my fate recorded generations ago. You and I—we are descended from women whose lives have been degraded into common folktales. We live their lives, echoing their stories, but not their greatness—only their stupid tragedies because that is all we remember of them."

I wanted to laugh, but I needed Chris. It took both of us to make our mother into a joke.

"They speak to me, Elsa. I've written down their stories as they truly lived, not as they're written now—I don't want for you the same bitterness—should've been so much more in this life. The stories will prepare you—I give you this, now that I'm leaving you."

"My God, Mom! You tell me all those dark, messed-up stories when I'm way too young, then you tell me to forget them. Now when I'm finally—you want me to—what is your problem?" I couldn't breathe anymore in the heat.

Sighing, she ran a finger over her eyebrow, lightly tattooed and severely arched. Her eyelids were also permanently inked so she wouldn't need to line them in kohl every morning.

"Chris would say you're being manipulative. Now that I have a chance to be free, you're laying all this crap on me. All your suffering—all I can think about, how not to be you, how not to drown in you—now you're talking crazy?"

"This doesn't concern your brother," she replied primly. "This is about us as women." She stood over me while I curled myself smaller on the bench. "I don't know which story your life will follow, so I've written them all down—for both of you."

"For me and Chris?" I mumbled. "Thought you said—"

"For you and your sister."

"The stillborn one?" The one we never spoke about, who came after Chris and before the baby she'd removed. Two lives between Chris and me, the ones who got out early. A bead of sweat rolled down my nose. I lifted my face to keep it from splashing loudly on the floor.

"No, Elsa, the other girl was sent away, for hiding in a far-off land."

"Ho-ly fuck! That baby was born dead! Please, don't do this to me, not now."

"By hiding her with another people, far away, I meant to save her. But I had you in this foreign land, and you turned out like me anyhow." She shook her head in dazed wonder, then clamped her hands over her ears. "Those bitches won't shut up! If you find her—maybe together you can stop—I didn't have anyone—my sister died long ago." Her voice trailed off as she stared into nothing, tits saggy and pointing down. Fever gone, everything withered. I brushed my fingertip against the bench, hoping for a splinter to pierce me.

In the silence, I ventured, "How did your sister die?"

"The war," she said quietly, head bowed.

"Yeah, but how—what happened?"

"I don't want to talk about it." She shrunk into herself, and I had more space to breathe.

"Please," she said from her corner, "do not blame us for how our lives have turned out. Perhaps it's not just the women in our family anyhow—our entire people have been telling the wrong stories, making a wretched mess of our history. As if anybody wants to be told that their ability to endure is their greatest virtue. No wonder we get invasions and occupations, war and asshole husbands. What kind of stories, I wonder, do the white countries tell of themselves?"

It was the first time I'd seen my mother step out of her solipsistic misery. Somehow, by extending her folklore curse to other women—all of Korea even—she seemed aware and prescient and therefore terrifying. Her personal nightmare became a bigger reality that the rest of us couldn't see or were willfully ignoring. She became a truth-teller instead of a tale-spinner.

Then suddenly, as if sensing the temperature had become bearable, she snapped back into character. Gripping my shoulder, she gestured around her in the cramped space. "The others are here for me now," she said. "All my story sisters. You'll see yours, too, when it's time." Only her hand touched me, but I could feel all the heat of her naked body.

Finally, she opened the door. Still dizzy and confused, I let her lead me back through the foggy caves. We didn't stop at the slate ledges, facing an obedient row of stools and their buckets waiting to be filled. She moved us past the ghostly bathers too—forever pouring waterfalls over their heads. She escorted my limp, sweaty body to the farthest corner instead, where the hot spring pools were clustered.

One hot tub was curtained with ivy hung from the ceiling. Another, veiled with rain, lit with electric moonlight. The strangest was a humongous stone bowl, lined with hammered copper that glimmered underwater. Dry-ice smoke spilled over the edges, like a cauldron. A woman climbed the ladder and slipped into the steaming pot, willing to be cooked.

My mother directed me to the pool in the darkest recess. A small, rock-ringed lake that bubbled, framed inside a dew-slicked grotto. She led me into the water. I pulled my hand free and sat on the bench that ran along the inside of the pool. She waded across to the innermost hollow, where the craggy wall looked like a giant's cupped palm. Falling against that hand, she shuddered. She was far away enough that I couldn't see her tears or hear her sob over the gurgling, jet-streamed water, but I could feel the force of her sadness, pushing waves to slap at my chest and pull me under. More than her ridiculous stories or my father's outbursts, her sadness frightened me because it was powerful enough to erase her mind, rewrite her past, and connect her pain to that of all the women before her. I hugged my knees and waited for the moment to pass, but the froth and foam rose above my chin, tasting of metal.

An old woman joined us in the pool. Over her shoulder hung a wisp of a silver braid, tied with red string. I willed her to comfort my mother, but she stared at me instead.

Mom didn't bother to cover her face as she wailed. Hot water funneled into my ears and nose as I kept my eyes down.

"You believe me, don't you?" she cried. "I can prove it!"

I curled into a tight ball, rolled over the bench's edge and slipped headfirst into the water. The bottom was tiled in mirror. My face slammed into itself.

Calm and quiet below the waves. My mother's pale legs and those of the old woman—this perspective close to the ground was how I saw the world as a little kid. *What if I stay this young forever? Never be kissed, never fall in love or get pregnant? Then Mom's sickness would never pass through me to another.*

I sat crisscross on the floor and waited for my mother's legs to move, but they stood rooted in place. My lungs burned. Couldn't hold my breath much longer. Still, I refused to come up. The old woman's legs approached instead. Their reflection in the mirror tiles changed, now smooth and young as mine. Kneeling, the old woman smiled underwater. Her silver braid thickened and darkened. Tied around its end, the red string bled crimson, settling into a ripple around us. Her body became firm, her face unlined. She was my childhood friend, come back to me at last.

I smiled, showing teeth, sucking water into my mouth. I laughed, drinking deep into my belly. The red ribbon wrapped around me, trying to lift me. But I wriggled loose and slapped it away because it tickled, making me laugh even more.

My mother finally moved toward me—but I was mad at her for not paying attention earlier, for talking about some other long-lost daughter when I was the one going away, for giving up on Chris, for letting herself go crazy, for staying with Dad and letting him be so mean toward everyone but me.

So I kicked at her legs because they weren't her face, weren't really her but some weird wobbly things. Too many hands grabbed me. I flipped myself over, laid myself facedown on the floor, like a kid throwing a tantrum. But my body rose with the bubbles, and I couldn't avoid my mother anymore, so I kicked at her reflection instead, slamming my toes into the glass, stomping on her like my father did to her once.

Muscular red tentacles coiled around me and lifted me out of the water. My friend looked at me sadly, her face half hidden in the foam. She slipped below and disappeared. Only then did I notice my mother was gone. I panicked, but strong arms dragged me over the pool's edge and laid me on slick tiles.

Naked screaming women carrying sloshing buckets. Hadn't even begun my folktale yet, but my story sisters would soon pour their endless water over me. My head on a woman's wet thigh. I vomited and watched it flow into the shiny drain near my face. The women cried and prayed. At first, I thought it was for me, but they were staring at something else. I pushed myself up to see my mother being lifted out of the water. Women flanked her on either side, joining their arms underneath to heave her dripping body and pass it to those outside the pool waiting to receive her. Whispers of Korean echoed throughout. "Fainted," "drunk," "shame," and "disgrace." But the only words I cared about were "breathing" and "alive."

Lights were turned on, revealing fake rocks and bruised bodies. The woman whose thigh my head had rested on, who'd pulled me out of the water, was the one in the daisy bikini who'd scraped my body raw. She held me against her chest, rocking me.

A woman claiming to be a nurse propped my mother on her side, pulled her mouth open, and pointed her jaw toward the floor. She bent my mother's arms and legs to secure her side position. This was best for recovery, she said, whether for drowning or seizure. The same pose my father created with my brother's body. I remembered how awkward and rude it seemed when Chris's face was so lifeless.

But my mother looked graceful, with her slender body, curved hip, and daintily crossed ankles. One arm draped across her breasts while her other cushioned her head. She stared at me and breathed softly, a thin line of drool streaming from the side of her smile.

According to the paramedics, my mother suffered complications of post-intoxication, dehydration, and overheating, leading her to fall, hit her head, and almost drown. They promised she'd be okay, just needed to rest for a while at the hospital.

In the locker room, a medic with a slicked-back pompadour examined my feet while I stared over his black hair at a white metal door I'd never seen before.

"Can you check my toes?" I asked. I was terrified I'd made my mother fall, had maybe kicked her in the head. I needed to explain that not even my dad would do that, that I never got in between to push him off her like Chris did, that I always avoided physical contact, affectionate or not.

Kneeling, he held my feet in his latex-gloved hands. "Do they hurt?" His quiet voice and the thick black frames of his glasses contrasted with his tattoos peeking from beneath his uniform sleeves. Around one forearm, writhing along his smooth brown skin, was a stone-carved serpent, feathers around its head and down its back. The other arm was tattooed with a rockabilly woman, busty in a long white dress. More interesting, her face under the Bettie Page bangs was a bejeweled skull, with a gauzy veil draped over her hair.

He caught me staring.

With my eyes fixed on the white metal door again, I asked, "Will my nails turn black and fall off?"

He cradled my feet in his warm hands—the first time a man, or even a boy, had touched me—and my lower belly buzzed. "Nah, stubbed toes happen all the time in a place like this," he said. "Nothing's broken. I don't think your toenails will fall off." Then he offered an ice pack, in a tone similar to handing me a lollipop or a sticker.

Standing tall and tightening my robe belt, I thanked him for his medical advice and told him I'd wait for the social worker in my hotel room.

Alone again, I searched for evidence that could be dangerous. I set the empty liquor bottle in the hallway, in front of a door far from ours. Nothing incriminating inside my mother's suitcase.

But in my bag, tucked at the bottom, was her notebook of stories. I picked it up and out fell a quarter-folded sheet. Scrawled across the top in Korean: "Four stories carved in wood" and something else about "echoes." In each creased block, a folktale title and below it—isolated words, scattered phrases, story fragments—with empty spaces in between.

A knock on the door.

I was about to slip the folded sheet back into the notebook but decided to pocket it. No reason, only impulse. Or maybe it was the nerd in me who couldn't resist a puzzle in quadrants. The spiral-bound stories went under the mattress instead.

The concierge entered with a tall Black woman with honey-colored curls.

"Is my mother going to die?" I asked right away. The paramedics had told me she was okay, and so had the hotel manager, owner, and lawyer. But I wanted to ask the social worker because I wanted her sympathy. Because I wanted to be told again I hadn't killed my mother.

"Oh sweetie, your momma's resting at the hospital, and she's gonna be just fine. I'll wait with you till your dad gets here, all right? Your brother's on his way too. In the meantime, let's order some food and get to know each other, OK?"

For the next hour, we talked while I ate fries and slurped my milkshake. I was used to serving as interpreter during parent-teacher conferences, tagging along with my mom since I was eight. Didn't matter if I was mistranslating the questions. I was the only one giving answers.

While we talked, I kicked my bare toes against the hardwood floor. When she asked why, I said it was my nervous tic, that my mother hated it, that Koreans believed fidgeting, like shaking your leg, meant you'd shake all your wealth away. She told me again my mother would be okay and wrote something in her own notebook while I rammed my toes into the floor. Her hand over my knee, but not touching, she whispered, "It's OK. You're OK."

When the social worker used the bathroom, I grabbed my mother's stories and fled.

Underground, in the locker room, I found the white metal door. I passed through into a tunnel. At the end of this, another door. Through it—steps leading up—out of shadow and into light. Finally, I entered the courtyard. Above me hovered the cutout square of a bright blue sky. I walked in the desert sunshine toward the tree—sculpted of metal, white like bone—somehow cool, despite the scorching sun. Smooth and aloof, lovely to touch. Unlike flesh, not needing anyone. I sat next to it with my mother's notebook in my lap.

I opened to the first page, relieved to find her usual calligraphic writing. No drunken tremble, only elegant symmetry. I couldn't understand all the Korean in "Sister Nymph," but enough to recognize the folktale, enough to know which victim my mother believed she was and what the rest of her stories would be like. No need to read on. I used the notebook as a pillow and slept in the shade of the unliving tree.

When my brother found me, with the social worker and hotel staff behind him, stars winked through the deepening twilight. Chris wedged the notebook into his coat pocket and lifted me in his arms. He carried me across the courtyard, over the tangled shadows of moonlit branches, through the secret passage leading to steps deep underground.

My mother, still asleep, was transferred to a hospital near home. The spa gave us money to help with medical costs as well as other things. No lawyers, just an envelope passed between hands. It was time for all of us to leave the desert. I rode with Chris in his car while my dad took Mom's. After some time on the road, Chris asked about the stories. I hadn't seen them again after he'd taken Mom's notebook from me. I tried to explain but stumbled over the details.

"Mom's very sick," he said. "With this elaborate delusion, she can compensate for feeling worthless and powerless. If she told you we're the descendants of—"

"Not you. Just us—Mom and me."

He snorted with derision, but something else haunted his eyes.

"Is it true about the other daughter?" I asked.

"She was stillborn. In Korea. Before you were born. Mom was visiting family, and when she returned, she said the baby was in a better place. She's a very sad, very sick woman. That's why she's dangerous. Even this last play," he scoffed. "After *I* get you out, she pulls this stunt, ending up in the hospital. Master manipulator—kinda baller."

I glanced at my feet in flip-flops. My toes were purple, toenails black. Only mirror tiles could bruise them like this—not flesh and bone.

"Leave all this bullshit behind, Elsa. You've got a chance I never had. Go to your school. Get into another school, then another. Get as far as you can and don't come back."

I withdrew the folded sheet of paper from my pocket. Tore it into pieces, rolled down the car window, and let the desert wind take them far from me.

Sister Nymph

This Woodcutter had saved the life of a Deer God from a hunter. So in exchange for saving his sacred hide, the Deer God had told him how we nymphs bathe in the mountain lake and that without our robes, we cannot return to the Heavens. The Deer God had betrayed us, one of his kind, just to avoid becoming a handsome pair of gloves.

The Woodcutter spied on me while I bathed. He stole my clothes. When my sisters ascended, I was left naked, alone on shore, unable to return home. Then he appeared with his dirty coat to wrap me in. Dressed in his clothes, I'd become his. That's how I became his lover, serving maid, and captive. That's how he made a water nymph into his wife.

After the birth of our first child, my husband guided me through the woods while my baby slept strapped to my back. He led me to a cave, whose opening was blocked with boulders. He rolled them aside, crawled inside, and withdrew a bundle. He unwrapped the cloth and revealed my nymph robes folded within. I lunged for what was mine, but he held me back. "I'm sorry, I can only give you one piece," he said, presenting my underdress to me as a gift, what he'd stolen from me. I grabbed it and watched him tie up the rest of my things.

I held my underdress, a long simple shift, draped across my arms. It swelled with breath, then dropped again, resigned. A jagged rock sat at my feet. I could have struck my husband dead, but I had a baby bound to my back. He shoved the bundle deep inside the cave, then rolled the boulders back into place. I set my jagged rock on top of his stone pile.

That night, I gave him my body. It couldn't budge underneath his weight, but my true self floated high above. He cried in my hair, telling me how sorry he was for stealing me. "The Deer God told me not to return all your clothes until you bore me three children."

For the next few months, I wore only my underdress and wandered through the woods, leaving my baby home to lie in her filth and cry in my bed. My shift became dirtied, torn, and bloody as I stumbled and fell. Finally, I found the cave, but could not move the stones. My husband found me, lying on the ground, and carried me home.

My baby cried for me, but I didn't care. Not until I felt another growing inside me. So I took off my underdress. I washed and mended it and put it away. I took care of my child and waited for the second to be born. When I presented my husband this new baby, he gave me my gown skirt, which was all I wore while we made love. On top of him, I kept my legs buckled around his hips, but still we hovered close to the ceiling.

When I gave him a third child, he gave me the rest of what was mine. I slipped on the underdress first, then tied the full skirt around me. When I put on my robes, tying the sash over my heart, the silk breathed at last, pulsing once more. I held my baby in one arm and picked up my son with the other. I began to rise.

My husband grabbed our eldest, the daughter I'd left hungry and crying at home while I'd wandered as a mad-woman through the woods. I walked out the door and rose even higher. I called for my daughter. She ran to us and leapt, clutching my leg like a monkey climbing a tree. We ascended as one, my children lighter than air.

5

My last night in Antarctica, I lie in Jesper's bed. I haven't seen my friend since she walked away from me on the ice, haven't heard from her since she called my name in the garden. Haven't heard from Chris either, about our mother supposedly speaking again or Dad's reaction. No more ringing bells, no more fritzing detectors. And yet—I can't wait to get out of here, what would otherwise be my icy refuge, my own Fortress of Solitude.

I keep things light with Jesper, but he senses anyway that I'm detaching myself for reasons unrelated to my imminent departure. Trying to get me to open up, he indulges me in postcoital work talk. "So I wrote to the DOM designer," he says, "and he claims it's impossible for the flasher to go off if disconnected. What an asshole. Totally Swiss. They're the most nationalistic white people for a reason." He expects me to laugh, but I don't. "A little mystery keeps things interesting though, right?" He's trying to provoke me, and I fall for it.

"We're here to *solve* the mysteries, not add to them. Scientists are supposed to—"

"Conquer, monetize, weaponize—sorry, not about you. Some American asked me today if I was wintering over to postpone my job hunt, if I had the luxury to do so because I was Swedish with a 'socialist safety net.'"

"Why *are* you wintering over, for realsies?"

"To fully confront myself and surrender to the unknowable—to be in awe."

"Yup, you're a product of the Swedish welfare system." I laugh, shaking my head.

"I've missed that sound. What's up, Elsa. What's going on with you?"

"I just need to sleep." I pull the blanket over my head.

"Maybe if we'd stayed friends—it's an inverse thing with you, isn't it? Confess all to a stranger, hide your face from—whatever I am to you."

"You'd rather I screw the stranger?"

"You never explain—your moods are all over the place. I have no sense of what's coming either—I can only take it like the weather and all I can do is be here for you. Sometimes, you're like a Bergman film—but with more slapstick."

While most men use the dark to get frisky and fresh, this Swede uses it for more probing, discomfiting intimacy. "Well, your people," I say, "are as neurotic as the Jews but without the wit—or deli meats!"

"There you go again, reverting to the general, avoiding the personal. We were friends for a year before this happened," he says, waving his hand between our naked bodies. "Only when I leave Sweden for Madison, *then* you're all over me, but only on *your* terms."

"But the collaboration meetings are conducive to this." I echo his hand gesture. "Nice hotels in European capitals and a decent per diem, all courtesy of our universities. That's like lots of free dates in a compressed period of time."

"Right, we date twice a year—in the company of hundreds of other physicists."

"We also summer together at the pole," I counter. "Though I guess it's not as romantic as wintering over with someone.

It's OK. I like Sasha." I use her as a wedge because it's convenient, because part of me still wonders.

Jesper's obvious hurt is more surprising and reassuring than expected. "You think—what the hell—what reason have I given you?"

"It's those other people," I say, to deflect his anger. "They see you talking to her and they assume—sometimes say it to my face—other times, I just *know* what they're thinking. But I can't always tell when it's the voice in my head or all those other voices telling me what I am, what I'm worth, why I'm desired or not." I try to shut off the lamp, but Jesper catches my hand.

"Do you want to be boyfriend-girlfriend?" In his shy hesitancy, his Swedish accent and sincerity reveal themselves in the pauses between his words.

"We're not in high school. I mean, you've got another two years in Madison, and that's after the winter-over. I've got another year in Stockholm, then if I'm lucky, an Oxford postdoc. Who knows where we get tenure-track, if we both stay in academia?"

I can afford to toss another bone. "I like you a lot, Jesper, but I don't want to tell you things. Don't wanna know stuff about you either. I'd listen, but I'd feel bad, like I owed you. My family, even far away—you're different, but still—people and their needs, their sadness. I gotta streamline, get my head in the game. Maybe in the future—but right now there's too much I need to accomplish first."

Jesper can tell he's not the one I'm trying to convince. His silence conveys his annoyance at first, but soon turns to pity. So I reframe my argument. "You can't understand, sweetie, because you're white, plus Nordic. The Nazis thought you guys were the überest of the Aryans."

He sighs. "Sometimes I'm the Swede, other times, the white guy."

I shrug, flop back onto bed. "I see the world the same way it sees me."

After a while, he says with his typical untroubled earnestness, "I hope you meet the right person, who'll get to see all of you. I could, if you'd let me."

Jeong, according to my mother, is more dangerous than love. "Attachment" is my closest translation. Jeong, insidious and inevitable, keeps you stuck, beholden. Jeong is more powerful than love because it doesn't need affection or admiration to grow. Only time and proximity.

I tell Jesper I don't want him to be lonely, whether in Antarctica or in Madison. I tell him I'm going to do what I want, and he should do likewise. This way, it's easier for me to ignore him when he sends emails, easier for me to ignore him when the emails stop coming.

We make love for the last time. I keep my eyes closed, which I usually don't. I can't chance seeing another woman in bed with us. Afterward, I kiss every part of his face. My kisses tell him everything I can't—goodbye, thank you, wish I'd met you as a different woman.

But wishing I were another girl is what got me in trouble in the first place.

Sister Princess

I should have known there were more young men beyond. But I was surrounded by uncles and magistrates, and the first beautiful boy I saw was the shepherd, almost as pretty as me. Wanting to caress and hold what I glimpsed outside my window, I wove his fields upon my loom. I pinned him with my needle, stitching his body in place. My hair got tangled in the threads as I rewove the world beyond my reach. My lust soaked through like dye. When the shepherd finally glanced at my window, he must have seen himself reflected in a tapestry mirror. He moved toward the vision of his embroidered self. When he stepped close enough to reach his hand through my window, I pulled him into my room and ensnared him in the silk of my hair.

We were soon discovered, however. My shepherd threw his cloak over my head and told me to run away with him. He thought I could live as a commoner or in the wild like some savage. So I pushed him out my window. My father still vowed to punish us both. So I drank the poison he'd set aside for a mistress grown heavy with child. I intended to only drink enough to become ill, but a few drops on my tongue killed me. My father tore out his hair. I grieved more than anyone else.

Bounty hunters were hired to find the boy. Then one day, a cloaked figure appeared. He asked my father the cause for his search and learned how I'd killed myself for love, as the story goes. The figure threw off his cloak and with knife in hand ran toward my father. The boy fell, plunging the blade into his own heart. At least he didn't cut his lovely face.

The villagers mourned us, and my father joined the monastery. The monks prayed, and though I was content to no longer exist, the gods decreed that our love be eternal. I was plucked from heaven, and the shepherd, who'd attempted murder, was torn from hell. But I'd seen not only beyond my father's fields but also beyond life's borders. I didn't need him anymore to tell me what I was missing.

We were placed on opposite ends of the universe and commanded to come together again. We made our separate journeys but were hindered by a cosmic river of stars, a luminous band across the sky you now call the Milky Way. The monks prayed more fervently. We had to unite our bodies to satisfy their wishes, but there was no way to cross over. I stood there weeping, afraid of what our disobedience would conjure. I cried so much, my tears flooded the earth. Homes were washed away, the paddies ruined, and the children drowned.

Then from the earth, a black wave rushed toward us—a great swathe of furious speed. I feared the darkness would swallow me. Instead it stretched into a slender bridge that fluttered at my feet, tickling my toes with feathers. All the magpies in the world had come to bring us together to keep the world from drowning.

I walked over their tiny heads toward my lover. We embraced as the gods desired, as the birds believed was what we wanted. But the feathered bridge grew weaker. The shepherd and I rushed back to our separate sides and watched the magpies fall to earth, some recovering mid-flight, but most hurtling to their deaths.

Every year, I return to the edge of the Milky Way and weep once more because it is my duty to release the summer monsoons with my tears so that crops will be threatened and humans will pray and magpies will offer their little lives. I cry because what can sustain us but the stories told over and over again, through the beating wings of so many birds?

6

I fly from the pole to McMurdo in a propeller plane rigged with skis. To Christchurch, I'm strapped inside a military cargo plane. Then to Frankfurt and finally Stockholm. Along the way, I jettison Jesper, bells, and bedtime stories.

But waiting with my bags in the taxi queue outside Arlanda Airport on a February midnight in Sweden, my chilled bones demand a clearer demarcation between then and now—the sleep-deprived, snow-blind consciousness I left behind and the career-focused present that will determine my future. It's the end of summer at the pole, winter's last kiss up north, but I've exchanged one frosty vista for another, a mirror world with me belonging to neither.

The taxi driver, a woman with frizzy black hair tinted magenta, greets me in accented Swedish. I reply in English. She smiles, easily switching languages. We drive along an empty highway. I stare out the window, peering beyond the snowy fields into the darker smudge of forests at the horizon. She asks if I'm on holiday, and I explain I've been working in Stockholm for two years as a physicist.

"I studied some physics at university," she says, "but too many formulas to remember. How do you remember them all?"

"Well, we don't write them on glass. That's just in the movies."

"I prefer to remember people and their stories. I was a journalist in Cairo. What kind of physics is your specialty?"

"Neutrinos, but I'm pivoting toward sterile neutrinos. Will need to extend my postdoc for it—not that I love it here." I glance at her, remembering not all exiles have a choice in returning home. "But the long, dark winters are good for something."

She laughs. "You go from studying something neutral to something impotent?"

"It's sterile because it doesn't experience the weak nuclear force."

"Yes, yes, okay. So tell me why you are interested in this sterile neutrino."

"If we can show that sterile neutrinos exist, then that means the neutrinos we already know can change in new ways."

"I see," she says, nodding. "Being able to change is useful."

"Let me put it this way. Neutrinos come in three flavors: muon, tau, electron. As they travel through space, they oscillate, changing from one flavor into another. They change identities, like shape-shifters. There are strict rules for how they can change according to the Standard Model, but"—I pause for dramatic effect—"in some observations there've been *discrepancies*."

"It is OK, you do not have to explain," she says, smiling politely.

Clearly, she doesn't understand the exciting implications. I lean forward as far as the seat belt will allow so the cabbie can hear me more clearly. "So theorists have come up with a fourth neutrino state of being, the sterile neutrino. This theoretical particle would only interact with other active neutrinos, and only through the gravity force, so it'd be even harder to detect than the typical neutrino. Some call it 'the ghost particle's ghost.'"

Chuckling, the driver eyes me in the rearview mirror. "How do you catch the ghost of a ghost?"

"It doesn't remain a ghost forever."

"It comes back to life?"

"No, as I've said before, it changes flavor."

"Like ice cream." She nods.

"Ice cream doesn't change flavors, jawbreakers do. Anyway, point is, if we can show evidence for the sterile neutrino then that means the Standard Model—which our current physics is bound by—is incomplete, insufficient. Even now, neutrinos don't always abide by the same old rules of the Standard Model, but it's like we keep forcing them to fit, even though the data shows these *anomalies*."

"So you wish to free the neutrino from this standard model tyranny?"

I can't help myself with a captive audience. "By limiting the neutrino's story, we've constrained our own cosmic existence. But if we can show a fourth state of being for the neutrino to morph into—that would upend everything! We'd have to build a new understanding of physics, a new understanding of the entire universe!"

She grins at me in the mirror. "You sound like a revolutionary."

"Yes, it would be revolutionary indeed."

"So this is why you became a physicist?"

I nod absently, staring out the window. The simple question throws me off because I can't remember. Initially, I must've gotten into science for its reliable, stable certainties. Because the rules and empirical evidence diminished my mother and disenchanted her, got me further from home. The meticulous work and the discovery still thrill me, but ever since grad school, I've become more strategic, a careerist intent on job security with ample funding and a travel stipend. So why the sudden revolutionary zeal?

My last night at the South Pole, while Jesper slept, I went

over the work I'd done for that season and found it safe and unassailable, but also uninspiring, lacking vision and ambition. Career freak-outs weren't unusual in such a competitive environment as particle physics, so I tried to calm myself by striding through the station corridors while reciting my CV accomplishments.

Then on impulse, eschewing my usual coping strategies, I ducked back into the hydroponic garden. No voices. I walked out onto the ice at the edge of our buried neutrino observatory. No bells. I spun around, scanning the horizon. No woman with a braid down her back. But instead of feeling reassured over my regained sanity, I felt more alone than before and confined by my own fear. And whether it was the voice from my childhood or the lullaby refrain from my mother's story, I started to remember what it was like to wonder beyond what was known. Physically, in my childhood, I rarely ventured out beyond the walls of the house or even my room, but there was so much more that I explored inside in closets, cabinets, and secret portals. The curiosity and hunger to see what others couldn't, the willingness to believe in the unexpected—that's not why I became a physicist, but it can make me a better one now.

"Like artists," I murmur, "physicists find inspiration in unlikely places. But often, it's just the energy or direction that's useful. You must discard the rest. So yeah, sterile neutrinos. A pivot in my research. I'm using the same data, just looking for something different."

Then in my most chipper American voice, devoid of scientific mysticism, I ask, "So what about you?" I stop myself from asking what brought her to Sweden, a question posed to me by many native Swedes, but not so much from immigrants. Perhaps they assume the stories of flight are similar enough, or they're not interested in sharing their personal tales yet again.

"I was a revolutionary too, once—a lifetime ago," she says.

"Now, I drive a taxi. But you know this?" She taps a blue lotus medallion, edged in silver, hanging from her rearview mirror. Fan-shaped petals, inlaid with lapis lazuli. "This means rebirth. It is an earring, but I lost the other one, so now it is a symbol for thinking. Because I have changed flavors too and will again in the future, I am certain."

"Why does it symbolize rebirth?"

"So the scientist does not know everything! Well, the lotus closes every night and sinks to the bottom. Every morning, it rises to say, 'Hello, I am alive!' and opens petals to the sun. Also, in the beginning when all was darkness, in the ancient water a flower come up to open petals, and sitting inside was Ra the Sun God, creator of all. Many world stories are similar to this."

Indeed. I remember now a Korean folktale about a girl who dove into the ocean, and a sea turtle took her to an underwater kingdom. There she was reunited with her mother, who instead of being dead, as the girl had been told all her life, was married to the Sea King. The mother sent her back up, enclosed in a giant lotus. A Land King sailing nearby netted the blossom. At his touch, it bloomed to reveal the girl, and he took her as his wife. Is that why she was sent back, decked out in petals—to nab a rich husband? Such a Korean mom thing to do. At least, that's how my friends describe theirs. I wouldn't know because mine's been catatonic since I was fourteen.

But if it's true that Mom spoke again, asking about the other girl... What if living underwater is a mental state rather than a literal aquatic realm? Could I also reunite with my mother, however briefly, if my life was a retelling of this ancient tale?

I crack open the window for fresh air. The wind whistles sharply. Tentatively, I ask, "Do you believe in reincarnation, past lives?"

We speed into the night. The wind sings—high-pitched, discordant.

"No, no, I am a rationalist! I am only talking about symbols for thinking."

Shivering, I close the window, but can't shut out the piercing wail.

"Ancient Egyptians, however, not so rational," she says. "In the *Book of the Dead,* there are spells for transformation so you can change into a lotus, come back from death, and—"

Collision in the night. Driver slams the breaks, lurching me forward.

On the car's hood—the splayed body of a black-feathered bird, one wing fully extended. Blood smeared across the cracked glass. The bird's gleaming eye stares at me. Its neck, snapped at a sickening angle. A closed beak, but still the keening threads through my ears, curls throughout my body.

7

My sublet tenant has left everything tidy and anonymous, leaving only the IKEA furniture passed down from one visiting researcher to the next. My personal things are stored in the attic, and the lease is in my name, but I still feel like an interloper. Then again, I usually feel that way in Sweden.

Fun fact: the Swedish word for immigrant is *invandrare,* literally "in-wanderer" or "in-rover," which fits the hobo-drifter that I am. My father has called me a gypsy in English for my nomadic career. But tonight, I'd rather not be walking the earth like Caine, the faux-Chinaman. I just want to be enclosed and untouchable, lest anyone expect me to bloom.

I unroll my sleeping bag on the mattress. Tonight, I'll play the squatter in my own flat. Tomorrow, I'll retrieve from the attic my bedding and towels, my books and mugs, and other accessories of home.

I'm grateful to be in my own space again. I only wish it were quiet as well. The bird-crash has re-triggered my tinnitus —but it didn't start immediately.

Right after the collision, the cabbie drove her car to the roadside, then stepped out to crunch through the snow. Lit up with high beams, she cursed in a language I didn't know, all while facing me. She tugged the sleeve of her puffy coat over her hand then knocked the dead bird off the hood with a single backhanded strike. She was silent the rest of the journey. When she raised the heat in the car, the blood on her sleeve tinged the air with smoldering iron.

The driver emitted a quiet rage, as if I'd drawn the bird to me, as if it were my fault her car was caught in the cross fire. This was all my projection, of course. She was probably spooked like me and annoyed or just tired, but I avoided her eyes in the rearview mirror anyway. Instead, I stared at the back of her dark head, rigid and angled forward, as if that would speed her to her destination, as if she wanted to crash through the glass as well.

That's when my tinnitus returned—the ringing bell.

Maybe it was sense memory mixing time and addling my brain—this backseat position and vantage was so familiar—an older woman driving me around to whatever math club or tennis lesson that would secure me a better life than hers, while she radiated determination, envy, resentment, and steely maternal ambition.

Or more likely, I'd suffered a concussion too—not just the kamikaze bird.

Back in my flat, I snuggle in my sleeping bag, tugging the drawstring hood around my face. At least the ringtone of my tinnitus has been set to "resonant bells" rather than "bloodcurdling avian wail." It's almost meditative as I lie in my puffy cocoon, and the ice on top of Brunnsviken Lake cracks and shivers outside my window.

But a moment later, I'm jolted awake as a frigid wind blasts through the balcony door, swinging it on its hinges. Wet footprints lead across the floor to my bed. Melatonin-induced sleepwalking? Still in my sleeping bag, I shuffle toward the balcony and peer below.

Moonlight limns the frozen lake. Dark shapes quiver on the ice. Broken bodies, crushed beaks, and twitching wings. The shattered lake top writhes with feathers. A group of magpies is called a charm, tiding, or murder. But what do you call dozens of dead birds strewn across the ice in an arc, connecting shore to shore—like a bridge?

Birds fall out of the sky because of sudden weather changes or collisions into power lines. Migratory nocturnal birds get disoriented by storms and fog. Pareidolia—seeing patterns in what's randomly created, like a face in the clouds. Apophenia—detecting meanings and linkages between unrelated things.

But why is it so quiet? No more bells, not even wind, chiming through icicle-tipped trees. Then, in the deafening silence, a lone voice emerges—but only in my head.

My green lab notebook is already open to the last page where I'd written about sterile neutrinos. The facing page is blank. I write as though another hand moves through mine.

The monk asked my mother if she had anything to give for a great bell for Buddha. She joked she had no money, nothing to offer but a daughter.

My mother thinks the story is about her, the moral being not to joke about your kids to strangers. The monk thinks he's the hero—when in doubt, toss a girl into a vat. A little child sacrifice goes a long way, and Buddha will be pleased.

But the story is about me, obviously, and the lesson is—never be born female.

I drop the pen in horror and rub my fingers over the words, hoping they're not real.

A therapist I saw for a few months in grad school had me

jot down intrusive thoughts in a notebook. They would be separate from me, contained. I could see how irrational and meaningless the words were, however disturbing in my mind, and shut the book instead of letting the thoughts grow wild and monstrous in my limitless mental terrain.

But the pages in my lab notebook are meant to be shared, to support my work and rationale, to be analyzed and assessed alongside my research by others. The book is bound, so that pages can't be ripped out, thereby preserving the integrity of the experiment and its process. No gaps are allowed in case false data is later inserted. Everything is numbered, dated, time-stamped. So I can't tear out the intrusive folktale. Can't redact with Wite-Out. Can't accuse someone of tampering. It's all in my handwriting.

Locked in my bathroom—I google the Emmileh Bell. One site details measurements, metallurgy, and acoustics. I find a couple of history articles and even a few pictures on tourist sites. But none of this satisfies. I require work that's peer-reviewed, in a respected academic journal or a book published by a university press. Harvard and Stanford have decent East Asian Studies departments. Any UC library would do, but I don't have access. There's JSTOR, but it's no arXiv. After some rabbit-holing, I end up on the website for Stockholm University's Department of Oriental Languages or Institutionen för Orientaliska Språk. How quaint and colonial. Learn how the Orientals speak, spake, sproke. There's a small Asienbibliotecket, but nothing in the library catalog about singing Buddhist bells.

Frustrated, I give up and return to bed. I'm terrified and in need of answers. When I turn to face the wall, I end up nose-to-nose with my friend instead. At least I'm not alone anymore.

She must be cold, still wearing that shift that now only comes to her knees. Why can't I imagine a more decent outfit for her? Looking at her makes me shiver, her arms and legs all bare. And yeah, it's annoying how her figure is a lot better than mine, as if my psyche is taunting me with my inadequacies. "Did you make me write that story?" I ask.

"That one's not mine to tell."

I'm a kid again, desperate for any kind face when voices are seeping through memory's walls, when things I don't understand are happening outside my bedroom. "For tonight only, you may stay. But I've got an important meeting tomorrow with my advisor, so you can't be here in the morning." After a moment's hesitation, I add, "Why'd you go away when my father was arrested? Why've you come back now?"

She says nothing. I should be screaming, running to the nearest psych ward, but I'm too tired and cold. Besides, I've kicked this habit before—just let me have this one night with her. Tomorrow, I'll be sane again, no longer hungover from the South Pole and whatever sickness I've dredged up from staring into all those holes in the ice.

In a quieter voice, I ask, "When did my mom go crazy? I need to get tenure before my shit hits the fan."

She sighs. Her disappointment is pitying, almost tender and familial, making me hungry for redemption and eager to punch her in the face. A very Korean relationship dynamic. Taught or inherited? Adaptively speaking, these traits can push a people to survive no matter what, to improve our lot and better ourselves, so long as we don't kill each other first or kill ourselves.

"Oh Elsa, she never loses her mind, she only slips and falls between worlds. At least for her it's only for a little while. Because she can't let you go." Then ruefully, she adds, "For such a seemingly capricious woman, her hold on her children is ferocious. But for now, her folktale is finished. So yours must also reach its end."

"Never mind your very confusing use of verb tense. What do you mean her folktale is finished?"

"That's why I'm here—to take you home."

I grab my phone, checking for texts and email. Nothing. Why am I feeding my anxiety, giving it face and voice? Still, for tonight at least, I'd rather be crazy than lonely. "I don't do folktales," I mutter, sticking my lab notebook in my drawer.

"You've run away from your family, but that's how all the stories begin," she says. "All your ancestors were teenage runaways."

I write Chris an email: "Back in Sweden. Keep me updated about Mom." I delete "about Mom" and press send.

"Listen, Miss Blue," she says. "It'll get worse if you resist. The magpies or things from other tales. Wouldn't want another monsoon or shipwreck."

"There are no monsoons in Sweden, and I don't do boats either."

Although I'm peeved, I can't help smiling. It's been so long since she's called me Miss Blue. Her odd, occasional nickname for me when she thought I was being overly dramatic. Sometimes though, when we played family, with me being the mom and her as the baby, she'd whisper "Miss Blue Miss Blue" in a singsong chant, even though I told her she wasn't playing the game right because babies can't talk, much less sing.

But what am I doing? I've been losing all sense of time. Popping melatonin, flying from one end of the world to the other, stuck in a waking dream.

A while later, I slip out of bed, leaving her behind. Her eyes are unexpectedly closed, but she looks troubled with her worried brow. Do hallucinations dream of reality when they sleep?

In the locked bathroom again with my laptop, I return to the Department of Oriental Languages website. No history or archaeology professors in the Korean Department, only those focusing on language and linguistics. Only one Korean name; the rest are Swedish, German, and Anglo. One name strikes me as familiar—Oskar Gantelius. MSt in Korean Studies at Oxford, MA in Korean Literature at Yonsei, PhD in Viking and Old Norse Studies at Aarhus.

Most Swedish names blur for me, all those Sven Svenssons. But even in supposed egalitarian Sweden, the rarer surnames connote a certain class. Some medieval families didn't wait to be ennobled by the king. They appropriated Latin-ish surnames, including the clergy and the wealthiest merchants. The national ethos purports to be all about Jantelagen here, but even longtime expats know of this name game, though the Brits care the most. One acquaintance, upon learning that Jesper had won a top physics prize, asked me what his last name was. "Johansson," I replied. The Englishman scoffed, disappointed, "Oh, a mere Johnson."

Oskar Gantelius, cousin of Aurelius, why does your name sound so familiar?

8

Entering the Stockholm metro, I push through the turnstiles, and my friend follows behind like a scabby fare-dodger.

Sterile neutrinos can be their own antiparticles, theoretically. Particle and antiparticle pairs can annihilate each other—how will it end between my double and me?

On the conveyor belt walkway, through a tunnel carved from granite, I glide with commuters, ghosts passing underground. I tell my shadow to scram. The person ahead of me turns to stare. "Sorry, not you," I mutter. "Can you at least shut up while we're in public?"

More people edge away. How annoying that Swedes are so fluent in English and several other languages. What's the point of living in a foreign country if I can't talk about people behind their backs or converse with imaginary friends? Then again, this isn't the first time I've talked to myself. In the beginning, I would do so just to hear English in an American accent to make my surroundings less alienating. But even after I could understand some Svenska, I kept talking to myself while swerving around the other human objects in my way. Who cares if people stare? They do anyway, even when I keep my mouth shut. Might as well give them something else to look at besides being exotiska and clearly an utlänning, or "outlander." No wonder Swedish boys love high fantasy—it's already written in their native language and they're usually cast as the elvish heroes anyway.

"And making me think something happened to Mom was very shitty of you," I hiss. "I can't go home right now. And besides, 'the other girl' wasn't about you."

When I try to lose her by pivoting, though, I shiver from scalp to heels. Something's been torn. To reject is easy; to be abandoned, terrifying. I change my mind. My glimmer of madness should stay by my side rather than run amok in a city that'll never be mine.

Unfortunately, here at T-Centralen, all lines intersect and it's the most diverse, a mini-London. Would be easier to spot my double along the red line, near whiter Östermalm. I follow her onto a train, through the cars. She gets off before I can grab her braid. The exiting hordes sweep me into an orderly Nordic parade. She dashes upstairs, then, above ground, she climbs a hill. I struggle after her through the bushes. At the top, I fall on my knees, ripping a hole in my tights, blood soaking into Lycra. Stretched before me is my university—but the other side of campus, where the humanities lie.

She skips downhill. Back on level ground, I keep better pace. Finally, she stops in front of Institutionen för Orientaliska Språk. She leads me into a lecture hall and sits near the front while I slip into the back. Most of the heads are dark in hair color. How disorienting to be once again among so many "blackheads," a Swedish slur conveniently covering multiple ethnicities.

At the lectern, a tall Asian guy faces the audience, long hair bound in a topknot, black beard trimmed close to the jaw. He looks like the scholar-poets featured in my father's favorite historical dramas, missing only the silken blue robes, scroll, and brush. But dressed in a fitted vest over a button-down with rolled sleeves, he looks like a Brooklyn hipster, an artsy Asian guy. Maybe an architect, gallerist, or restaurateur.

Then it hits me—this is Oskar Gantelius—and I've already met him.

Surely this isn't kismet. Still, how unnerving—I'd grown up thinking of my life as some immigrant's kid bildungsroman, but then things took a sci-fi supernatural turn in Antarctica with some recent feathery flourishes of gothic horror. Now I'm tripping into a rom-com setup.

How do I seize control of my life when I can't even maintain a stable genre?

The breeze blew in through the open terrace doors of the faculty club. Interdepartmental mixers aren't my thing, but open bars certainly are, especially in this country with its 25 percent VAT rate. "Sidecar, please," I ordered, and the blond bartender with the David Niven 'stache stared back at me. Close-cropped hair, neatly combed and slicked with a side part. Stockholm hipster or neo-Nazi? His mustache hinted at whimsy, but the blond tidiness was so very fascist. When my Trinidadian-Swedish hairstylist told me to watch out for "wire-rimmed round spectacles," I'd laughed at first, then filed away the info to add to my list.

Yellow-'stache swiveled around, then took out his phone. Another bartender arrived, a deeply tanned woman with dyed black hair and pale blue eyes, like some gorgeous Arctic wolf. Yellow-'stache asked her in Swedish, "Hur gör man en sidecar?" *How do you make a sidecar?*

"Ingen aning." *I've no idea.*

Behind me, I heard in English, "Allow me to be of service." Then in Swedish, "Cognac, apelsinlikör, och citronjuice. Fem, två, två."

Five, two, two. The perfect ratio, the perfect man.

I turned around, very surprised to see a bearded Asian man, dressed in a summer suit, his shirt unbuttoned at his throat. Long hair combed sleek and tied at the back of his neck. My eyes roved down his chest to his nametag—Dr. Oskar Gantelius.

My first thought—Korean adoptee. Sweden had adopted many, part of its global humanitarian mission after remaining neutral through two World Wars and emerging with its architecture and populace intact, going from one of the poorest in Europe to one of the richest. Maybe there was a little guilt, survivor's and otherwise—i.e., letting the Nazis use their rail system to transport troops and weapons in their fight against Norway. So when the Korean War started, Sweden set up a Red Cross hospital and stayed there long after the armistice. When Oskar scanned my face, which facts and figures scrolled through his mind?

"Tack så mycket," I thanked him in my nasal-twang American Swedish.

"My pleasure," he replied with a slight bow. Then glancing at my scooped neckline, he read my nametag aloud. "Dr. Elsa Park."

Go ahead and ask, should be obvious that I'm Korean.

Instead, he offered his hand, saying, "Oskar Gantelius."

His British accent meant he was of that older generation of Swedes, when "proper English" was taught and mimicked, instead of its vulgar colonial offshoot, popularized by American TV. That made him midforties? More intriguing was a slender scar, running from the corner of his eye across his temple, pale against his tan skin, parallel with the sharp cut of his cheekbone.

"Five, two, two," I repeated like a secret code. "Nice call going for the IBA ratio."

"It's how I like it myself. Dry, strong, sour balancing the sweet."

And how I like my men! That's what I'd say in the US, but being too American here with strangers, especially men, can get one in trouble, especially if one is an Asian woman. Though I wondered if expectations and assumptions might be different for us?

Oskar told the bartender, "Samma för mig. Och ett glas rött, tack." *Same for me. And a glass of red, thanks.*

"Sorry," the bartender replied in English, glancing at me, then Oskar. "Only one drink per person at a time."

I took an exaggerated step to the side. "We're not together."

Oskar tipped his head toward a Hitchcockian blonde leaning against one of the terrace doorways. She had that wounded but icy reserve that certain men found attractive.

"Ursäkta," Yellow-'stache apologized.

Oskar smiled with a subtle shake of the head, an elegant "*no worries, happens all the time.*" With a similarly graceful and barely perceptible gesture he directed us a few steps away into a pocket of privacy.

"If I may, to which department do you belong?" he asked quizzically, no doubt parsing me as I did him.

"Experimental particle physics. And you? Are you hard or soft?"

Oskar blinked, a faint flush in his cheeks. "Pardon?"

"Theoretical, applied, or soft sciences?" I asked, finally realizing why he was embarrassed but relishing it anyway. It really was too easy to disrupt a Swede's equilibrium since I played by different cultural rules.

"Ah, literature and language," he replied, regaining composure, "both theory and application of. Specifically, I teach Korean language and history, poetry when I'm allowed. Lately, epics inspired by myth and lore."

My turn to blush. Asian guy—I just assumed. "Sorry, should've asked."

"Educated guess." He smirked, scanning the rest of the room. The few nonwhites I recognized were in the math and sciences, foreign visiting researchers like myself. We knew each other by face, not always by name. Passing them on campus, I'd try to give them the "ethnic nod," though friends tell me it's not a thing, especially when coming from an Asian woman.

"To make matters more confusing, Dr. Park," he says, "my doctorate is actually in Old Norse."

I laughed, then realized he wasn't joking.

"Yes, my face is the punch line." He picked up our sidecars, leaving behind the wine. When he handed me my drink, our fingertips met around the chilled glass. Oskar looked me in the eye, holding his glass to the middle of his chest, the rim of it hovering above the parting of his shirt where it was unbuttoned.

"Oh, Swedish style." I'd only done the proper Swedish toast with old professors at formal department dinners, never with a guy I found attractive.

"You may slam your glass against mine if you like," he said. "Like a frat-boy barbarian."

I raised my cocktail to my chest, meeting his gaze in challenge. "Let's skål, motherfucker."

"Skål," he echoed. Then in silence, we stared into each other's eyes as the ritual required, nodded in sync, angled our heads away while we sipped, then locked eyes once more and nodded to finish. "Perfekt," Oskar deemed, impressed, patronizingly so. I did my best to appear aloof. The traditional Swedish toast was too intimate despite its formality. Stylized and soul-baring, like the Argentine tango, like eye-fucking in a crowded faculty lounge.

The Hitchcock blonde, with her glass of red, inserted herself between Oskar and me. "Hej," she said, jutting her hand like a blade. "Vendela."

"Elsa," I replied.

"You're American!" she said, greatly amused.

I wanted to leave before the threesome skål—looking into each person's eyes like some creepy-kinky suicide pact—but Oskar stopped me with: "Dr. Park is a physicist. Vendela teaches Old Norse philology. This is the sort of intersectional opportunity promised in the email."

"I'm just here for the open bar," I replied. "I don't know how to intersect."

"A funny American scientist," she said. "Have you learned any Swedish while here?"

Noticing her Gantelius nametag, I blurted, "You're married."

"No. Why would you assume—?"

"She means us, Vendela," said Oskar. To me he explained, "I'm adopted from South Korea. Vendela's my sister. Hence, our surnames and the fact that we both have PhDs in Old Norse." I was grateful for Oskar's matter-of-factness. Undoubtedly, he was used to putting others at ease after their awkward assumptions and questions. "Most important," he added, "we're all here for the open bar."

I racked my brain for something to say, to show him I wasn't always this graceless, something to hold him here longer with me. But his sister was not only distracting, but also wanted him elsewhere.

Vendela said something to him in Swedish. The only words I recognized: "tenure-track," "Minnesota," "Toronto." Oskar's annoyance was clear in his bored gaze and tight mouth. "Excuse us," said Vendela. "There are important people Oskar needs to meet."

"I'm sorry, Dr. Park," he said. "I promised my sister I'd make more of an effort. Perhaps I'll see you around campus?"

When he was a few steps away, I blurted, "I'm Korean too!" He turned to smile. "Korean American," I continued, unable to stop myself. "Not adopted, but—" I shrugged, gestured around me at the Swedes in the room, and tossed back the rest of my drink.

He nodded, almost laughing, then raised his glass to me in salute—while being pulled away by a sister who hadn't even bothered to glance back.

Oskar Gantelius's lecture is about Yi Sang, a poet from the 1930s. He projects a poem on-screen, the Korean original and Swedish translation. My spoken Swedish is limited, but my reading is better, as many words resemble their English counterparts. My Korean is also limited. These days, I rarely speak it—with my dad mostly, and at Korean restaurants. Between the two texts though, I can pick out words from either language and piece something together.

One poem is about a porcelain cup resembling a skull. Someone holds this cup when his arm branches another arm, and this new hand grabs the cup and smashes it against the floor. I learn that Yi Sang was imprisoned by the Japanese police for "thought crimes" during its colonial rule, that the poet died at age twenty-six. In another poem, someone cuts off their arms to use as candlesticks. Much easier to comprehend, at least, are Oskar's face and form because he is mathematically, empirically attractive. But that makes me feel guilty about Jesper, so I stare at my friend's head instead. The red ribbons undulate, hypnotic...

As I start dozing, a familiar name pulls me from sleep—Shim Cheong. She's the speaker in the poem that Oskar's discussing. Author: Anonymous. Shim Cheong is the girl who throws herself into the ocean so that her blind father might see. The girl transforms herself into a giant lotus, rising to the surface. Oskar analyzes the language's violence, defamiliarization, self-alienation, and transformation as resistance and rebuke against Japanese colonization.

Didn't expect *that* narrative turn, but now I've got a name—Shim Cheong. I don't think the others had names, not in the picture books anyway. Not the nymph left behind in the lake, nor the princess who must drown the world in her tears.

So many girls tossed into oceans or vats of molten bronze—drowned or smelted. One myth flowing into the rest. You all have your own stories, but something common flows throughout. Korea is a peninsula, after all, surrounded by seas. And considering how the ice is melting at an alarming rate, this remix of lore is probably inevitable after so many decades of outright denial. Maybe that's how my friend appeared at the bottom of the world, as the waters moved from shore to shore, transfiguring their states of matter along the way.

Neutrinos are also shape-shifters, though in physics we call it oscillation. These ghost particles change identities along their lonely, infinite journeys—between electron, muon, or tau. However, we've never observed them in the *process* of transformation. We can only detect and deduce, observing them in one form here, another over there. Even then, we still can't see the ghost particle itself. We can only trace its shadow and echo upon collision with another.

I always felt like a shape-shifter too—moving across America, across class, from Gardena to my blue-blood patrician schools, and now among the NordicTrackers. But it's not code-switching—I don't adapt in order to fit in or translate myself back and forth. I can't peel off my Asian face anyway. But how else to explain why my skin feels false, ill-fitting, or suffocating—depending on which borders and spaces I cross?

The lights come on and students file out. None is my friend. Soon, it's just Oskar and me. Tugging my skirt's hem over my torn bloody tights, I approach.

"Vi har träffats," he says. *We've met before.* A moment later, "Sidecar?"

"Five, two, two. The perfect ratio." The lectern is a barrier between our bodies, but its lamplight touches both our faces, holding us together in its warm glow.

"Maths," he says. "No, you're a physicist. And American."

"And you're Oskar Gantelius. Dr. Gantelius, I mean."

"What was your name again?"

"Dr. Park. Elsa Park."

"Yes, of course. Are you auditing?"

"Just wandered in. I liked your lecture, what I understood of it. Also, there's a *lot* of Asians in your class!" I sweep my arm toward the empty hall. "Like holy shit, the most I've ever seen in Stockholm, including the three Korean restaurants in the city."

Oskar laughs. "Many of them are adoptees, taking my class as an elective while pursuing more lucrative careers. They're friends, really. We explore and discover—together."

My mind instantly calls up facts I've learned while living here. With a population of 9.5 million, Sweden has over 9,000 Korean adoptees since the war, the highest per capita in the world. In absolute numbers, Sweden ranks third. Scandinavia as a whole has the second biggest population in a homogeneous land with very little Asian immigration otherwise.

Out of the corner of my eye, something black and red blurs outside the window. I turn and see only falling snow. "The Emmileh Bell," I say. "Do you know the real history of it?"

"If I may ask, Dr. Park, why would a physicist be interested?"

"The physics of bell acoustics. Vibrations, wavelengths, oscillations."

"Ah, the tonal qualities of child sacrifice."

"The Shim Cheong poem, that's a folktale too. Do you know a lot about folklore?"

Oskar gathers his notes, looking down, retreating. "I dabbled in translation when younger. Wrote some retellings. Small press, when multiculturalism was en vogue."

"Dr. Gantelius, do you have time to talk right now? Or I could come by another time."

He pauses. "My schedule's clear until noon. Shall we have coffee in my office?"

My advisor will understand if I'm late. Better to arrive with a clear head after contextualizing my ghosts in history and culture, where they belong. Plus, when else can I talk to this man without any hot blondes around? For a moment, it almost felt like home, at least how others talk about it. Mine was always something to escape or forget, but I like the abstract concept—seems cozy, being sheltered from outside elements, belonging, possessing, and being known.

"I should inform you," says Oskar, as we walk down a corridor, "my doctorate is in Old Norse poetry."

"I remember. From the mixer."

"Of course, I told you already," he says, looking straight ahead. "A social reflex of mine, especially when meeting other academics."

"But you teach Korean poetry now?"

"I still publish, translate, and consult on runic inscriptions, but there aren't many full-time university positions.

Competition is fierce, and my appearance, rather distracting." He opens his office door. "I already had two masters in Korean studies, and with this"—he waves his hand over his face like a magician—"easier to sell myself to this department. Right packaging." He gestures toward two armchairs, then excuses himself to get us coffee.

I've always kept my own offices stark naked, without even an xkcd comic on the wall. But some colleagues use their workspaces to intimidate with publications on their shelves, along with some Polish poetry to appear well-rounded. Splashes of personality are conveyed with toy figurines or memorabilia from Burning Man. Oskar's no different.

There's a wall of books on one side of the office, and on the other, posters of Im Kwon Taek films, including *Seopyeonje* and *Chwihwaseon.*

Beside these, there's an old Korean map, atlas-sized, set in a deep frame. Moldering sepia parchment and faded colors of green and blue. If not stolen from a museum, it's an uncanny reproduction. Amoeba-shaped landforms, labeled with Hanja characters. China, Korea, and Japan clustered in the middle, surrounded by ocean. Around these ancient kingdoms, a narrow ring of land signifies the rest of the world—mountain ranges, ponds instead of seas. Encircling all, an outermost ring of blue dotted with islands and symbols. A flat circle Earth, with the Orient no longer defined by its eastern relation to whatever else considers itself central. A title card in English reads: ATLAS OF ALL THE WORLD UNDER THE HEAVENS, C. EARLY 19TH CENTURY.

Then, in a corner alcove, I discover a vintage French poster of the original *Planet of the Apes*, lovingly lit from above. Blond, blue-eyed Charlton Heston in bordello-bondage, the human interloper from an Earth long gone, flanked on either side by simian black-haired overlords. The palette in aqua, orange, and lurid green evokes '60s sci-fi, à la Toulouse-Lautrec.

Oskar returns with two coffees and hands me one as we stand in front of this vision, like a couple on an awkward first date at a museum.

I quote the film's line about all men looking alike to the apes, then explain how Dr. Zira is the true hero. "Taylor's a total dick. Who's your favorite?"

"Nova," replies Oskar.

"The hot, mute woman."

"Dr. Park, I'm joking." He holds my gaze, rendering me speechless. "Friends assume Cornelius is my favorite. But it's really Dr. Zaius, who knows that power lies not in science or religion but in crafting the story the simians want to hear. Secretly, I identify most with Taylor."

I raise my eyebrows as high as they can go.

"He's the tragic immigrant," he continues, "the ultimate exile who can't return home, who suffers considerable demotion in his new land."

"But he's not an immigrant," I counter. "He's still on Earth, so the real tragedy is that he left home, in a freakin' spaceship, but ended right back where he came from." Though Oskar's taller and we're on his turf, I'm not backing down. I sip my coffee loudly to show I'm done arguing, that I'm right.

"I never realized how many things Americans can do so audibly," says Oskar, gesturing to the armchairs. I continue to sip loudly as I settle into the bigger chair.

Oskar launches back with, "He's a *temporal* immigrant, out of his time. Home is forever lost, for the way to the past is not traversible—never mind the sequels. Yes, he's a tragic superhero, an alien on his own planet, the last of his kind."

"No superpowers, so *not* a superhero. Just a super-dick, for never thanking Dr. Zira."

Oskar smooths his shirt with a palm down his chest. Swedes are coolly elegant and restrained, so it's easy to ruffle their feathers with sass and vulgarity. He's enjoying this though, I hope. And I suspect we're both revealing more than usual.

"Consider this," he says. "Like Kal-El, Taylor is common where he came from, but among the apes he is Superman and very much alone. Yes, I also identified with Kal-El, fellow immigrant and adoptee. But while he and Diana and others could belong through their secret identities, Taylor was reviled despite the blond hair and 'bright eyes.' Yet he doesn't hide his conviction of superiority. He's my *personal* superhero. Or was, when I was young."

I want to touch some part of Oskar, let him know I understand. So I clink my mug against his. "Well, we're all fugitives now." I lean back, pondering. "One thing though, I never liked it when the apes rode the horses."

"Yes, yes, I've bored you enough with my nerdy teenage self-pity. Shall we discuss the Emmileh Bell instead, Dr. Park?"

"I bet the horses are like: 'Watch your back, tree-climber. Someday *we'll* get opposable thumbs.'" Oskar's gaze makes me feel like he can see all my cards, peel them off my chest even, so I deflect with: "Doesn't Dr. Zaius look a little Asian around the eyes? Never mind. So, Dr. Cornelius, I mean, Gantelius—may I call you Oskar?"

"Please do."

"Cool. You can call me Elsa. Anyway, the Emmileh Bell. Made in 771 CE, twenty-five tons in bronze—I got the numbers, but is the legend inspired by any historical truth?"

"My God, it's like conversational whiplash with you!" He playfully clears his throat and sets his mug down on a side table. He steeples his hands under his chin, giving me mock professor-face. "You're wondering if the girl of legend was truly melted into a bell? Not much different from ritual child sacrifices in other cultures, I suppose."

"What about the girl who jumped into the ocean? In your lecture—"

"Shim Cheong, whose filial devotion is her greatest virtue. Whether based on fact, well, human sacrifices were rarely properly documented."

"Girls," I say.

"Pardon?"

"They were all girls—in the stories my mother told me."

With an edge, he says, "Throughout Korea's history, both male and female children were sent as tribute to the dominant kingdoms. To China and Mongolia, and most recently, the West." He looks down into his coffee. "According to my colleague anyway. Used to be an activist, rather militant, arguing against transnational, transracial adoption. A long time ago."

I nod, hoping I haven't upset him. "In a lot of the stories, children are given up, mistakenly or not. Like the bell girl offered to the monk. Or Shim Cheong sold to the sailors."

Oskar smiles. "Your mother was quite diligent with passing on these tales."

"That's one way of putting it. But more than the details, I remember how disturbed I was, how she whispered these in the dark, lying beside me in bed. Like the bell girl—what the fuck, Mom? Why are *these* girls, doomed and sacrificial, the ones in the picture books?"

Without missing a beat, he replies, "To inculcate the most virtuous Korean values among its children, so that the nation and its people may remember and survive. That is the party line, isn't it?"

Our knees almost touch. I slip my hand over the blood-stained hole in my tights. He notices.

"Or like this map on my wall," he says, breaking the tension that perhaps only I'm feeling. "The stories remind us of how the world looks to those from other cultures—how we're similar, how we're not. In a way, these characters are time-travelers, even finding their twins in distant lands. Cinderella is found the world over, though many believe she originated in ancient China—bound feet, smallest shoe, foot fetish and whatnot.

"Better yet," Oskar said, striding across the room to his shelves. He reaches to the top, and his shirt strains around the shoulders. A swimmer perhaps, with a body long, lean, and smooth. "I present data for your perusal. You can examine the source material yourself. Perhaps you'll find another reason for their appeal." The hardback is old, with yellowed pages, a faded green cloth cover. "That was a gift, for when I first arrived."

"Arrived?"

"Before I was adopted. I arrived when I was five. Was formally adopted two years later."

"Two years? So you were just roaming the streets of Stockholm till then?"

"Like a Dickensian foundling, a child pickpocket. Tried to join the circus, but the clowns wouldn't have me."

"Really?"

Oskar's so serious I can't tell if he's joking. Plus, my father told me how orphans formed kiddie gangs during the war, thieving for survival. He wasn't even referring to his little sister, my aunt, who wasn't that much older when she was lost. *Remember your father's name and hometown and that all roads lead to Seoul,* he intoned in Korean, as if echoing the chant that all children were taught during their passage south, as if to teach it to me now for my own travels around the world.

"No, Elsa," says Oskar. "I lived in a big house on a beautiful island with a Swedish woman and other orphans from Korea."

I still can't tell which was his reality, which was a smokescreen.

Sitting on the edge of his desk, Oskar unwinds his topknot, then tucks his loose hair behind his ears, transforming from Shilla dynasty scholar-poet to Lou Diamond Phillips circa the '80s, when brownish-yellow men with long black hair passed for Cherokee.

"Anyway, it's in English," he says. "There weren't any Korean folktales in Swedish back then, not that I could read Svenska. Truth is, I didn't bother to read this until I was in uni. Translated by a missionary, so it's a bit stilted. You may prefer this other one."

It reminds me of my own childhood books, with their translated dual texts and bland watercolor illustrations. Were these made by the propaganda office for the children of diaspora?

"In the early '90s," he continues, "it was fashionable for nations to apologize to their minorities and displaced. So President Kim came to Stockholm and apologized to all us Korean children for sending us away. There were cultural events too, showing how wealthy Korea had become. Also maudlin documentary specials about adoptees meeting their birth parents."

"I've seen one on PBS."

"A Korean movie was also filmed in Sweden about a real-life adoptee—I knew Suzanne, a little." He's remembering with sad fondness. Jealousy flares, then is doused with shame.

"Some of my friends attended the protests," he says, returning his attention to me. "I picked up this book among the souvenirs. No Swedish versions though. We got the leftovers from the American Apology Tour. I liked the cover."

It's a picture of a bulbous-eyed tiger lounging against a tree and smoking a long pipe. Smoke escapes his nostrils in curling plumes. I recall—instead of "Once upon a time," my mother sometimes began her stories with: "In the old days, when tigers smoked tobacco pipes..."

He presents another book, *Koryo Kayo Songs.* Professorial again, he's taking up more space, enjoying the sound of his sonorous voice. He explains how the songs were originally transmitted as oral literature. "These may reference a prewritten form of myths. They contend with the mortal world, so you might find child sacrifices and flesh metallurgy in these pages."

"But these are all written by men. Why would fathers, monks, and sailors tell the truth?"

"You're still keen to believe the bell girl and Shim Cheong were real." His smile is bemused but not patronizing, as if he too wishes he could believe the world was once riddled with wonder and magic, however gruesome at times. "Well, some do speculate on historical antecedents for European fairy tales too.

"As for female creators," he says, "this early poetry was transmitted for hundreds of years before it was written down." He's sitting on the edge of his desk. I glance away from the pull of his slacks against his thighs. "Literary fairy tales, such as those by the Grimms, were written by educated men to create and curate a folk culture, a national identity. But these same tales descended from much older sources, many of them women tellers, the majority illiterate. Such tales were born on the field, in the kitchens, around the hearth—embellished and personalized—passed across villages and down through generations."

He winds his hair into a topknot again, securing it with an elastic snapped off his wrist with a kind of vicious elegance.

"Furthermore, much of oral literature," he continues, "especially if conveyed by women or others without power, allowed for vocalizing lament and grievance that was socially acceptable—or encoded. Consider the lullabies sung by American slave mothers to their children, while they could still keep them. You see it throughout history the world over. I'm sure *your* mother also had her own spin and agenda in what she passed on to you."

"Sure. Maybe. Thank you—but this is all too much." I dump the books on his desk and retreat from their suggestive power.

Geeky bantering is fine, but what did I expect—that this guy could reassure me the stories weren't true, that my mother is simply crazy and my hallucinations temporary? As if he could sign off on my papers, so I could resume my real life? Flirting with Oskar was dangerous. Bad enough I wrote down that story in my lab book. Why fan the flames?

And why are we pathologizing being Korean? Us together—that way madness lies. In college, my Jewish boyfriend cheated on me with his Korean ex. I couldn't sleep and couldn't stop crying from the shame and betrayal. So I signed up for a counseling session at University Health Services and was assigned a Korean American grad student. The therapist-in-training interrupted my unloading about my mom's constant sadness and her obsessive warnings about first loves with: "OK, but how do you feel about your eyes?" The grad student's eyes were slender, mono-lidded like mine. I replied, "I have no problem. My mom always told me my eyes were beautiful just like hers had been, uncut and un-botched before her eyelid surgery, which had been the trend at the time in Seoul. My mom envied that I had the eyes she was born with. My nose though—now that honker I'd love to shrink into the small, cute button noses that all the other Korean girls have."

But how do I explain to Oskar that it's not him I'm distancing from? Instead, I'm running from all the questions we stir up in each other, contrapuntal and resonant, even if one of us doesn't know his parentage and the other feels burdened by ancestry. Weren't we both trying to assert our own identities through physics, runic poetry, and simian sci-fi?

"Like I said before," I say, "I just wandered into your lecture, killing some time before—I'm a physicist—not looking to reconnect with my roots—certainly not in Sweden."

"I didn't mean to presume—you'd have more first-hand knowledge anyhow, unlike me."

"That's not what I meant—fuck, I didn't mean you weren't a real—or any less—you mentioned writing your own retellings. Are they in English?"

"I don't have any copies. And please, no need to soothe my ego."

"Sorry, I've taken too much of your time." I reach for my coat, but he places his hand lightly over mine, barely touching. He's about to say something, but catches me staring at his almost-touch and whisks it away. Decorous and proper once more, he holds my coat open. I slip my arms into the sleeves, never realizing how intimate it was to slide backward into this near embrace, especially in silence. With my back to his chest, his breath skims along the top of my ear. "Perhaps another time," he says.

"So many girls drowned, burned, or smelted," I whisper. "How could our people be so cruel? Did my ancestors really suffer like that? I mean, generally, not literally."

Still behind me, his nearness palpable, he says, "Several European stories feature children baked, fried, and eaten. In fact, there's a classification system for folktales. Tale types, grouped according to major common plot points. And one tale type is known as 'My Mother Killed Me, My Father Ate Me.' So, it isn't just *our* people who were so strict with their young."

"It's amazing any of us are still alive."

"Think of it this way," he says as I slowly spin to face him. "The terrors of childhood are mysterious, rooted in the inexplicability of the world and its people. Easier for a child to process her fear if it's about being eaten; best if the child overcomes it by sticking the witch in the oven. Childhood is its own dark, wild wood, Elsa—fairy tales help us through it."

I notice his scar again, from the corner of his eye to his temple—so rakish at first. But now, I imagine someone slicing his eye into an exaggerated slant, that maybe he'd done it himself. It was hidden before, behind long loose strands, but is now pronounced. Its trail disappears into his hair, making me wonder how far the cut extends.

"Oskar, would you like to have dinner with me—tomorrow? My treat. Or maybe some other time—"

"I'd love to, Elsa. Tomorrow."

I sweep the books on his desk back into my arms, hurry out of his office and down the hallway. Bursting through the doors to the outside, I'm grateful for the chill against my burning cheeks.

In the falling snow, I don't see my friend, but she's not the ghost I need to confront. The voice in my head I ignore, the face I forever turn from—if my mother is finally coming back, I need to be ready. If I'm going to force her to play by my rules of reality, then I must know the territory and define those boundaries for myself.

9

Back on the right side of campus, running toward the Alba Nova building where the real work gets done. Not even the soft scientists get to play here. Time to focus on my future.

Panting from the exertion, I enter my advisor's office. The entire back wall is glass, a floor-to-ceiling window facing a snowy forest. Dr. Linnea Lönnrot's study is spare and pristine as an art gallery. White walls, white furniture, no curtains for the glass. But Linnea's dressed like a Stevie Nicks groupie—wavy beige hair, velour skirt, and a pashmina covered in cat hair.

"Sorry I'm late—"

Linnea crushes me in a bear hug. She's one of the architects of IceCube, also on the Nobel Committee for physics. A brilliant and generous mentor, she's why I came here for my postdoc. She holds on to my fingers in her vein-snaked hands, adorned by a heavy opal ring, the milky orb flecked with phosphorescent green. "Is it still as thrilling as the first time?" she asks.

"Yes, always."

"Kaffe? Milla has also baked some lovely kanelbullar."

Fika, both noun and verb, is a coffee break with pastries, typically cinnamon buns. With at least two fikas a day at work, across all industries, I'm baffled how Swedes stay so slim and how they get their work done and why they need six weeks of vacation.

At a conference table next to the glass wall, we fika with my proposal. Linnea nibbles a bun and reads my pages, her opal glimmering like a mood ring.

Nervous, I look out the window. More snow has fallen. Nothing but white-skinned birches, luminous and ghostly. The overcast sky and snowy ground provide little contrast. The trees in the forest, like alternating bars of pale and paler. Unclear which is the negative space. Like staring into wallpaper with a depth that's both illusory and unstable. My Park Slope friend papered her baby's nursery with an expensive version of this pattern, but I blanched when she sent me the pictures. What baby wants to be wrapped in a forest prison?

"This is all very good, Elsa, but why sterile neutrinos? What about your binary stars?"

"No one at IceCube is leading a group on sterile neutrinos yet. And with the data from Fermilab and Daya Bay, this could be the next big thing. Clock's ticking. I need to stand out from the pack."

"I can always put in a good word for you with most of the EU universities, if you are feeling stressed about—"

"Thank you, but I can't stay here long-term." I lean back and sigh. "Took me thirty years to learn how to be 'ethnic' in the States. Don't have time to figure it out again here. Postdocs are fun, but I can't immigrate for reals. I mean, you're white, but you've told me that you got crap sometimes for being Finnish."

"Yes." Linnea smiles proudly, raising her chin. "We are primitive drunk barbarians, former subjects of the empire, a blonder shade of Russian."

"So what hope do *I* have? By the way," I whisper, even though it's just the two of us, "it's because you're Finnish and probably some Sami that I can say this to you. You get me."

Linnea is confused, trying not to laugh. "I am not of Sami descent, Elsa."

"Close enough though, right?" I reason that the Sami are kinda Asian, by way of Siberia, and Finland's next to Russia, so Linnea could be a long-lost aunt, several millennia removed. Also, didn't some race biologists back in the day dismiss Finns and the Sami as cousins of the Mongols? Talk about splitting blond hairs when it comes to a white-off.

Linnea takes my hands in hers. "If it makes you happy, Elsa, less alone, to believe that I am Sami, of course you may. But I must press—are you sure about the sterile neutrino? Yes, there are some proponents among the theorists, but you know the theorists—always nattering on, with little consideration of how experiments—"

Behind her, through the window, I see a woman deep in the forest with her hand outstretched, stroking the paper-white bark as she loops through the woods. Her skin and dress, pale as the trees. Black hair dusted with snow. I pull my hands away and screw my eyes shut. *Not now, please, not now.*

"Oh Elsa, I don't mean to upset you! I only want you to be certain, passionate even."

I *am* passionate, but I can't reveal that it's driven by an impulse I can't shake. What's worse, I'm skeptical about this as a career move too. Other physicists seeking the sterile neutrino are zealous, truly wanting a revolution in physics. But me—I'm more cautiously curious about this realm of possibility, where the foundation upon which we've built our understanding of the universe might actually be wrong. Moreover, in this liminal space, I won't have to work so damn hard to rationalize what doesn't make sense in my life lately. And the more challenging puzzle of sterile neutrinos is a welcome distraction when I need a break from red ribbons and singing bells. But for Linnea, I present my rehearsed speech instead.

"We're using point source analysis," I say, "to map the universe, but there's so much we don't understand about neutrinos themselves. We detect it in one state here then observe its changed identity later in its path, but what happens between those points, how does it change identities in transit?"

"There's very little proof of the sterile neutrino thus far," says Linnea. "You'd be willing to spend years on this, stake the next stage of your career—only to possibly end up with mounting evidence against it?"

"That's our job. 'The religious have their culture of faith; we scientists have our doubt.'" A catechism, anchoring me to this world.

"Richard Feynman," she says, recognizing my quote. "Bit of an ass, but clever."

"If my work closes off the possibility of the sterile neutrino's existence, then I've done my job as an experimentalist," I say, ignoring how my friend slips deeper into the woods, but stops momentarily, red ribbon caught on a branch. Then she keeps going as the crimson curlicue unspools throughout the forest. I scoot closer to Linnea so that her beige bouffant obscures the view. "At least, I'd get rid of one ghost."

"Ah, the ghost particle's ghost. Those journalists are so witty with their nicknames. And how can I help you with this endeavor, Elsa?"

"Postdoc extension. Then with your help, a second postdoc. Oxford, I'm hoping. Then publish, publish, publish. After that, I'll get a job and settle down."

"I was only waiting for you to ask. Who knows, maybe a Nobel down the line?"

"Don't tease me, Linnea. You haven't even taken me as a date yet to the ceremony." The snow has fallen harder outside the window, blotting out the view, not a hint of red.

"Play your cards right—" She pauses while riffling through my notes and removes a folded sheet of paper. "What's this?"

It seems to be a page torn from my green notebook, which is locked in my desk in my apartment to prevent the bell story from oozing out. Linnea smooths the quadrants. Across the top is scribbled: "Four tales carved in wood, most common in our blood." I snatch it from Linnea and stuff it in my bag, telling her it's nothing, that I need to go.

She knows me well enough not to push. "Before you go, Milla packed you some buns." As she retrieves the container, she adds, "Even the snake lets the sleeper lie in peace."

"What's that supposed to mean? What snake?" *Did she mean my friend?*

"Something my grandmother used to say. Figure it out. Aren't you a rocket scientist?"

Maybe this Finn really was an inscrutable Scandi-sage, spouting cryptic wisdom through Uralic koans. Then again, Linnea's favorite Finnish proverb, one quoted by a couple other Finns I've met, was: "A weak fart doesn't rip the ass."

We hug goodbye and I sink into her pashmina embrace. So easy to be with her—not a rival, nor object of desire, nor someone who needs me to redeem her. But then over her shoulder, I see that the floor-to-ceiling window has suddenly been replaced with birch forest wallpaper. I move toward it to stroke a slender white tree with my fingertip, marveling at what little grip I seem to be having lately. "You don't have a window," I whisper.

"But I still have a view. Milla insisted on using the leftover paper from our lake house. Very Stockholm, this accent wall, but I like it anyhow."

"Lovely." I turn to leave and hide my agitation.

Linnea grabs my hand, studying me with concern. With my thumb, I stroke her opal in a tiny circle. It doesn't change color, doesn't reveal my mood either. I wish I could rub it to change all that I'm feeling instead.

Once outside, I open the folded page. At first glance, I'd imagined that the torn pieces I'd tossed out the car window sixteen years ago had awakened, finding each other across the desert, whirling like tumbleweed to re-form and follow me across the ocean.

But the graph paper tells me this is ripped from my notebook and the handwriting is mine. Must've written this after the bell story dictation and bathroom googling. My subconscious, desperate for something tangible, must've reconstructed this—and translated it unfaithfully. Folktale titles are written in my own voice rather than my mother's: "Bell Girl," "Sea-Diver," "Fairy Housewife," then a large "?" in the fourth quadrant. Something else is missing too—those scattered islands of words in the blank, empty sea.

Well, though it's certainly unnerving not to remember recreating this, at least it's more data to work with—to invalidate, refute, and dismiss. And now that the floodgates are opening...

I've argued theology with Chris before, to explain with Biblical sources why he can't be the brother of Jesus. But his faith is impervious—even when knowing the Jesus delusion isn't entirely uncommon among stress-triggered schizophrenics in hyper-religious immigrant families, even when confronted by the fun house reflection of other mentally ill Asian dudes. "I've met two crazy fuckers who thought they were Jesus," he told me once. "One guy isn't even diagnosed with anything, just a weird-ass. I keep them away from each other lest their heads blow up. But even with the one freak, I had to argue with him like a Pharisee. I don't want him as my holy brother. Never claimed to be Jesus anyway. Just another child of God."

At least Mom can't argue back, even if it's true she can string a few words together. Her asking about the other girl won't require me to get into an ontological or metaphysical debate, not that I actually know what those words mean. More to the point, I have other skills as a scientist. Unfortunately, the most straightforward experiment is impractical because my mother's theory requires a longitudinal study across decades, and I don't have the patience nor stamina to test whether my life adheres to folkloric fate. As for my mother, my dead aunt and dead grandmother and all those before her—I don't know enough and never will.

Of course, if the theoretical family curse goes back further, there'd be plenty of cousins out there now living these destinies. Which of these women cry out when struck? Which have lost freedom and power through marriage to become trapped? Which have fled for a different life, only to be sent back into the bed of a man? I don't need Ancestry.com to tell me these story sisters are legion across time and space.

But Mom's delusion, however elaborate, didn't accommodate these considerations of genetic spread. Instead, her fantasy, like her suffering, was solitary and therefore distilled. The curse, as she described it, passed through the simplest direct bloodline. Thus, she'd siphoned all the pain that came before into herself, trying to keep it from spilling over into her children.

Maybe I should start with something more obvious instead, to find the hole in her story—the mythical sister. But how do I track down a girl who doesn't exist in order to disprove her when I don't know my relatives in Korea, when they might not know what a deranged pregnant woman was doing while on the lam from her husband?

More salient perhaps—what about my friend? Was she a subconscious manifestation to unlock memories or evidence of a biological fate, another kind of blood curse of familial inheritance?

Piblokto is an Inuit ailment, called Arctic hysteria, typically applied to women. When the white men explorers first met the Inuits, they witnessed the women going crazy in winter.

They'd run naked across the snow or jump off ships, diving into icy water. There was screaming, sometimes seizures. Then they slept, forgetting all, while the white men scribbled in their books.

My brother also stripped naked a few times during his episodes. He also passed out after seizures and slept deeply after, but it was my mother who wrote while her son drooled.

Piblokto is a culture-bound syndrome—like how only Americans suffer brain freeze after ice cream or feel existential dread after bingeing a TV series to completion. Korean menopausal women often exhibit hwa-byeong, fire sickness, the result of decades of pent-up rage unleashing itself, usually upon husbands, mothers-in-law, and ungrateful children. The psychosomatic symptoms often arise from an overflow of Han—itself another culture-bound syndrome. There's no English equivalent, but it seems to afflict all Koreans—a mournful sorrow and railing against fate's unfairness, an aching of the soul.

Piblokto only exists among Arctic people, according to some doctors, but there's no such word in any Inuit language. A hundred fifty years after it was first recorded, it's still written that way in the Diagnostic and Statistical Manual of Mental Disorders under "culture-bound syndrome."

But if a bunch of foreigners barged into your world, dragged your men away on dangerous expeditions, studied you like you were some alien, and demanded you explain every word you had for snow—wouldn't you also run naked and dive into the frozen sea?

Folklorn: a more narrowly defined culture-bound syndrome—family-bound.

10

Walking toward the city center, I want to be surrounded so that any hallucinated friend could ostensibly be another blackhead like me. I keep my eyes down. I've done this many times here, averting my gaze when I couldn't stand being stared at anymore—usually by men of a certain age. Sometimes they leered, swiveling heads as I passed. One old man just stood in front of me as if I were an exhibit. Which is creepier, smiling or not? Sometimes, a "konichiwa" whispered in my ear, but more often a "ni hao." Got a "Thai massage" remark a couple times, once it was "whore." Unfortunately, these words in Swedish are near identical in English.

Of course, I get comments like this in the States too, even in LA or Manhattan. All women in the world get sidewalk harassed, mine's just Oriental flavored, like from a ramen spice packet. But in America, I can read the perp—dick, racist, frat boy, skeezoid. Whereas in Sweden, everyone looks the same—clean-cut, Nordic-preppy, coddled by a generous welfare system. So I can't prepare or avoid beforehand or categorize and cast judgment after.

I realize—this was how my mom behaved around white men. She kept her distance from white fathers of classmates, crossing the street even. I'd assumed she was being demure, immigrant, Korean. But here I am at thirty, the woman whose combat boots were the loudest on campus, along with her voice, as she stomped into lecture halls to stand in front of the whiteboard, now moving through Stockholm with head down, mincing steps—the shy, frightened, meek Asian girl she vowed never to be.

This is partly why I never took the next step with Jesper while he was still living here. From the start I felt like myself with him. He saw me, understood who I was. But us walking around together—other people, men and women, Asian or not, looking at us, judging and assuming—kept me from seeing him for who *he* was or could be if I gave him a chance. But a couple of the lewder comments I got were while I was with him in public, so I kept us as friends here, something physical once he left, but he never got all of me in one place.

Right now though, it's not creeps I'm avoiding with my turned-down gaze. I'm no longer scared to be seen by them. I'm afraid of who I might see instead.

I leave my brother a voicemail. I text and email. "Call me—I'll reimburse." But no reply.

I have a few friends and colleagues here, but I plan on seeing them again after I resolve my present condition. Don't want them wondering what's wrong with me now or remembering it in the future.

In Jesper's recent email: "Let me know how you're doing. Tonight, Kate's making everyone watch *The Thing*, both the black-and-white version and Carpenter's adaptation.

I write back: "Wish I was there with you guys." Then replace it with: "Any news on DOM 1? Linnea okayed sterile neutrinos. Have fun."

At three in the afternoon, dusk settles over the city. After the eternal sunshine of the South Pole, being in Sweden with its six hours of meager light is more than disorienting. The cold I can handle; it's the darkness that isolates.

I cut through Norrmalm and stop at the stone bridge leading to Gamla Stan, the medieval "Old Town." Stockholm's an archipelago of fourteen islands, laced with Lake Mälaren's fresh water. The low salt means that in winter, you can walk from shore to shore across the ice. But here, under this bridge, the water always thrashes, funneled between stone pillars with radiant heat. For the first time, I'm nervous about crossing because the wild, foaming water conjures so much from memory and story, so I make a wager with the universe. If I can pass in reasonable time, then I'm neither genetically nor narratively cursed. If I can avoid stepping on the cracks, then my mother is still sleeping, mute and enchanted but alive. Shuffling steps, eyes cast down, magical thinking, one two three. What usually takes a minute, takes fifteen. Wager won.

With its original medieval foundations and restored seventeenth-century façades, Gamla Stan is a trip back in time. In the summer, the streets overflow with cruise ship tourists, but now in winter, the island is hushed, a snow-dusted labyrinth. The alleyways, strung up with fairy lights, draw me into nestled courtyards. A statue of a boy guards a cemetery of only five tombstones. Narrow Renaissance buildings huddle against each other like gossiping women.

At the heart of the island, I end up at my favorite bookstore—a sci-fi bookshop selling the usual figurines and comics but also boasting a diverse English collection, including novels by John Crowley and Shirley Jackson. I wander toward the myth section and find both Tibetan and Egyptian Books of the Dead and illustrated erotic guides on the occult and black magic—but nothing Korean-related except one academic text on shamanism.

Taking a chance in the Japanese aisle, I find—underneath a shelf full of goggle-eyed nymphets and beside the Murakami translations—a few orphaned books, including *Stories from the Peninsula: Korean Legends and Lore* by Oskar Gantelius. In his author photo, his long hair is parted in the middle, falling over the sides of his face, covering his temples.

Sense memories take over as I read and remember how I originally heard these tales—heartbeat slows, limbs sigh heavy. I'm holding a book I understand without looking at the words. The next moment, a Black woman wearing glittery blue lipstick with hair braided in a coronet explains how everything is closing up all around me. I smile, thinking she's also American, also a minority. But no, she's speaking Swedish. She translates herself, asking if I want to buy the book. "I love fairy tales from other countries," she says. "Like learning a new magic, yeah?"

That night, I read Oskar's stories out loud in bed. So long as I keep chanting, my friend stays away. Perhaps she's the jealous type, like me. Or maybe—if she's one of these characters—she could be self-conscious about hearing me narrate her truncated, trope-fulfilling life. Thank you, Oskar, for helping me sleep alone.

And thank you, Swedes from animal control, for clearing the bridge of dead birds from off the frozen lake. No need for a crossing to the other side tonight.

The day after I wandered into his lecture, I'm supposed to meet Oskar for dinner in Hornstull, the part of gentrified/hipster Sodermalm once nicknamed "Knive Soder" because of its crime and violence. But switchblades only make me think of *West Side Story*. In my childhood neighborhood, drug deals took place in the church lot across the street, police helicopter searchlights swirled overhead, and everyone in my family but me has been mugged. But here in Hornstull, there's a skater bar called Brooklyn, an old-timey barbershop, and a bar serving steamed baskets of Chinese dumplings. For dinner, I suggest the Hungarian restaurant overlooking the water. I'm in the mood for goulash. I'm also fifteen minutes late.

Oskar's waiting outside in a funnel-neck black coat that skims his knees. He's got on black leather gloves, a freshly trimmed beard that shows off his jaw, and hair braided in a modern queue. I didn't have time to go through my attic storage—so I'm wearing jeans and a grey cowl-neck sweater, unwashed since Antarctica. Couldn't muster enough energy to put on makeup, but the wine I drank all day blushes my cheeks and make my eyes shine.

When I see Oskar, I greet him with, "You look like a Chinaman assassin!"

"Hello, Elsa." He knows I'm tipsy and surely regrets coming. "Our table is ready."

Heavy wood furniture as if carved from tree stumps, candles everywhere including an iron-wrought chandelier, and bouquets of dried herbs tied above our heads make everything cozy and faux Central European. Oskar offers to take my coat, but I tell him I'm cold and keep it on as well as my knit cap. I also ask him to order us a bottle while I hide behind my menu. He chooses a cabernet, then asks about my day, the normal pleasantries. Too bad, I would've liked being his friend, maybe more, but I'm not capable of being normal right now.

"I watched all the *Planet of the Apes* movies today," I say as my opening.

"Hope you didn't think you had to prepare for our dinner."

"It wasn't about you." Our wine arrives. I finish my glass and gesture for more.

"Zira's not even in all the sequels." Oskar plays along. "Why the marathon?"

Out of nostalgia, I downloaded the first film and watched it on my laptop. Drew the curtains and opened a bottle for the next. No Asians in the future—not until Sulu—so I let the drama unfold, comforted my race would be spared the war between human and ape. When Zira and her decoy chimp baby got shot, and she threw the dead creature off the ship, I mulled over Shim Cheong and how she threw herself overboard for her father. That's when I saw my friend again—in the corner of my bedroom, her face to the wall. Her back was ramrod straight, her ribbons waving like blood-soaked seaweed. She was silent, but I kept on my headphones, downloaded the next films and emptied my bottle.

By the time I'd finished the fifth movie—with its closing lines musing that perhaps only the dead knew about the future—it was too late to cancel dinner. I wanted the distraction of a real person anyway. And when I got on the subway, for the first time here, I was grateful to be the only visible Asian woman. My friend, creepy and coy, remained in her corner all day.

But I can't explain all this to Oskar, so I ask him what he thinks of Caesar the intelligent ape, orphaned, who can't communicate with the simians who resemble him, nor with the humans, except for his adoptive circus-daddy Ricardo Montalban.

"Don't much care for the sequels," Oskar says. Sipping his wine, he glances out the window. Fairy lights garland the trees. Across the water, party boats glimmer on the waves, including a ship that hosts a reggae dancehall. It's Friday night, payday, and the streets are full of more attractive, considerate dining partners.

"He's 'last of his kind,' like Taylor," I say, pushing buttons, pushing everything. "Orphans figure a lot in fantasy stories. What about endlings?"

"I've wondered, if I remain childless, is there a word for me, an orphan without progeny?"

I exhale long and slow. I'm not in the mood to talk about anyone's theoretical kids. Plus mentioning kids on a first date, even for an older guy, raises red flags. Unless he didn't consider this a date?

Oskar orders goulash. I echo, but with sour cream to be different.

"What intrigues me most about Caesar," says Oskar, humoring me at last, "is that his parents are from the future. Thus, the orphan fathers the apes that will eventually produce his parents, courtesy of the time loop. Poetic in a way."

"I thought you hadn't seen the sequels."

"I said I didn't much care for them. You should pay attention to what I'm actually saying, Elsa, as well as the subtext." He smiles just enough to be playful, though still enticingly sharp.

I shrug off my coat and remove my hat, unleashing all my kinks and frizz.

"So you are staying for dinner," says Oskar, refilling our glasses with *grape juice plus.*

"It's not a perfect closed time loop though," I insist. "Caesar creates a branching timeline, a different narrative from what his future father quotes in the Sacred Scrolls. That's my interpretation anyhow, despite what the original screenwriter intended."

Oskar seems genuinely surprised. "How hopeful of you. So he breaks the cycle of trauma for his family, for his entire kind. He rewrites the Sacred Scrolls and forges a new future."

"Nej, nej, nej. An altered timeline leading to the same shitty outcome. Caesar repeatedly tries to broker peace, but the world fails him every time. Earth explodes yet again, and the blast sends his refugee parents into the past, where they die and leave Caesar all alone to keep trying to make things better for eternity. So, yes, it's looped, but a multiverse of looped failures."

Our goulash arrives. I bow my head to breathe in the onions, paprika, and caraway, and imagine a trio of Hungarian grandmothers stirring a cauldron in the back of the restaurant.

But before I can dig in, Oskar says, "Caesar knows who his parents are. He hears their voices, albeit a recording. Even knows why his mother left him in Armando's care. By the end, he creates unity among his kind and becomes a leader. For an orphan who's also last of his kind, it's mawkishly ideal, naïve wish-fulfillment that's so romantic it's insulting, insipid, beautiful, and moving." He gracefully lays his napkin in his lap. "But if you insist on hiding behind pop-cultural minutiae, Elsa, I'd much rather discuss Pierre Boulle, the actual author of *La Planète des singes*—"

"Say what?"

"Monkey Planet, the novel upon which the film was based. Boulle was also a spy and POW captured by the Japanese, forced into manual labor. He also wrote *Le Pont de la rivière Kwaï.*"

I hold up my hand to keep him from translating. "Yeah, I got it. Boys and their bridges. I'm a fan of whatever depicts the Japanese as war criminals. Now *that* country knows how to spin PR—they're like white people's favorite Asian—talk about branding. At least the Germans own up to their history, actually teach it to their kids."

"Ah yes, I've noticed how young Korean Americans are rather vehement about the colonial past, much more so than Korean nationals their age. I gather it's because of their immigrant parents."

Sure, we were raised in a specific cultural time pocket, determined by whenever our parents had left, further bound by their class and regional background and personal vendettas. The Koreans back home, though, evolved alongside their Japanese counterparts across the narrow sea—to make amends, forget, or just not care anymore. Still, I hate to be categorized to support some hypothesis, by a humanities guy no less, not even a soft-science sociologist.

I point my dripping spoon at him. "Do you think Frenchie was drawing on his POW experiences, slaving away in the jungle for the yellow-skinned creatures, for his monkey book?"

Oskar smiles. "The thought did cross my mind. But the novel's racism isn't that crude—as a sci-fi writer he's examining the human race from afar, as an entity in itself, with cultural mores and prejudices more often mirroring than not. The British and the Japanese, after all, both go to tragic lengths to 'save face.' His other novels also show a more nuanced—"

"I bet you read him in the original French. How many languages *do* you speak?"

"Scholar's French. Academic, mostly for reading and writing. Same for my Korean. May I ask how fluent you are?"

"I only speak it with my dad."

"So your mother is fluent in English?" Oskar prods. "Or—?"

"She's a woman of few words." *The other girl—where is she now?* "My Korean's garbage anyhow. Left home for boarding school at fourteen. But I don't need to get into a pissing contest with you—you're more Korean than me in all the obvious ways—sorry, that sounds—"

"You'd rather talk about Caesar and his ape revolution."

With my spoon, I swirl the sour cream round and round in my goulash, white trails melting into the broth. *Can't stir things apart. Must go on mixing, disorder out of disorder.* I stare into my soup so he doesn't feel scrutinized. "Do you remember anything about your birth parents?" It's rude and cliché to ask this of adoptees, but it's his turn to feel vulnerable and defensive.

"My mother was probably one of the many young girls to move from the countryside to the city, to work in factories during the industrial boom."

"Probably?"

He sighs. "The rapid urbanization imposed by Park Chung Hee's authoritarian rule ripped apart the social fabric." He exaggerates his precise diction but reveals no emotion. "So many young women living in the city alone, exploited in more ways than one. Illegitimate children are personae non gratae in Korea, but the bastard of a poor woman is an additional burden and stigma. Also a detriment to society. Better to be rid of the child completely."

Before I can think of a reply that's sympathetic and not too clumsy, he turns on me with: "Judging by your age, I presume your parents were also affected by the military dictatorship. When did they flee Korea?"

"Early '70s."

"Right, of course, after the '65 Immigration Act. So they were most likely not dissidents nor academics. Probably college-educated anyhow or skilled laborers, who sacrificed career and class for opportunities in the US, becoming"—he tilts his head and assesses me—"grocers or—"

"My dad owns an auto body shop."

"Yes, he works to the bone to send his daughter to an Ivy League college so she can join the rank of the model minority, the more dignified coolie laborer, one of many in tech, finance, medicine, the sciences. Your parents must be very proud of how you've repaid their sacrifices."

I'd take this as an insider's joke, but Oskar, with his seemingly posh Swedish background, even if adoptive, didn't grow up working-class. And his academic remove underscores the sociological condescension, telling me he doesn't consider himself an insider either.

"Well, fuck you too! Don't textbook-case me, even if you got most of it right. What the fuck, man—bad enough my Euro colleagues all assume immigrants everywhere are refugees 'cause that's the only narrative they know. My dad didn't come to America 'cause of the war, wasn't fleeing no dictatorship either. His people were hard-core merchant class from Kaesong, focused on money and surviving throughout dynasties, not just measly presidential terms. That's how my dad's jokbo lists over sixty generations."

I realize too late how impolite it is to flaunt this in an adoptee's face, the fact of my genealogical book. But I'm drunk-monologuing all the things I meant to say before in similar social situations, when put on the spot by presumptuous white folk. I'm not even looking at Oskar anymore as I wave my hand and hold forth for all in the restaurant to hear.

"My grandpa already had a second wife and house in Seoul, later on a third, so he wasn't your typical storybook refugee either, more like a polygamist who knew how to spread out his assets on both sides of the border. He also carried Red money and papers in one side of his coat and Blue on the other, playing both sides, the Crips and the Bloods. When the war started, he brought down his eldest son, my dad, to live in Seoul, and only went back North to get his first wife and other kids because my dad pressured him to.

"So the two of them," I continue, "pushed up against the escaping hordes to bring down the rest of the family, along with a coffin that Grandpa used to smuggle his gold. Not exactly war-movie heroics, right? Not the stuff you get from history books. My dad doesn't fit some tidy immigrant model either. He was a party guy on a motorbike, hitting up dance clubs until his factory went bust, the one his dad bought for him. He lost my mom's dowry too, fat chunk of land, and also his brother-in-law's money. So, of course, he had to come to America, even though Grandpa offered to set him up with another business. Dad wanted to stand on his own two feet, supposedly. But truth is, he couldn't stay behind with all that bad blood, not after some other shit went down that I still don't know the full story of."

I'm finally done, and Oskar is troubled, not meeting my eyes. Silent, jaw tense. Then he looks up and extends his hand across the table. "I'm sorry, Elsa," he says with so much grave sincerity. "I'm sorry for being such an ass. I'm not usually. I meant no insult when I—"

Now I feel embarrassed for overreacting. The open hand waits for me, so I touch my fingers to his palm, hesitant and shy. He grips my hand. The heat and pressure surprise me.

"Elsa, everything I know about Korea—theoretical models, statistics, first-wave or whatnot—all that was learned from books, just as you say. I'm academically Korean, and Korean by genotype and phenotype, but—"

He lets go, and I finally exhale.

"How I form a picture of my mother, Elsa, all I have is based on the year I was left at the orphanage and general economic trends of the decade. I've been told my documents from my time before were destroyed by a flood in City Hall. The Swedes who facilitated my adoption had very little information. They got the same story given to many Western agencies, given to many adoptees. We find out on internet forums how the same tropes appear in our origin myths. Official records destroyed by fire, lost in a move. Parents depicted as college sweethearts. Often the father died in a car accident or the birth mother couldn't afford a child but wanted the best for her baby in a rich white country. At least, the story I've crafted for myself—for how and why I've come to be—hints at tragedy, yes, but it's couched in a larger national history, which is itself another myth." He looks out the window. The candlelight kisses the scar at his eye.

"I remember a little from the orphanage," he says softly, "a few songs. But my foster mother—feels strange to say that in English—she also sang these songs to me when I lived on her island, so I associate them with the Archipelago." He sighs. "I didn't mean to presume to know you and your family simply because—well, you must be familiar with a certain academic type, especially male and insecure? Can you forgive me?"

Only the most secure of men would admit that. How can I not fall for him? His frank vulnerability chastens me, and I murmur a shy "no worries," unable to meet his gaze.

We eat our meal in semi-awkward but companionable silence as I wonder about this Swedish woman on an island, singing Korean songs to children, and my own mother's lullabies. Emmileh, Emmileh—did you want me to never forget your voice, Mom, or did the girl in the bell haunt you too, demanding you sing her song? Maybe you were crying out for your own mother. You were only a kid, after all, when you lost her.

"Your birth mother," I ask Oskar, "did she leave you anything in writing? Or was everything lost in the apocryphal flood?"

"Not even a photograph. And there aren't many first-person Korean sources from that perspective, far as I know, so I can't create a fictional composite either. There are many adoptee memoirs, of course. I wrote a book of folktales instead."

"I've read them," I say, holding Oskar's eyes with mine. "They're beautiful."

He doesn't believe me, so I pull his book from my bag.

He studies me, unsure. "You really didn't have to prepare for tonight."

"I already told you—it's not about you."

"Good, then I won't ask you about neutrinos or the 'visible echo of collision.'"

"Did you read my—"

"The abstract. Some articles. Can't pretend I could understand much. Please, put that book away. It's like looking at one's teenage diary."

I point to his author photo. "We did have the same teenage hairstyle. You wore it better though. You still do."

Oskar swipes the book onto the chair beside him. "Finish your soup. And please, drink some water."

I'm about to confess how I read his stories to myself aloud in bed, as if to recreate childhood memories, but then I realize I wasn't trying to resurrect what was lost—it's not in her voice anyway. Instead, his stories provided the censure I needed so I could luxuriate in my guilt. I never read her folktales, written for my journey away from home, and on top of that I lost the notebook. I was fourteen, desperate to leave, but I could've indulged her exactly because I was leaving. Could've promised her I'd read her writing, promised I'd find my sister too, participated in my mother's fantasy so she'd feel less alone. Could've let a sad, sick woman believe she was preparing me, doing what her own dead mother couldn't for her. Should've thanked her for being a good mom. Assured her I'd be better off for what she'd figured out and presented for me, revealing the shape of our interlinked lives.

Over the years, in my darkest thoughts, I'd wondered if she'd intended to drown that day, if that's why she entrusted me to share her words with some long-lost sister. I don't believe that anymore—my mother's will was strong enough to reassemble her mind, to impose patterns and reasons over generational tragedy.

But her speaking again, after sixteen years of waiting—not even about me, but about some other daughter—am I still being the stubborn fourteen-year-old refusing to listen to my mother and pay heed to her warnings?

"Elsa, are you all right?"

My eyes feel hot. Soup dribbles from my mouth. I wipe with my sleeve. Oskar's probably repulsed. Honestly, whether hallucinatory or supernatural, my friend could beckon outside the window and I'd come running. We'd make snow angels on the bank, step out onto the ice, and see how far we can go before we drop from sight.

The fairy lights in the trees quiver. The night is pricked with bright snow. I wipe away my tears, but still the orange streetlamps blear and the party boats shudder across the dark water. I need to lie down and sleep off everything. Someone touches my hand. Oskar's beside me, on bended knee. "Elsa, what is it—what can I do for you?" he asks with so much sweet concern.

His black sweater, cashmere, soft and thin against his shoulders, nothing underneath. His throat is bared, and in the candlelit shadows, his neck is sculptured—the slope of a back muscle there, the angle of his tendon crossing in front here, meeting the graceful curve of his clavicle. So many strong lines to trace with my finger and vulnerable hollows into which to press my lips. Must've been some goulash. I whisper, "How about a walk? I could use the fresh air." When we leave, I grab his book of folktales, hugging it to my chest.

Once outside, I notice the nearby stone bridge leading to forested Långholmen Island. On the other shore, white beams shine from the heavens to the treetops. Light pillars—created by moonlight reflecting off ice crystals with horizontal parallel planes. A phenomenon similar to the parhelia, or the mock suns, that I saw in Antarctica.

Grabbing Oskar's hand, I lead him away from our now. "Hurry, hurry, we've got to catch the beams before they close the bridge to the other side!" I muster enough wonder and enthusiasm to almost fool myself.

11

The moon is too bright, the trees bereft of leaves. I'm holding Oskar's hand, but would rather slip inside his black coat. Or better—climb his braid and join my sad prince in his tower.

Looming in front of us, an imposing compound of elegant yellow buildings, enclosed by a stone wall. Haunted or enchanted?

"In the early eighteenth century," he says, "this was a women's prison, a 'spinning house' where homeless or unemployed women and prostitutes were forced to spin wool or linen. Later turned into a men's prison."

"They had a nice view, at least."

"The island was rocky and barren back then. The prisoners were made to haul in mud and plant over three thousand trees. Now you have cafés and playgrounds. The prison itself is a trendy hostel."

My finger over his lips. "No more lessons, professor. If they hear us, they'll disappear."

"Who?" asks Oskar with genuine alarm.

"The little people," I whisper, "the wee folk. Come and see. A village has been built for them, right on this island."

I lead him off the frosted path through a dense forest, toward an orange plastic latticework fence. A friend, a real live one, told me about this place. A passage appears where the fence has been sliced and curled aside. I slip through onto a field of tough green, fiercely even. Joining my side, Oskar surveys this unveiled world. He's unimpressed, saying something about a miniature village, a playland for young gophers. An American import. "Hasn't officially opened yet. We're trespassing."

Can't he see I've magicked us into some other dimension? I walk toward a thatched-roof cottage. But as I approach, it shrinks. At my touch, it's as tall as myself. A giantess with no shelter, I bend to peer into a window. "How can anyone live in a house so small?"

A hand touches my shoulder. I turn to face Oskar. I hope he'll lean me against the thatched roof and kiss me, but I worry about straw in my hair, about the little folk inside screaming at the sight of fornicating gods. I close my eyes and offer my lips anyway. But Oskar stifles a laugh, saying, "Maybe we should get you home."

How dare he refuse to ravish me in the dark when we're the only two giants left in the realm? And how can one man shrink the world all around with just a touch and a smile?

I slip away, tripping on the brick border of a cottage driveway. I hit my crotch against a flag. Nearby on the rolling plain is a windmill, and over the hills, a castle. I stop at the river's edge. I dip my toes, hoping the water will return me to my proper size and place in the universe.

He's the only one big enough for me, so I allow him to take my hand. I peer up to the sky, wondering if our heads will crash into the stars.

"How about some coffee and cake?" he asks. "I know a place in Mariatorget."

I don't know if this other world of his still exists though. I follow him anyway, entering the wild green beyond the windmill, leaving behind this meager one, sized for gophers, a mini-world for mini-lives. It wouldn't work between us anyhow because we'd terrify the locals with our gargantuan fucking, and how would we unite our bodies when the universe is shrinking into nothingness? Then again, what else is there to do when the world defies your control, when it refuses to stay still long enough for you to catch your breath and plan your next move?

We emerge through the woods and step onto the shoreline path, common-sized again in a static world. Approaching us, four men with beer cans. One shouts in mock-Asian gibberish. I stiffen, shocked, not from the ugliness, but because it's a playground taunt, passé and childish. I'm confused about where I am, when I am, if I'm still just a kid.

Oskar maneuvers himself between me and the men who are still jeering. My heart's pounding—I'm no longer fun drunk. As stress cortisol and adrenaline flood my system, I become stone-cold sober—more reason to be enraged. I quicken my pace, but Oskar grips my hand, keeping his same rhythm. He's staring them down.

One says in accented Swedish: "*Which one girl? Which one boy?*" Another says something in a language I don't know, though the tone is perfectly clear and the laughter universally comprehensible to women. Then one guy juts his face, squinting in exaggeration with a serene smile. I recognize it also from childhood, but without the fingers tugging back the eyelids, I don't know if this is more elegantly subtle or just fucking lazy.

Oskar and I reach the footbridge and the drunken laughter fades. I want to reach up to touch his cheek, but he's removed, locked in his tower. "I'm sorry about that," he says.

"Whatever, they're drunk assholes."

"I'm sorry I didn't say anything—I would've—if they were white." Oskar looks over the railing. The ice-top is shattered, jagged pieces outlined with dark water. "But I assumed from their accent that they're recent. One spoke in Rinkeby Swedish."

Jesper explained to me once about this new "dialect"—a dynamic mix of Swedish, Turkish, Arabic, and English, cultivated in neighborhoods dominated by immigrants. Conservatives thought it vulgarized, but many of the children of immigrants have co-opted it as a linguistic badge of honor, coded language. Even some white Swedes who grew up outside of immigrant housing have adopted it for its swagger, defiance, and creativity.

"I grew up with a rich family on Lidingö," Oskar continues. "The right accent and address. I'm a foreigner still, but a hard-working Oriental." He's still not looking at me. "I was angry like them for much of my youth. Misunderstood, lonely, violent. They only want a bit of power, the illusion of it. But you were with me, and you're not from here, so I'm very sorry."

He keeps apologizing, but I feel it's about something other than what just happened.

"One time," he says, "I was out with friends, all white. A group of men were nearby, none of them white. One stumbles toward me and asks why the Swedes like the Chinese. 'You think you're better than me? Or just better at kissing ass?' He says all this earnestly, calmly, in perfect Swedish. His friends laughingly pulled him away." Oskar sighs. I can see his breath in the chill. "The first generation who come are grateful, certainly. They can endure much, swallow their pride. Their children want more—the freedom not to be grateful, indebted, and beholden."

From my side of the bridge, I offer: "Took me a long time to fight back, do anything more than just stand there." My mind flashes to images of my father shoving my mother to the floor, me whimpering for him to stop. "But it's tougher for me here. 'Ice cracker' is the best I can think of. Also, 'herring-fucker.' Found 'snow honky' in a novel set in Antarctica. According to *Deadwood,* we're Celestials living among the squareheads. But I'd need another minority friend with me to laugh when I say these things. Doesn't have the same effect if I'm alone."

"I'm not hassled so much anymore—but when I'm with an Asian woman—maybe I'm more aware—do you notice—"

"Me, notice what it's like to be an Asian woman here, with or without a man, white or not? I've no fucking clue what you're referring to. Look, I know I've got it easier than others, including my brother and maybe you too—but living here does make me miss the racism back home. Rather be mistaken for a doctor or accountant than a vacation souvenir or email-order bride. Wait, don't you get bullshit when you're out with a hot blonde, even if she's your sister?"

Oskar smiles wanly. "There's no question of where my home is." He crosses over to my side. "But why did you choose to come here?"

"White people exposure therapy. Kidding. Came here for my advisor. Also, had things figured out in America, thought I could transfer the same strategies— What? Should I go home because I can't deal? I *can* deal, mostly. I'm just pissy all the time."

We're side by side, but I'm not nervous anymore. Don't feel like kissing either.

"The secret to time travel," I say, "is to cross borders while ethnic. Suddenly I'm in the '80s, ski-slope noses all around and blond men. Do you know how rare it is to see blond men in America now? Sweden is Hollywood's vision of what California's supposed to look like. It's more *Children of the Corn* here to me, but anyway, I get how my brother felt growing up in '80s SoCal. How the only Asian women in the movies were hookers or Vietnamese snipers, or both at the same time. I even get why my dad was so angry and mean all the time. Must've felt like a nobody shit after being a rich man's son inKorea. And after being stared at like an object so much—I see Swedes as objects too—want to punch out the next leering face I meet on the sidewalk. Imagine what *I'd* be like if I'd grown up here."

I'm surprised I've told him this much, but this isn't a date. It's commiseration, impromptu therapy, whispering confessions in the dark, the stuff minorities talk about when the whites aren't around. Maybe this is why I don't date Asian men. We're too combustible, echoing each other's rage, fearing we'll rehash our parents' bullshit, reenact their fucked up dynamics and raise kids who chase after approval and achievement rather than love.

Oskar wasn't even raised by Koreans, and yet we're still—no wonder it's easier to escape into the pale white void when it comes to dating, falling into the laid-back negative space of those whose existential struggles can be deemed universal, human, and multi-genre, rather than ethno-specific, suffocating, and separate. Did I really need to see my dislocation and neuroses mirrored in another? Wasn't it easier to be alone or with someone who could never even begin to understand?

Also, in the mini golf park—why the fuck didn't he kiss me?

My phone rings. It's my brother finally calling back. The playground tussle with bullies, the teenage trespass into the park, the freshman-dorm conversations about race—it was fun pretending I was still young with Oskar by my side, but I can't hide anymore from my present.

I can, however, send it directly to voicemail. Chris has been ignoring my texts anyhow.

I turn to Oskar, trying to look as sober as possible. "Can we go back to your place?"

He hesitates. "The café I mentioned is only a few—"

"Christ, man! I'm not going to jump your bones. Never mind." I turn to look over the bridge. Getting rejected twice in less than an hour would try any woman's patience.

The ice below cracks and shivers, setting my nerves further on edge. As the shards creep away from each other, bubbles rise and froth to the surface. I don't wait to see if it's a lotus from the black lagoon or the bloated face of a drowned hallucination.

Lacking feminine wiles, I appeal to his gentlemanly protective instincts instead. "Please, I can't be alone right now. Those men—what they did, so stupid and trivial, but it's all these little things every day that build up over time. I'd go home, but I don't want to take the subway or even deal with a cabbie. Don't want to walk around, being so goddamn visible."

Oskar's apartment features a brown leather sofa covered in woolly blankets. Books stacked everywhere—the dining table, on chairs and ottomans, though not on the desk tucked in a book-lined alcove. Elephant leaf plants and frilly ferns arch toward the ceiling.

One thing stands out immediately—in front of his sofa, set on a low table, is a long glass case, beveled and framed in brass like Snow White's coffin. Instead of a body, however, a stone slab lies within, jagged around the edges, the surface engraved with rows of angular markings. I kneel before it, not wanting to get my fingerprints on the polished glass. "Is it real?" I ask.

"Got it off eBay," he replies.

"Right, you examine runestones on-site or at museums, not in your apartment. Looks so cool, wanted to believe it was real."

"I use digital photos too." Still smiling, maybe laughing, he turns on a lamp that spotlights the stone.

"Do you impress all the ladies with this, Scandinavia Jones?" I sit on the sofa, still wanting to run my fingers over the mysterious carvings.

Oskar heads to his kitchen, saying, "It's a knock-off of a knock-off." He pops the cork of a wine bottle and returns with two glasses. "I wasn't kidding when I said I got it off eBay. Described by the seller as an 'Authentic Reproduction.' Though this is smaller and nowhere close to two hundred pounds. Have you heard of the Kensington Runestone?"

"Nope, tell me." I settle in, hugging a cushion as Oskar sits beside me and pours.

"In 1898, in the backwoods of Minnesota," he begins in his sexy lecturer's baritone, "Olof Öhman, a Swedish immigrant farmer, while clearing his land, found a stone slab with markings entangled in the roots of a tree. Minnesota was full of Scandinavians, so it wasn't long before it was identified as a runestone. At this time, there was talk about the Vikings being the first white men in the Americas, so this discovery was embraced as proof. The transliteration tells how a group of Scandinavians sailed west to Vinland. But one day they returned from an expedition to find ten of their men dead. This is a memorial stone, year marked 1392."

"The Vikings did come to North America. Newfoundland, right? Like in AD 1000?"

"L'Anse aux Meadows, but that settlement wasn't discovered until 1960." Oskar takes off his sweater, revealing a grey, vintage-thin T-shirt. I'd been wondering about his arms. My swimmer theory still holds. Then again, he could be kettle-belling runestones.

"How come Swedes have always been drawn to Minnesota?" I ask. "Were they following their ancestors' footsteps?"

"That's the thing—it's a fake. From the start, scholars and linguists have all said so. The runes directly transliterate into modern Swedish, not Old Norse. There are other historical anomalies too. Many believed that Olof the farmer had carved it himself, as he was known to be a prankster and also owned a few books on runes."

I glance at the stone. Somehow, it looks cheap and tacky, though only a few minutes ago it was glowing with Spielbergian light.

"And yet for over a hundred years," continues Oskar, "there's always been passionate opposition, mostly American. There've been renewed examinations and publications. One Norwegian American scholar, in particular, was its champion for authenticity. So much debate and controversy, with most European scholars befuddled why so much academic energy was being devoted to this obvious falsarium. The runestone was even displayed at the Smithsonian in the mid-century, in the natural history wing, as possible proof that the Northern Europeans had come here a century before Columbus. Also"—he leans in to whisper—"it was displayed here in Stockholm at Historiska Museet only a few years ago."

He sips his wine, waits for my reaction. I widen my eyes and nod, a reaction that works for most conversational pauses in my experience, especially with men.

"Yes, exactly," he says, grinning. "It caused much controversy because out of 2,500 actual runestones in Sweden, this Kensington rock had its own exhibit with dramatic staging, describing both sides of the argument with seemingly equal weight, and leaving it to the viewer to decide if it was real or not. It angered linguists, historians, archaeologists, and many others who viewed it as a publicity stunt, irresponsibly contextualized and marketed, especially considering this is a state-funded museum."

"Why do you have a copy then, if you think it's ridiculous?"

"I don't find it ridiculous at all," he says. "It is beautiful and meaningful *because* its origin is a myth, and like all great myths, the story endured because it allowed people, including immigrants—those struggling to survive and wondering if they'd made a mistake in leaving—to become part of a grander narrative that unites them with each other *and* with those in their past." Oskar holds my gaze, enraptured, a preacher on fire. "It may not be medieval authentic, but it still has a real history that's also important."

"But can't myths also be dangerous? Used as justification or prophecy, self-fulfilling maybe. Didn't the Nazis believe the runes hold magical power?"

"Nazis and fantasy nerds, yes," he replies.

"You're neither, maybe the latter. Anyhow, it's quite the focal point of your interior design."

Sighing, he leans back on the sofa. Swirling his wine, peering deeper into the stone, he says, "As an adoptee, I appreciate the romantic imagination, the need for self-created myths. It surprises my sister, when meeting Americans who describe themselves as Swedish or Italian, though they speak no Swedish or Italian and are more than three generations removed. But I understand the hunger for claiming a people and a past, the ease of claiming it in the US—if you have the right look."

I want to touch some part of him, but I'm not sure how. I push up my sweater sleeves instead and run my fingers lightly over my forearms. The lingering sensation of skin on skin—I spark my own desire.

Finally, he shifts closer but peers at me with a side-eye glance of shy wonder. "How did I get from fraudulent runestone to adoptee sob story? When I'm with you—maybe because you're American or because we're speaking English—or have you bewitched me?"

As I bring my glass to my lips, I brush my arm against his, not daring to meet his eyes.

"According to some historians," he says, hushed but with more gravel in his voice, "the Norsemen weren't allowed to write love poems about women."

"Why?" I lean my ear closer to his mouth as if trying to hear more clearly, but of course, I can hear him perfectly, including his breath and the quickening of his pulse.

"Because it was feared that the words would tarnish her reputation or a false reality would be created about her, the words serving as a kind of binding spell."

I whisper back, "So that's why men started writing on bathroom walls."

"Of course, poems about women were still carved." He places our glasses on the table. "They carved their words into any surface." I suddenly feel queasy. "Stories of longing and loss," he says, "carved into stone or wood."

The quarter-folded sheet that I unconsciously recreated from memory. Now I remember the original heading written by my mother: *Four story-fates carved in wood that echo most in our blood.* I still can't remember the fourth story, but I have a clearer grasp of the strange, scattered words. Must be an outline, plot points, the story twists and turns my life would follow.

Oskar brushes the hair away from my neck. I try to focus on his touch only. I command myself to stay in this body, to respond to his breath and his mouth hovering over my skin.

"In proto-Norse," he says, "the word *rune* means 'whisper' or 'secret.'"

I draw him to me. His warm lips taste of wine and salt. As I sink deeper into his kiss, I climb onto his lap, straddling him. His hands slide under my sweater around my waist. I arch closer as his mouth travels down my throat.

With his face tilted to the lamplight, his scar running from eye to temple gleams golden. I trace it with my finger. *Who carved you, and what secret did they leave?*

Fates engraved in wood and stone—a mind excavating buried artifacts without permission—this man whose lore-spinning leaves me dizzy. I thought I was the one working him for intel, but instead of dispelling myths, he tempts me to wonder and almost believe.

I clamber off him and grab my things. I thank him for dinner and the wine, but claim I've got a headache and need to get home. He's more concerned than confused and offers to call me a cab or escort me back to my place. No need, I assure him, I live close by and can walk from here.

When he holds the door open for me, I intend to say something like—we should do this again or I just left a guy at the bottom of the world and returned with another woman—but all I can do is mumble about so much work and time running out and ghost particles everywhere.

On the sidewalk, I take out my phone to call a cab and see that Chris has left two voicemails and a text telling me to call him back.

I'm not ready to hear that my mother has awakened at last. How disappointed she'd be to see how we've fared without her. Can't rely on her useless, disobedient daughter, so she's shaken off her sleeping curse to find her missing daughter herself.

Leaving Oskar's building, I walk through Kungsholmen Island toward Stadshuset, a favorite haunt of mine at the edge of the water. Technically city hall, it's more regal and imposing than it sounds, where the Nobel laureates are feted and newly minted citizens are welcomed in ceremony. What draws me, though, is behind the statuary garden, where wide stone steps lead into the water, as if the temple is sinking. In the summer, Swedes lounge here and dive in, but I love it in the winter, when the ice is thick, forbidding access to what lies beneath.

With phone in hand, I stand just above the ice. The dark glass stretches before me toward the city lights on the opposite shore. The stone under me tilts toward the frozen sea. I kick a rock, and it skitters across. The phone lights up. Chris has called again. "Why haven't you been picking up?" he says with irritation.

"What'd she say now?" I ask dully.

"Mom died—that's what I'm dealing with here. Mom is dead, finally."

"When?" I step onto the ice.

"Early this morning."

I walk farther out. I don't want to ask Chris if Mom said anything before she died, if she was alone, if there was anything to do to prevent it, if she should've died long ago and we've just been needlessly extending her blank-faced misery.

"Natural death, according to the doctor," says Chris. "No struggle or suffering."

All this time, I've been dreading her return, preparing for it—expectant. So my fear was merely hope in disguise, longing dressed in lies.

"Cremation's tomorrow," he says. "You didn't want one last look, right?"

When I first left for Sweden a couple years ago, Chris and I'd made arrangements with the hospital and mortuary just in case, so everything would proceed smoothly. Still, I'm surprised he's already made an appointment and booked the funeral for next week. He hasn't shown this much initiative or efficiency in a long while.

As for one last look, maybe Chris was doing me a favor being so quick. In all my visits, she'd never looked completely gone, more like someone enchanted—what my child self would've believed. Even as an adult, I admired her bone structure and complexion, so lovely still in suspended animation, as if she were busy living some other happy life, hidden from us. So I don't think I could handle seeing her now—emptied, unfulfilled.

"Did she know how I got her into the best nursing home?" I ask. "Did she know—should've visited her more. Should've talked to her—did she know that we loved her?"

"Can't hear you. You're mumbling."

"What did she look like, when you—"

"Same," says Chris. "Been dead for while. This is just a different kind of death."

"The final kind."

"Anyway, need to crash. Dad and I were at the hospital all night."

"I thought she died this morning, that she didn't suffer?"

"Hospital was for Dad. He wanted to do a job over, claiming Javier messed it up. So Dad's working at midnight, doesn't wear a mask as usual. Spark tools burn his eyes. Lucky I was upstairs, heard him screaming. We went to the ER. Old man's all bandaged up, dosed up on painkillers—that's when I get the call about Mom. When it rains, it's a goddamn monsoon."

"How bad is it?"

"Should be better in a few weeks, maybe longer. What a fucking mess, blind bastard. At least, one less parent to worry about."

"When's the last time he saw her?" I ask.

"Yesterday. He's been visiting a lot more since she talked. Not that she's said anything since. Nor will she now."

"Why *did* she ask about the other girl in English? Was she

talking to the nurses? Did she think I can't understand Korean anymore?"

"Whoa, calm down. You didn't believe me last time—we still don't know for sure. Maybe she was asking about a shift change, wondered where the other nurse went, who the fuck knows? It don't matter. Let's focus on the funeral—when you coming home?"

"Need to take care of some things first."

We don't say anything for a while. Then he asks, "Anyone you can talk to over there?"

"I've got people."

"Sorry I couldn't call earlier—what did *you* want to talk about? That weird message you left—anything else going on with you?"

"Should I talk to Dad?"

"He's sleeping now. I might take a couple of his painkillers too. He got good ones."

"He knows, right? He understands she's gone?"

"When I told him, he said nothing. When we got to her, he put his hand over her chest and told her in Korean: "*All right, let's end this. You did good to leave.*"

After hanging up, I don't repeat "Mom is dead" over and over in English and Korean to force my mind to accept what's happened. The city looks the same as it always has—foreign, unreal. I'm sure it saw me the same way. I don't feel different because the part of me that truly understands my mother is dead is separate. She's walking around Stockholm in a slip. She's the one sick with nausea, the ground giving way and dropping her into a chasm. It's her lot to deal with the confusion, to feel inconsolably alone and unseen.

I can't get through to the sea below, so I lie on the ice, grateful for the painful freeze on my face. Halfheartedly, I scratch the surface, all for show. There's no one on the other side. My skin grows numb. I puff clouds of breath and will myself to become something that can't think or feel—bell, lotus, particle.

I thought I had enough memories to wish for more space between us, but now with my mom gone, I realize I don't have much at all. When I left her, was she all alone in her fantasy world? Or did she also have a special friend?

"There, there, Miss Blue," says my own friend, lying beside me on the ice.

I close my eyes. "Please, help me."

Red silk dangles above my forehead, then strokes down my nose to the tip. Starts at the top again. I feel the ribbon's movements as a brush of air, a whisper of tenderness. This is how she calmed me when I was a kid. As an adult, I've tried to do it myself, rubbing my fingertips down the centerline of my face, but only getting pimples the next day.

My friend can soothe me though, even after all these years, so I allow her to linger and console. Besides, this subconscious vessel probably bears for me the more banal memories of my mother—braiding my hair into a crown for a piano recital, buying me a cheap watercolor set, then spending a quiet hour by herself to paint a bowl of fruit. All those boring stories of her college classmates reuniting with their first loves. Dear God, that woman could go on forever about first loves, telling me to be careful because you never forget your first. That's why I shouldn't have sex before marriage, 'cause it would be like first eating an orange but then marrying an apple, and for the rest of my life, I'd always remember what that orange tasted like but could never have it again. Who was your first, Mom? How often did you crave oranges? If my friend were indeed an externalized repository, I had access to more memories, at least. It isn't new time with my mother, can never get that now, but I can have more of her.

Most important, I still have the handwritten stories somewhere at home, or with Chris. They weren't diaries or love letters, much too personal, potentially devastating. But her stories would also reveal a part of her, even if they were ravings of a madwoman in fairy-tale form.

But there was something else too—the four fates carved in wood. Memory divulges more. Some of the words and phrases, despite being scattered under different story titles, echoed across the quadrants. Should've noticed before, the similar elements: girls discarded or submerged, transformation and reckoning.

Was this a sketch or blueprint for something my mother had yet to carve? Her own Kensington Runestone, something she'd try to pass off as an authentic artifact, waiting to be found again. To what lengths was she willing to go to convince herself she was folklorn, to persuade me as well?

12

The next morning, my friend and I take the metro together. If anybody stares, I tell myself it's because of the barefoot, half-naked Asian girl beside me. Not because I'm newly motherless.

"Don't be weird," I remind her when we get to my advisor's office. "In and out, drop off forms, a longer than usual hug. I let you come with, so you gotta behave."

This time, my friend stays out of the wallpaper and waits by the door as I explain to Linnea why I must leave so suddenly after just returning.

"Yes, of course," she says, cradling my hand in both of hers. "My mother was ill for quite some time before she passed. For months, I was so distracted, impulsive too, even quit my PhD program for a spell. Yes, I see now—your sudden new proposal—"

"I found out last night that she died. My proposal on sterile neutrinos has nothing to do with her."

Linnea and her watery blue eyes regard me kindly, careful not to reveal anything.

Ignoring her scrutiny, I ask, "Your mother died when you were young? Then you became a great success?"

"Correlation, not causation." She laughs. "Or perhaps, it was despite losing her at a tender age, I went on to pursue my ambitions. Are you concerned? Take all the time you need.

You'll be granted an extension, without any interruption in funding, even if you are in the States."

"How long before you felt like yourself? Before you got back to your real life?"

"My dear, losing a parent isn't something you catch and get over, like a cold. You're in shock. That's why you sound like an idiot. You'll figure out what you need to do."

"By the way, sterile neutrinos isn't considered fringe anymore. Self-interacting sterile neutrinos is a very plausible candidate for dark matter. With another postdoc, I can—"

"Dark matter, schmark matter," says Linnea with a shrug. "I remember when it was all about superstring theory and feathered hair, then M-theory and those tiny little backpacks." She snorts. "Chasing glory, I say." She fans out her voluminous Scandi-boho skirt, then sighs, pulling my rolling chair closer to hers. "Oh Elsa, I'm not belittling your ambition, but now's not the time to fuss over career. Even if it's easier, even if you tell yourself it's what your mother would've wanted. Your proposal is promising, but how will any of this help you now?"

The sterile neutrino, with its ability to morph identities, could be a candidate for dark matter. Other possibilities include mirror matter, which is also known as shadow matter and Alice matter. Some theorize that mirror neutrinos can oscillate into ordinary neutrinos, so it's not just the ghost particle, or the ghost particle's ghost, that's a sneaky, shape-shifting bastard.

Tangentially, not related to sterile neutrinos but also evocative and dangerously allusive: self-annihilation is the mechanism through which we can detect dark matter—the stuff that the universe is mostly made of. Dark matter cannot be directly observed, but its existence is implied in numerous astrophysical observations. Unseen yet abundant, unknown yet integral to the universe, dark matter shapes its structure and evolution. It's probably the thing that's keeping galaxies from flying apart.

So how does any of this help me now? Well, Linnea, considering I've chosen my imaginary childhood friend to be my plus-one at my mother's funeral, I think we're past the point of finding a healthy work-life balance.

I resolve, however, to find my way back.

For my mom and for sterile neutrinos—my job is to demystify. I can't bury Mom now that Chris has burned her to ash, but I can put her and her fantasies to rest and finally say goodbye. I'll banish my friend then too—when I can be alone again, when I don't need these illusory binds to my mother, her story sisters, and her myth of ancestral heritage.

"I'll see you in a couple weeks, Linnea." I leave her my documents for the extension. I've already checked through for any errant pieces from my past that might've snuck in.

"It's the love that I want to see in you," she says after we hug goodbye, and I wonder how this Finnish hippie has gotten this far in Sweden. "The passion for physics, it's in you, I know—but it's missing in your current proposal."

"A weak fart can't rip the ass."

"It is a fact."

"I need more sisu?" I ask, clenching my raised fist, unsure about my usage. Tricky to translate, *sisu* encapsulates the Finnish spirit of gutsy courage, grit, and tenacity. The Finns use it to describe their national identity, their people's soul.

"You certainly have sisu," replies Linnea, "but not always applied in the right contexts. Sisu will not help you grieve and mourn."

But juche certainly will! Also untranslatable, embodying North Korea's self-reliant willpower. Kim Jong Il—Dear Leader and Beloved Father—describes *juche* as how woman is the master of her destiny, that she decisively shapes her world—pronouns obviously mine.

(

As my friend and I exit Alba Nova's rotunda, we run into Oskar and Vendela on the entrance bridge. What an awkward foursome. Vendela tells me she remembers me from the mixer and shakes my hand again. Oskar nods hello and explains he was intending to drop off a note in my department mailbox before going to fika with his sister. He doesn't offer his hand or a continental kiss on the cheek or the Swedish hug, which still throws me off in this chilly emotional climate. He keeps his distance instead, cool and professional.

"A handwritten note?" I ask. "How old *are* you?"

Vendela smiles. "Not many men these days are friends with their stationer. At least he's not delivering a runestone."

I want to laugh, but I'm too self-conscious for various reasons. Vendela's surprising warmth is not helping, as it makes me wonder what exactly Oskar told her about me.

"It is precisely because I study runestones and manuscripts," he says, "that I value tangible documentation." He looks over my head while speaking, ostensibly to appreciate the science building's glass and steel modernism. "Besides, it shows more care, consideration, and style." He deftly removes an envelope from his inner breast pocket and hands it to me.

It's still warm. I restrain myself from smelling it. "Do you want me to read it now?"

"Later, when you're alone," he says, locking eyes with me at last.

"I've heard there's an observatory here," says Vendela. "Aren't you curious, Oskar?"

He answers her with some quick, irritated, brotherly Swedish.

"The telescope's in that dome up there," I explain, "but mostly used for astronomical instrumentation and confirming supernovae. I helped confirm one last year, actually. A supernova 1a." A few people try to squeeze by on the entrance bridge, and we step aside to let them pass. I'm apologetic that we're three Asians rudely blocking the way. Then I realize there's only two of us, in fact, plus Vendela.

"Type 1a," echoes Oskar. "Not very poetic for the explosive death of a star, its final luminous breath." He's clearly pleased with himself for knowing what a supernova is.

"Poetry." I snort. "When Swedes talk poetry, I think about how the areola around the nipple is called 'vårtgård' in Swedish. Literally 'wart-garden.' Imagine what the Viking love songs were like. Anyhow, supernovae 1a would be tricky to name because it's specific to a binary system." I pause to gauge their reaction. Vendela is curious and eager to hear more. Oskar seems uncomfortable being the one who knows less.

"A binary system," I explain, "is when two stars orbit around each other's barycenter. From far away, it might look like a single star. The dwarf star gradually accretes mass from its larger partner, then reaches a limit of core density, surpassing its Chandrasekhar limit. It explodes, leaving nothing behind. More rarely," I add, glancing at my friend, "two white dwarf stars orbit closer, then finally merge together, creating a supernova in which both are destroyed."

Vendela grins at Oskar, trying to hint something. He studiously ignores her. "I just remembered," she says to her brother, "I have some emails I need to send. How about I go back to your office to work and you fika with Elsa instead, if she's available, of course. We can catch dinner later before my flight? Are you free now, Elsa?"

What a good question. How free can I possibly be when I'm increasingly dependent on my friend? There must be other ways to deal with a mother's death across the sea.

"Yes, I'd like that very much, Oskar," I say decisively, a bit too loudly. "I've got a flight to catch myself, in a few hours. But I'd like to ask you a few things before I leave."

"Oh?" he asks, clearly disappointed. "Back to the South Pole?"

I shake my head. "Something else came up."

Vendela hugs me goodbye without my consent and peels away from the group, leaving the three of us on the bridge. Two Asians make a couple, but three is an invasive horde.

I both want and don't want to be left alone with him, wanting most of all to reassure him he did nothing wrong the other night. I glance at my friend for indication of what to do, but she's already gone, as if Vendela took her with her.

After a few minutes of wordless walking, Oskar and I reach a street on the edge of campus, full of cafés. He chooses a teahouse I've never visited before, with apothecary drawers built into the walls. As we pass by the glass-encased pastries near the register, I spot a tray of curious round bulbs, the size of brussels sprouts, capped with a splash of hot pink.

"Ursäkta, what are these?" I ask the young guy behind the counter. He's wearing a neon blue keffiyeh artfully draped around the neck, over a tight black T-shirt that shows off his intricate sleeve tattoos of moths and beetles. All the cool kids were wearing this scarf in Stockholm this season, except for maybe the Arab-looking kids.

In annoyingly perfect English, he replies, "Flowering tea. Huā chá," he adds in a tonally precise Mandarin, probably also perfect. "We just got them in from China. The tea leaves are sewn around dried flowers, and the whole thing blooms in your pot."

I bite my tongue. No need to specify that I'm not Chinese, in response to being schooled by a white Swedish boy. Is it always this exhausting for me to be in my foreigner's body, or am I more hyperaware because I'm with Oskar? An imaginary friend's so much easier—looking enough like me so that I feel less like an outlier, but hallucinatory still so we don't seem to be taking over a space in which we don't belong.

After giving our orders, Oskar and I sit by the window. He asks where I'm headed off to, and I answer that I'm going home to my family, which stuns me when I say it out loud, as I didn't intend to share this with him.

"A short visit," I add. "What about your sister? Also flying out?"

"She teaches Old Norse at Cambridge. Been trying to get me out there in the UK market for a while, but I'm too old to play the game. Still don't have the most marketable look anyhow."

"Oh, are you looking to teach elsewhere?" I ask as casually as possible.

"Not really. She doesn't believe me though when I say I'm content with my position at SU, a mere Lecturer in Asian Studies and part-time consultant with runes. My big sister"—he sighs—"encouraging yet disdainful, wanting more for me and not respecting what I actually do."

"So you *do* have an Asian mom."

"Is that what your mother is like?" he asks with a disarming smile.

The server arrives, the guy from the counter. I turn my full attention on him. He places an empty glass pot in front of me, with its green bulb nestled at the bottom. When he pours in hot water, the bulb rises, spins, and swirls. The clenched fist of green loosens. Leaves unfurl; the pink blooms into many sharp petals. He advises me to let it steep before leaving us again.

"I'm sorry for being so weird the other night," I tell Oskar. "I was planning on emailing you to apologize, but then—" I stare at the tempest in my teapot, waiting for the blossom to rise to the ocean's surface. Can't help wondering if a tiny girl will emerge. What would she want from me? "My mother died," I say. "That's why I need to go home. She was sick for a long while—years—so it wasn't sudden, but—" I swirl the teapot. The tendrils sway like seaweed.

"Oh Elsa, I'm so very, very sorry."

With perfect timing, the server returns to set down a black teapot for Oskar. "Authentic Yíxīng clay," he adds, pouring for us from our respective pots. I'm grateful for the ceremony's disruption, appreciative of its ethnic irony. When he leaves, I study the tea leaf fragments in my cup. Why are people so desperate to know their future, reading patterns into any fucking thing?

"Thank you," I tell Oskar, "but I'd rather not talk about my mom." I take my first sip, surprised by its saltiness. "Actually, there's one thing I've been meaning to ask—growing up I heard that a family friend in LA went to Korea when she was like six months pregnant and ended up giving her baby up for adoption there. She came back alone. Never made sense to me, but what do you think?" Something tickles in my throat. I drink more salty tea to wash it down.

After a moment, Oskar says, "There's not much domestic adoption in Korea. Bloodlines are so important there culturally, hence the high rates of transnational adoption. I suppose it's possible, if—"

"That's the thing. The story was that she went all the way to Korea to have the baby adopted to a foreign country, a white country probably. It's so convoluted, a major hole in the story, right?" I cough, trying to clear whatever's lodged, drinking more to drown it altogether.

"I see," he says thoughtfully. "Forgive me for the indelicacy, but was this woman perhaps living in an abusive situation, in LA?"

I look at him in surprise. "How did you—"

"Well, that would be one reason—it is quite the circuitous journey, but it's never a simple trajectory for either the birth mother or for the child. Consider what an immigrant mother would do, for example, if she didn't think she could provide a safe home for her baby in a country where she didn't speak the language or know the system. How would she navigate the process without her husband's knowledge? Perhaps, this family friend of yours would know the right people in her own country, would be able to hide it from her husband over there, so to speak. Maybe she'd trust her 'own people' to ensure a better life for her child, to find the right parents."

"But then why send the kid to a Western country—even if Koreans don't adopt?"

Oskar sighs, tugging his beard. "Well, it's not only Western countries who believe an orphan is lucky to grow up there. The fairy tale is used to console desperate birth mothers, but also serves to assuage the guilt of others—relatives who persuade the mother that this is best for her and her future, for the other children she already struggles to feed. It's a story wielded by those who shape policy, who handle transactions with foreign agencies. It's a fantasy for those not even involved—the ballad of the Korean orphan growing up in the exotic, romantic West—never mind the loss of identity, language, or the right to exist in a particular place. It is simply enough that the fairy tale happily ends with the baby delivered into the arms of a deserving white couple. But this is only the end to *their* story of childlessness. It's the beginning of another for the one who'll be a visible foreigner within his new family and throughout his youth."

He looks into his cup. "The fantasy persists for some Koreans who find us romantic in our otherness, as if we're some rare cultivar. Some of my female students from Korea fancy me precisely because I'm more 'authentically European' than an immigrant, but still familiar and safe with my Korean looks. A limited-edition model. Quite discomfiting." He shakes his head. "Many Swedes don't even think they themselves are truly European anyhow, not in the historical, continental sense. Sweden was somewhat a backwater back in the day."

I'm pleased that Oskar doesn't seem the type to exploit or be flattered by these student crushes. But I too am guilty of finding him more interesting than the Korean American boys I know from home. Out of our diaspora, who were the most exotic, rarest, loneliest?

Oskar drums his fingers on the tabletop. A deep wrinkle appears between his thick raven-wing brows. Bitterly, he says, "Some who insist that the child is lucky to grow up in a rich, white country also would vehemently object if their own daughter wanted to marry such a rootless creature without lineage, homeland, or heritage."

I tug him back from wherever he's gone by laying my fingers over his. "I dug up some of your old essays online. I found them beautiful and moving."

He covers his face with a hand and groans theatrically. "You really need to stop researching me, Elsa. I'd much rather you get to know me as I am now."

"Why would you be embarrassed?"

Oskar grimaces. "I was not the most ethical journalist."

"Did you lie?"

Staring out the window, Oskar unties his hair, rakes his finger through, and ties his mane again. Still not looking at me, he says, "When I was younger, when people asked where I'd come from originally, all I had were facts and figures. I used my knowledge as defense, to ward off questions I couldn't answer or didn't want to think about. So at a party, I'd reply to some insipid question with: 'Allegedly, the first transracial adoption in Korea came about when a female North Korean soldier handed her baby to a Swedish nurse.' Or: 'The suicide rate for transnational adoptees in Sweden is nearly four times higher than that of non-adopted Swedes.'

"It wasn't graceful," he adds with a smirk, "but better than the pity or expectation I should be grateful. But I wasn't understanding myself any better, and my facts didn't help anyone else to understand me either. Or my friends.

"So in my essays," he continues, "I included personal details.

Except they weren't mine to share. One friend felt like the exotic pet of the family. Another told me how her adoptive mother turned cold, jealous even, when she became a teenager, attracting unwanted attention from men, and her father became distant, uncomfortable. Another had a lovely childhood, but a reporter interviewing her adoptive parents thought it worthwhile to mention in the article how much they'd paid for her. The neighbors were duly impressed. Clipping's included in her babybook. All the ways in which we are constantly reminded—the accumulation over a lifetime—"

He pauses, catching himself. Finally, he turns to look at me, worried he's gone too far.

"Go on, Oskar. I'm listening."

"I was young and arrogant," he says, "and hated that any critical analysis could come across as ingratitude, especially from someone who looked like me, when what I wanted was dialogue, consideration beyond shelter and even love, yes love, for those idealists who believed that family affection could protect a child from—but the stories of abuse and violence also distracted from the damage that was more subtle, though still lingering and unacknowledged."

I can't help also feeling Oskar's rising emotion, his tumult of words rushing through me. When he stops to catch his breath and calm down, I ride this dissipating wave with him.

"I'd learned some Swedish with my foster mother," he says softly, as if others might overhear, "while living on her island. But I was more stubborn than the younger children, holding on to my Korean. She indulged me too with her own rudimentary Korean, because I was with her longer than the others, as most who adopt prefer babies. So when I was finally placed into a Swedish family, I couldn't understand my new parents, nor they me. I was adrift between languages, losing one while barely gaining another. I couldn't tame or give voice to my mad, wild thoughts. Couldn't explain or even understand how I was feeling. Felt like I was losing my mind. Not until I acquired a new language could I make sense of my own thoughts. That's why, though I came here when five, I don't remember much. Later, I learned to speak Korean again, but—my memories feel fictive, unstable and untrustworthy. Never was comfortable sharing my own life because of that. Above all, I was too afraid to confront my feelings, to truly examine myself. So, I used what my friends had confided in me, used them in the way I saw fit. How can you not judge me ill for this betrayal, this cowardice?"

"I'm a physicist. We don't judge. We observe a holy shit ton of data, and then come to a clearer understanding, we hope. But never final, never conclusive."

He sighs. "I lost friends; trust. Lost any right to speak out—I hurt many, including those who'd facilitated our adoptions, whom I deemed dangerously naïve and simplistic in their idealism. I'd failed to make these people understand because I didn't—" He cuts himself off. "Maybe that's why I teach poetry these days and spill my heart to physicists. Why am I so open with you, so shamelessly garrulous? Because you're American? Because I'm not speaking Svenska, the language of repression and fear of judgment? What have you done to me?"

"I'm a witch. Isn't that what you said last time?"

"I said you've bewitched me. Connotation matters." He reaches for my hand. "But I apologize for going on and on about myself—especially when—your mother—I'm so deeply sorry, Elsa."

"Stop apologizing so much." I withdraw my hand, but when he reacts with surprise, I pick up my teacup as an excuse. "You sound like a woman." I tease to deflect, knowing full well gendered jokes don't fly with Swedes, but it lands differently because now I'm thinking about my mom again and can't hide it in my voice. "I didn't want to talk about her anyway, really. Too soon, too sober, too much daylight." I want to tell him I'd rather learn more about him, but I can't because something is crawling up my throat, creeping across my tongue. "I'm gonna be sick," I mumble, running to the restroom.

Inside the locked space, I retch and heave and finally get the thing out of my mouth. A perfectly formed pink blossom with serrated petals. It plops into the toilet, bobbing on the waves. I flush it all down.

From the other side of the door, "Are you all right?" asks Oskar.

I look into the restroom mirror and see my friend. She tells me, "Playtime's over, Elsa. Now it's time for us to get back to the right kind of story. Say goodbye to Asian Darcy."

"Please," I tell my friend in the mirror. "I can't right now—not with you. Just please leave me alone. Let me get through this by myself?"

Footsteps retreat from the other side. The girl in the glass remains.

When I return to the table, Oskar's gone. The server explains that he had an emergency and brings me my bag and coat, adding that "the gentleman has already settled the bill." On the table is Oskar's business card with a note in the tiniest script. The first line is written in runes. Below that: "Not a binding spell, but a promise. If ever you need me, I'm here for you."

I open the envelope he handed to me on the Alba Nova bridge. Inside are two tickets for the fortieth anniversary screening of *Planet of the Apes* at a Stockholm art house theater—for next Saturday. Also, a note stating: "This is only pretext. Doesn't matter to me if we view the film or not. I simply wish to see you again."

A few hours later, I'm in a cab headed for the airport, my friend beside me. I rest my hand on the seat, extending my pinkie toward her. Red ribbon loops around it.

Sister Shim Cheong

I'm not sure what's more extraordinary—the sailors' stupidity or savagery. What a perfectly good waste of a virgin—to toss me overboard into the Indang Sea because the waves were too choppy. Or maybe my blind father was the idiot. He believed the monk's claim that three hundred bushels of rice given to Buddha would grant him sight. Most will suspect, however, that I was the biggest fool to have sold myself for the required payment.

Mind you, I didn't do it because of faith in Buddha or suicidal desperation. My concealed plans, however, were thwarted when the sailors tied me up once we set sail.

Unlike the previous girls, I didn't kick or scream while being dragged to the docks. It unnerved the sailors when I walked calmly onboard. Maybe they feared I would jump into the sea before the ritual prayers were completed. In any case, I couldn't persuade them to exchange me for another virgin at another port, and being bound hindered me from swimming to shore. And when they threw me into the waters, I couldn't escape the sea turtle that came to get me.

The creature took me to the Sea King's palace, where I

discovered my mother was Queen. She'd died when I was born, or so I'd been told, but I learned now she was originally from the Sea, rejoining her kind and remarried to its King. Did my blind father know of this? I was happy to meet her at last, but couldn't shake the betrayal. Moreover, I longed for the surface, as half of me was land-born. So my mother transformed me into a giant lotus. I rose to the surface as a monstrous bloom, bobbing on the waves until I was claimed by the Land King as his freaksome treasure. His men hauled me by net and delivered me to his chamber.

At night, I cried and shed my petals, crouching naked next to his sleeping body. At dawn, my eyes dried and I became a rotting lotus once more. The King didn't see my true form until weeks later, under a full moon so bright no one in the palace could sleep. He explored my body, making me his wife. But night after night, he could not feel how I was shedding so many petals that I was drowning in them. One morning, he noticed me choking. For three days, he kept vigil as I translated myself from flower to girl, from woman to flora. Finally I told him, as seeds fell from my lips, that I needed to see my father once more.

To be exact, I wanted my father to see me. If the rice he'd gotten in exchange for me had not granted him sight, he could feel me at least, how my body bore the marks of so many journeys as I was handed off from man to man, world to world. So I agreed that if the King brought my father to me, I'd become his Queen. But the emissaries sent to my village discovered he was no longer there. The villagers told them that the old man had learned too late what he'd lost. He'd waited for the ship to return every day, standing upon the shore surrounded by the three hundred bushels that diminished day and night as others came to steal their daily meal. When the sailors finally returned, the blind man offered all his rice to buy back his daughter, but the sailors saw only a few grains scattered around him and whatever else was washed in by the tide.

With the King's permission, I threw a banquet for all the blind men in the kingdom. For a month they trickled into the courtyard and feasted as I walked among them, searching for my father. At month's end, the banquet was over. When the last of the blind men were escorted through the gates, I heard the guards jeering at an old man who'd arrived too late for his meal. I knew what kind of man this must be—to miss an entire month's feasting by a day. I ordered the guards to let the straggler through. The beggar fell to his knees as I rushed to catch him in my arms. We knelt upon the ground, and I brought his filthy hands to my face. His blindness was removed from his eyes, and I waited for my father to see me.

I am still waiting.

Part II

The Body Shop:

A Korean American Cali-Gothic

1

Outside the gates of my father's auto body shop, I expect helicopter searchlights or Dopplered sirens, but the graffiti-laced neighborhood with its bungalows and palm-spiked apartment complexes is quiet, sedated. It hasn't been dangerous for years, but whenever I return, I expect it to be as menacing as I remember in childhood. The shabby, dirty smallness of it all is underwhelming, even eerie in its calmness.

I've often thought of my hometown as "the poor man's Compton" because our local gang was an embarrassment, tagging playgrounds and hanging out with underage girls in the 7-Eleven parking lot. Their guns idled in the glove compartments, bullets rotting in the heat. Even the cops felt sorry for them. Unlike our more famous neighboring town, we produced no prophet-rappers and couldn't claim any cultural capital that could grant us swagger rights or street cred.

But the Hustler Casino and other card clubs, courtesy of a gambling loophole, attracted Chinese tourists by the busloads and the occasional Hollywood has-been too lazy to drive to Vegas. With the steady stream of revenue, Gardena eventually drained the swamps where Chris had chased rabbits as a boy and transformed them into an eco-reserve with benches and walking paths. New strip malls were installed, and in the gleaming Krispy Kreme, former gangbangers wore do-rags under their retro paper hats.

The Japanese parts of town were always nice and still are, with graceful landscaping and artisanal restaurants catering to salarymen from the mainland. But I had little access to this community growing up, with their roots going back a century to when the issei first settled here. The Japanese kids in my school were third- and fourth-generation, with grandparents and great-grandparents who'd been incarcerated during WWII, their houses and strawberry farms confiscated. After the war, some of these Americans returned to start over with nothing. Eventually, when racist immigration restrictions were overturned in '65, Asians from other countries came, many settling in Gardena, with their own hatred and suspicion toward the Japs, or jjok-bali as my parents called them, for the jjok-jjok sounds of their slippers. So not only were there generational differences to contend with, but also ancient animosities and more recent war crimes to navigate and let fester, even in the locker rooms or playgrounds.

But I don't think Chris's bullies or my own Nipponese tormentors a decade later knew any real history. They were parroting white racists instead, calling me "slope" and "flat-faced." Their disdain proved their loyalty and the dues they'd paid. If relegated to second-class, make sure there's a third and fourth class beneath you. Plus, what's more American than shitting on foreigners and new immigrants?

My best frenemy, proud of her Okinawan ancestry, told me her uncle lost an arm in the Korean War, with the cold glare that only an eight-year-old alpha-girl can summon. I didn't reply that my dad lost his homeland in that same war, that my mom lost half her family. Didn't know how to explain that the war wasn't really fought *against* Korea, but *on* Korea instead, using Korean bodies. Probably moot, as I left home at fourteen and still avoid these neighborhoods now. I grew up literally on the wrong side of the Union Pacific train tracks, after all.

But while the seedier parts of Gardena cleaned up, my dad's auto body shop became a grimy, decrepit eyesore. Used to be the most imposing, proudest building in the neighborhood. Its origin story was also full of promise. I wouldn't believe its romantic Americana-mythos, except it's all true.

A Jewish auto body shop owner, who felt bad about Japanese neighbors getting carted off to the camps, hired my Dad as an apprentice in the early '70s and had his Black employee teach him everything he knew. After years of scraping and saving, Dad wanted to open his own shop. He found an old gas station to transform. A white family friend, whom I used to confuse with Jack Palance, lent the money to buy the land. We called him Ah-jussi, "mister." He'd been a GI and married a Korean woman, a family friend Dad had grown up with back in Kaesong, a fellow refugee from the old country.

Before I went off to boarding school, my mother revealed that Ah-jussi's wife had "sold her body to the GIs to feed her family and send her siblings to school," that she sacrificed herself and God rewarded her with a good husband who brought her to America. From anyone else, the story would've been too cliché to believe. But Ah-jussi was the only white man Mom liked and trusted. And she capped off her story with a warning for me to never fornicate with a white man because my face would turn green, our parts not matching. So I knew the preceding tale to actually be true, despite my pushback, asking if Ah-jussi's wife's face had ever turned green. Mom admitted no, not to her knowledge, but she *had* heard of such cases.

My father paid off Ah-jussi's interest-free loan and became his own boss, an immigrant success story. When I was in kindergarten, he'd bought the surrounding land to build larger and higher, the biggest building in the neighborhood, with the intention of leasing the upstairs loft and some of the garages to complementary businesses so he could finally move his family into a safer town. Instead, after a few years of fielding offers while using the upstairs as a party space for his friends, Dad moved out of the house into the "upstairs" and never left.

The black gates still enclose the seven adjoining garages, forming an "L." A second-story loft stretches above half the garages. The windows are tinted black, except for the one in the corner that's boarded up after being shattered by a rock or bullet, with no one bothering to repair it since. Rusty cars rest on cement blocks, cluttering the once expansive parking lot. Abandoned auto-restoration projects are hidden under tented coverings. Random graffiti on one wall and sun-faded Korean signage on another.

The hoarding is more evident inside the garages. Only half are used for actual work by the lone employee Javier, who's been with my dad for over a decade, the only one keeping the business alive and my father and brother fed. The other garages were never leased, used as storage for Dad's undriven cars. A '60s Studebaker big as a boat and a '70s black Mercedes, the kind favored by Pyongyang's elite and third-world dictators. Alongside these are assorted fenders, doors, and uprooted backseats leaning against the wall like kitschy sofas. A pile of headlights and side mirrors with tangled nerves, tilting towers of stacked hubcaps. In case of emergency, another war? Or in response to the loss accumulated over a lifetime?

My father has crossed so many borders, even those that moved incessantly until finally set by the powers that be. He told me once that many Koreans in America were from the North because they already knew how to leave home and start over with only what you could carry. No wonder he wanted to stay put and surround himself with so much junk, to be buried under its weight. Or maybe more simply, after having his wife committed, he'd walled himself up too.

Bar in each hand, I shake the black gates, sending tremors down the tracks. Neighbors shout: "Quiet the fuck down, you crazy bitch!" Finally, feels like home.

A garage door rises, revealing a silhouette—my brother, dressed in boxers that hang like a demure apron beneath his taut, round belly. He yells, "Was I supposed to pick you up?" He's gotten paunchier since I saw him last. He's flushed, hair damp with sweat, matting the white streak at his temple.

"Are you sick?"

"Working out," says Chris, miming bench presses. He unlocks the gate, rolls it aside.

My friend has accompanied me thus far, but as I'm about to cross the threshold, she walks back into the street as a car passes through her. "I'll be at the house," she says, and runs toward my childhood home, a block away.

"Come on in," says Chris. "My balls are freezing out here."

When I was eleven, Chris was finally in college, commuting from home. On this night, he was dressing for a student drag show at USC.

"Where'd you get those?" I poked his spongy breasts. Our mother's silver dress hung over the small peaks, jutting high on his chest.

"Nikki's favorite padded bra."

"If you're wearing Nikki's bra, why you wearing Mom's clothes?"

"Nikki's punk rock," he said. "Mom's Greta Garbo."

"How old is she?"

"Same as me, twenty-one. But she's a junior."

"So even at twenty-one, I might still be this flat?"

He picked up a slinky gold belt, shaped like a snake, and fed its tail into its mouth. "Get yourself out of this shithole with scholarship money." He applied lipstick, having studied our mother just as I was studying him. "Then you can buy your own boobs. Get a nose job too."

"What's wrong with my nose?"

He swept his bangs over mascaraed eyes. "Put Mom on the sofa and play something jazzy." While I butchered Gershwin on the piano, Chris sashayed into the living room. Our mother gasped with wonder. As my brother shimmied, she laughed, no longer the broken beauty. I kept playing to keep my brother dancing—that's how I made my mother happy.

"Shameless! And absolutely glamorous. You wear that better than me." She clutched her belly. "Am I getting fat?"

Chris wrapped his arm around her waist. Their reflection in the sliding glass doors behind them—two women, the smaller one leaning her head on the larger one's shoulder. Only my face reflected in the glass, no friend by my side—what I'd been working so hard to achieve.

For dinner, Chris wore our mother's apron like a bib. In high school, he'd drive around with his friends waving a Korean flag out the window, scouring plazas and strip malls for any "Jap bastards" they could beat up in order to avenge colonial crimes and middle-school bullying. The teen vigilante was now handling chopsticks with more grace than our mother, whose women's university in Korea had basically been a finishing school with a degree. Her major had ostensibly been music, but her proudest achievement was being mistaken for her classmate, Miss Korea, who in postwar 1963 had placed fourth runner-up in the Miss Universe pageant.

"Have you decided your major yet?" asked Mom.

"You know what the doctor said," he replied in Korean. "I need to ease into things."

"Too much stress isn't good for his—nervous system?" I glanced at Chris for approval.

"Yes, I can get overstimulated by new environments."

"You both get your sensitivity from me." She placed some mackerel in his rice bowl. In English, she added, "Fish is good for brain." Chris transferred the same piece to my bowl.

A few years ago, Chris had graduated from high school but needed to save up for college. During this time, he lived in and out of the house, sometimes with friends, sometimes by himself in the desert. I wouldn't know if he'd be gone for a weekend or months.

My father's departure had been more definite. Instead of leasing the body shop loft, he set up a bachelor pad, inviting other strays to crash, like newly divorced friends or husbands kicked to the curb. My parents' bedroom became Mom's, the house her domain. She delivered lunches to my father, called him home for dinner.

"You check out the book I got you?" Chris asked me.

"Picked out ten schools. Typed up letters and asked for catalogs. Real expensive though."

"Rich schools. Lots of scholarships."

"You fill her head with unrealistic notions," said Mom.

"You want her to end up like us?" He struck a tragic, glamorous pose—the back of one hand on his forehead, the other on his hip. He waited for her to laugh, but she didn't. "Anyway, gotta go. Spending the night at Nikki's."

"Never mind your father's dinner. I'll take it myself. You go and have fun, and try not to ruin my dress, please."

"I promise to return it before the party."

My brother glimmered across the moonlit driveway with heels in hand. Mom watered the lawn, but when Chris's car rounded the corner, she dropped the hose and reached into her apron pocket. She withdrew cigarette and lighter. A flicker of a flame charged a firefly in the night. The hovering glow kissed her lips, then darted away. She directed the tiny ember toward different windows in the apartment complex across the street, aiming for one target then another. "Wrap the leftovers. Then call your father and ask when he wants to eat. I'm visiting friends." She untied her apron strings and then yanked them tighter around her waist, a brutal crisscross double wrap. She walked into the street, another firefly chasing her in the dark.

I wondered which of her Korean friends she'd visit—the one who'd almost paid Mom back everything but needed another loan or the one who'd disappeared for months before showing up with a fruit basket? Maybe it was the woman who sheltered us while we hid from Dad last week during one of his Tuesday Tempers.

But usually, the housewives knocked on our door during the day, their white envelopes thick with money. If Mom wasn't home, they handed their envelopes to me, always reminding me not to tell my father. I was old enough to know this was Mom's thing anyway. She got money from Dad for groceries and the house, and also my private school tuition, piano and art and tennis lessons, and whatever science or math thing I wanted. Even when I won scholarships, she asked him to fork over the full cost. "Anything having to do with you," she told me, "he hands it over, no question. One of his few positive attributes."

When Chris pointed out how he'd gone to public school, Mom said a girl was safer at a Christian academy, adding that the neighborhood was worse now and we couldn't afford tuition back then. When he pointed out my extra classes, she reminded him that he'd run away from piano to play with friends and quit painting despite all the supplies she'd gotten him. She even had a family friend pose as his aunt so that Chris could register as living with her in a superior school district. But Chris quit this high school because it was majority "preppy white boy" and all the Asians were "nerds competing against each other with literal scorecards for their GPAs." He came back to his local public high school instead, where there were enough "cool Asians" to form a club, with letterman jackets and cute girlfriends, ethnic solidarity and protection.

In contrast, I was the lonely kid who stuck with her lessons, whether in a rec center or with a private teacher at home. I didn't have neighborhood friends anyhow and I enjoyed achieving. So over several years, Mom got to skim from these funds earmarked for me. She amassed, then loaned the money at high interest to other Korean women, mostly newer immigrants, a few of them in the apartment complex across the street.

But whatever compelled my mother to call on these other wives at this late hour must've been important because of the great risk—when *their* husbands might also be at home.

Now, in the body shop loft, my brother drops my bags and heads for the fridge. My eyes adjust to the overhead fluorescent lights. All three TVs blare the same Korean soap opera. Embassy-size Korean and US flags stand sentry on either side of the biggest flat-screen. The flags were displayed downstairs in the office after the LA riots in '92 and again after 9/11.

Crowding the space from here to there—the leftover furniture of the last thirty years, marking our immigrants' assimilation, like layers of geological strata. From floral brocade in avocado green, to brass-studded leather, to glass and gold metal—mazelike with narrow aisles carved between the furniture. Makeshift rooms were formed by office cubicle walls that Dad bought brand new, never for offices though, only for bedrooms. Had he ever intended to lease out the loft or was this his secret plan all along?

From the doorway, I can see the top of his head over the low, padded walls, in the middle of the hoarder's labyrinth. The blind minotaur with his bandaged eyes barks in Korean, "What the hell was making all that goddamn noise?"

"Your daughter!" yells Chris over the competing TV voices. He stands in front of the open fridge, stocked full of soda and sports drinks, bought in bulk like the food in the kitchenette.

"Bullshit. Firemen again?"

"It's past midnight," says Chris.

"Saying I've got no permit for living. It's my building, isn't it?"

Chris places his empty Gatorade back in the fridge. He picks up the remotes next to Dad and mutes each screen. "Your daughter Elsa is here in this room."

The old man grabs Chris's shoulder and pulls himself up. His belly protrudes like his son's. His flimsy undershirt hangs from bony shoulders. Both men wear boxers, though my father's are more threadbare. Silver stubbles his chin.

Blindfolded, he holds out his hand. As if summoned, I come to him silently. Grabbing my wrist, he jerks me toward him, his body collapsing into mine. Chris turns off each screen, and my father's tears seep through his bandages to coat my skin. He runs his hands over my face and tugs on my ears, which he'd always said were just like his own well-shaped ears. "Is she here to stay? Has she really come home?"

He's so pathetic, I need to be firm, lest his expectations work their guilt on me. He never played that game with us though; Mom was the master. But old dads can learn new tricks, especially with their wives gone. "Ah-bbah, I'm only here for the funeral." I guide him into his chair. His hands won't let me go, until I pull away.

He sighs. "Nothing sadder than a girl without a mother. Your mother was motherless too. That's why she never knew how to receive my love." We've heard this before. Usually, it pisses me off, but right now I only notice how his blanket—a comforter with a pastel geometric '80s pattern—pools around his feet, making him look so small and frail.

"Where does he sleep?" I ask Chris.

"In that chair, then his bed."

"Doesn't he need help getting around?"

"He knows every corner of this place. Built it himself."

Chris disjoints a cubicle wall and swings it open, revealing Dad's clothing racks—tailored three-piece suits in garment bags and monogrammed French cuff dress shirts. These are relics of his flashy heyday, when he made good money in the '80s, was a member of the Playboy Club, when he wore a gold chain and a diamond-encrusted gold nugget of a ring like a minor mafioso.

"Ever since Dad's latest accident," says Chris, "I've been staying here full-time. Just in case the old man falls down the stairs," he adds with a grin. He connects the wall with another, forming a new cell adjoining his own. From the time Mom had been institutionalized, Chris had been living at her house. But he also had this second residence, when he couldn't stand sleeping in his childhood bedroom with all its smothering memories. He shoves a mattress into this new cubicle. "Tomorrow, we'll get nicer stuff from Mom's. Or do you want to sleep there tonight?"

"You can sleep at Mom's tonight," I offer. "I'll take this shift."

"There are no shifts. It's just me, all the time."

"I meant—"

"If you want to talk shifts, you could live with him for the next few decades. But let's not get into it now. After working out, I'm totally beat," he says, cracking his neck.

So our mother did have an observant disciple after all. I ignore the barb. It'll just be the two of them now. My visits to Mom were dutiful, curious. I owe my father less.

If anything, I owe Chris more, as he likes to remind me. So I'll tell him that after Dad's gone, he can have the house and the body shop. I'll make that clear after the funeral.

In his cubicle, Chris does some deep, deep squats. We all mourn in our own ways.

"You sure Dad can manage?" I ask.

He cocks his chin. "There, watch the old man go."

Our father maneuvers through his maze to the bathroom. Leaving the door open, he pisses in the dark, then wends his way back. Before climbing into bed, he says, "Elsa, you've been away for a long while. You should rest now. You need to sleep for a very long time."

"Sorry there isn't more of a homecoming," says Chris, still squatting up and down. "With all the meds, we follow a strict schedule. Got some good ones for Dad too. He's super mellow now." Chris bends over, trying to touch his toes, but his belly blocks the way. "Too bad we couldn't dose the old man when we were younger." With his face upside down, flushed red, he whispers, "I got extra. If you need help falling asleep or whatever."

Coming through the front door, my mother caught me frying Dad's fish for dinner. "He's coming now?"

"I don't know. He called twice about Chris. Asked where you were too."

"Why are you frying now? If he's coming later, it'll just get cold."

"It's almost nine. You want me to stop?"

"Too late now." She took the phone into the living room.

I poured more oil. The fish sizzled, but my father's voice was still audible over the hiss. I turned the knob, growing the flames.

"He wrote a theatrical piece for his university club," she said over the phone, "you can't expect him to be around whenever... How am I supposed to know when you want dinner... Decide what you're pissed about before you scream at me." She hung up, then locked the doors.

I peered at my fish. Gutted but not skinned, with head still attached. Its gelatinous eye, "grievous" and "affronted," words I recently learned from vocab books that Chris bought me. But no one could tell me if I used them correctly. So the fish and I glared at each other.

The phone rang again. "I hung up because I thought you were done," said Mom.

I poured more oil. It spattered onto my arms. Smoke clouded the kitchen. Couldn't find the spatula, so I grabbed the next best thing—the pink plastic fly swatter. The right shape, but I couldn't wedge it underneath. Mom shut off the heat and took the swatter from me. The edge bubbled and curled at a diagonal. Pink plastic, flecked with black char and scales, glistened with oil. "Open the back door," she said. She rinsed then patted the wet plastic against her thigh.

I opened the sliding glass doors. Dead flesh thumped into the trash. I wanted someone else's voice to deafen my ears, her red ribbons to blind my eyes.

Headlight beams shone through the windows. The slam of the car door. Kicks at the metal front door, deepening the dent already there. Keys clawing at the lock.

Handing me her apron, she said, "Hide this under your bed." I took it to my room and heard the Monster enter.

"If you need him to translate," she said, rooted in the living room with wide stance, hands on hips, "ask him in advance or wait until he returns. Elsa could help, but it's her bedtime now."

I came out to volunteer, but I couldn't see or hear my father, only my mother framed by the hallway where I stood.

"He's three years behind," she said, "because he had to work to save money."

She doesn't need to remind him that Chris took time off to help with the family while Dad recovered from the assault, when the thief smashed his head, leaving him unconscious on the body shop parking lot. She doesn't remind him that their savings had been depleted for hospital bills because immigrants can't afford insurance, that the shop barely survived while Dad learned how to walk and talk again. That Chris shouldered the stress and forms and bills and was told to be the man of the house for Mom, as well as a father to me. That even though the Korean pastor urged his congregation to have their cars serviced at our shop and my parents' friends and relatives probably helped in ways they could, these were lost years for our family. My memory of this period is spotty too. Mostly because Mom and Chris shielded things from me.

"Him making money?" Dad scoffed. "What kind of money could he make at a bookstore? Tutoring? He should learn a real trade."

"We went to university in Korea," she countered. "Just because you're now a body man—your own great-uncle was a scholar! Just because we're immigrants now—no, especially because we're immigrants—he did well in high school, but his sensitive nature, his lack of discipline, his outlandish ways—this country is too soft on their boys perhaps. You were spoiled too until you left your father's wing. Our son lives here because it's cheaper, but we should pretend he doesn't. I'm helping him get an apartment closer to school anyhow."

A man's foot stepped into view, but I couldn't see my mother anymore. Dad had been muted, while Mom had been erased.

"I've got shit for brains?" she screamed. "One would assume so for marrying you. But wasn't my choice, was it? I've got shit for destiny too."

I heard the thump of dead flesh landing in trash. An echo of the burnt fish.

"You stole my life, but I pushed you out," she said. "I've got money of my own now!"

"Don't be ridiculous on top of stupid." He laughed, ugly and mocking.

Headlights beamed through the house again. My father turned toward them. My mother, lying on the floor, propped herself up on shaking shoulders.

Click-clacking on the driveway and falsetto-singing, Chris waltzed into the house, still in Mom's dress. After one glance, he grabbed Dad and pinned him to the wall. He'd kicked off his heels, but was still several inches taller. As their bodies struggled for control, Chris in his molten gown and my father in his greasy uniform stumbled and swayed.

Watching the two men dance, I thought of my parents at parties. In a tailored suit and Italian-made elevator shoes, my father would spin my mother, using steps he'd learned in Seoul when the war was finally over and his father still a rich man. My father could twirl her with barely a touch. But now, he was the one dragged around by a monstrous beauty whose dress strained at the arms. Chris pushed him against the wall. Our father spat in his face.

Chris wiped his eye and examined the black smear on his fingertips. "You know how long it took to get my makeup right?"

"Speak Korean!" Our father grabbed a fistful of dress. "What shit is this? Take it off!"

Laughing, Chris slowly slid the gown off his muscled shoulders, as if in a striptease. "Relax," he answered in English. "It's my costume for a musical revue I wrote. A total success." Only wearing his boxers, he draped the dress over the grand piano, which blocked our father from the door.

"What the fuck are you? Whose son are you?"

Chris slapped his chest and lunged toward him. "I'm the thing you made. If I'm a piece of shit, as you love to say, take a bow 'cause you are the maker of shit."

My brother had hardened his body with his backyard bench press. He'd toughened his fists with the punching bag hanging from the patio roof. The bag's chains would rattle the house rafters, the chandelier crystals chattering like loose teeth.

"This is what you do at that university? So reading all those books all these years were what—just for show, to play the fool?"

"You mean the books you ripped up in front of me because they provoked you? You who only got into college because of grandfather's money? He gave you a factory too and it went bust, right? He even got Mom to marry you, turned her head with all his money and gifts and promises you'd be a grand success someday?"

I feared Chris had gone too far, even keeping his English simple, clear, and slow so that Dad would understand every word. Our father seemed poised to attack, but then after a long and tense moment, he sighed instead, exhausted.

"You wanna be some kind of scholar?" he said. "You're just like my uncle, worthless poet posing as revolutionary, no better than the peasants who pretended to be soldiers—that's how the Japs took over, how we lost everything. The supposed thinkers, playing with ideas better left to bigger countries. My uncle and his sons all dead in the North. Along with all their stupid dreams of a new Korea. You'd be dead too. Wouldn't last a day of what I've been through."

Dad shoved past him, then stopped at the piano where the silver dress melted over the edge. I expected him to hurl it at either wife or son, but he stroked it instead, remembering.

This moment of surprising quietness and Dad's posture of an overworked fiftysomething-year-old man, who kept surviving despite the odds, must've humbled my brother. Chris, suddenly aware of his nakedness, crossed his arms and shivered. "Father, after I wash up," he said in Korean, "I will come to the body shop and help you with whatever you need of me."

Nodding, our father lowered himself onto the piano bench, his back visibly aching. He reached for his leather work shoes. I wondered why he'd taken them off in the first place midrampage. Was it because of Korean custom, removing shoes before entering the house? Or a courtesy granted to my mother before kicking her?

At the door, he added without turning: "Bring my dinner with you."

In honorific Korean, Chris replied that he would do so.

After Dad left, Mom approached Chris with a washcloth for his face. "I told you not to ruin my dress," she said, pointing at the torn shoulder seam.

"I promise to buy you more when I'm rich and successful."

"A lawyer, then maybe a judge. You never had the temperament to be a doctor, but you're good with words, yes? Good at arguing, certainly? That's what you're doing at school, besides having this silly fun, right?"

"Yes, Mom. Yes, you're exactly right," Chris replied in Korean.

She took the apron from my room and into hers. My brother finally noticed me. He winked his smeared black eye and said, "At least I still look pretty." He left me to wash up.

In the kitchen, I transferred the fish I'd saved for Chris to plastic containers for my father.

After Chris left the house with Dad's dinner, Mom called me to her. Seated at her vanity table, she asked, "Why didn't you protect your own mother?"

"I'm sorry," I said, thinking how the most dangerous place in this house was by her side.

"What kind of a daughter—whose daughter are you?"

When my father asked this and I replied I was my mother's, he would feign heartbreak. Always a joke to him, never for her.

"Whose mother are *you*?" I tried to make her laugh, like Chris did so easily.

"Wish I weren't." She picked up a foundation compact. She dug her fingers into the cream and slapped it onto her cheek, rubbing in circles.

"Wish you weren't what?" I asked.

"Cruel—"

"You're not—"

"Cruel to be a mother." She piled on the makeup, but I could see the handprint blooming underneath, throbbing pink. He must've given it to her when I couldn't see or hear. But I knew, things I couldn't see still happened, still existed. "I hope that other one got away," she said.

"You mean Chris?"

"What do you two talk about? Anything you're hiding from me? So what if the boys make fun of you? What about Eugene? I know his mother."

My mother had eavesdropped again, overheard my crying to Chris earlier that day. How Eugene, normally nice, the only other Korean kid in my class, had shyly passed a note, asking if I stuffed my bra, that maybe I should. When I opened it, the

Japanese boys all started cracking up, but Eugene hadn't. "Please, don't make it worse, Mom."

"These boys are insignificant."

I expected her to tell me that things would get better, my future bright. Instead, she said, "You must be strong because you'll face much worse. Can't be avoided. You must learn to endure. Deadly, if you're unprepared, like I was." The red handprint winged across her face. It pulsed and fluttered, struggling to take flight beneath all that powder.

I didn't want to be alone, despite her strange muttering, so I followed her through the house. She picked up the melted swatter and stepped into the backyard, where our lone palm tree had shed its orange, marble-sized fruit that fell like heavy raindrops. If we didn't sweep them, they coated the ground and attracted flies. I stepped on the fruit with bare feet. Its juices seeped. Sweet rot rose from below. My mother closed her eyes, tapping her thigh with the swatter, searching for rhythm and tune. Feasting flies, their bastard-fairy wings tickled my toes.

I wander to the corner of the loft while Chris takes a shower. This is where Dad set up his shrine for a lost daughter. From the time I left for boarding school, he'd scavenged scraps from my room. Trophies and ribbons, a thrice-used lacrosse stick, photos of friends I no longer spoke to, love letters from boyfriends long forgotten. Each summer, I'd bring home more stuff for storage, and he'd root through my things. Journal publications were shelved along with alumni magazines, while news clippings and their xeroxed duplicates and trivial documents on university letterhead were filed in folders.

But this wasn't fatherly pride or his attempt to hold on to me. Chris explained to me once that in Confucian culture, the child is an appendage of the father. He was showing off his own accomplishments. This was *his* dissertation and those were *his* diplomas, and he proudly displayed them all, including the Jewish prom date and the spelling bee trophy. But he couldn't pin up my neutrinos, sterile or not.

He had plenty to be proud of too, what he built for himself and his family. The body shop, literally the most concrete proof of his life's work, was my rival for his affections. No wonder he refused to vacate, despite the firemen's multiple visits warning him that his commercial property wasn't "coded for living." My father appeased them with the special cabinet for flammable chemicals, improved ventilation for the paint garage, the fire exit no longer blocked by stacks of yellowing newspapers. He claimed the bed was only for naps, that the loft was for storage, not the remainder of his years.

But the firemen don't know he's prepared his own mausoleum—no one's going to box up his belongings and burn him down into ashes to fit into a decorative jar. He won't rely on delusion and catatonia to escape, like his wife. He'll rely on steel and cement to remain standing.

They say the last time you meet your parents is when they die—through the things they leave behind. My father's been diligent with his hoarding, leaving us several garages to sift through. My mother's effects are more elusive. Like her quarter-folded plans for wood carvings. Her folktales were also coded, laying out all the ways my life could be like hers or fucked up in the ways of my dead aunt or dead grandmother or dead sister.

But maybe she left instructions in how to defy like she did—a nymph ascending to heaven *without* her children. Maybe I need to learn the rules of my fate in order to break them. Anyhow, through these stories, I'll meet my mother for the last time—or more likely for the very first.

Not long after Chris goes to bed, I hear both men snore. Moonlight shines through the vertical blinds. Shadow bars stripe my body. Leaving the men in their padded cells, I head home to ransack a three-bedroom bungalow for a dead woman's fairytales.

Later that night, after Chris had washed off his makeup and taken Dad's dinner to the body shop, I heard angry sobbing through my bedroom wall. I imagined Chris was crying because he'd really been transformed into a woman. I cracked open the door. Mom was packing a suitcase. Chris passed her his clothes. So, they were running away without me.

Mom withdrew the envelope from her apron and gave it to Chris. He noticed me first. His face without makeup was splotchy-red, his nostrils smeared and crusted with dark blood. "I'm staying with friends," he said to me. "Then I'm getting my own apartment. You can visit whenever. Here, in case you don't win any scholarships." He handed me the padded bra—lavender, beautiful, and dangerous.

"It belongs to your girlfriend," I said.

"She's got lots, all shapes and sizes. You take care of Mom, OK?"

"No one will believe I grew them overnight."

"Sometimes it happens that way."

Our mother rushed back and forth to pack the car with blankets and kitchen appliances. Chris stopped her and drew her close. In his arms, she stopped shaking. Like the other times when he had to flee in the night, we watched him drive away.

The next day at school pickup, just after I'd slunk into the passenger seat, Mom stepped out, engine running, holding up the other cars. She'd spotted Eugene on the upper floor balcony and yelled at him in Korean.

"Mom, please!" I tugged her sleeve, begging her to get back in the car.

"You're a Korean boy! You're supposed to watch out for each other! You think you're one of these Japs?" my mother shouted, shaking her fist. "You think you do what they say, they'll treat you like one of them? You're supposed to protect her from them! What kind of Korean man are you going to be?"

The white teachers emerged to see the commotion. The Japanese boys whooped and hollered: "Dude! Elsa's mom is cussing out Eugene! She's totally cussing him out in Korean!"

The next day, I wore my lavender padded bra. No one would believe I'd grown them overnight. It was for me anyhow—my own beautiful, dangerous armor.

2

The garage floodlight shines on the front yard. For years, the lawn's been merely yellow bristles stuck in the dirt. Recent rains must've nurtured this jungle—knee-high desert dandelions with serrated dagger leaves; bushes of spiny thistle with purple flowers and needle-pricked Hellraiser bulbs. The most virulent weeds, made sinister in the electric light.

But inside the house is more alarming. While she'd been hospitalized, all of Mom's things, including cracked eye shadow palettes, electric blankets, and church sermon cassettes had been left untouched. But now, the family photos are gone, along with her landscape pastel prints, dusty silk flowers, the Korean knickknacks and Christian tchotchkes. Only the furniture and the TV remain. Boxes of energy bars and protein powder canisters replace the throw pillows. Shiny barbells line up against the wall where the piano once was. Chris hasn't wasted time finding a buyer for the grand. I can still see the carpet indents where the instrument stood for decades.

I check the rooms. My princess daybed's still there, along with the girlhood junk my father deemed unworthy for his shrine. Chris's bedroom was still lived-in, though his desk was recently organized. My mother's bedroom—I hesitated, afraid to find it scraped empty—was left just as I remembered on every visit, preserved as if she'd return any day.

And waiting for me here, more natural and at home in this setting than in Antarctica or Sweden, was my friend, seated at my mother's vanity, her face unreflected in the mirror.

"Why'd you ditch me?" I ask. "Am I compartmentalizing?"

"They can't see me. I hate being ignored. Worse than being forgotten or never known."

"Some emotional support animal you are. Can you at least try to be helpful in my search?" I tie my hair back and literally roll up my sleeves.

"The stories aren't here, Elsa. Not in this room, not in this house."

"Where'd I last see the notebook? As my external hard drive, you should be more useful."

"You already know who has it."

Maybe once I find the stories, my guilt—this walking, talking, braided manifestation of it—will finally leave me be. In the dresser, lavender sachets are tucked among silk slips and wool sweaters—they've retained their scent, her scent, all these years. In one drawer, I find a stack of birthday cards, some addressed to me when I was a baby. Others are blank. Mom must've bought in bulk for all my future birthdays. This is too much. Haven't slept, eaten, or showered since—I face the mirrored closet doors. Instead of a jet-lagged thirty-year-old woman, all I see is a scared little girl.

I also remember what it was like to be lonely and terrified to go outside, with nothing to do but stay indoors to discover buried worlds and secret lives.

And the only thing my mother locked in her room, what she repeatedly told me to keep hidden from others—especially my father—the wood-chest.

When I first found the wood-chest and its Korean hanboks inside, I immediately tried on the silk gowns. Mom never wore these, preferring blouses and pleated skirts. But I knew how to put on the crinoline petticoat first, then tie the voluminous skirt around my chest. I slipped on the top that closed in a V-neck. The bell sleeves extended past my fingers, and the ribbons tying the lapels trailed down my front. I raised my arms, stood on tiptoe, and held my breath.

The next moment, a car sped up the driveway. Heels clicked frantically. Mom entered the house, locked the doors. Another car sped up, followed by kicks to the door and a curse echoing down the street.

My mother came into the room and I fell into a heap. She lifted me, a bundle of crushed silk, and placed me inside the closet. She stuffed the other hanboks in the chest and squeezed in beside me, sliding the door shut. Her hands clamped over my ears, but I still heard doors being thrown open, plywood whimpering on hinges. As my father yelled louder, her hands pressed tighter. He entered, but didn't open the closet, not then or any other time.

Only now do I wonder if he'd been shamed or troubled by his reflection, if that's why my mother hid us there behind the mirrors.

When my father finally left, Mom released my head, and my ears throbbed. "Don't put these on, not even for playing," she said. "Your body may not be yours anymore when you're married, but you can choose the clothes the world will see you in."

After she'd told me someone else could own my body, I didn't want to play dress up anymore, pretending to be another. I didn't have to anyway because after she left me in the closet, I discovered beside me a little girl, her braid tied with a red ribbon.

Now, more than two decades later, I burrow again to my corner. Right where I'd left them are my flashlight, *Highlights* magazines, and a Ziploc of teriyaki beef jerky. My kiddie survivalist bunker. Lying underneath the hanging clothes, I peer up into the many skirts of my many mothers. Back then there was Housewife Mom, Church Mom, Party Mom, and Immigrant Mom whom I accompanied to serve as interpreter. Now, these only belong to Dead Mom. I turn from such intimate views, striking my forehead against something hard.

I push aside the pillowcase stuffed with tangled pantyhose and peel off the crocheted blankets to rediscover the chest. The lock's open. I don't know if Chris found the key, or if my mother had unlocked it before taking me to the spa.

Inside, still folded neatly in tissue—my mother's trousseau, symbolic of the life promised then stolen. That must be why she couldn't bear the sight of these gowns. I empty the chest, then run my hands inside. No carvings, no secret panels, not even a line of engraving, courtesy of *Things Remembered.*

Most disturbingly, I'm tempted to stuff my entire body into the wooden box.

Ignoring the weird impulse, I examine the hanboks, flapping a petticoat. From the crinoline, an envelope tumbles out, stuffed with hundred-dollar bills. Inside the deep hem of a skirt, more money. Cash tucked into a padded jacket or stitched within wide pleats. Seventy-five thousand dollars in all. So, neither my father nor brother has been here.

I slip my fingers into the slit hidden behind a seam of a velvet skirt's lining and withdraw a palm-sized address book. The pages are filled with names and addresses, along with dates and dollar amounts in the hundreds and thousands. Sometimes the values decrease steadily; sometimes they vacillate. When they increase, they grow at a 25 percent uptick.

Chris often spoke about our mother's loan-sharking and her network of desperate women—some undocumented, some acting on behalf of their husbands, or for the family businesses, or for relatives back home. Some trying to build runaway funds of their own.

For the names in my mother's ledger, the last value is zero. The dates next to these zeroes were in the last months before our desert trip. With one exception: "Mrs. Kang of New Jersey," with a former address in Seoul and a previous name in Korean, redacted and illegible. Her numbers were denoted with a positive, unlike the negatives for the others. Mrs. Kang's values increased over inconsistent intervals, beginning in the early '80s, lasting over a decade. No interest accrual. Last value: positive fifty thousand. This must be what my mother owed her.

I turn to ask my friend how Loan Shark Mom fits in with all her other identities, but she's not with me anymore. How many different moms were you—to me and Chris and to this woman in New Jersey? Will I ever see your real face—do I even want to?

For the next few hours, I sit on the floor, studying the names and numbers and dates, graphing them in my mind in search of a pattern. But really, I'm waiting for 4:00 a.m. when I can reasonably call the number. It'd be 7:00 a.m. on a Jersey weekday. High probability that an old Korean woman would be awake, not yet at the park for some power walking with her sun visor and white gloves.

I dial, not knowing what I'll say. I'm simply following the money like a good detective. The answering voice, however, speaks without accent. She sounds young like me. "Am I speaking to Mrs. Kang?" I ask.

"Well, this is Hannah Kang. I'm not a Mrs. though, not anymore. Who's this?"

I hang up, heart pounding. Mrs. Kang morphs into a little girl, tracked down by my mother, her long-lost daughter given up in Korea, who then immigrated to the US with her adoptive parents. According to the ledger, Mom's been sending her money, ever since Hannah was a young girl to when she was a married woman.

I was fourteen when Mom took me to the spa. The supposedly stillborn girl would've been eighteen or so. Was this last seventy-five thousand Mom's final gift before dying? A graduation present, along with some handwritten stories, maybe some wood carvings, all conveyed through a sister who'd be her link to a mother she never knew?

The air smells sour and briny. The carpet feels damp, its sogginess seeping through my jeans. I look up and see my friend before me soaking wet, her shift clinging to her body, her legs sheathed in velvety moss.

"Stories first. Sister later." Her expression shifts from sorrow, then fury, to dread. Her eyes flash green, of fiercest envy.

"But this woman in Jersey could be the sister Mom talked about, the other girl."

Her voice, like a wild creature, scrambles up into the highest registers, shrieking, "Not yet, not yet, not yet! I don't want to be alone!"

Shivering, she stares at her arms, gloved in lacy algae, rapidly blooming toward her shoulders, unfurling tendrils up her neck so that her blue-veined cheeks and purpling lips—so cold she must be—are overlaid with virescent filigree. The sea-green luster drains from her eyes, leaving them colorless, horrified. Her gaping mouth opens and closes like a fish. And over her trembling shoulder—the sopping black braid drips along the red ribbon, weeping something brackish and foul onto her muddy feet.

I wedge my face between bent knees and breathe slowly until I no longer feel the cold on my neck or smell the rot in the air. When I finally lift my head, I'm all alone.

3

In the morning, Chris enters the house, shouting my name. I roll out of the closet onto the carpet. In daylight, my mother's bedroom looks dusty, sad, and sane. I charge into the living room, blustering my anxieties away. "What'd you do with Mom's stuff?" I demand.

"Found a company online to haul off the junk. Left her bedroom for you, but the jewelry's been sold off long ago. You sleep OK? You look like shit."

"You supervised? Made sure—"

"All junk. I need to go tutor now. But heads up—Dad wants to have family dinner here tonight." Stepping closer, he adds, "You sure you're okay? You look puffy—squishy, even."

"I'm just jet-lagged. So how long's tutoring, couple hours? Wanna hang out afterward?"

"Booked all day, lots of errands. Dad's not going anywhere though, if you need company."

"No, I'm really busy too, lots to do. See you at dinner."

But later that night, I'm still on edge. Haven't seen my friend all day. Part of me wants to see her in normal mode, to make sure that she and I are both okay. I keep myself distracted, rooting through Mom's things. Stories first. That Jersey woman, Hannah Kang, was probably not my sister anyway. She sounded much too alive.

*

Chris brings home Korean takeout, and I help my father eat. Medicated, he dribbles rice while jutting his head closer to the Korean TV news. After a while, he lays down his spoon, resting chin on chest. We move him to Chris's bed. He's never been so easy.

While clearing the table, I ask Chris how Dad's handling things.

"The old man's reckoning. Now that she's gone, he can smell his own corpse rotting."

"And you?" I ask. "You barely touched your dinner."

"Went to early service and ran three miles at the beach. Why ruin all that?"

"Going to church again?" What I meant though: *Weren't you excommunicated?*

"A little disagreement over interpretation, got blown out of proportion."

The first time Chris got booted from our family church was because he'd called the pastor a fraud and Philistine. When the pastor replied, "Why you calling me Palestinian?" Chris laughed in his face. Or was it because he'd said the women were using church to find a husband, as evidenced by their "clubbing attire"? Even going so far as calling one girl a slut? For that he was knocked to the ground by the other guys. I happened to see across the lawn, how he got up on all fours and grinned up at the angry faces around him, the braces on his teeth glinting through the blood. There were multiple banishments, but Chris would beg, and they'd let him return until he pulled some other stunt, like the time he brought his samurai sword, the one I'd bought for him in Little Tokyo for his birthday, because of our shared love for *Highlander*. He used it for performance art at church, he claimed, to drive out the moneychangers.

"How *you* dealing, Elsa?" He drinks beer while watching me clean up.

"I'm just sad." I place the leftovers in a fridge full of takeout containers. I shut the door and stare at the white squares on the dingy yellow surface. The newspaper clippings and recipes have finally been removed, as well as all of Mom's handwritten notes.

Wiping the counter in endless circles, I ask, "When Mom had her accident at the spa, I had a notebook of her folktales—ring a bell?"

"Don't remember."

"She used to fill journals—maybe it's with her hospital stuff?"

"Never saw any notebooks."

"You took it from me—I mean you hid it from the social worker when you picked me up at the spa. You know where it is now?"

"My depression and whatever else I got makes my brain an Etch A Sketch—shake, shake, blank." He pulls out a six-pack. "Have a beer. Brother knows best—isn't that what they say?"

Even before the on-screen warning about epileptic seizures, I ask if gaming is okay. Chris assures me that his modern meds are better, that he can sense how much his brain can handle before pulling the plug. Besides, this is boxing, not a psychedelic role-playing game, he adds.

"Not like messing with a loaded gun?"

I grip the controller, tense about his recklessness and his caginess about the notebook, about everything bubbling up now that Mom's left limbo for a more permanent state of absence.

"This is fine," he says, "nothing like the old Nintendos."

"These graphics are more insane! I can't handle you seizing all over me."

"Like you ever had to deal with it. Or anything for that matter. Just suck on your bottle."

"I may not have been around for as long as you, but I saw stuff. Stuff he did to Mom."

"He never hit you," says Chris.

"On that trip to—"

"Yeah, that one time, Grand Canyon."

"I was just a kid."

"So was I," he says. "Then I wasn't a kid anymore, so he used his words to beat me down. Fine, I get it, he was treated like shit out there in this country, but how much better did he really feel after taking it out on me?"

"There was that time I had to go to the police station with Mom," I insist, "and explain Dad's hit-and-run. Really messed me up for a while."

"Seriously? You, the one with the cushy childhood, are going to steal mine just to make yourself feel what—part of this fucked up family? *I* went to the police for Dad's hit-and-run. Mom got *me* out of school, *I* had to argue with the cops. Dad yelled at me for not explaining right, then we all came home and I told you what happened."

"Not true," I lamely counter, wondering if my entire childhood was secondhand, patchworked from that of others.

"Guess I'm just too good a storyteller. I can install fake memories into your head." Palm out, he grabs my face like a smothering starfish. Peeling his fingers off me, I growl at him to stop fucking with my head.

"What about that time," I start again, "after Dad got his head bashed, and I went to the hospital billing office with Mom and explained how he'd been mugged. I was there, right?"

"I did the talking. Only brought you along for pity points. Some people thought you were cute back then. I handled all the forms and bills, the Victims of Violent Crimes application."

"When Dad wanted to drive in the carpool lane," I say, "he'd make me ride with him with his dirty cap on my head. I'd sit like a dummy while he ran errands downtown."

"Yeah, I can see how that would scar you."

"He took me to Vegas," I say, grabbing for vaguer memories. "I played in the basement carnival all day. Don't know where Dad was, but we must've stayed overnight. Did you and Mom know where I was? Weren't you scared he'd kidnapped me?"

"You were Dad's last chance—thought he could make you love him, have someone in the family not hate his guts. He played you, she did too. But you played them both by busting out of here. You're welcome, by the way. But even with a PhD, you still suck at video games."

"It's not me!" I hurl my controller across the room. "Gimme the other one."

Chris fixes me with his big brother stare. "Want some of my pills? I get them real cheap from the state. Could do you some good."

"What are you, a goddamn drug pusher? I don't need your antipsychotics."

"Was thinking of the antidepressants, actually," he replies. From the Korean apothecary chest, he removes a pill bottle, shaking it like a baby rattle. "Kicks in after a few weeks."

I pull out random drawers and find several full vials. "You skipping your meds again? The funeral's in a few days!"

Chris stands close, smiling. He whispers, "Now that Sleeping Beauty's dead, I'm finally awake." He turns off the TV and shuts off the lights, leaving us in the dark. "One body down, one more to go. It's my turn now, but I need your help."

My brother fancies himself an Ivan Karamazov but sometimes admits he's really a Smerdyakov, the "stinking one," the bastard with the shaking fits.

"I'm not helping you commit parricide," I joke, hoping to dispel my unease, but my brother's smile remains mysterious, his silence menacing.

"Look, I've got Mom's stupid book of stories," he says. "You want 'em? I've gotta proposal for you then."

"What is this—extortion?"

"You owe me big-time anyway. But first, some grub. Know how to drive yet?"

"Don't need to, not in Sweden or the South Pole."

He snorts. "For someone who likes to keep moving, you sure do limit your mobility."

Even with the beers and gaming, the history of mental instability and hoarded pills, the crazy brother is the only one fit to drive. I'd never wanted to learn. My nursery had been an automobile morgue. My playground was built of crushed cars and dismembered vehicles. I was surrounded by wrecks. I was raised by them.

Entering the Korean pub, we bow as the barmaids sing their welcome. Posters of Korean models shilling beer are strung across the ceiling like Tibetan prayer flags.

While Chris orders, I observe the clientele's trendy glasses, slim builds, ironed dress shirts, and fancy handbags. Obviously, recent immigrants. Chris is less slobby than usual with his white polo and minimal stains, but I'm rocking Mom's paisley caftan, which she only wore as a housedress. Used to be that we American Koreans were the more stylish, sophisticated ones. Now we're just fatter with poorer posture.

When the server leaves, I ask Chris how much money he wants for the folktales.

"Never asked you for money." He regards me with disgust.

"Your business proposal?"

"Dad's wasting his property. I just want a few garages, an advance on my inheritance. So I'll trade my birthright for whatever Mom's stories mean to you."

"How would I—"

"You're the favorite, Cordelia. Tell Dad you're broke, that you're in debt from all your schooling. Ask for a couple garages, propose I manage them for you."

"Why now? Because she's dead?"

"The global economy's just collapsed—now's my time!" He slaps the table with both palms. "Little Uncle in Seoul, the multimillionaire—the one Grandpa intended to leave behind in the North, the one who wasn't sent to college like Dad—Little Uncle told me that chaos is when fortunes are made, when you must seize your chance to flip your destiny."

Our father, as eldest son, was gifted a factory that he ran into the ground, and he lost Mom's dowry too, land that the Olympic Stadium was later built upon. But Chris was the most obsessed with these losses, with his alternate life as a rich man's son. He was haunted by what should have been, this other reality, however tenuous.

"The playing field's equal again," he says. "All my friends who surpassed me have lost big-time. I lost nothing 'cause I had nothing to begin with! I can finally get ahead now."

"Very sympathetic of you."

"The house and shop are paid off, so we're in perfect position. We lease out the garages, transform this place into a multi-service auto center. Nobody will be buying new cars now, all about upkeep. Paint jobs, replacement parts, wannabe Lexus trim. The shop's always made the most buck during the holidays with all the drunk driving. Well, this is *our* holiday when everyone's freaking out about gutted stocks and 401(k)s, crashing home values, tanked careers, all the stuff I didn't have in the first place. You owe me 'cause I'm George Bailey, and it's *my* turn to lasso the moon. Look, I get it, you were young when you lost Mom. All you have are her stories. With my venture though, you'll get a decent cut. We'll actually make something of our inheritance."

"All right, all right, I'll ask him. *After* the funeral."

He hasn't been this driven and goal-oriented since I was a kid, when he orchestrated my departure from home. I'm uneasy about what this change in energy foretells—what part he has in mind for me. So I'm grateful when our fried chicken arrives to shift the focus.

Chris cracks into the breastbone, tearing off the hot skin with his teeth, releasing steam from its flesh. He washes it all down with a cold pint. "Dad's not doing anything with the shop. Should be a family trust. He doesn't even have a will."

"It's his property," I mumble while enjoying my own garlicky wings.

"How'd he build it, at what cost? Bullied us, made me and Mom go crazy? Look, I'm asking you because Dad thinks he's wronged you the most. Sent you away when you were young, thinks you're practically an orphan, boarding school then Sweden then off to the Eskimos—that's what he said. You have power over him. A while ago, we were watching a World War II movie, and Dad says out of nowhere, in English, 'Nobody love me.' I busted out laughing. Then in Korean, he said, 'I thought Elsa might have, but no.' I told him, 'That's right, old man, nobody loves you! Why should we, after what you did to us?'"

Chris chuckles, his lips gleaming with grease. His eyes glaze as he settles back into the booth. His paunch in the white polo catches the light like a full moon, echoed by the pale streak in his hair.

When Mom called home frantically from church, telling Dad how Chris was acting out again, my father went to retrieve him. I waited in the car's backseat, in the parking lot, and saw how my father walked his son out of the church. Dad held his head high, his arm protective around Chris's shoulders as angry faces glared behind them.

When Chris had worked installing car batteries at a service center across town—earning money instead of helping Dad for free, while taking another break from college—our father would leave the body shop to spy on him. Dad would later tell Mom how pitiful he looked, lugging those heavy batteries, how his son's hands were not meant for such work. It was the same thing Dad's cousin visiting from Seoul had said about my father. Cradling his scarred hands, she remarked how they'd once been so soft and pale. Dad jerked away from her hold. This cousin was another Kaesong refugee who'd become rich, flipping her destiny. My father, who'd started off with all the advantages of a firstborn son, had reversed his fortunes too. I doubt he could've ever returned to Korea, even if he wanted.

"Dad loves you," I tell Chris. "But he doesn't know how to show it. It's cultural."

"You think he didn't know how to show Mom? Or is that cultural too?"

"It's easier to love your kid. Clear vector, one way. Him and Mom though—I was only there for the end. Don't know what it was like before—how often did he hit her? Must've been more than— I was afraid all the time, couldn't sleep till he was out of the house. You say I don't remember—what am I doing to Mom if I can't? Like I'm hurting her all over again."

Gently, he replies, "Just a few times. Not like some of my friends' dads. Mostly, Dad yelled a lot. Verbally abusive. Mom knew how to play up her end too. She screamed before contact, made sure we noticed. Just a few times, Elsa. In my childhood and yours. You're lucky if you don't remember. Don't beat yourself over it. I know, poor choice of words."

This time, I'm thankful he's lying to me.

"Easier if they were both dead," I sigh. "If Dad died long ago, he'd just be Monster."

"Oh yeah, Monster!" Chris grins with chicken flesh in his teeth. "That was my nickname for him. You stole it from me. Or I taught it to you."

"Point is, now that he's this feeble old man, it's hard not to feel sorry for him," I say. "But that makes me feel guilty after everything he did to her."

"Biological strategy—babies are cute, so we take care of them and don't eat them. Parents get old and pathetic, so we also don't eat them."

"Maybe that's why I don't want to remember. I'm bigger now, but how can I hurt an old man?"

Chris refills our glasses. "Mom was pretty wacked-up too. Something runs in the blood—look at me! My doctors say high stress can trigger schizophrenia, if you're susceptible. Even if Dad weren't an asshole, she might've— They both grew up during wartime. Dad vented his trauma through us—very cliché. Mom was more *imaginative,* with more flair."

I steady my voice. "Do you remember what she said to me in the spa?"

Chris studies me in the lamplight. "Why *do* you want her stories? You don't believe—what else she tell you at that spa?"

"Why have you kept it all these years?"

"For your own good. Wish someone had done me the favor." Chris shoves a drumstick in his mouth and scrapes his teeth against bone, sucking off flesh, tendon, and skin.

"Why?" I persist. "What else is in there—did she write about my sister?"

"Oh fucking Lord, not this again—not from you too."

"What's important is that she believed, and I want to know why *this* fantasy? What patterns did she see in herself, her mom, her sister—in me? This is all I have to understand her. The other daughter—why did Mom say—"

"She was born dead, Elsa! Mom was wrecked, dreamt up this story as consolation."

"Like the story you tell yourself, about being God's other—"

"I didn't tell myself a story!" he shouts, slamming a fist on the table. Others in the bar turn to judge us. More quietly, he adds, "God himself told me in my dreams that I'm his other son. Hearing is believing, isn't that what they say?"

"It's 'seeing is believing'! Fucking A, I know English is your second language, but you came here when you were like five!"

He shrugs, calls for another pitcher. We drink in sibling silence. After a while, I ask, "Have you ever hallucinated *before* seizures—or *without*?"

"I've *never* had auditory or visual hallucinations, yet I still get diagnosed as schizophrenic!"

"Because you believed your dreams were holy visions. Do you still? You promised you'd stop at age thirty-three."

"When my brother was crucified." He snorts, leaning back out of the lamplight. "A while ago, I came across this article about the God spot. There's this study on epileptics whose temporal lobes fire up during seizures. They have religious visions, full-on, visual and auditory. Even the most devout atheists see the face of God. The part of our brain that lights up most—that's the God spot. So maybe there's rhyme and reason for my crazy. From the moment of birth, when the 'Made in USA' forceps pulled my head into the world. You know they tested that model on foreign babies first? Never made it to the domestic market. They stopped using it in Korea too. Always a sore point for Mom. For me too," he says, tapping the side of his head.

I knew what was next. I let my brother finish his origin myth.

"Then the car accident," he says, "in case the first brain damage wasn't enough, right?"

At three, he ran into the street and got hit by a car. His left temple has sprouted white since he was sixteen.

"I wonder," he continues, "what if Dad had coughed up the money for the recommended surgery? Would I've still become epileptic? Become a vegetable like Mom? Cheap bastard. Why'd I fight so hard to get him the best care, when it was his turn to crack his skull?"

I keep the focus on him and his illness. "Your seizures might explain your religious dreams, but do you still believe, and why?"

He shrugs. "Mom considered herself a Christian despite the Korean mystical shit. Wasn't contradiction for her. More like hybrid faith. I just know I'm a son of God. Used to think I'd kill myself if it weren't true. Now it's this secret identity that keeps me going." He lays his hands on the table. His knuckle scabs bleed fresh around the edges.

Like my brother, I've done some amateur research into our family's mental illness. One theory I've got is that we became addicted to neurochemical hormones in our childhoods. Mom grew up in wartime, her developing brain brewing in adrenaline and fear and the desperate need to survive at all costs. This hormonal cocktail became the norm, so she thrived during trauma and crisis. A useful state of mind for an immigrant, especially with buffets and items on clearance. But when there wasn't danger, she became uneasy, jonesing for a fix, the next adrenaline spike. So she conjured unseen enemies, a war between her and forces even more powerful than the ones who'd severed her country in two. For what was a war among men and their ideologies when there were ancestral curses, ancient stories that would never let her go? That's how she swerved and snapped, from a woman scrounging and harvesting thousands through loan-sharking, to someone who transcended the common street fight among immigrants, to something more sublime—wrestling with the ghosts of goddesses.

As for Chris, he never claimed to be Jesus or on par with the Holy Trinity. He considered himself a Ringo, "the lesser child of God." How could I strip him of such meager divinity?

Ignoring me, he turns his attention to two women playing pool. One leans over, cue in hand. The sharp V cut of her dress mirrors the triangle of racked balls. The other girl in white passes behind in the shadows. Her lips are bright red. "Asians are good at geometry," says Chris. "Still hot when chicks can play pool." The girl with red lips ties her hair back into a ponytail.

"For those who have hallucinations triggered by the God spot," I ask, "is it possible to activate that spot on command?"

"You *want* to see things? Or do you already? Hey, didn't you used to have an imag—"

"I'm scientifically curious is all, if it's possible to self-induce a seizure, if there's an architectural similarity between our brains."

"Well, for a simple-class partial seizure, you can be totally cognizant and awake while you're seizing and not even notice."

"So I could be seizing right now?" Just hearing him say it was possible made it true.

"You feel it as a memory glitch or déjà vu," he says. "Or emotional disturbance."

"That could be everyone in the world all the time!"

"It's more intense, like a bright light. Some people smell burnt toast. Or you hear something from an object that shouldn't be making noise."

Like a hole carved in the ice, or a friend lying in your bed?

"It's called phantosmia."

"That sounds pretty," I say.

"Who do you want to see? Whose voice you want to hear?"

I can't tell him I want to see and hear Mom because I never got to say goodbye, because he was so quick to burn her to ash. Can't tell him I'm already seeing a woman from my past, because he'd feed me pills and be smug about how I ended up like him despite all my running. Haven't told anyone about my friend. Like a wish—utter it and it won't come true. Like a sin—confess and it'll wash away. I need her mine to define. She's proof I'm like my family. Makes sense I reunited with her at the bottom of the world. That I snuggled with her in a country where my own reflection surprises me, so unlike the other faces all around me.

"Well, for activating your God spot, my PS3 won't cut it," says Chris, finishing his beer. "We'll need to go old-school if you want synaptic fireworks."

"I was kidding," I slur, listening to the simple clacking rhythms of Newtonian physics on the billiards table. My childhood physics, before the relativistic and quantum uncertainties.

"Let's bounce! I don't wanna be around all these new immigrants anymore. Makes me feel old and sad. Why do they keep coming? Nothing's better over here, not anymore."

4

In the loft, Chris opens cabinets, revealing disco cubes and strobe lights. "Don't look at me like that," he snaps. "I used to throw dance parties up here." He stumbles downstairs for an extension cord, leaving me with the remnants of my father's party days, the kye gatherings.

The kye was a communal lending and savings club, a Korean economic strategy a few centuries old in which twenty or so families kicked in funds to join. Every month, members would take turns collecting the kitty, with variable interest rates depending on how soon and desperately they needed the money versus how long they could afford to wait. The kye was easier to establish and navigate than an American bank loan, and would enable immigrants to make a down payment on a house, liquor store, or dry cleaner's. In return, the family receiving that month's bounty hosted a party, and all would sing and dance, eat, drink, and gamble. These shindigs were about trust and community, first held in homes, then banquet halls. When the loft was finished, my father lent the space for the parties, even when it wasn't his turn to host.

Of these late nights, I remember swishing skirts and hands that would swoop down and throw me up into the smoky, whiskey-soured air. The members were young and good-looking, at least in the '80s—part swingers club, part support group. Their teenage kids, like my brother, were several years older than me and would thus be off doing their own thing. I was left behind with the partying adults. Sometimes—while I played in the corner with the bingo set, rolling the balls in the cage to see which of my cards would win—I overheard their drunken war stories.

My father, like Chris, was a storyteller, and could even make wartime sound fun. "I rode the train like a goddamn surfboard, like the yellow-heads at Redondo Beach. I surfed on top of the train at night and held on as the wind screamed in my ears. In the morning, I saw on either side and far back along the tracks—bodies, riddled with bullets, their blood frozen in the snow."

The others would also regale, eliciting nods and laughter and clucking tongues. But this generation, in this party setting, was boasting and one-upping with tales of cunning, luck, or savagery. My dad had seen combat, had even witnessed the Chinese coming over the Yalu, "swarming like cockroaches," but he'd only been a lackey to the GIs. The older Koreans, teen soldiers who'd actually fought in battle, were quiet during these swapping of childhood reveries.

But one by one they all left the kye. With businesses thriving, they sought to leave behind a shared past and seek new class distinctions among themselves. The accountant and real estate agent joined white golf clubs. The shoe shop owner established two sister stores and won a church deaconship. The kye secretary set his sights on leading the homeowner's association for his gated community.

And the one who threw the lavish parties held on to the mirror ball and karaoke machines, now gathering dust. He didn't follow his friends' footsteps, too tired after so many uprootings. He didn't want to climb anyone else's social ladder, not when he'd already built himself a citadel.

I rearrange the light cubes. What's the ideal radius for self-induced seizure? Should I focus on the strobes? I sit lotus-style and wedge the disco mirror globe in my lap. It's cold and sharp against my bare thighs, but I feel powerful, having given birth to a tacky but fabulous planet. I peer into my mirror ball and see myself reflected, shrunken and multiplied.

One face, however, is my friend's, trapped in a single gleaming tile. She's tiny and no longer a drowned green-eyed monstress. I whisper, "You're a symptom of brain damage, but I'm stronger than Chris. I can overpower my genetic fate."

"Stories first," she says. "Let their voices speak through yours. Then you will find your true sister. That's the way we're supposed to do this."

"Chris says she's dead, and I'm no ghost hunter."

"Since when do you take his word? Which of us has lied to you, manipulated you?"

"You mean, who's done it more? Don't be jealous. He knew a different side of Mom. They'd laugh without me, felt like betrayal. But he knew her better than you ever could."

"No, Elsa. She's a mystery to him too. That's why he has her locked up in a trunk—"

I press my thumb over her face to blot out the image of Chris cramming Mom's corpse into his car trunk. I press harder, mirror edges slicing into flesh. "You're sweet and K-pop pretty, but you're the sickest part of me. What kind of a son do you think he is? What kind of a daughter can't dream of her dead mother? I need to see her face one last time to say I'm sorry." I remove my finger and see only my own face. I suck the blood off my thumb. Shouldn't Chris be back by now? I pack up the lights in a suitcase and head downstairs.

The stairwell is dark—concrete floating steps with steel railings, cement walls closing in on me. The door to my left is open, leading into a series of garages. I can't find the light switch, but metal cans of auto spray paint lie scattered, glinting. I follow these breadcrumbs—any mess or destruction marking my brother's wake. But inside the first garage, there's only another within—an auto paint booth. The modular design with pristine white walls and small windows in the double doors reminds me of the South Pole Station. Sense memory chills me, and I shudder. In the shadows, this room-within-a-room shines like a secret, like a glowing garden in the middle of the Antarctic. Past and present overlap. I've already been here before.

The paint booth's windows light up. What is Chris up to? Always creative, he used to make art as a teenager, soldering spare parts into sculptures. He also used expired auto paint for stencils and murals. For all these projects, Dad would scream at him for stealing from the shop.

I approach the window. Inside, the brightness is blinding. A figure steps forward, wearing a vintage gas mask. Not the kind used for painting cars but used during old wars or the end of the world. Hooded in leather, round dark lenses for the eyes, staring blank and impassive. Over the nose and mouth, a round metal filter and drooping nozzle. Like a bloodsucking insect's head on the body of—a woman dressed in a hospital gown. Stoop-shouldered, halting crooked steps.

I'm not ready. Never visited her alone, not even as an adult, couldn't be in the same room with her, not without Dad or my brother to anchor me, to remind me I was still alive, that Mom hadn't taken me with her through some underwater passage into this other liminal existence.

The gas-masked figure comes closer. I hold the doors shut. She reaches behind her head to pull off the leather hood. I'm shaking but can't look away. When she peels off its insect face of glass eyes and metal mouth, I don't see my mother. All I see is smoothness all around, like an egg wrapped in human skin. No features—faceless, empty, and horrific. I scramble backward, trip on a paint can, falling on my ass and crying out in pain.

"Is that you, Elsa?" I hear my brother in the dark. He's far away, his voice echoing in the metal caverns. A flashlight shines my way, like a lifeline.

In the next garage, I see Chris seated in a wrecked car, half-skeletal with much of its body missing. What couldn't be saved must be crumpled like aluminum foil. The wheels have been removed, the entire thing propped on rails. He doesn't ask why I cried out, why I'm still trembling. Whether indifferent or oblivious, he allows me to also ignore and deny.

"I thought you were coming back with an extension cord," I say, my voice unsteady. "And why are there paint cans on the floor? Some opened, total fire hazard." Nagging him makes me feel grounded. I must've inhaled the fumes. This on top of jet-lagged drunkenness.

"Got sidetracked. Thought we were goofing anyhow. You don't really believe you can induce a seizure, do you?" he says, sneering.

"What are you doing here anyway? And where are the fucking lights?"

"I was looking for the cord, but then saw this beauty. Can you feel it? How this absorbed the impact of collision? You can feel the reverberations, still shivering through the metal."

"Shit, did anyone survive?" I meant to be facetious, to hide my jangled nerves, but Chris's silent headshake makes me regret my question.

"Sitting here," he says, "takes the edge off wondering what it'd be like to ram this fragile body into a wall. I'd go full force, like a warrior." Hands on wheels, he screams, wild-eyed, then laughs with head thrown back. "Sometimes, I fantasize I can walk away afterward. Not a scratch on me. Don't worry, all just pretend. But you can feel it, right? A collision like this soaks up all that crazy energy, and it needs to be released somehow."

"I don't want to be here anymore. Paint fumes are giving me a headache." Was Chris ever a huffer? Wouldn't that be redundant?

"Yeah, whatever. My buzz has worn off anyway," he says, climbing down. "So, Dad's at the house, I should be there too when he wakes up. You can stay here though."

"No fuckin' way, I'm coming with."

The backseat of Chris's car is piled with a gym duffel, clothes, camping gear, and a brand-new boxing bag sheathed in plastic. "Your trunk full?" I ask.

"You're the first person to ride shotgun in a long while. Don't need the backseat."

"We gotta talk about hoarding. Pop the trunk, lemme see how bad it is." I slap the rear.

"Leave it the fuck alone! I don't go prying into your stuff. This is *my* car, not Mom's, not Dad's. Let me have something of my own."

The fried chicken is angry in my belly. My mind, sodden with beer. But one clear thought emerges—my friend told me where I'd find my mother.

Later, after Chris passes out, I sneak out and unlock his car trunk. It's his mobile office, with Dad's old briefcases and leather binders. Enclosed are documents regarding living trusts, estate and inheritance taxes, and power of attorney. Cardboard file boxes are stuffed with moldering pamphlets, books, DVDs, even VHS tapes—a library of get-rich-quick schemes, delivered in lecture and how-to format. I skip past the SAT curricula and illegally xeroxed tests and pick up another folder. Inside, a business proposal detailing how to transform the body shop into an auto center. Also a petition of grievances, labeled with a note: "Grant proposal, to be written in the style of Oscar Wilde's *De Profundis*, except the gay parts."

I pick up a fat leather binder—his anthology of greatest hits—college admission essays ghostwritten for others. Divided by topic, some with blank spaces like Mad Libs. I read a few under the garage floodlight. Some are familiar because he's read his latest immigrant tearjerkers over the phone. All the essays touch upon the psychic trauma of the refugee or exile, even when the subject is "The Day I Won the 1,000-Meter Race" or "What I Learned from Being Model UN President." He combined the best here, for reference and exhibition, the closest he'd ever get to publishing a book, he'd once said. "I've gotten into all the Ivies, some of them more than once!"

But despite his bravado, Chris couldn't handle college because for the first time, he wasn't easily the smartest guy in the room. He impressed a few of his professors, but seemed to shirk at being challenged, changing majors once he got the top grades in the intro-level classes. Moreover, the allure of K-Town next door—"Harlem to a Black man during the Renaissance," he said—tempted him with a subcultural paradise in which he could strut and swagger as a Korean guy in a world that catered to him, his gender, and his money. Maybe hedonism and stress weren't to blame though. Family concerns still yoked him, being called back by his parents for whatever they needed. And schizophrenia—a disease that, like my brother, is widely misunderstood, slippery, and contradictory—has its own triggers and demands.

Then, flipping past his essays, I notice pages similar in formatting and first-person perspective, but disguised somehow—or disfigured. I read a few lines then recognize the true voice hidden by another's. I've found my dead mother at last, locked in my brother's trunk—exactly where my friend said her stories would be.

These are Chris's translations, and at the back of the binder are her handwritten originals. They smell of mildew and gasoline, musty and combustible. The folktales have been sliced from their spiral notebook, three-hole punched, and inserted behind Chris's one-size-fits-all essays. The water rings on paper, like booze-embossed seals. Here was evidence of my memory and her conviction that these stories would help me endure, with neither of us to blame.

But these strikethroughs and slashes aren't hers. Neither are the words pasted in, paragraphs excised with razor blade and attached elsewhere. My revulsion coils inward. I let him take the stories from me, never bothering to reclaim them until now.

In my mother's room with door bolted, I stay up all night to reverse my brother's edits and restore her words. I resurrect Mom's voice, for how can I mourn her if she died a stranger? I dig and exhume for the truth—how to avenge, whom to punish, and how.

And as the hours pass and sentences pile, I consider how my friend led me to these stories. Finding them in the trunk wasn't some repressed memory. Furthermore, my brother constantly lies to me, while my friend does not. I let my brother determine who Mom was from the beginning, even though he's dismissed her as crazy while stealing her words. Maybe for once, I should consider what my mother told me herself—and peer with her beyond the observable universe.

5

The day after the funeral, I'm alone with my father in the loft. I unwind the cloth, uncovering tender skin around his eyes. Never held his face before. The softness surprises. But I need to remember that despite his sorrow, he is the Woodcutter who kept my mother captive.

My father ordered large standing wreaths of lilies, roses, and chrysanthemums. A scheduling mistake brought the wreaths too early. They wilted in the parlor, especially the lilies, their sticky scent reminding me of apartment showings where realtors used their florid stench to mask stranger, intimate odors.

My mother was contained in a silver urn beside her blurry, blown-up photograph. The soft-focus effect was dreamy, softening her jaw, which I knew was tense because of the man's hand, cut off at the wrist, resting on her shoulder.

The stained-glass window slashed my arms with shards of red and blue light. I sat separate from my family, claiming I wanted to be alone. I wasn't—my friend was by my side.

We hadn't invited anybody except for Javier, who'd told Chris long ago that his strategy when working with my dad was to stay on the opposite end of the body shop, far from him as possible. He advised Chris to do so as well, adding, "That is why your sister is so smart, not because she is scientist, because she run away to other side of world." I didn't know him well, but I was grateful he'd come for a woman he never met, whom he also probably deemed clever for keeping her distance. As for why he stuck it out with my dad for over a decade—he was an immigrant and my father begrudgingly respected him for that. This and his hard work and tolerance for Dad's tempers won him my father's trust, enough to become de facto manager. Maybe that's why Chris directed him to sit in the pew behind theirs.

As for my mother's relatives in Korea, they'd been uncommunicative since before her accident. Maybe they'd given up. Maybe they thought she died long ago. In the years since, my father had disowned siblings and burned bridges with friends. He'd become a recluse too.

Still, people heard. The gossip used to be about who was going bankrupt, whose kid got into which Ivy, how much was spent on a wedding. But now, the updates were about death. They must've known my father wouldn't appreciate their showing up without permission. So dozens, from the kye and church, sat in the back. My father didn't hear them rustling or pretended not to notice. But at the end of the service, the old Koreans formed a line in the aisle. Chris took Dad by the elbow, whispered in his ear, and guided him next to Mom's portrait to face them.

I hadn't seen these old Koreans in decades—ghosts from my childhood. Some missing teeth or hair. Many shrunken, stooped, and frail. I'd remembered them as cantankerous, scrabbling, feisty sons of bitches. They approached, bowing first to my mother's portrait, then to my father. They nodded to Chris and me, some smiling with a wave as if I were still a little girl. They streamed toward us, then away.

After the service, the Korean funeral director appeared beside me with bowed head to nervously whisper that someone was waiting for me in the ladies' room.

I recognized her immediately. With her botoxed brow, tight jawline, and the same chic bob, dyed brown—she looked just as I remember from her early '90s real-estate ads in the Korean newspapers. This realtor was one of the few among Mom's friends who spoke fluent English. She became a scandal when she divorced, a sensation when she got rich flipping houses. Opening her arms, she compelled me to step in for a perfumed, bony hug.

Her English was only slightly accented but overdone somehow, as if mimicking the forced optimism of American saleswomanship. She said the usual things one does at a funeral, glossing over the fact that Mom had been ostensibly dead in the Korean community for years, and not explaining why she hadn't come down the aisle to pay her respects along with the others. Had she been hiding in the bathroom all this time?

She pulled out a thick white envelope from her Louis Vuitton. I explained that the funeral director was collecting the condolence money on Dad's behalf. A Korean custom, I figured that even if Dad didn't want it out of pride, Chris definitely would.

"This is for you only," she said. "Don't tell your daddy or your brother. This is what Mrs. Rhee owes your mother. Your mommy, she gave too much to her, and Mrs. Rhee ran away to Busan, never pay back. I warned your mother because Mrs. Rhee, she was, you know—her husband, like your daddy, you know? But your mommy—heart too soft. Sometimes, no business sense. When I heard your mommy died, I use my network and find Mrs. Rhee and tell her she must pay back everything now—with interest! So this is for you only, Elsa. Mrs. Rhee is in Busan now with her own ddeok shop. She has nice new husband and is so sorry this is late. Ten thousand, plus extra for interest and for funeral donation. I counted for you."

I emerged alone, dazed with heavy perfume and heavier secrets, the envelope in the inner pocket of my blazer. Dad and Chris, both wearing white gloves, were waiting for me in the lobby. My father held the urn while my brother carried Mom's portrait. Chris directed me to stand beside Dad. I didn't realize we had to perform for the uninvited guests. I guided my father out as Chris followed behind. The old Koreans, lined up against either wall of the lobby, bowed in unison as we walked between them, as my father escorted his wife's ashes out the door.

While Chris helped Dad into the car, Javier pulled me aside. "I'm very sorry about your mother," he whispered. "I'm sorry for your father and Chris. But you should not stay too long. They need to be alone, and you too—but not together. I know men like them, in my family too."

My God, was everyone going to give me a piece of their mind today? This was like the inverse of a funeral—attendees delivering their eulogies and revelations to the family in mourning. Though maybe I was the only one being addressed—and warned.

Chris looked over his shoulder at us with curiosity, suspicion. I thanked Javier, patting his shoulder, then got into the car. "He's just being kind," I explained. "Said something about memories keeping the dead alive." We headed for the ocean.

"Medicine first," I say, slipping two pills between his lips. I give him water with another crushed pill mixed within and set him in the armchair by the window. "Now for my questions."

"Be quick about it. Need to be in my office or Javier won't do his work."

"Javier's already opened the shop, like he's been doing for the last decade. He's been working all morning. It's noon, don't you know?"

"But how can it already be—?"

I don't explain it's because I can dictate time, hurry or reverse the hours by whim. Instead, I open my green notebook. "What happens at the end of 'The Woodcutter and the Nymph?'"

"What the hell?"

"The folktale. How does it end?"

"At the lake. No, it begins there. Who the fuck cares?"

I want to tell him the story is about trans-world abduction and forced marriage that preps girls for leaving behind one life for another of confined servitude. But my Korean isn't good enough to explain this, so I only say, "Drink more water."

My mother's version ended with the Nymph taking her children to the Heavens. In reality, Mom left us twice, first at the spa, then a more final ascension. She not only truncated her folktale but also defied it. What kind of ending did my father deserve?

I give him a run down. He nods along, nestling into a more comfortable position. I lay a blanket over him. I sip bitter water from his glass.

After the funeral, we drove to a pier in San Pedro, climbed down the wooden steps to the docks, where the captain was waiting for us in his boat. Thirtysomething male, Pacific Islander maybe, with jade-colored eyes and a ponytail of curls. His black shirt and pants were faded from sun, sea salt, and countless ash scatterings. The Korean mortuary set this up, so he knew to bow deeply to my father. Twice as big as my dad, the captain helped him aboard. Then he took the urn from Chris and helped him as well. Finally, he took my hand, but my feet wouldn't leave the dock. "It's all right, miss, I got you. Water's choppy here, but it'll steady once we get out."

I yanked my hand back, saying, "I'm sorry, I'm sorry, I can't."

Dad and Chris thought I was overcome with grief, couldn't bear this final farewell. They said I could stay behind. Truth was, I was worried what I might do on the boat. Call it déjà vu, or the opposite—a premonition. So I waited on the dock. When the boat sailed far out, I saw a woman standing at the prow. A blanket wrapped around her shoulders. Her dark hair, long and loose, whipping in the wind. It was the braver version of me who'd complete this ritual, scattering ashes into the ocean that connected two lands—where my mother was born and where she died. What I should've done, would've done, in an alternate reality.

But also, I didn't want to say goodbye because her death didn't seem entirely real. I never saw her body embalmed, face caked with makeup. These ashes could've been anything.

When they returned, the captain told me everything went smoothly. Beautiful sunset, even a whale's spout and flicked tail in the distance. "That's a good sign. Means something real good in some cultures." Chris added that the red rose petals were a nice touch, but there was a plastic coffee lid that floated though the remains.

On the drive home, I sat in the backseat and saw on my father's shoulder, pressed into his black suit jacket—a woman's dainty handprint of ash.

In my mother's retelling, the Woodcutter never gets his second chance. In real life, she left it to us to deal with him. The Nymph had three children, whereas Mom had only two who survived. Counting the stillborn sister, I was the third, allowing her to fulfill her folktale.

"The other daughter—Mom believed she's still alive. What do you say, Dad?"

He's already drooling, so I get to work. I use the internet, Oskar's book, and my mother's Korean-English dictionaries, the same ones she used to unlock my diary. While I was away at science camp, she deciphered my angry teenage words that railed against a mother who always compared me to imaginary, idealized girls back in Korea. Who were these perfect daughters in the homeland? Why not go to them instead? My mother wrote beside my teary scrawl—her apologies in Korean, as well as promises to be a better, more loving mother—with assurances that I was her only daughter in this world. Even back then, I couldn't be angry at her for betraying my trust, not when I realized how painstakingly slow and arduous the process must've been for her—to translate me word by word.

But I only get down a few lines of folktale translation before I'm too tired to think between languages. Dad's asleep anyhow. And what use are words in punishing him, when "guilt" and "atonement" aren't even part of his vocabulary? Besides, wasn't he also fated to play his part?

I wander toward the funeral wreaths in the loft's corner. The windows are closed and the A/C off, so the petals are shedding. Lilies droop; pollen dusts the carpet with gold. I twist their necks, and their juices seep between my fingers. I wrench off blossom heads, then root through the shrine for my Hello Kitty sewing kit. Letting my mind rest, I give my hands work to do instead.

At eight years old, I was a Missionette, a Christian Girl Scout, earning badges for baking, prayer, and proselytizing. Mom left Dad alone at the shop to pick me up. If she'd stayed with him, would she have stopped Dad from confronting the thief? Or would she have been bludgeoned as well?

A man was stealing a paint gun from the shop. My father ran out to stop him. The thief bashed his head with the tool, worth a few hundred bucks, and drove off. My father was left bloody, unconscious. Neighborhood kids called 911. He was in the ICU for weeks. A family friend advised Mom to build a backyard shed to house my father.

But surprising everyone, my father not only survived, he also learned to walk, talk, and use the bathroom again. Doctors called it a miracle, how it only took him several months to recover. However, though he didn't end up a vegetable like many predicted, everyone said he was different afterward—even quicker to anger than before, set off by little frustrations or the most minor of perceived slights. So much rage. Traumatic brain injury can shift one's personality and he was temperamental to begin with, but his fury wasn't just neurological. His savings, over a hundred thousand dollars, was wiped out while he'd been indisposed. This wasn't the first time his fortunes had been reversed. How many times would he have to start over?

One thing I remember clearly—the flowers kept coming even when Dad left the hospital. In his office, the wilting arrangements remained when at a doctor's suggestion, my father was strapped to a high-backed chair at his desk with a typewriter. Speechless, bound to his throne, he summoned his focus to peck at the keys on his electric Smith Corona while garlands withered all around. Mom claimed this brought him back, but she couldn't recall what he'd typed.

Some things didn't correspond though. I must've been eight when I made my brother's graduation lei, a local tradition among the Japanese whose great-grandparents had worked on Hawaiian sugar plantations. But the graduation had been a happy day, and I was proud of my hand-sewn lei, even though his was the only one with a red and white pattern that couldn't be continued because there weren't enough among the hospital flowers. Did Dad miss the graduation because he was at the hospital or bedridden at home? At least, I remember Chris being charmed, though I was embarrassed when his friends posed beside him with massive bouquets and smothering leis strung with flowers much fancier than his secondhand carnations.

But now, a day after my mother's funeral, I've got a better grip. I thread the lilies and chrysanthemum with a needle, bunching the blossoms along the string. I make two wreaths for a blind father and his daughter, placing one on his sleeping head, the other crowning my unwashed hair. Below us, the parking lot is cracked, weeds growing along the fissures. I describe the sunset for him. It's still morning, but I can make the sun go down with my words.

My father clutches my hand. I retrieve his pill bottle and his half-empty glass of clouded water. I swallow a couple of seeds to silence the unusable voices, so I can concentrate on just one.

Hearing him breathe, so vulnerable in my hands, I remember more. When my mother was out of the house, I answered his cry for water. When he fell out of bed trying to reach the bathroom, I held the plastic bottle to his crotch. I wore slippers when walking over the shards left from a bowl hurled against the wall. What I did though was nothing compared to how my mother cared for him. Those were intimate moments, deadly, glimpsed through a door, cracked open. She could've ended things, but she had a teenage son, a little girl, and no means of support. So she bided her time. Pragmatism in the guise of compassion moved her hands to attend to his body, which he'd used to hurt her many times—and if it ever healed, would do so again.

The bitter seeds I shared with my father dissolve in my gut. Sitting at his feet, I lean my flower-crowned head against his knee. Pollen dusts my lashes. In the corner of my eye, I see my friend—no longer a drowned monstress. She looks younger than usual, or maybe it's her shy pose, spying on us behind a door, cracked open. My father and I fall asleep with conjured moonlight on our faces. His fingers become tangled in my hair. The loft is a hothouse of shredded flowers.

But warping the hours—much like casting lies—often backfires on the one who thinks she's in control. The cab for the airport comes and goes. Days and weeks pass, and I remain by my father's side. Despite knowing full well how parents can be inescapable black holes, absorbing light and bending space-time around them—I didn't account for this much gravitational time dilation.

At least we've been productive. My mother's stories—once just bones—have now grown flesh. Dressed in my language, they sing my words.

E—

Hope it's not too cold in Stockholm. *The Thing* was a lot scarier than I expected. Keep thinking all winter-overs should be replaced by alien doubles because we'd have more fun. Kate and I started a film club, might even try making our own movie!

BTW, after test run, DOM 1 malfunctioned again. We killed the connection permanently. Rest of fifty-nine DOMs functional. Requires recalibration but shouldn't affect data too much. Conclusion: defective from start. Probably made that way. So please don't stress. You always find something new to obsess over, especially when it's not your fault.

Sun's lower on the horizon. I find myself staring at it, following its path. I'm saying goodbye, preparing myself for the next stage. I know what you're thinking—what kind of Swede commits to a half year of darkness? You'd say I was setting off to explore somewhere far from home, ending up in a place just like it. Like the Scandinavians in Minnesota.

Truth is, it's not the darkness I'm worried about, or the cabin fever, or the isolation. I'm afraid I'll get used to living here, even prefer it. It's easier in some ways than living out there. Ever wonder why people come back to winter-over? Do they know which one is the real world?

—J

"If I'm Shim Cheong, shouldn't I be with the King in his palace?" I ask. "Why am I here?"

I'm working on my translations again, beside my father. He's perfectly dosed, eyes still wound with a bandage, ready for his execution and lacking only a cigarette.

"Why does she hate me so much?" He speaks clearly, no slurring or mumbling.

"Why does *who* hate you?"

"My daughter. Please, don't fill her head with any more lies. Not about the other girl. You promised you'd stop. I have no other daughter." Then, as if he's only been pretending to be half-conscious all along, he walks across the room without stumbling. He shuts the bathroom door for the first time and weeps over the running water.

Sometimes when I check in on him napping in the afternoons, when I'm the one peeking through a door cracked open, I see my friend seated at his feet. I asked her why she does this, and she replied, "That's when he talks to me." I explained early-onset dementia, that he mutters while asleep. But she shines brighter anyway, feeding off him too.

My friend looks so vivid lately. Sometimes I wonder which of us is more incorporeal, which is doing more of the haunting. Maybe that's why I'm eating so much, why I've let my hair grow dirty these past several weeks—to be anchored in reality with greasy locks and a heavy heart, sinking my feet in the mire.

6

Dear Elsa,

Not the email I expected, but very happy to hear from you and hope your time with your family gives you the comfort and solace you need. As for your questions, I'll do my best.

In traditional versions, after losing his wife, the abandoned Woodcutter learns that the nymphs don't bathe in the lake anymore. They draw a bucket by golden rope instead. So he climbs inside and is pulled to the Heavens, reunited with his wife and half-mortal children.

I didn't include this folktale in my collection because there's yet another narrative act. Although the Woodcutter is reunited with family, he still misses his mother, hitherto unmentioned. The Heavenly King grants him a winged horse so he may visit. A Confucian touch? He's also warned that if his feet ever touch the earth, he can never return.

His mother rushes to make his favorite soup but spills it on the horse. The creature bucks the Woodcutter to the ground, then flies to the Heavens without him. Eventually, the man is transformed into a rooster—and that is why the cock crows at the sky every morning. What does this say about Korean sons and their mothers? Was the soup-spilling accidental or his mother's checkmate? (I wouldn't put it past my own Swedish mother.) Many Korean folktales feature reunions between parent and child as the happy ending, but I couldn't write this one without Western-skewed, Freudian ridicule—about a man who, because of his hankering for his mother's soup, loses his wife and becomes a wailing cock.

Instead, I imagine a different ending: The Woodcutter returns to the lake and sees his wife bathing alone. He strips off his clothes and wades out to meet her. He begs for forgiveness because shame as much as loneliness made him cruel. He confused cowardice with power in keeping her beholden and bound. But this mountain lake, the highest in Korea, is where they can meet between the Heavens and Earth. From afar, no one would know who was the Nymph and who the mortal. They wouldn't notice either, both naked, each the only one of their kind.

Again, I am very sorry for your loss. Regarding folklore or anything else, I'm here for you.

Your friend,

Oskar

P.S. Yes, there is such a faceless folkloric figure as you describe. "Dalgyal Gwishin," literally Egg Ghost. Sounds comical in English and Swedish, but quite eerie in Korean. Some believe they are childless ghosts, with no descendants to honor them and conduct memorial rites, and so they become faceless. No mouth, yet ravenous. No eyes, yet always seeking a victim. No worse fate than to be childless and unremembered in such a Confucian culture. An unappeasable ghost with no one to haunt, so it consumes everyone in its path. One look causes instant death. But don't worry, they live deep in the forests, high in the mountains, far from us.

Dear Elsa,

How fascinating! I'm not familiar with this author and am curious, but I'll respect your secrecy and am delighted to help.

A few notes: Both in my retelling and in the one you've shared, the father sells his daughter, but in most contemporary versions, Shim Cheong lies, claiming a noble family wants to adopt her in exchange for the rice. I omitted the adoption, as it seems a recent sanitization, and wonder why it was removed in yours. Must be in line with older tales. Adoption was rare then and still is in Korea, family bloodline being paramount.

Also different, in my version, like most, the King touches the lotus, and it blooms, revealing Shim Cheong inside. Your story emphasizes her back-and-forth transfiguration, making this a variant of the shape-shifting wife. Somewhat a sequel to your nymph tale.

Most versions oddly gloss over the mother-daughter reunion. You'd assume there'd be much to explore when Shim Cheong discovers that her mother, presumed dead, has been living underwater, remarried to the Sea King. Most likely, the story has been mangled over time to exemplify Shim Cheong's filial piety, and thus the girl worries so much about her blind father that she returns to the surface. Even being a Queen herself is not enough, not until she is reunited with him. More curious, I've wondered how does a mortal end up with a Sea King on her second go? Your story resolves this by making the mother originally from the Sea, thereby complicating Shim Cheong's migrations, heritage, and loyalties. (And both women marry Kings?)

Also, in this version, unlike the other magical-wife tales around the world, the King witnesses his wife transform, but they remain together. Perhaps this man is the exception because he didn't force her into one form only, simply waited for her to tell him what she most needed from him?

Dear Elsa,

No, I don't think the story was "a recruitment video for sacrificial virgins, serve your country, serve your father bullshit." But Shim Cheong is certainly the exemplar for filial piety.

As for historical antecedents, I recently came across a nineteenth century account written by a Westerner. He claims that before the Joseon Dynasty, there was a custom of tossing a virgin girl into the water, as offering to the sea demon, to secure rain for crops and safe journeys for sailors.

But when a different royal house came into power, the new prefect witnessed a screaming girl being dragged by three shaman women. He asked if they truly believed a virgin sacrifice was necessary, if the demon would accept nothing else. They said it was so. Then he had one of the old women tossed into the sea. The villagers expected the demon to churn and protest, but all remained calm. So, the other two were thrown in as well. After that, no more sacrifices, least not in that province. So perhaps these stories honor and remember those victims of past ignorance?

Oh Elsa, I don't know if Shim Cheong is based on many girls, only a theory. If it helps, it was also believed that fish and snakes that lived in the mountain lakes for a thousand years transformed into sea dragons. Maybe the drowned girls also became powerful, monstrously so. But perhaps then they'd demand sacrifices too. An endless cycle?

You seemed quite distraught over my fanciful supposition. Forgive me if I'm crossing a line, but how are you doing? I haven't experienced the death of a parent, but I do know loss when it comes to one's origins and connections to the past. If you ever want to talk about it . . .

Dear Elsa,

Thank you for sharing your mother's stories and revealing her as the author. What a tremendous gift for you and your family. I understand now why you've been so immersed, and am honored you've asked for my help. I admire your dedication to your mother's legacy . . .

Downstairs in the garage, I've got my laptop in my dad's Studebaker, what he drove cross-country on his first tour across the US. I can't keep postponing chat sessions with Jesper. It's obvious he wants to tell me something. After some exchanges, he jumps right in and informs me, sheepishly, that he and Kate have gotten together. I type that I'm happy for him, that I was never really there for him. He denies this, as he would. A part of me is relieved it's Kate and not Sasha he ended up with, though I don't like admitting this even to myself.

"Besides," I write, "I'm diving deep into my sterile neutrinos. So no monsoons of tears will be shed on this side. Have you seen the auroras?"

He offers to send pictures, but I tell him I'll see for myself one day. I'm relieved that gossip hasn't spread, that he thinks I'm still in Stockholm. I imagine myself in this alternate reality that we conjure together with our words. I like that his mind hosts a phantom me, doing what I'm supposed to do. I wish him well, adding a goodbye for Kate, and Sasha too.

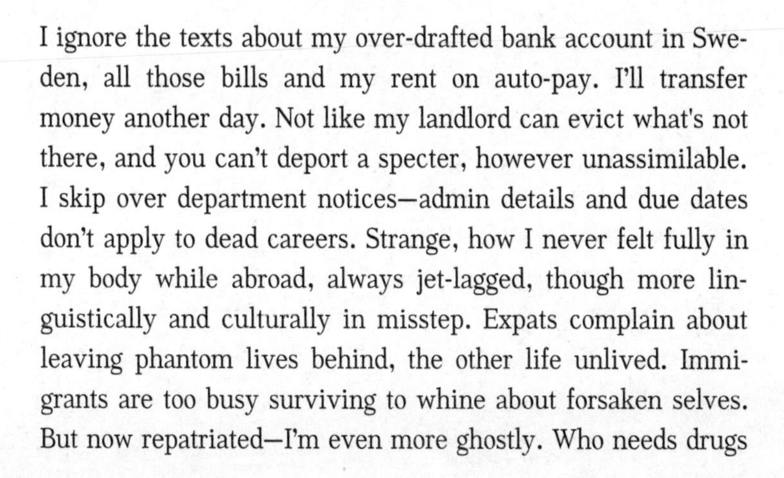

I ignore the texts about my over-drafted bank account in Sweden, all those bills and my rent on auto-pay. I'll transfer money another day. Not like my landlord can evict what's not there, and you can't deport a specter, however unassimilable. I skip over department notices—admin details and due dates don't apply to dead careers. Strange, how I never felt fully in my body while abroad, always jet-lagged, though more linguistically and culturally in misstep. Expats complain about leaving phantom lives behind, the other life unlived. Immigrants are too busy surviving to whine about forsaken selves. But now repatriated—I'm even more ghostly. Who needs drugs when you've got depressive out-of-body experiences, time warps forward and back, being trapped with other ghouls, reliving past traumas in a never-ending loop?

Finally, I delete Linnea's latest email unread. The recent data on sterile neutrinos isn't promising anyway. My proposal isn't worth pursuing, neither are these folktales. What's the point? I can't tell my mom, I'm sorry I couldn't protect you. Wish I could've been your confidante, but I was too young and so was Chris, though you told him plenty. When you told him you wanted to run away, did you assure him you'd take him too?

If she were here, I could show her my work in my notebook—Look, I've transfigured your stories into the English you never mastered. Through translation, I've made these stories mine and disenchanted yours. I've dispelled you. You can't tell me what I got wrong either. Dead moms tell no tales—isn't that what they say?

And just because Oskar's much more fluent than I and has multiple degrees doesn't mean he knows you any better. I wrote to him: "You can't understand because you never grew up in a Korean family, never had a Korean mom, and you can't have mine."

I was probably drunk. At one point, I'd even wondered if he was falling for my mother through her writing—an incestuous love triangle complicated by language, family, and death.

The next day, I apologized: "I've been frustrated because I thought I'd understand her, that I'd finally see her face and be done. But I've only been writing down my own voice, seeing my own reflection in her stories of girls lost, abandoned, and trapped."

Usually, Oskar answered quickly, but he didn't reply for several days. I considered sending a gift basket of dark chocolate and spiced nuts. But I see now, on my screen—his reply.

Dear Elsa,

Thank you for your apology. I'm being trite when retorting you only had one mother, while I've had grievances with three. Vendela advised me never to reveal this, especially with women I'm interested in. But here goes it.

Though my three mothers have known me at different times of my life, I was angriest with them when most alone in my adolescence and twenties. A volatile period when I was destructive, quasi-militant, and embarrassingly prolific with op-eds. Never met my birth mother, so I could spare her, and I've made amends with my adoptive mother, though it's ongoing.

She and my father were naïve, wanting me to be thoroughly Swedish—a Gantelius, Lidingö-bred—expecting everyone else would see me as they do. They didn't bother learning about Korea, or teaching me about it, equipping me with pride and self-defense. Inadvertently, they instilled in me a shame born of ignorance. They didn't want me to feel different, to be confused. But they should've known that despite my diligence and lack of any alternative role model, I'd always be different, never considered truly Svensk.

I grew up ashamed of my heritage, though it was written on my face. I thought my parents knew so little about Korea because it wasn't worth knowing. That I'd been saved and was better off here. But I didn't understand the source of my shame until I was older, couldn't make my mother understand either. She felt under attack, that I doubted her love and criticized her as a parent. My sister also felt betrayed, though she's since come around. My father claims to comprehend intellectually. He says he only did what was advised at the time—to assimilate me, forget my past, provide a home.

I used to think my mother was unwilling to listen because she couldn't bear thinking she'd been a bad mother. Her defensiveness comes to the fore. But perhaps she can't bear the thought I had such a sad childhood, burdened with feeling false, always insufficient.

For so long, I'd played along with her lie of a happy narrative for her sake. Even as a child, I felt her happiness was more important. I had painful notions of powerlessness and worthiness, earning my keep and their love and my right to stay. To be insecure of one's place casts a long shadow. Doesn't matter how kind the parents. I was adopted not only into a family, but also into a country, one with little history of immigration compared to others, even less of integration, with a culture valuing egalitarianism that is often misconstrued as conformity and homogeneity.

How could I broach this when she refuses to think race could complicate our family? Most Swedes don't like to discuss racism at all, believing it unnecessary since they are not racist, of course. They fear talking about it might make them complicit or guilty by association, or that saying anything more nuanced than "racism is bad" might reveal something untoward. Conflict avoidance, repression, and denial—such cultural characteristics make for calm dinner conversations and ineffectual discussions.

My mother was also the type to be incapacitated when her children skinned their knees, so I learned to hide my feelings early on. But now, at my age and hers, I'm willing to let her believe her version of my past, uncomplicated by race, history, society. Perhaps if I had children of my own, I'd try harder for the sake of her grandchild, who while growing up in a different Sweden than mine, would still be marked with difference. It helps to have Vendela. I don't need her to have had a similar childhood. She supports my memories, even if so very different from her own.

As for my foster mother, I hurt her with my writing, not engaging with her before or after. Took me many years to realize she was a product of her time and place, just as I was—except that most other children of my time and place did not end up alone in the Far North. Still, I didn't mean for her to bear the brunt of my pain or feel responsible, but this is what she perceived and some others as well. Anyhow, too much time has passed to address it now with her.

All this to say that my mothers have known me at different stages in my life. I've also revised my understanding of them. Maybe now's not the time for your mother's folktales to be understood. The stories will come back to you—more resonant, revealed anew—then again and again.

My mother once woke me at dawn, hustling me into the station wagon while I was still in pajamas. There was a rainbow, and she drove all over town chasing it. Lying in the backseat, I looked up through the dirty window, trying to see the same beauty she described, the beauty she said was so important for me to remember, to know she'd wanted to share it with me.

But all I saw was reflection and refraction of light through water droplets in the sky.

"Elsa, do you like being home with family?" asks my friend, keeping me company in my mother's room. "Do you like being with others who look like you?"

"Wish they'd look a little less like me, to be honest."

I'm sitting on my mom's bed. All around me—the restored original folktales, Oskar's translations, and my scattered notes. The door's locked with its sliding bolt. Dad's eyes still haven't healed, weirdly enough, but today's my day off.

"Must be nice to be wanted by your family. Guess that's why you don't have time for me."

"Chris can't know I've taken these from his trunk. I have to steal time to work on these."

She turns away, obviously hurt. How can she frighten me one moment, then guilt me at another, and now break my heart? "I'm doing the best I can," I tell her.

"I know, but that means we don't have much time left together. Soon, you'll forget me, and I'll be alone again. It's so hard, Elsa, the waiting—in between."

"What do you mean?"

She hesitates while her red ribbons swish and flick the air like insolent cat tails. "When your mother told you that your life would repeat the story, she should've said the story would repeat in your life. She plays her tale, and you'll echo yours—forever. Like me, like all of us, we complete the tale and begin again. But while none of you remember, I always do. I'm always alone, waiting for that moment between eternities, when you—"

Groaning like a moody teen—"Why are we like this?"—I fling myself backward onto the mattress.

Sighing, she climbs off the bed to walk toward the mirror doors of the closet. Unreflected, she says, "I suppose it started long ago, in the olden days, when tigers smoked tobacco pipes." She steps into the glass. I only see the back of her.

"Well, I have a fairy tale for you too," I say, looking up at the ceiling. "Most of the drowned girls of ancient Korea ended up being eaten by scavenger fish, bacteria, and worms—but a few who survived for a thousand years transformed into lotus monsters or sea dragons. According to Oskar anyway. Well, in the Antarctic, the ice creeps toward the coast and calves into the ocean. I first heard the bell, then saw you in the water, so maybe you're like a manifestation of these girls, the ones who cycled through the seas, ascended then fell from the clouds to become snow, then ice—is that who you really are?"

For the first time in forever, I want to take a long, hot bath, undisturbed. In my mother's house, I use bleach, rubber gloves, scrubs, and toothbrushes to clean the tub and tiles. I remove the shower curtain along its J-track so I can wash it. That's when I notice black mold blooming in a Rorschach pattern on the wall where tiles have fallen off. The mold is plush, deep black, like Victorian velvet-flocked wallpaper. I'm tempted to gaze on it while bathing—but the hypnotic, serpentine curves won't lie still, filling me with nausea. So I rehang the curtain, shielding me from the mysterious fungal design, which at one angle looks like a benevolent smiling face, and at another, like two naked women writhing in dance.

When steam veils the mirror, I undress. I skip the shampoo and soap. I only want to be immersed, nestled in this enamel vessel. Seems pointless to have scrubbed the tub when I'm the thing that's dirty, sweaty, and sad. Whatever's released from my pores clouds the water with greyish-green scum. The white painted ceiling above peels and bubbles. Later, I'll scrub the dead skin off like a good Korean girl. After I'm pruney all over, I'll wash the oil from my hair. But right now, I'm exactly how I want to be—curled on my side, sinking to the bottom as water rises over my face to slip over mouth and nose. I press my palms against the walls. This porcelain container gives me rigidity and definition, serving as barrier. Without it, I'd dissolve.

Oskar's right, I'm not ready. I thought I could avenge her, but I'm just bullying an old man. And what can I do to Chris that he isn't already doing to himself? I should leave, return to Sweden. Some people aren't meant to belong anywhere.

Soft moss grows between my fingers, under my breasts, between my thighs. How pretty my hair, swaying like seaweed. My friend sits on the tub's edge, rippling her fingers in my bath. "I was wrong to call you Miss Blue—you're not like her." The waves warp her voice. "Please, don't give up now. You've given us the stories, now's the time to find the sister. Call the woman, whose name you found. I won't stop you this time."

Her black braid plunges into the water, and her red ribbons slink around my neck. She's a good spirit guide, but she's wrong—I don't want a sister. Why would I subject someone else to this godforsaken, mother-haunted family?

In the distance, I hear ringing. Crimson silk wraps around my throat, tightening, squeezing. The noise is louder, insistent and shrill. Ribbons yank, and my face breaks through the surface. I gasp, gulping, then cough up silty bathwater. There's no one with me except for the faces in black velvet mold above. The ringing persists, dragging me out of the tub. I drip naked down the hall and pick up the phone. But no one answers.

Dear Elsa,

My retelling is rather conventional—tears of joy, Buddha's grace washing away the blindness. Over the years, however, I've realized that the happy ending lies not in reunion, but in how the blind man can finally see his daughter's face. That after all she's endured, she wants to find him, to show him who she's become. That she does so without spite, simply wishing him to understand and be forgiven—this allows him to truly see her.

As for Korean stories carved in wood, I wonder if you mean woodblocks? Most woodblocks were for printing religious, historical, legal, and royal texts, and poetry, of course. Legends and myths too, if part of the classics, but not common folktales.

However, a contemporary artisan might be inclined. Probably out there somewhere, even if I've never seen it. Why do you ask?

7

Mom never told me how her sister died in the war.

Some historians estimate nearly five million casualties, including the non-Korean soldiers who waged a three-year war on this small peninsula. Not a soldier, my aunt was one of the three million civilian deaths. Commies killed Christians and America-loving traitors, and vice versa. Ideological purges and mass killings on both sides were expected, as borders continually shifted. There were US military–conducted massacres, including of women and children, since enemy soldiers could've been hiding among them. On and off the battlefield, starvation led to a kill-or-be-killed mentality, to survive at all costs.

My aunt probably died in the bombings or crossfire, since her hometown Seoul changed hands four times. And the American scorched-earth policy resulted in more tonnage of bombs dropped on Korea than what had been used in the entire Pacific theater in WWII, more napalm than what'd been used in Vietnam. At least, this is what I'd gleaned from books. There was a lot that my parents didn't tell me and much more that I didn't want to know.

I sensed there were other ways a teenage girl could die though, in a city overrun with fearful, desperate soldiers, many also teens. Especially so in a bloody civil war commandeered by foreign powers, who like gods had descended with weapons and forces that could split the ground in two. That's what I imagined as a kid anyhow, when Mom told me that an American general with stars on his shoulders had divided her country. A John Wayne–looking Zeus, hurling ninja stars at the earth.

My grandmother's death, however, first described as a consequence of war, was later revised.

"In my childhood backyard," Mom told me after I'd gotten my first period, "there was a tree that would shed seeds that, when dried into husks, could be blown like a whistle. I'd whistle all day, but never at night, for that's inviting bad luck into the house. I followed the rules, but still one day, my mother fell ill. We rushed her to the hospital, the new one built by the Swedish Red Cross, where she later died. My sister told me she'd brewed the same special seeds into a tea, to poison the baby she didn't want forming in her belly, but ended up killing herself as well. Who'd want a new baby at a time like that anyhow? The next day, my father had the tree cut down."

I only half understood, not even sure the story was meant for me. Then a couple months before I'd leave for boarding school, I overheard her ask Chris about a birth control shot for me that would last for years. He thought it unnecessary, potentially alarming, and confusing for me.

I thought it was ridiculous too, because no boy had ever liked me or thought I was pretty. But our mother had thrown condoms at Chris when he entered high school, though he was a virgin and had never been on a date. She'd also quiz me: "What would you do if you got pregnant now? You know you can rip it out, and you should, when you have your whole life ahead of you." I'd quote what we'd learned at my Christian school, that life in its earliest forms was still life. In response, she slapped me upside the head and called me a fool.

These days, I'm more certain I heard her correctly about how my grandmother died.

A Korean male doctor told my mother to have me, to heal her body from her previous decision to exercise her choice. To redeem herself. My mother, her mother, and all those before didn't have control over their bodies. Couldn't decide how many children to have and how many would survive beyond birth.

What if my mother used that sad fact to hide the one who did survive, who did get away?

Hidden in my mother's wood-chest—unworn hanboks, secret money, and a book of women, whose addresses revealed only one geographic point in their many migrations. The amounts listed for their debts and payments conveyed another story of hope, strategy, and wished-for future. My mom's network was mostly bound to LA, but not all. There was Mrs. Kang of New Jersey and also Mrs. Rhee, formerly of Torrance. Beside her name, written in Korean in my mother's hand: "Busan, Korea" with "USD 10,000" crossed out. The first time I'd glanced through the address book, I didn't pay attention to it. But after meeting the realtor in the ladies' room, at my mother's funeral, I'd reviewed this data point many times, wondering about the bigger story behind it.

I couldn't imagine that my mother—as cutthroat as the other war survivors—would use her "soft heart" rather than her "business sense" in her moneylending, as the perfumed realtor put it. But maybe there were a few whose loans my mother "forgave," including Mrs. Rhee who is now selling rice-cakes in her Busan ddeok shop.

And maybe, just maybe, my mother had other reasons for amassing money on the side, secret from her husband and children—to make amends and provide a story of a wished-for future for another girl, far away.

After several rings, Hannah Kang picks up.

"My mother was Hae Rim Park," I begin, "maiden name Song. I found your info in her address book listed under Mrs. Kang—does any of this sound familiar?"

Silence on the other end. Then, "Maybe."

"My mom died about a month ago, maybe it's been longer. My sense of time has been off lately. Anyway, before that, she was hospitalized for a long while, but she told me she had a daughter before me."

"Your mom's dead?"

"Yes." Should've held back on that. I might've crushed her hopes.

"Well, Young-Ah Kang doesn't live here anymore."

"Who?"

"Mrs. Kang. My mom. This is my mom's house. I moved back home years ago to take care of her and 'cause I was broke. Guess I never really left home actually."

I feel so stupid. Why did I assume? But still—the money. Hannah could still be my sister, she just didn't know it. "But my mom paid yours fifty thousand dollars over ten years," I say. "Why would she do that?"

"Who the fuck knows? Maybe my mom was your mom's bookie."

"Can I talk to your mom? Where can I reach her?"

"Lakeside Nursing Home, but she's totally senile. Look, I've had to deal with a lot of my mom's shit already. That's why I'm still living here in this loser town. So let's just move on with our lives, yeah? Whatever was going on between our mothers shouldn't concern us."

I didn't want to let her go. "I think my mom owed yours another seventy-five thousand."

Silence, and then, "I doubt that. Mom was always in debt. Big time gambler. She would've told me if someone owed us money, and I would've paid a visit with a bat."

"Maybe they were friends back in Seoul?" I grab for anything. "What'd she do there?"

"Mom was a nurse in Korea, but all she did in America was lose shit tons of money. Look, my kid's going nuts. Next time I see her, I'll mention your mom's name."

"Hae Rim Park, maiden name Song. When's your birthday?"

"What?"

"When were you born? Do you know?"

"Christ, you wanna know my sign too? June 10, 1984. Gemini."

1984 means she's too young to be the sister between Chris and me. I had no evidence she was my sister, yet now that I knew she couldn't be, I mourned the loss of her. I realize I wanted to believe in her without proof—because of clues left by my mother, especially for me, how the personalized revelation of mysteries made me feel chosen, beloved.

I hear a sickening, high-pitched yowl and then sweet gurgling laughter, both disembodied.

"Get off the fucking cat, Sheryl! Look, Elsa, if I find out anything, I'll let you know."

"How did you—did I tell you my name?" I ask.

"Must have. What did I just say, Sheryl?"

"Let me give you my number."

In response, she hangs up. I should let her go anyway. Hannah Kang is not my sister.

Sister Fox

My father wished for a daughter, so he prayed me into existence. He begged the spirits for a girl, even if she be a fox. By winter, I appeared. He had no wife, only three sons, and he welcomed me as one of his own.

On the morning after the first full moon in my seventh year, my father discovered a dead cow in our shed. One brother, who sometimes watched me as I slept, told our father he'd seen me dance naked in the moonlight, slather my body with sesame oil, then plunge my arm into the animal's anus to remove its liver. He told our father that I ate the liver while the cow slumped to its haunches, dying as it lowed. My father beat him for the lie when, in fact, he'd told the truth.

On the night of the next full moon, another cow was found dead and another brother was beaten and banished for telling the truth.

Finally, there was only one brother, the youngest, whom I loved most. I bound my stomach, but when the full moon shone, my desire was too strong. So I hid myself in the shadows, I did not dance in the moonlight, I did not smack my lips when I ate the cow's liver. The next day, this brother told our father all he'd witnessed. He saw me walk toward the outhouse then disappear in the shadows. He later saw the cow's dead body. Thus, he surmised that after I'd relieved myself, the full moon in its brightness had frightened the creature to death. He wasn't the cleverest boy, but he was the sweetest.

My father promised us two all his land when he died. I was happy to share with this brother, and this kept me full enough. The animals stopped dying—for a while. I was still a growing girl, after all.

Years later, my disowned brothers came home as monks. They found me sitting alone in the kitchen, playing with my cow-bone dolls. They asked where our father and youngest brother were. "They're no longer here," I said. "I am all alone and have no one to play with." They asked what happened to the house, to the village. I looked up at the roof, the thatch moldy and rotten. I glanced at the shredded paper that paneled the doors. I peered out the window at the rest of the abandoned village, unable to remember the last time I heard children laughing.

I asked my brothers when they'd eaten, if they were hungry still—for father's land, for wives and children of their own. Did they harbor a desire so strong they'd be willing to compromise? To settle for something ill-wished, malformed, a counterfeit daughter and sister?

We are not hungry, they said. We are without desire and thus we are sated.

I poked their ribs and pinched their flesh. "I can see how hungry you are. Come brothers, stay and I'll prepare a feast. If you do not join me, I'll have to find another."

A family reunited, we ate our rice and dumplings, but they did not drink the wine. They refused to sleep, vowing to keep watch and guard me instead. So I lay in my corner, but when the full moon shone through the window, the leftover rice in the bowls turned back into maggots, the dumplings into shriveled ears, the wine into blood. I showed my true face as well.

When my oldest brother woke up, I was straddling the younger one, chewing on his liver. "Please go back to sleep," I said. "I only need one more, and then I'll be a real human girl."

My brother ran out of the house. I chased after him, and we ran through the village. He threw a white vial—thorn bushes caged me. I changed into my fox form to escape and gave chase again. He threw a blue vial—a lake swallowed me whole. As a girl, I swam across. When I was close at his heels again, he threw a red vial. Fire engulfed me. I burned in the brightness, changing from fox to girl, girl to fox. Finally, I became only ash.

My brother, the sole survivor in our family, ruined my chance of becoming a real girl. He suffered alone. If only he'd given me his liver, at least one of us could have been happy.

8

The body shop loft is built on top of two garages, while the other garages are one-storied, leaving a large, empty rooftop, accessible through the upstairs bathroom window. On this warm night, my brother and I spread out a picnic under the stars, like old times.

Chris wears only board shorts. Paunch gone, he's looking more like his former self. My body has changed too. He's told me one too many times how bloated and puffy I look, like I'd been dredged up from a lake. Every time, I punched him in the gut, and he laughingly apologized, but I've caught him staring with concern that's more insulting. Funny how much can happen in a month (or two?) and not happen as well. Mom still dead, Dad still blind.

"Lookie what I confiscated from a student today." Chris dangles a baggie with a weed nugget. "Homeboy was wearing the same jeans and Vans I wore in the '80s. Trippiest thing. Sometimes I see a face I recognize, then realize it can't be Johnny Wong 'cause he'd be over forty."

"How does smoking interact with your meds?"

"My meds already numb me. This'll just make me sleep. Could be good for you. Mellow you out." From his other pocket, he pulls out a lighter and our grandfather's tobacco pipe.

"Here, let me." I don't want to witness his awkward fumbling. "The theoretical physicists are all basically stoners, so I've picked up a few things."

Chris plays his favorite Depeche Mode CD on his old boom box. Under the lavender-bruised chord progression, he hears something I can't. My brother can sit in his car for hours listening to music in a parking lot, sobbing and beating his chest to the rhythm. Or walk through the more dangerous parts of town in the middle of the night, headphones clamped over ears, singing and air-drumming in the streets. Even the gangbangers leave the crazy-ass Chino alone.

"Wave the flame over the bowl while you suck," I instruct. "Make the embers glow."

Chris erupts into hacking coughs, then rips into a bag of In-N-Out burgers. Handing me a beer bottle, he says, "You've been working real hard lately—thought you were on sabbatical?"

"Working on an independent project. Two projects actually," I realize, briefly wondering what Linnea's latest email was about. "But I'm taking a break on both."

"Was worried for a while, considering your hygiene, lack thereof. You were smelling pretty ripe, briny even."

Ever since the black mold hallucination, I'd been reluctant to bathe. Even moved into the loft with the men, into my own padded cubicle. Then after the phone call with Hannah Kang and learning she was too young to be my sister, I took my first shower in weeks. I also stopped seeing my friend, as if washing her away too down the drain. My fantasy sister and my hallucination could only exist in relation to each other, codependent.

Probably a good time to pack up and return to Sweden, except I can't seem to leave. Some of my former classmates have had to move back in with their parents because of the financial crisis, but I'm in a different boat.

Cleaner now, though no less unmoored, I stretch out on the blanket and smoke up like I'm on a rooftop opium den, the stars quivering above. Meanwhile, Chris regales me with funny stories about his job. He tells me how he wrote letters to the Educational Testing Service to rat out his hagwon bosses, how he alerted ETS of the copyright infringements on SAT prep books, how teachers were sent in to pose as students, how tests were taken in Asia by affiliates and answers relayed stateside before the same test was given twelve hours later. He tells me about embittered hagwon teachers setting up rogue academies, stealing software and test answers and client lists from their bosses, who had no actual fluency in English or math but had the church connections and immigrant network. It's his stand-up routine and soapbox diatribe.

"This was supposed to be *our* time, but the older generation won't give way." He dumps the ashes from our grandfather's pipe. "We need rolling papers. Hold on, got something better."

Chris crawls through the window and returns with a black hardbound book, the size of an encyclopedia, with delicate pages printed in Hanja characters and diagrams I can't parse. He tears out a sheet, balling it in his fist. "Our genealogy book. Don't worry, we've got two copies." He pops the crumpled paper in his mouth and chews with relish. "Nothing but names, our bullshit lineage. Already in our blood anyway."

"How many generations?"

"We're the sixty-second. You're not in it. Ha-ha. Probably 'cause you're a girl." He tears out a page and hands it to me, along with the weed.

"So these are only the men." I sit up and roll with origami dexterity and pass him the joint. Flipping through the book, I find cigarette holes, sliced-out names, sometimes rows—excised generations. "What do you do with the pieces?" I ask.

"Art projects. Papier-mâché casts. Theme being—molded by

ancestry, etc." He exhales forgotten and never-known lives through his nostrils.

"Or you just chew them up."

"Yum, tastes like rage and despair. Don't be sentimental. They were all assholes like Dad. Haven't done jack shit for us except pass on degenerate genes."

I nod. Smoking my ancestors seems honorable as I lie back down to puff clouds to heaven.

"Speaking of family," I say, not looking at Chris. "I called up a woman in Jersey who I thought was our sister. She's not, of course. Just the daughter of one of Mom's old friends."

"Why'd you think—"

"Found Mom's address book and something about the name, I don't know. It's over now—need to get back to my real life."

He stands over me, looming. "You promised you'd stay until Dad's eyes have healed." His posture would be threatening, but I'm so high I'm simply fascinated by the reddish glints in his black hair, mingling with the white—a fox dancing in moonlight.

"Yeah, it's weird right?" I murmur. "How his eyes haven't healed yet? I asked some of my doctor friends and—"

He crouches beside me and says, "Maybe Mom was telling the truth, and the other girl survived. I found some of her letters, whole bunch she never mailed to Korea. Maybe you can go through them, find something about the other girl?"

I sit up to face him. "Why do you have them?"

"Years ago, I was hurting for money. Mom used to hide jewelry and shit all over the house like a medieval peasant. Bet there's gold in kimchi jars buried in our backyard. Didn't seem like she was coming back, so I tore the house up. Found some jewelry in a false dresser bottom, a Rolex in a busted Cuisinart. And thick envelopes I was hoping was her loan-sharking cash."

"You read the letters?"

"Skimmed. Not as interesting as her stories—yeah, I know you took them from my trunk."

Of course he knew. How could I hide anything from him when the three of us were living in the loft, separated only by cubicle walls? "If you knew I had the stories," I say, "that you had no leverage over me, why didn't you confront me earlier—"

"I was happy enough having you here."

"And now you want me to stay longer, in exchange for the letters?"

I'm curious about his shifting motivations, his true end game. But he deflects by reverting to his classic stance. "Fine. If you're set on leaving, then ask Dad for my share first. I deserve something for everything I did for you. You've got a life elsewhere, help me get my piece."

"OK, I will. Soon."

He's surprised by how easily I agree. "Let's drink to it then and seal the deal." He slips through the window for more booze, leaving me alone on the roof with the ketchup-stained remnants of our meal and a mouth fuzzy with weed.

While waiting for him, I riffle through the genealogy book like it's an old issue of *Us Weekly* at the dentist's office. Ancestors—they're just like us! Which of these bastards can I blame for my hobbit feet? What's the gossip—murder, incest, rape, illegitimate kids with Mongol or Japanese invaders?

Then I find tucked within—a single sheet with scattered typed lines and lots of white space. The fragments include "two sisters," "a drowning in a lake," "many murders," and "a vengeful ghost." The phrases don't resemble anything in my mother's originals, but I recognize the formatting. This could be the fourth story-fate carving, echoing most in our blood. Had Chris glimpsed the quarter-folded sheet all those years ago, transcribing it before I'd torn it up? Was this homage or something else stolen? I slip it into my pocket when he returns with whiskey.

I ask, "Did Mom ever mention stories carved in wood? Maybe woodblocks?"

He doubles over laughing. "I don't know what the fuck you're talking about. Even if I did, I still wouldn't tell you." His voice darkens. "Poisoned, everything she touched, including me."

"You're not poisoned—"

"How would you know? She got to you too. I mean, what the fuck—you called up some rando thinking she's your sister? And the way you obsess over her stupid stories like they're Talmudic passages. I guess I was like that too. Thought I could figure out how I failed her, but there's nothing in those pages but her."

"That's not why I—"

"Never satisfied, impossible to please. Fucked up immigrant culture, combining the worst of two countries—all about social perception, can't find worth in herself so she depends on her kids to reflect it for her. But I could never redeem all the shit's she's been through. Never had the right start. Don't even know how I graduated from high school when Dad couldn't even piss in the toilet, when I was asking teachers if I should join the army so I could support the family. How could I just go on to college and complete some checklist for success made up by some immigrant mom who never had a real job, who didn't know the first thing about making it in this country as an outsider? Twenty-one-year-old freshman—I could never catch up."

Sensing he's not done, sensing he hasn't had anyone listen to him in ages—I keep quiet.

"One time," he continues, "I made the mistake of telling her I was stressed, thinking of dropping out. Asked her what my life was going to be like—work, struggle, then death? She said some people are born with a sprawling canvas, while others like me are born with just a scrap. All depends on what you do with the piece you're given. I was pissed off—the look on her face—like she already knew my limits. I started bawling. That was her gift, making me—and Dad too—feel like shit, like we weren't the son and husband she deserved."

"Oh Chris, that's not what she—"

"Both you left me anyhow," he says, steamrolling me with his anguish. "Then Dad went back to work and Mom kept sleeping. So I held on longer while you went farther and farther."

I don't tell him that I can't be blamed for my gender or birth order or for taking advantage of these in our family, or that there was no way I could've taken him with me anyhow.

"What's most fucked up," he says, "is that even with her in a coma, I could still hear her voice telling me to protect you—but what about me? Who's gonna protect me? At least I didn't have to keep lying to her about being a lawyer. Funny thing is—these new immigrant moms pay me beaucoup bucks to get their kids to reflect their worth too. They don't even know I never finished college. They just know I got my kid sister into the Ivies with lots of scholarships. They all think you're working with Nobel laureates in Sweden. Though I guess now that you're home doing God knows what, you're ruining my platform and sales pitch."

"Linnea isn't a—"

"I listened to Mom too much—that's how she got in my head, expecting a child to be her savior. You're not firstborn, not a son, so you don't have to redeem her. Alls you gotta do is not end up like her. Don't worry though—you're more like Dad anyhow."

Chris walks to the roof's edge. "Dad seems content in this tiny world of one. Maybe I could be happy too. Block out everyone else, and no one can tell you you're wrong." His back to me, he says more quietly, "I thought I could rework her stories, make some place in them for me—back when I thought I could write my way into making sense, write myself a better role in this family. I get why you're obsessed though." He stretches his arms out wide. "Some are born with a sprawling mother, ever oppressive. You only have scraps."

"Speaking of scraps," I say. "Do you really think the body shop will be enough for you? She's not coming back and you don't need to take care of Dad. Stop lying to yourself. Give yourself a chance to really change things instead."

"Why the body shop," he echoes. "Reparations, safety net, what else of worth does he have to give me? It's what's most important to his life, and if he entrusted it to me—"

"Someone to believe in you—that's what you really want?"

"Ach, too cheesy. But faith does work wonders, I've heard. Or maybe I'm just a covetous son of a bitch. Maybe I want to hit him where it hurts. He'd be horrified—his shop in my hands—handing me his *other* precious baby." Hunched over with his face in his hands, he's rocking on the balls of his feet.

"Please, Chris, not so close to the edge."

He swivels around, crouched like a gargoyle. "Kinda impressive though, how she's still making us sick, even while dead."

"I'm not sick—"

"Oh please, I hear you talking to someone who's not there—you sound so fucking disturbing—I don't need that shit in my head!" he says, slapping his skull.

"Reasoning out loud helps me to—Jesper used to hear me out, check my logic—"

"The Swedish guy? The one you were—"

"We're not together anymore. He found someone else, in Antarctica."

Chris laughs, loud and ugly. "Yeah, we're fucked when it comes to relationships. Better if we don't have children. Too late for me anyhow. You're still young enough, but probably a gamble with our genes. Could end up like Mom, with a kid like me." With a sly grin, he combs his fingers through his hair, which like him is lush, dark, and vulpine.

Leaving my brother on the roof, I head for the window.

"Hey," he says softly, grabbing my arm. "It ain't all so bad staying here, is it? Past couple months have been the happiest I've been in a long while. 'Cause of you."

It was the saddest, most frightening thing he said to me that night. I couldn't let the evening end like this, on this note—not again.

"Hey, you know what I'd love to do right now?" I say with a sweetness that disarms, with enough mischief to tempt him. "Let's whack some balls like old times. Do we still have the clubs? Will you do this for me, please, Oh-bbah?"

At Hermosa Beach, Chris heaves Dad's golf bag out of his trunk. Our father used them only once in the early '90s when he was invited by Mr. Yang to his fancy Palos Verdes country club. For this one visit, Dad bought a brand-new set. He wasn't sporty, didn't have any hobbies besides watching K-dramas. I'm guessing his intention was to eat a nice meal, drive a cart around, and laugh at his friend pretending to be one of the rich whites. I don't know what transpired at the club, but the golf bag was tossed into the garage afterward, never used by Dad again, and we never saw Mr. Yang again either.

But over one Christmas break during college, after a particularly stressful night, Chris took me to the beach with the golf set. We made a ritual of it a few more times, even buying extra balls. So here we are now, teeing up on the moonlit shore, channeling all our frustration into metal clubs to wallop white plastic spheres into the dark sea.

Stronger and angrier, Chris easily drives his arcing into the night, while mine only reach the cresting waves, spitting my balls back to me.

"Do you practice?" I ask, envious and suspicious of his power.

"No, Elsa, you just suck. You're like the only Korean woman who's not a PGA pro. Wasted your biological destiny."

"We're descended from farmers and merchants, not athletes." Another swing, another fail.

"There were a few scholars, too, and a magistrate," he says defensively, "but yeah, we descend from the dilettantes and womanizer line. That's not what I'm talking about though. Our people are good at golf because they got those long Korean torsos, more torque when they twist up. Lower center of gravity with those short Korean legs. Thick calves help too, the same calves that helped us run up the hills whenever the Japs invaded." Chris slices another ball into the sky.

"How come it's only the women who dominate? You got a long torso, short legs too."

He has no race biology explanation for this. Mutters something about men's Olympic speed skating. I can feel his mood lightening though, and when I finally hit a ball over the waves, I jump and scream with exaltation, spiking my club deep into the wet sand like a reverse King Arthur. After that, I manage to strike a few more into the ocean, each time thrilling at the perfect moment of contact, blasting these little white planets across the universe.

"We're out—no more balls," he says.

"Sorry for littering, Mother Nature, but holy shit that felt good!"

Afterward, we walk up to Pier Avenue for pizza. It's like a mini-spring break with palm trees wrapped in lights and thronged with so many drunk kids, frat boy types. More diverse than Stockholm, but still surprisingly white for the South Bay, which had become more brown and yellow over the years. In these parts, the California valley girl and surfer guy were relics of the '80s. The blond, blue-eyed descendants of dust-bowl migrants from the Germanic-Scandinavian midwestern states had moved on again.

These kids were probably out-of-state college students anyway, judging by how they were mimicking behavior usually seen on reality TV. I typically avoid this scene, but Chris is curious. He finds all this exotic 'cause he's only partied in K-Town. The one time I went to a sports bar, I heard "me so horny" and "never been with an Asian chick before." No wonder I prefer hipster lounges where white guys try to impress with Wong Kar Wai references instead.

With golf bag beside him, Chris sits on a bench, shaking chili flakes onto the pizza slice I got for him. While waiting for my own at the counter, a sexy hot mess of a girl with long red hair teeters on her strappy heels toward my brother. Her gaggle of girlfriends follow behind in a wobbly V-formation, drunk birds struggling to keep the flock together.

I'm tense because she's getting closer. Chris is intimidated by hot white women, so I hope he won't gawk or do anything embarrassing. I feel more nervous for the girl though because she's bending forward in front of him, with her intimidating rack contained only by a drapey handkerchief top. She asks in her loud, drunken lilt if she can have some of his pizza.

Stunned, Chris turns his uneaten slice around for her. She takes the end of it into her mouth and chomps down. Mumbling thanks with her mouth full, she totters off with her arms raised in victory. "I fucking love pizza!" She swings around to point at Chris. "Thank you, sir!" Her giggling friends follow, curving their flock's movement around my brother.

I join Chris on the bench. I'm relieved and irritated, not wanting to get into why. "She was fucking hot!" he says. I let him replay the moment, then remind him I was right there, witnessing everything. I cut him off when we're done with our pizza and point out a cotton candy stand.

"This one's on me. I got you, girl," he says, thumping his chest, as if it was him and not the pizza that the redhead was drawn to.

Stuffed, drunk, and buzzed from skank weed and unknown ancestral histories, we amble down the boardwalk together. I'm the only woman in a hoodie and pajama bottoms, while Chris is wearing a faded Tommy Bahama shirt and board shorts. He's more fit now and finally got a haircut, but still looks old and out of place, especially on a Saturday night on this Greek Row by the sea. I want to get my pink fairy floss and go home.

Across from the cotton candy shack is a two-story Irish pub, pumping progressive house from its upper veranda. With its neon shamrocks in the windows and dancers waving glow sticks, it's a McPaddy-on-Mollies. Chris hands me a fiver, telling me he never gets out, doesn't even watch TV. He and the golf bag lean against an empty bike rack. With his hands on the railing, he surveys the scene, a captain at the prow.

What would a stranger make of him, this schlubby, middle-aged Asian guy, brazenly checking out the white kids like some shameless anthropologist? Could they tell he used to be obsessed with being ripped and cut, dating the most beautiful Korean girls at school? That his philosophy profs quoted his essays on Kierkegaard and Wittgenstein to the rest of class? Did he seem like a guy who'd lie on the roofs of cars with arms outstretched, gripping the edges of the window frames and howling while his friends drove donuts in the parking lot? "Like how Dad rode the tops of trains during the war!" he told me.

He pulled other stunts too, slightly less dangerous. Like sending secret admirer letters and roses to his English Lit TA, "a gorgeous Rosetti redhead." The department secretary who'd seen him deliver these eventually told him, "The letters are beautiful, dear, and have made quite the stir among the grad student ladies, but you should fess up now or cease altogether." When he revealed himself, his TA turned him down gently and appreciatively. He was fine with that, as the admiring was the point, and he derived the greatest pleasure in that his prose style had dazzled more than just the recipient.

I idolized my brother when I was a kid. He basked in my adoration too. He presented himself to me and others as a Dally with the soul of a Ponyboy. It was only when I got older that I feared he was really a Johnny at heart.

Superficially, it seemed that he shaped his persona to outright defy ethnic stereotypes. But actually, he didn't care about societal expectations or even polite social norms. During one unbearable heat wave, he'd walked around his college campus wearing boxers as shorts and laughed when a friend noticed his dick hanging out. Dancing at a K-Town club, he'd split his pants up the ass, Dad's three-piece white Travolta suit. So Chris ripped the tear further and kept dancing with pant legs flapping as the crowd gathered around him and cheered. Of course, none of this I witnessed, but as a twelve-year-old I'd lie in bed hearing his outrageous stories while he lay on the carpet, telling me all about this life outside of home.

Chris's friends loved his flamboyance, but he wanted to be admired more for his "profound, aesthetic intellectualism." Truth is, he felt stifled among the Asians, where he was considered the pretentious weirdo acting so free and fruity—as if he were white—spouting poetry and talking about writing novels.

"We should be pipe-smoking dilettantes, supporting the arts." He claimed that *this life* should've been our right, as we were descended from Kaesong yangban, specifically "degenerate aristocrats." History and a change of dynasty moved the capital to Seoul, forcing these ancestors to become traveling merchants. The womanizing gene couldn't be curbed by circumstance though. Grandpa had three wives; Great-Grandpa, five. Some other dude before them had fourteen. "I was bred to be a skirt-chaser. Grandpa died penniless in the arms of his youngest wife. Dad had no game with the ladies, but that's how he lost his inheritance. Partied and danced and frittered away his opportunities. No business acumen whatsoever. That's why he's so pissed at the world. Especially here—blue-collar gook—talk about downward mobility."

Chris felt unseen when his friends dismissed his yangban roots or didn't take his artistic side seriously. To them, he was something more familiar—at times histrionic and fanatically religious like their mothers, or depressive and suddenly violent like their fathers. His friends understood and forgave him, up to a point. It wasn't his epilepsy or religious manias that pushed them away though. They finally left because of his selfish despair and inability to deal with *their* pain. This is what he once told me, ostensibly to warn me of my fate, if I kept up my loner-ish tendencies.

Finally, I'm at the front of the line at the cotton candy stall. The teenage server dips a paper cone into the whirlwind of sugar, gathering my pink cloud around it. My mouth is already watering, my teeth aching from the coming sweetness. Then I hear behind me on the boardwalk, a guy saying, "Look! It's Tiger fucking Woods!"

"Tiger's Black, you idiot," says another.

"He's got an Asian mom, dickwad," says the first.

Four bro-ish white guys, one wearing a lime-green polo

with a popped collar and puka-shell necklace, another sporting a barely buttoned linen shirt over pink madras shorts. All with 40s of malt liquor duct-taped to their hands. They're playing Edward 40-hands on a street full of cheap liquor and patrolling beach cops—what a cocktail of stupidity, recklessness, and fearless entitlement. I'm so very envious.

"If he's Black *and* Asian, what you think Tiger's got hanging down there—driver or a putter?" says the shortest guy, also the most muscular and broad, square like a mini fridge.

"You're such a fucking herb!" The other boys laugh. My cotton candy is handed to me, but I can't cross over to Chris because the boys are in my way, sloshing and shouting compliments to the girls passing by. One guy swings his arm around his buddy and slurs, "I dare you. Go for it. It'll be fucking hilarious."

Chris is leaning forward on the bike rack, his back to the boys. He must've bummed a cigarette off someone. Supposedly he quit cold turkey years ago, but on occasion, while drinking, he enjoys a rare one. Taking deep drags, he's basking in the night, his mind elsewhere. Wherever he is, he's not here in the present and thus hasn't heard the boys talking about Tiger, or doesn't care.

Suddenly, Mini Fridge runs up behind him and humps with gusto, creeping his pelvis closer and closer to my brother's ass. Back in my clubbing days, this was an acceptable dance move that was both a greeting and invitation to grind from strange men, but Mini Fridge's performance doesn't really acknowledge my brother as a reciprocating partner. Hence the pantomimed ass slaps.

I try to warn Chris, but can't find my voice, like I'm a kid again. A couple onlookers join in the laughter. But still, my brother doesn't think it's about him, so the boys whoop it up and Mini Fridge thrusts closer—then makes actual contact, bumping into my brother.

Chris whips around. "What the fuck?"

Mini Fridge keeps humping because his friends are laughing harder. I'm sure that his beefy arms, made even more disproportionate by his jug hands, make it difficult for Chris to ignore or avoid him or even process what the fuck he is. Chris backs up into the bike rack away from the thrusting pelvis. He's more confused than anything, and I know why—he's in a time warp because these preppy frat boys with their '80s revivalist clothes are the low-rent Steffs and Blanes of his youth, the sandy-blond predatory Socs. Never mind that *The Outsiders* was written in the '60s; the movie Socs who beat up Johnny dressed like John Hughesian assholes. A certain type of white boy bully lives eternal, with only slight modifications to hairstyle.

My brother sees that strangers all around him have been ridiculing him, that they shared in the joke with these kids. He finds me across the way, holding my pink cotton candy. We look at each other for a moment before he turns on Mini Fridge with a ferocious, "I said, what the fuck you doing, homeboy?"

"Just messing around! Chill, dude." The kid stumbles back to his friends, who yell out, "Can't help it if our boy's a fucking rice queen!" They all strut away together with their arms outstretched on the crowded boardwalk. Their hands dribble and spurt, marking their territory, jizzing their hoppy scent all over the scene.

After they leave, my legs can move again. I approach Chris slowly, giving him space. But I still don't know what to say.

"You saw them coming at me? You saw the whole thing?" His face is flushed, his eyes veined with shame.

"I tried to warn you but—whatever, they're just dumb fucks. Let's get out of here."

Chris turns toward the golf bag and I expect him to

heave it over his shoulder, but he stares at the set thoughtfully. Then he draws out a club, one of the sleek irons that can slice through the night. He jauntily pops it over his shoulder and strides after the boys. "Hey, crackerjack fuckers!" he shouts. The boys look over their shoulders. So does everyone else.

"Oh shit, Tiger's pissed!" says the guy with the puka-shell necklace. He means to be mocking and pretends not to be concerned, but quickens his pace anyway.

"Think you all can mess with me then just walk away?" Chris says, moving with long, loping steps. "You think I'm just gonna take whatever you throw at me?"

I can't leave my brother hanging again. Awkwardly, I sling the golf bag over one shoulder while not dropping my cotton candy. I lose precious seconds because of my anxiety and lack of coordination. Chris is already far ahead as he stalks his ghosts of white bullies past.

The boys mutter, "Whatever, man. Fuck off, weirdo."

"I want a fucking apolo-geeeee!" screams Chris, turning more heads, setting off gasps and a *Holy shit!* and *Crazy motherfucker!* People edge away, leaving my brother on the boardwalk to face down his enemies alone, bars and saloons on either side of him, like in some never-filmed Western—the Mad Chinaman at Midnight vs. the White-Heads.

A couple Black guys in beanie caps and skinny jeans, carrying their skateboards, yell for my brother to "Put down the club, man! Put it down!" Shaking their heads, sad and solemn, they wave their hands in dismissal and skate away, not wanting to be anywhere near during the fallout. But the white partiers are keyed up. Can't look away, some are even trailing behind Chris to see how things will play out.

"I'm not gonna apolo-giiiiize!" Mini Fridge whines like a child, privileged and petulant.

His friend with the linen shirt and bared chest says, "We didn't do nothing, you psycho chink!"

"I'll show you how fucking psycho this chink can be!" Charging at them, Chris howls at full pitch while wielding a golf club two-handed over his head like a kumdo master. He's missing the caged mask, leather armor, and the flaring, wide-legged pants, but his Tommy Bahama floral shirt similarly billows behind him as he flies over the boardwalk with steel sword gleaming. His warrior cry—both piercing and guttural—is thrillingly, defiantly un-American.

The white boys are running, their beer streaming from their palms—loops and arcs of amber liquid glittering under the twinkle-lit palm trees. People around them get splashed, jump back, curse and stare in wonder at the crazy Asian guy giving chase.

I lug the golf bag more securely in preparation to run also, but the weight of it threatens to pull me backward. I'm the most pathetic caddy, a worthless Sancho Panza, as I struggle to catch up while holding my cotton candy aloft. I yell for my brother to hold up, but he can't hear me. The only reason I'm able to finally get closer is because Beach Patrol, already in the neighborhood for another licentious Saturday night, pulls up at the end of the avenue. Two police cars block the path. Four cops step out and point their guns at my brother.

The crowd moves back just a bit, sticking around for the drama. I can't help wondering if the few people of color are on my brother's side without needing to know what went down. Isn't it enough that the four white boys are young and good-looking, with expensive clothes and 40s taped to their hands? What about the police? One is Asian, while the other three are white. The drunk kids are already stumbling toward the white cops to make their case, even though guns are pulled out. How fearless of them, how self-assured.

A white cop orders Chris to "Drop your wea—drop the golf club now!"

Chris complies. Hollow metal clatters on the boardwalk. But instead of holding up his hands in obedient surrender, he shrugs with outstretched arms. "This ain't no weapon. This is for self-defense. That guy assaulted *me*!" My brother's eyes shine with righteous fury, but I'm the only one who can read the cunning that flickers as he scans the crowd and delivers his next statement. "That man *sexually* assaulted me in public! I've got *all* these witnesses." He sweeps his arm in a wide arc as he plays to his audience.

The police holster their weapons, confused and annoyed, as the white kids complain and appeal to the white cops. They point at Chris, yelling about him chasing them, while my brother remains alone, the only one with his hands raised.

Chris shouts, "You really think *I'm* the one causing trouble? There's four of them—one of me! I just want a fucking apology!"

"Calm down, sir," says the Asian cop, silent up till now.

Chris points his finger at him. "You know *exactly* what I'm talking about, man. These white boys, they've been ragging on us all our lives, treating us like shit, disrespecting us to our faces. You know the bullshit we put up with, what they get away with, what they *know* they can get away with. Fuck man, I know you know what I'm talking about!"

They lock eyes, and so much passes between them that I'll never understand. The Asian cop is rigid, forcing himself not to look at his white colleagues, willing them not to look at him either. But the white cops, they don't scoff or roll their eyes or tell Chris to calm down. Sheepish, they seem to know exactly what he's talking about.

The Asian cop, after a long moment in which nobody speaks, finally says with evident exhaustion, "You just gotta let it go, man. Just walk away." There's more he wants to say, but he shakes his head. I can't see if Chris is let down, betrayed, or if he understands that he put his Asian brother on the spot—what else could he have said at that moment?

I finally step up, dragging our father's golf bag while clutching my cotton candy, still uneaten. When the cops see me, they change the story in their minds. My presence, whether as sister or girlfriend, means that Chris isn't some solitary madman, unhinged and unloved. He's no longer the creepy-nerdy ostracized Asian student who flips into the campus sociopath on a rampage—the lone golfman. The two of us with a full set of clubs between us made us more legible—Asian couple doing an Asian sport. Hell, maybe Chris was defending my honor from these white boys, regardless of my slovenliness. The cops confer while the white kids whine and threaten to call their fathers' lawyers. Ultimately, Beach Patrol tells us all to go home, reminding the boys they're getting off easy with the public drinking.

From far away, I hear, "Fucking bullshit! We woulda got shot!" The young Black men have circled around for the finale, but are keeping a safe distance. "Told you nothing woulda happen to the Ko-rean. Them and the cops in cahoots! Fucking funny as hell though watching him go after them punk-ass white boys." Their slender silhouettes skate away, gracefully serpentine down the street, in and out of lamplight and shadow. I can't tell from their melancholy laughter or the leisurely pace of their skating if they're relieved or disappointed, if they feel more alone and reviled than before.

We've all gotten off too easy tonight, but my heart rate won't come down. Not even after a cop watches the boys pour out the beer next to a palm tree then drop the bottles into recycling. Not after I dump my cotton candy too because I feel like throwing up instead.

The golf club remains on the ground until I pick it up. Chris takes the bag and leads us to the car. The adrenaline doesn't dissipate until we reach the body shop. With the fight-or-flight chemicals finally leaving my body, clarity brightens and blooms instead, along with the urgent need to prevent something like this from ever happening again.

My brother steps out of the car, ready to call it a night. I tell him I've got around eighty-five thousand dollars to give him. Chris asks how I have that kind of money.

"My travel and most of my living expenses are covered by the university," I say, adding that I'm frugal like an immigrant, which is all true, but stretching it. "I'm guaranteed another postdoc, then tenure-track. Housing is also subsidized for professors, plus there's the dining hall. It's a racket. I can spare the money." My lie has become the most fanciful fairy tale of academia. I don't know if he believes me, but he's clearly interested in hearing more.

"I'll give it to you, but on one condition—you gotta leave this place. Not just the shop, but this city, this entire geo-cultural-temporal area. I'm giving you the same advice you gave me—move forward, see who else you can be out there."

"But you came back. What was the point? Maybe I was wrong to push you out."

"I'm leaving too. Back to Sweden. Then wherever the next opportunity takes me."

"What about Dad?"

"I'll figure it out, make sure he's OK. But you've done more than enough. Eighty-five thousand just for you to do whatever—as long as it's not here."

"You'd really do this for me?"

"I'm sorry I didn't do it earlier. It's time for us both to move on."

9

Chris drops me off at UCLA. He thinks I'm meeting an old physicist colleague. I'm not ready to tell him the truth.

Off campus, I find the appointed teahouse. My entrance sets off a little bell hanging over the door. Not what I expected inside. Clientele's heavily Asian, as is UCLA, but the café's not even LA Zen, more Mad Hatter, with mismatched Victorian furniture and shelves packed with tea tins and porcelain. So much fragility—I'm She-Hulk in a china shop.

The space is dimly lit because there are no street-facing windows. Instead, the wall is plastered with various doors. A circular one, upholstered in brocade. A metal hatch of thick steel. Tiny double gates of filigreed brass, fit for a Versailles mouse-queen. There's even a door-within-a-door-within-a-door in the upper corner. I claim a table in the back where I can sit and watch them all, as I no longer recall which portal I came through. Then, setting off the bell, Oskar walks in through the middle one. Dressed in a dove-grey suit, hair wound in an elegant topknot, he spots me right away, even amid all the other Asians. I thank him for coming.

"Are you certain you don't have time for dinner over the next few days?" he asks.

"This is the only free time I have," I lie.

Weeks ago, Oskar had mentioned in an email that he was

attending a conference at UCLA. Initially, I'd told him I was too busy to meet, but in the last few days, Chris and I've been dreaming up plans. He's thinking of traveling, visiting friends in New York, maybe going farther. He mentioned returning to school, but wouldn't reveal what he'd study. Meanwhile, I researched in-home care nurses, luxury senior apartments in K-Town, which universities were most generous. Briefly, I looked into leaving academia altogether for a lucrative industry job. Data scientists were a new thing on the horizon, promising salaries that far outstripped those of mere professors. Of course, there was my postdoc and Linnea and—sterile neutrinos, was it? But who needs the ghost of a ghost, seemed like overkill. Perhaps I could pivot back to my original analysis with high-energy neutrinos. For an industry job, it's easier to demonstrate my data science, AI, and machine-learning skills with those particles. What's not theoretical is typically easier to market and sell.

More important for my fantasies of the future and my return to Sweden, I needed to see Oskar to remind myself where I'd been before my mother died, and where I could be again, when ready. Luckily, I haven't missed my opportunity. I wrote him only yesterday, asking if he still had time and interest in meeting me. Still, I need to be careful with my transition—between worlds.

"Let me get you tea," I say. "Then you can tell me all about your presentation on the palindrome runestone. Read in a loop, multiple embedded messages, right? Story changes as one cycles through?"

"Yes, I'm flattered you remember, but I've got something more interesting, Elsa. A recent discovery—about the Emmileh Bell."

Oh, that. I'll have to lay down some ground rules if we're to go any further. "Black tea, whichever is the most expensive and authentic?" I leave to order before he can reply. From the counter, at this safe distance, I watch him. Oskar drapes his jacket over the chair's back and angles his crossed legs to avoid bumping the table. Even without the suit and manner of folding his limbs just so, he stands out as foreign. More precisely, he's so very Swedish.

When I return with our tea, Oskar shows me an old, clothbound book. "You haven't mentioned the bell in a while," he says, "but I came across this. According to documented history, the Emmileh Bell had been used for seven centuries before a fifteenth-century flood destroyed the temple housing it. The flood carried the bell downriver. In effect, it was drowned and buried, resurfacing years later in another region, among the ruins of Kyongju's river."

"Zombie bell," I murmur, nodding, feigning interest. I'm at a dead end with the sister search, and my friend isn't around anymore. My mother's words are dutifully translated in memorial, her ashes in the sea. I've been gradually extricating myself from all this. But Oskar is luminous, a discoverer and teacher, wanting to share his excitement. So I let him continue.

"Exactly," he says, "and this undead bell was enshrined in a new temple and rung for a few more centuries. During the Colonial Period, the Japanese Governor-General wanted to melt it down for weapons against Korean independence fighters. But historians and scholars were able to save the bell, and now it's still hanging, only rung once a year. I knew none of this before I met you. The Emmileh Bell has more stories—and more lives—than just the girl who sings."

I can't help playing along, countering with: "Or it's the girl in the bell—with the many lives, many songs." Gears are turning. Once a nerd, always a nerd, no matter how fraught the subject and tangled in familial myths.

Oskar touches my hand. "Yes," he whispers. "I thought you might say that."

I glance down, expecting a burn where our skin made contact. There's no mark, but I can still feel the heat of his fingers over mine. After months of feeling nothing, of only wanting to lie down, Oskar's presence and attention overwhelm me. But there's nowhere to hide, so I point to the book. "You got the history from this?"

"No, but this is interesting too." He flips to a page, a poem in English. "The bell casting is recorded in the *Samguk Yusa* from the thirteenth century. But there's no mention of child sacrifice, even though it's a hybrid text blending legend with history. Yet every Korean knows this story. Most assume it's an oral legend, but I've discovered this printed record from 1906, written by Homer Hulbert, an American missionary."

"White guy?" I ask.

"Very white. But he wrote books on Korea and protested Japanese colonization in the States and the Hague, so we can consider him an honorary Korean. Here, he writes about the native poetry and includes his own translations."

I skim the poem. A "master-founder" desires the "rare metal" that the "spirits hide from mortal sight." A royal edict issues a prayer to all to "render up their treasure," lest the city "shall have no tongue to voice her joy or pain." A "mother witch" appears, carrying her child, promising that with this sacrifice, "That he who once has heard the bell's deep tone, shall ever after hunger for it more than for the voice of mother, wife, or child."

"So the mother willingly gives up her child."

"Hulbert was a missionary too. There's a tension between condemnation and fascination with the occult. And this, 'Unpitying are the hands that cast the child into the seething mass. Fit type of Hell! Nay, type of human shame—'"

"He calls her a witch-mother."

"The mysterious Orient and whatnot," he says. "But what I find striking is that Hulbert credits 'Justice' with ensuring the bell would forever sound, 'Emmi, Emmi, Emmi, Emmilé,' which he translates as 'O Mother, woe is me, O Mother Mine.' Most Koreans will tell you that *Emmileh* literally means 'because of Mother.'"

"My mother told me *Emmileh* meant 'Mommy.'"

"In the Silla dialect, *Emmi* is 'mother.' *Emmileh* is 'because of mother.'"

"So it's accusatory! The girl is telling everyone her mom did this to her!"

Oskar smiles. "There's the fire I remember."

"But why would my mom say it was the monk who had the dream, who took the child?"

"Some say the bell-maker cast his own daughter into the vat."

I stare into my flowerless green tea. What if Mom excluded the bell story from her collection because of guilt over the girl she gave up? This story, the first I'd written in my lab book, wasn't translated—it was dictated. As soon as I wrote it, my friend appeared in my bed, and in the morning, she led me to Oskar. Whose voice started all this at the bottom of the world, telling me "because of mother"?

Someone enters the café, setting off the bell over the door. Louder than before.

Oskar touches my hand again. "Are you all right? Where'd you go?"

I shake away my thoughts like snowflakes from my hair. "Bit far from runestones. Hope you're not researching all this for my sake."

"Not just for you," Oskar replies, unfazed by my rudeness, or already accustomed to it. "When the royal edict demands 'treasure' belonging to the 'spirits of the earth,' I can't help but think of the European changeling. In Scandinavian lore, parents could force the return of their real child by abusing the changeling. One method was placing the child in a hot oven. There are court cases from seventeenth-century Sweden about parents using the changeling defense to justify their actions. What if the mother was sacrificing not her own daughter, but a fairy child, the spirits' 'treasure,' in order to regain her true daughter?"

Oskar sighs. "But now I'm mixing my lore. Cross-cultural yearning, forcing connections that only exist in my mind." He blushes, the color rising past the golden scar across his temple.

"A while ago," I say, dusting off the memory for Oskar's sake, "I read how the Kyongju Museum was performing chemical tests on the bell, looking for calcium phosphate—evidence of human bone. But they only found copper and zinc."

The bell over the door rings again, deeper and more resonant. I try not to scream.

Oskar taps the plastic-sleeved sheet. "This is from a newspaper during the Colonial Period. A macabre fairy tale of a mute girl who throws herself into molten bronze to sing through the bell. Coded resistance. I've found others like it too. I believe this could all lead to a very interesting paper. Working with you on these folktales has given me new insight where I thought I had none. Your mother's retellings, the voice and perspective—"

I try to focus on Oskar and keep my own mounting anxiety at bay, but then in the corner of my eye, I see someone like my friend, climbing the spiral staircase, dragging her red ribbons behind her so they wrap around the railing like a candy cane. But it's not her. Not even another Asian girl. Just a persistent shadow burned into my vision, like the afterimage from staring at the sun. This is the first time I've seen any echo of her since her ribbons pulled me out of the tub.

The bell rings, vibrations deep in my bones. But no one has entered, the door remains closed. What's wrong with me? What's wrong with *him* for wanting to be my—whatever I was—friend? Pen pal? I stand, rattling the teacups. "Is *that* why you've been writing me? Am I research or test subject or source material? Are you just interested in my mom's folktales?"

He glances around with his Swedish self-consciousness. "Please, Elsa, not here."

I don't care. I only see people like me, Cali-Asians who don't give a fuck, who tell the most racist jokes about each other. These are my backyard Asians, my cousins from school and church and the mall.

"You lord your age over me," I say, "and also your Koreanness—all academic, by the way. Come on, it's still called Oriental Studies in Europe. But if you can convince me, you've got your lectures all ready for your adoptee students. I'm not fluent like you, don't know as much, so I make you feel more Korean—more—"

Bristling through me is defiance and desire, the need to challenge this man, provoke and command him because I don't want to lose him.

Oskar stands too, steadying me with his hands. "I wrote you, Elsa, because I want to know you. I helped you with the stories because you asked me to. But the folktales, I've had my own tricky relationship. My retellings, I wrote in English—not my mother tongue, nor my adopted one—but the language that feels most neutral and academic and safe from emotion. And why those stories of filial piety, family reunion? That book I lent you—that was from my foster mother. She didn't call herself that, but these are the imperfect words I have to explain who I am, how I came to be. I wish you wouldn't think so little of me, or so little of yourself. You're right—you do make me feel more."

"More Korean?"

"How can you be so brilliant and yet so daft? No, Elsa, you make me feel more, period. And you feel and think more than is possibly healthy for most people. Now can we please sit down? Our tea's getting cold."

I sit, tingling all over. Awake and brimming with desire.

Gently, he offers, "Perhaps you can tell me about your neutrinos? A safer topic for us both. The ghost particle's ghost, I believe?"

"No, no, you're clearly excited about your new research—please, go on. I'm listening."

"I keep trying to learn more about you, Elsa. Perhaps you don't want me to feel stupid, hate explaining to laymen. So how about you tell me what drew you to science in the first place."

Such a simple question, but not the easiest to answer.

"My mom used to eavesdrop on the other line when I talked to my brother. She once unlocked my diary. Translated it word by word with her dictionary. So science became my secret language and safeguard. The better I got at it, the more different I became from her too—that's what I first thought anyhow. Physics, in particular, at that age, seemed the most hard-core and badass, embarrassing to admit that now. But in college, I realized how *little* physicists actually know because every discovery leads to more mysteries, more locked doors. My advisor finds it exciting—'So much to discover, why we first crawled out of caves,' she says. It terrifies me though. Why I became an experimentalist probably, instead of a theorist."

"But you love it, despite the terror?"

I want to say I love physics because it makes me human,

both trivial and miraculous. My mother's misery isn't important in the big scheme. Whereas historians consider beyond individual lifetimes, to meditate on the birth and death of civilizations, of epochs and eras—physicists contemplate a cosmic time scale. Even then, I am infinite because energy cannot be created or destroyed, only changes forms, or shape-shifts. After my body dies, my energy will continue as always. We're made up of stardust from other galaxies, and a bit of our dead bodies will decay and form helium that'll journey across space again. I'm grateful. I'm in awe.

But then a group of people exit the café, holding the door open for each other. The bell doesn't ring this time. Through this opening, I see Chris in his car, parked at the curb. He's peering through the doorway, scrutinizing Oskar and me. I don't know why I panic. In a rush, I apologize to Oskar, telling him I need to go, that I forgot something important, that my father needs me. I gather my things and tell him how much I love his idea for a new paper.

The café door closes again. Hidden from view, I kiss Oskar, quick and chaste. Then I hold his palm open in mine. "I don't know whether you're the prince or a plot device," I say. "Is there a difference? But thank you for coming to wake me. The most important thing I want you to know—I'm coming back to Sweden. I don't want to give up physics, and I want to keep getting to know you. But I've still got work here left to do."

I cradle his hand in both of mine. My lips linger over his palm. I whisper words, close his fingers over them. "I'm coming back to you, so don't go anywhere, please."

"I promise," he says, holding on to my real kiss.

Yes, I know we'll see each other again.

Jumping into Chris's car, I tell him, "You're early, and you were supposed to wait for me at the gates."

"Who's the dapper Asian?" he asks. "*He's* a physicist?"

"Yeah. Were you following me?"

"No, you wacko. I was revisiting my old haunts. Then I spot you in there—getting all cuddly with the samurai hipster—Japanese?"

"Korean."

"Homeboy's Korean?" Chris nods appreciatively, then checks out his own reflection in the rearview mirror. "I'm better looking," he says. "If I lose more weight"—he sucks in his cheeks—"I could pass for Japanese. Back in the day when I was real cut and wore sunglasses—"

"Yeah, yeah, you looked Italian, like Stallone and Pacino. Can we go now?"

"Then I got all fat 'cause of my meds, looking like Ray Romano."

I ignore him, chanting the promise I whispered into Oskar's palm.

"What are you muttering?" he asks.

"A prayer."

10

The next couple days, while my brother and I continue to cook up plans for his future, Chris doesn't ask again about Oskar. He suspects I'm concealing something. I can't even explain to myself why I don't simply say Oskar's a Swedish guy I like, whom I hope to see again. Maybe it's like my friend—keep him secret, keep him mine. If I reveal, Chris might tell me that Oskar's also illusory, unrealistic and inappropriate. How can you emotionally invest in someone from another world? Isn't he too old for this—hasn't he already outgrown you?

The tension's festering though, especially when we're all living together, as if in quarantine from the rest of the world. So Chris proposes family karaoke—trapped in an even smaller room, but with microphones and tambourines and an hourly rate. Thus, on this weekday night, I'm huddling with my father and brother in a vinyl booth, taking shots of soju while riffling through multilingual song binders. Even out of the body shop, we can't escape the mirror ball and disco lights. At least the liquor is part of the culture—no need to hide from Dad.

Steering clear of my mother's standards, "Yesterday" and Korean torch songs, I stick to my usual Queen, Prince, and Bowie. When I'm drunk enough, I reach for Kate Bush. During my down-tempo cover of "Running Up That Hill," I choke on the high notes, my voice breaks, and I start crying. I wipe my nose with my sleeve, so Chris leaves to get tissues.

What if she saw us now—her blind husband rattling his tambourine while her daughter's synth-heightened sobbing echoes in heartbreaking '80s reverb, and her son bursts into the room with toilet-paper pom-poms? No wonder she left us. She never even really wanted me.

Mom didn't want the child before me either, but her doctor said she had to bear me to survive. Atonement or inescapable destiny? Before that, the stillborn baby. She couldn't prevent her body from bringing forth another girl into the world. I became the daughter she couldn't get rid of, who didn't die, who kept coming back to remind her what it was to be a Korean woman. Yet I turned out so foreign—another annoyance. Was I the reason that she imagined another daughter? This girl, born in the negative space between us, was the one who should've been, if our fates could've been swapped.

Maybe *this* nurtured her fantasy—each woman echoing her story for eternity. When her life ended and her folktale began again, Mom could reunite with her lost daughter, before the baby died as the men believed—or before she was sent away, as she claimed. Hannah Kang was only one dead end, but I had no other leads, and my hallucinatory friend vanished also, as if one supposition depended on another. Besides, I've been mourning a dead mom and searching for a lost sister while my brother's the one who needs someone to believe in him. Better if my sister were dead anyhow, so she could be with our mother and aunt, grandmother and ancestresses. I should let her go to them.

When my song ends, Dad finally hears me. "Why she crying? Stop crying!"

"Nothing, I'm just drunk."

"You're unhappy. I hear you crying in the middle of the night."

Flipping through the binder, Chris asks, "How about Tears for Fears? OMD?"

"An unmarried daughter should be home with her family, with her father. You can live in your mother's house. I can fix up one of the cars. The silver Benz?"

"I don't want your damn car! Don't want anything from you!" I rush out, stumbling through corridors. Moaning voices seep through walls. Each door I pass has a small window, like a lunatic's asylum. Through one, I see a man with a tie knotted around his head, singing his heart out. With him, a second man gropes a girl while the third thrusts the mic to her lips. Another window reveals a couple slow dancing, their child sleeping on the banquette.

In the last room, I see my faceless mother seated in a chair with microphone wires wrapped around her wrists and ankles. A spotlight shines on her head, highlighting its smooth, featureless curves, that exquisite pore-less complexion, the horrifying blankness.

In the bathroom, I splash cold water on my eyes, then return to my family, wanting Chris to take me home. But my father announces, "So, the little bitch is back." He's called me that before, a Korean word both slur and term of endearment. I'm not sure which one he means right now. "If you want something, go ahead," he sneers. "You want my building, my land?"

"What did you say to him?"

Chris shrugs, tossing nuts into his mouth. How stupid of me. He's not going anywhere. He needs my father to blame for his life, just as I need my mother to justify mine. And my brother would keep me tethered here too if he could, so he needn't wonder about an alternate life, a parallel world. The family that stays together, hides together from reality. Isn't that what they say? At the very least, if he can't keep me by his side, he'll make an utter mess of things just to watch shit blow up.

"What do you want from me, Elsa?" our father asks in Korean.

Fine. Let's see how far we can take this. "Chris is too chickenshit to ask for himself," I reply in English, too tired at trying and failing to communicate with family. "Can you give me a couple garages to rent out?"

"So—you will live at home, with us? You will use the money for—"

"No. Chris wants the rent money. I'm going back to Sweden. He wanted me to ask you, to pretend that I'm the one who needs the money, that I'm the one who cares you're sitting on all this, doing nothing with your life's work, to pretend that a little chunk of change will get me a do-over with my life, as if this was the only thing holding me back."

There's so much Dad doesn't understand, not just because I say all this in English. But he grasps enough. "Running off again and you just want my money!" He slaps the table but misses, knocking the song binder to the floor. "Better if I'm dead, right?"

"Oh, don't be ridiculous," I sigh. "Mom was the drama queen. I told you I didn't want anything. Give everything to Chris! I don't care!"

"What is it you're looking for—wandering all over the world like some damn forsaken orphan—meanwhile, the boy's the one who can't even—"

"Actually, Dad," I cut him off, exhausted by his casual meanness, seeking a change in key even if the lyrics remain the same, "Chris has a very solid proposal for an automotive center, worthwhile and lucrative. A solid investment. You should seriously consider it."

"I will give you nothing," our father announces with a curt wave of his hand. "No inheritance for you worthless pieces of shit!"

"That's not what I'm—fuck, I *must* be adopted! Maybe after Mom gave up her first daughter, she stole me from someone else." A bowl of nuts flies by my head. I scream, surprising everyone, mostly myself. "What do I owe you for what you did to us? Made me go crazy?" I slap the side of my head. It's my brother's speech, but I've heard it so many times I can mimic his performance, surpass it even. "You don't even know what you did to us 'cause you're too goddamn sick in the head!"

"Speak Korean!" he bellows.

I comply, calling upon another tired hit from the family songbook, in a voice befitting a woman much older than my thirty years. I am, after all, only an echo of all the women who've preceded me. "What kind of a man are you? What kind of a husband? Father? You should never have been let near any child, least of all your own."

"It's you!" He gasps, then rises from the banquette. He rips his bandage so it hangs beneath one eye that's puffy and shut, gleaming in ointment. The fallen gauze exposes injury and disfiguration. "What kind of a mother are *you*? How many babies did you send away?"

"They're better off, far from you."

"You took her away from me," he says, searching for his next object to hurl, but he only rattles the tambourine.

I step into the swirling rainbow lights. "The other girl was never yours. Neither am I."

He trips while swatting the air. "How did you make her disappear?" He swings his arms, but he's no shadow-boxer.

Crawling up my arms—the static of the karaoke machine. Liquored breath fills the room. My father's rage dissolves into pain. "What did you say to make her hate me so?" he asks. "Did you tell her about the baby girl?"

I step back, confused about which part I'm playing.

"You promised you wouldn't tell Elsa—did you?" He shuffles toward me, rests his hands on my shoulders. He heaves a great sob, then shoves me against the door. The knob gouges into my back. "Leave me and die!" He falls into Chris's arms. "I never want to see your face again!"

I finally realize—his bandage isn't for hiding his wound, but to blind him from what haunts him still. I stand silent, watching my father plead with the invisible figure beside me.

"Call a cab and go to Mom's," says Chris. "He's drunk and pissy. I'll put him to bed."

My father sits back on the couch, chin resting on chest. When I close the door, I hear him say, "Where did she go? Why did you send her away?"

For the last month, while we've been living together, I believed that the crying my father listened to in the middle of the night and the hand he gripped when I washed his hair both belonged to his dead wife. Now I realize that the face he's waiting to finally see when I unwrap his bandages belongs to my lost sister instead.

In my mother's room, I empty her wood-chest, tear at the lining, and rub my hands over the grain. I need the woodblocks because they're heavier than her dresses on my body and her ashes on my tongue. But I can't find the carved pieces that will unlock her.

However, maybe I can see her if I'm like Chris in ways that can't be fully understood...

I pull the disco lights from under the bed. I plug them in a semicircle with the largest strobe on the wood-chest so it's eye level. I'll jam my fingers into a holy socket, charging my God spot with cubes that pulse color and those that stutter white. If

Chris can hear his holy father, why can't I see my numinous mother? Primary colors tremble in brilliance, bathing my face. I wait for neurons to fire, so I can ask Mom if she notices my efforts or if I'm wasting my time at home, why Dad believes the other girl is real but Chris doesn't.

What must I do to absolve myself for all the ways I failed you, leaving you alone in your madness—or should I reconnect to my child self who believed my friend was made especially for me, when my mind could accommodate so many more truths? If I can reach this place again, beyond reason or reality...

Madness is like a muscle, though—if you don't use it, you lose it. Or is it like riding a bicycle? Haven't ridden one in years—wasn't safe biking around my neighborhood, so I'd settle for circles in my backyard till I got too big and left the family circus. Do bears in Russia pedal in their sleep? Unicycles can't repress their memories of inverse pendulum control theory, so if my friend's black braid is the massless rod in this equation, does an external force move the red ribbon?

But even after this disco-light baptismal, nothing happens. Not even a headache. Seeking visions, I'm caught instead within a shattering rainbow. I turn off everything except for the shivering moonglow of the strobe. That's when I see my friend stepping out of the mirrored closet. I kick her legs. "Stop looking at me like that!" Why does she look so weak, so beseeching? I want her as rageful as me, as my mother must've been. I want her horrific, frightening me with her drowned monstress beauty.

But she remains just a girl—sorry and lost, begging for mercy. So I shove her chest. The glass doors in their plastic tracks wobble. Her fragility makes me mean, makes me want to hurt her. With each push, the rubbery thudding gets louder, more comical and mocking. A sharp crack would be more satisfying. So I keep pushing my friend back into the mirror, warping the thin metal frame behind her. "You're not even the one I want to see." I hit her again with both fists. I shout because making so much noise fills my ears and empties my mind and what else is this thing good for but a punching bag who can't hit back, who looks at me like she knew this was coming, that this is what I needed all along.

"I've done everything you asked, but I'm still broken," I say. "Can't get rid of you."

Her image blurs, her features shift and ripple, settling into another's visage. She's replaced by another woman in the glass.

Finally, I see my mother. A swollen lip, a red handprint on her cheek, fingertip bruises along her jaw. She's no longer the faceless ghost, but her gaze—vivid with dark fury—refuses to meet mine. I cover my eyes and fall to the ground.

Chris comes in. "You done now?" He moves in the strobe light, flitting like an image cast by kinetoscope. He jerks the cord from its socket and yanks me up by the arms. "That's enough." His grip is painful.

"Yeah, Mom's real good with telling stories," he says. "Told me I was special too, but she didn't take me to a spa for that. It's why you're obsessed with her folktales, right? This is worse than I expected. It's all just her bullshit. Before her Korean mysticism rah-rah, she was really into God. Loved how Jesus suffered, told me I'd save and redeem her because I was God's child, his gift to her. You know what that does to a sensitive, brain-damaged kid? Watching her get beat up—'course I wanted to be God's son. Better than being Batman and the Hulk combined. I'd throw myself between them, sink my teeth into Dad's arm, and he'd hurl me against the wall.

"For you," he continues, "she dreamt up some feminist shit, but I was her holy freaking first. That six-year-old boy felt so powerful—how could I let that go? Hell, you're lucky you never failed her. Nothing's worse than having the one person who built you up in the first place, tear you down afterward."

"But you still believe? Even though you remember it as a story?"

"Meh. Dopamine overload. Hyper-religious background and childhood PTSD contribute to being schizo—high rates among Korean immigrants and the famine-fleeing Irish. Epigenetic trauma, yada yada, I've done the research. But I also know how *good* it feels to believe. In other languages, other eras, I'd be considered blessed or chosen. Mom's gift to us. At least, Dad reminds me I'm shit—keeps me grounded as fuck—usually."

Kneeling, I pick up a light cube and choke it with its own black cord.

"Look, I get how seductive her words can be," he says more gently. "But it was all about *her*, always has been. *She* was the mother of a holy child. *She* was the descendant of goddesses. Oh God, Elsa, I'm so sorry for the shit I pulled tonight. Stupid joke. I'm an asshole. I wanted to watch you squirm, wanted Dad to think that all you cared about—wanted to prove how you get everything so easily—you have a new guy, too, right? In Sweden? I was wrong to ask you to stay. I don't need your money, don't need Dad's garages. You're right, won't change a thing anyway. But you still have a chance—go now, before it's too late."

He grabs the original handwritten folktales off the bedside table, charging down the hallway. I follow, clawing at him, but Chris shakes me off, heading into the kitchen. He raises the stovetop flames and sets the stories on fire. I can't budge him or reach past him, as he forms a barrier with his body. With face hunched over the burning papers, he turns our mother's words—his revisions and my restorations—all to ash. Grey flakes drift to the floor like snow. He's crying from the smoke, from so much more. "She has no power over us anymore. Whatever she said you were, whatever she said or didn't say about me, it's not true. You're free, because of me."

I'm stunned, not because of his destruction but because he truly believes he's exorcised her, as if her pages had talismanic power. I see how my brother, so smart and cynical, can also believe in dreams of a holy father as well as curses and prophecies foretold by a once-loving mother. I see the effects of her redaction and erasure of her son. How much she hurt him when she demoted him from her champion and defender—to just another man who failed her.

From under our mother's mattress, I remove the cash. "It was Mom who left this for you. I found it the other day. She wanted you to know what a good son you were, how grateful she was for all you did for her, for Dad, and for me. It's all yours."

Chris takes the money, stares at it, then at me—saying nothing. I tell him I need to sleep. I know what I must do in the morning.

11

I wake before sunrise to catch the bus. My friend is already seated. Clutching my water bottle, I join her. I thank her for showing up, but I don't apologize for the night before.

Looking out the window, she says, "There's another lost girl in your family, not just in your mother's stories. Your father's sister was missing during the war. For two years."

"Yeah, I know. You're part of my subconscious, so whatever you know, I also—"

"Your father was fourteen when he ran away from home. Same as you when you went off to boarding school."

"OK—don't remember him being that young. Must be buried pretty deep."

"When he discovered his father had a second wife and family in Seoul, he ran off to work for the GIs. One day, your grandfather came to the army camp and asked for his son. He waited for many hours in the dirt road outside the base. Finally, your father emerged. Your grandfather said, 'We've lost your sister. Come help me find her.' They left together at once.

"She'd been missing for a year before your grandfather enlisted his son's help. They found her after another year. Afterward, your father returned to work for the GIs, never forgiving his father for the many wives. When your grandfather died, leaving his wealth to his third wife, your father, as eldest son, disowned his half-siblings and the younger wives, declaring himself head of the house and his mother as first and only wife. He vowed never to repeat the sins of his father."

"So he indulged in other vices? Saved his violence for just one lucky woman?"

"He never abandoned his family or started over with someone else. Even your mother appreciated that he didn't 'drink, whore, or gamble' like his father. Your story, though, ends with you, Elsa. No one will suppress or reject the traits they inherit from you."

I never really wanted kids. Rather, I didn't plan my career around their possibility, adjusting goals and settling for alternate realities, like some of my female colleagues have had to do. More than ruling it out though, it was a decision I put off till later. Like-minded girlfriends would whisper "thirty-three" with dread. That was the supposed cutoff year—so much to accomplish before then, before it got too hard or expensive to get pregnant. Biology was ticking against me, but I also feared the ticking of the bomb in my head. How could I pass *that* on? Despite my uncertainty, however, hearing I won't have children from some deeper, perhaps truer, part of me—saddens and unsettles me more than I'd thought possible.

We get off the bus and cross the street to the edge of the beach. Removing my sandals, I sink my feet into the cold sand. We walk toward the water. Her red ribbons lengthen down her back, trailing as they stretch across and widen like streamers. We step onto the wet, dark shore, strewn with kelp and embedded with broken shells.

"You seem to know what I'm about to do," I say.

"I'm familiar. You've done your part anyway. The rest will follow, the story unfurl."

I can't untangle her allusions to our looped folktale, can't argue about determinism and cyclical generational trauma and madness. Besides, she's being so amenable—despite my ugly behavior the night before. So we'll just make this a simple goodbye between old friends.

Before the waves reach my toes, I reach into my pocket for the pill from Chris's amber bottle. Research indicates that if I'm unlike Chris, nothing much will happen. I'll feel sluggish and slow, both in brain and body. If I *am* like him, my hallucinations should dissipate. I posted on forums, queried a college friend who's now a psychiatrist. She didn't think my questions suspicious. We were never that close. Dosage is low anyhow. Plenty of misdiagnosed patients, especially when schizophrenia was more a catchall, have been on it for years without too much long-term damage, mostly leaving them dazed, fat, and complacent.

But I'm not treating myself medically. I'm curing myself with symbol and ritual, the only way to fight mystery and magic.

I take my pill while my friend moves on, her red silks whipping in the winds. I call out, "I hope you understand." But she doesn't turn to look at me or wave goodbye. I didn't expect her to leave me so easily. I prepared arguments and pleas, but she simply walks into the ocean, her movements determined against the waves, dragging her banners behind her.

This is happening too quickly. She's already waist-deep. I grab armfuls of red, tugging her back to me, but the winds fill the sails, yanking me into the ocean with her. Cold water sloshes around my legs. I fall onto my knees as another wave splashes salt into my mouth. I release everything and crawl back to shore. The winds stop. The silk darkens and shrivels into ribbons twisting in the waves. Her head slips below, all traces of red melting into the sea.

Oh Elsa!

You are not a fraud or failure. This is merely a crisis of faith, and no physicist worth her salt hasn't doubted. The objective isn't to resolve all mysteries of Nature or even just one, and that includes one's family. To seek is enough, is the root of all fundamental science. Even when we think we know the answer, we must revise again and again. The history of science is all about revision, so there's more failure and error than anything. But think of the new fields of physics suggested by our data! So much that we can't even process it all now.

Remember! Every year, we collect enough data to fill shipping containers, those steel monstrosities. We send these by ship to two different locations on Earth, for us and posterity, because we don't know what to do with it all now, what signals lie amongst all the noise.

Also! The neutrino was only theoretical for decades before we could prove its existence. Even now, nobody has ever seen a neutrino itself—we only see its echoes of collision, isn't that how you put it? Faith in pursuit, over generations, has brought us here. All effort to seek and learn is worthy, however infinitesimal.

And that quote by your darling American Feynman—"If you think you understand quantum mechanics, you don't understand quantum mechanics." Actually, a misquote. Feynman was talking about his mother. Insider gossip. Please do reconsider. Summer will soon be here.

With Finnish-Sami love,

Linnea

E–

I had no idea what you've been going through. I've been a shitty friend. I'm sorry.

Yes, of course, I can contact your landlord and explain your situation. My brother can get your stuff from the attic and ship it to you. Let me know if there's anything fragile.

I'll be back in the States in a few months, but I can use my phone time to talk to you now. I'll say it's a family emergency. Kate sends her love.

You don't have to go back to Sweden, but you do belong in physics. No one else sees things like you do.

–J

Dear Elsa,

You keep apologizing for taking up my time. Allow me to explain how much I've gained from knowing you.

For the last several years, I'd been feeling resentful in the Korean department, teaching mostly language to K-pop fan-boys and finance careerists. I cherish my passionate students, of course, as well as fellow adoptees. I know I would've benefited, when younger, from my classes.

But my sister's ambitions for me have made me somewhat bitter. She means well, but... I used to have similar perceptions, that my academic work in Korean literature was not as intellectually rigorous or impressive, that it was merely my longing for connection and heritage. I used to be embarrassed of my fascination with Korean folklore, thinking it childish, mawkish. But why should we venerate the myths and legends of only a few cultures, recognizing how they are foundational to classical literature, whereas those little stories from other cultures are considered—lesser, quaint, and colorful?

I used to believe that only my work in Old Norse made me a true scholar, as if whatever I wrote about Korean poetry was merely an extension of biology, politically fashionable, a strategic ploy to appeal to a niche or dominate a tiny field, or utilize my ethnic background to professional advantage. Others have ascribed so many reasons for my interests in Korean literature, everything besides the simple truth that I find it rich and fascinating, with so much to explore and share.

I haven't left academia, as some of my peers have. And I haven't left Sweden either, for I am Swedish and this is my home and I'm proud of much of who we are and who we could be, despite all my frustrations with how some others define my identity and seek evidence for it. Still, I've compromised in little ways. For many years, I've focused my work in more modernist Korean poetry, letting go my previous interest in folklore. I also still research, translate, and consult in Old Norse and runestones, and I wonder if it's something I can never shed—the need to prove myself by somebody else's metric.

Meeting you, however, has undone me in more ways than one. But I can only chastely expound on one way, within this letter. I'll explain the other ways when next we meet.

Even before you revealed your mother as the author, I sensed the importance of this project. I was hesitant, at first, because these stories reminded me of my youthful doubts—what right do I have to these tales? Do I deserve to see myself reflected? They stirred up old questions I was not in the mood to confront, thinking them resolved long ago. But I focused on your needs instead, which allowed me a tentative reacquaintance that has grown into something so wonderful, enlivening. The paper I told you about is only one of many that I want to write.

We have full right to these stories of our ancestors, even more so because we are of the diaspora. These tales—like us—have traveled far across time and space, to be remade and understood in a new light. I'm sure I must've told you some version of this before, but these days, I truly believe it. I am waiting for you, with utmost impatience. Come back to me soon.

—Oskar

Dear Elsa,

I miss hearing from you. I've even been reading the latest Ice-Cube news, but it's a poor substitute for your lectures. Have picked up a few things, however. Fascinating how a single neutrino was traced to a blazar four billion light-years away!

I'm confused though. A blazar is a galaxy with a churning supermassive black hole at its core. I thought black holes absorbed everything, but apparently these blazars shoot out jets of high-energy particles across the universe. How?

My reading also says that neutrinos from this blazar are "messengers" carrying "secrets." Only a metaphor, of course, for the knowledge gleaned from these long-distance travelers, but I still can't help imagining . . . Much anthropomorphism used in these pop science articles. Helpful but also distracting to someone like me whose mind naturally veers toward the mythic and fantastical. I hope I'm getting some of this right. I'd love to ask you more in person. Until then, I'll try to learn more on my own—makes me feel closer to you.

—Oskar

Elsa,

I hope I haven't written anything that would offend. Still, I'd rather that the reason for your silence is a failing or misstep on my part, instead of any difficulty you might be facing. I will continue to write, so you know that there are those in the Farthest North who won't let you go so easily.

—Oskar

12

Over the next few months, the magpies keep bringing their messages from the other side of the world. I have no reason to step on their little heads, so I let them flutter for a bridge of birds that no one will cross.

While I sleep, the rest of the house awakens to transformation. Chris is spending Mom's money on renovations—new bathroom and kitchen, replacing the carpet with hardwood, new paint throughout. No more black mold. And with his own savings from his hagwon jobs, he's taken over the body shop, first promoting Javier to official manager, this time with raise and back pay. In return, Javier uses his own immigrant network to draw in tenants for the garages: a smog check and a mechanic's stall. Chris also hired a fluent Korean-speaking worker because even if Dad's old customer base had moved on, there were always new immigrants in the South Bay. My brother's dreams for a Korean-Latinx-American auto center is no longer just words on a page, rotting in his trunk. Through the internet, he's also selling off the decommissioned auto parts from Dad's hoarding and finding buyers for the vintage Benzes.

Yet surprisingly, Dad doesn't feel ousted or stripped or carved up for increased profitability. Maybe it's because I'm sleeping in my childhood bed again, while suggesting he take over Mom's room. With a filial daughter finally at home, he's willing to play the ailing old man, allowing his son to be his successor. Anyhow, Dad follows my meal plan and exercise regimen. In return, I've taught him how to stream K-dramas online and bought him every WWII or Korean War movie available on DVD.

"Yes, it was exactly like that!" he shouts. "All those bodies thrown into the ditch, their blown-off limbs tossed on top of them!"

One afternoon, Chris catches me again sleeping my life away. He pokes my cheek with a corner of a manila envelope. "Here, the letters I promised, the ones Mom never sent."

"No need, decided to stick around anyway."

He slaps the top of my head with the envelope, then leaves it on my face.

Vaguely curious and comfortably numb from the pills I've been sampling from Chris's stash, I read the letters. I learn that on one family trip to Korea, my mother tracked down her old matchmaker. Sounds familiar. A few years ago, Chris told me about how Mom had gone ballistic, cussed out the old woman for fucking up her life. "How many lives have you ruined?" The matchmaker replied that she consulted the dates and times of birth and astrological charts. "So why don't you curse the heavens and your mother's pussy too!" But in this letter to her friend, my mother only noted that the matchmaker had intended her to marry my father's cousin, the one who became an econ professor in Toronto. Throughout my childhood, Dad would joke how he'd tricked Mom into marriage. Whatever the word is for "bamboozle" in Korean.

Another discovery—on this same family trip, she snuck away to meet her old boyfriend, the one deemed too poor to marry. Once spurned, he fled to Germany to become a rich man, returning to Korea with wife and son. My mother wrote how they had lunch in a fancy French restaurant. Afterward, he'd driven her back to the hotel, and she'd stared at the back of his neck, knowing she couldn't have tolerated all those years married to those stubbly rolls. He'd had a temper too. "So did it matter who I married? The same man, no matter the face, just my fate."

In another letter to her cousin: "After we went shopping that Saturday, I didn't go back to meet my family. Instead, I went to the old Scandinavian hospital. Where did all the trees go? I hear golf resorts are buying up the old cemeteries, moving ancient family plots—all those souls pushed aside for little holes in the ground. Since I was last at the hospital, it's changed again. Makes me doubt my memories, for they've nothing solid to affix to. Like ghosts, free from bodies to become something else."

My grandmother died at the Scandinavian hospital, the first foreign hospital built in Korea during the war and lasting for decades afterward. Mom told me how in her youth she often passed this neighborhood institution where her mother had died—on her way to university, on her way to her wedding, perhaps when she left for the airport to emigrate, and now to reckon again, wondering where it all went wrong.

I don't know what my brother's agenda was in giving me these letters. I'm mildly intrigued, but fearful of stepping on such tiny wings beating madly to stay aloft. Still, something is tickling my mind—a long black feather with an iridescent sheen.

Then one day, lagging behind the others, another magpie arrives at my mother's house. It's traveled from much closer in time—but from an unknowable land called New Jersey.

Elsa—

I lied. Recognized your mom's name. My mom told me that Hae Rim Park or her daughter Elsa might call one day. Weird name for a Korean chick, so it stuck. When I took on my mom's debts, she told me she owed Mrs. Park in California a lot of money. Years ago, my mom gave yours the name of a woman who lived on an island in Sweden. Only connection I know, Mom worked for the Scandinavian Red Cross hospital in Seoul. For this, your mom gave mine $5K.

Over the years, my mom kept bugging yours for more money, again and again. All in all, your mom sent $50K, no interest. Mom called it a loan, but it was shadier. Not a bribe or hush money, but payment for stories. My mom's good at making up shit, and I think in exchange for cash, my mom told yours about the woman on the Swedish island.

This is what I remember, sketchy though. Mom's batty now too. Pumped her for more info, but she can't even remember my kid's name. Sometimes she yells at her in Korean because she thinks Sheryl is me. Funny thing is Sheryl doesn't speak a lick of Korean, but she knows what my mom's yelling because it's the same old shit I scream at her.

Anyhow, when I told my mom that yours died, she got all scared, freaking out, saying the "Blue Lady" was going to come after her. WTF, must be a Korean thing. She asked me to pay you back, keep the ghost away, but I can't. This was all over twenty years ago, nothing signed. You can't take me to court for this. I'm real sorry though. So here's a check for $200. All I can spare. Don't expect nothing more. I'm not a crook. Just my mom.

But isn't this better than what you believed—that your mom owed mine? Hope you can give this Korean sister a break.

Got a kid and a sick mom in a nursing home. My dad died a while ago, my ex is a deadbeat loser.

—Hannah

I void the check and mail it back with a note saying the entire debt has been repaid, that her mother needn't worry about the dead. I know it's significant, this Scandinavian connection, but I can't see how the pieces fit. So I translate and categorize. I sequence chronologically, chart her letter-writing frequency across seasons. Determine the dates of her Seoul visits and identify the friends she'd corresponded with. The data's manageable, nothing like sifting through cosmological readings of subatomic interactions, but I can't read between the lines.

I collect and collate rather than excavate and examine. But really, all I do is stack, underline, and highlight. My efforts to understand Mom through meticulous annotation look familiar.

Ever since I left home, Dad has rummaged through my stuff, sifting whatever I jettisoned from my nomadic life to take to the body shop and study like some anthropologist reconstructing a daughter, displaying her totems in his shrine. While hunting for more clues about Mom in the body shop, I'd found files in his cabinet labeled with all my schools and places of residence, random trash like love letters to crushes I couldn't recall, old syllabi and term papers, itineraries from conferences and hotel receipts. He'd gone through my college freshman directory and highlighted every Korean-sounding surname (some were actually Chinese). He'd filed away photographs, even ones in which I'd cut out ex-boyfriends. All of these perfectly sequenced and tabbed, like his neat stacks of body shop invoices and color-coded Rolodex.

Pathetic and heartbreaking, our attempts to peer into another life through obsessive organization, aided only with the usual office supplies. Then again, I'd always interpreted my father's OCD tendencies—how unexpected in such a volatile man—as reflective of his need for control, or his response to the lack of it. Wasn't that also why he tended to physical domination? What else did I inherit from him and how would it manifest?

The magpies keep coming from the Farthest North. I let most of them fall from the sky. Their bodies, soft and broken, litter the ground, and I lie in their nest of feathers.

But sometimes—they recover and take flight, slipping back into formation, for they are also characters in this story with their own duties to remain suspended—even if I'm not yet ready to cross. Months pass, but the bridge remains.

Then I sense a change in the winds. I assumed the birds would need to shift to accommodate this, then realized that the magpies were creating this breeze with their tiny but mighty wings, beating the air to stay aloft. A breath sent from the heavens—currents nudging me forward in a new direction.

Because of this or because my mind chafes at being bored, even when depressed, I think about my friend and our last moment together. Right before she slipped under the waves, I tried to yank her out of the water. Until that point, I'd mostly convinced myself that she was an extension of me, that my decisive will could submerge her once and for all. But when I was losing her to the sea, I felt her force as separate from me—both pulling away and pushing me back onto the shore, to safety.

Recently, I picked up my green notebook again. Skipping over my old proposal notes for Linnea and the story translations for my mother, I've turned to a new page to scribble and doodle and let my mind wander.

Particle physics experiments show that matter and antimatter don't always obey the same laws of nature, as previously theorized. Matter particles and antimatter particles are supposed to be mirror-image counterparts, but with reverse charges. Neutrinos are even more particular: Neutrinos spin anticlockwise, while antineutrinos spin clockwise. This is their opposing chirality—appearing as doubles, but not superimposable in mirror image.

All this time, I'd assumed the magpies and my friend would do my bidding because they were figments of my mind—wishes and what-ifs. But I've also been forcing Hannah Kang—as well as my mother and others in my family—into a narrative that worked only for me.

Enthusiasm for the sterile neutrino has waxed and waned over the years. Some experiments produce no evidence, leading the search to a dead end. But then others indicate promising data, resurrecting fervor. Skeptics consider it almost fringe and not worth pursuit, while adherents believe that the sterile neutrino is the key to unlocking a new physics.

Most investigations into sterile neutrinos until now have been focused on neutrinos because differences in behavior with antineutrinos have been negligible. However, in the last decade, detectors have become dramatically more sensitive and precise in measuring oscillation rates. Maybe with our newfound capabilities—refined over all we've learned, including all the assumptions and mistakes we've made in the past—it's time for us to reexamine.

The antineutrino's infinite journey seems to echo in trajectory with that of a neutrino—but from here to there, what if she undergoes more transformations unknown to us? What if it's the *antineutrino* that can shape-shift into the fourth state of being—beyond the Standard Model?

I send my revised proposal to Linnea, detailing how I want to analyze oscillation rates between muon antineutrinos and electron antineutrinos. She's intrigued, even encouraging. Mostly, she's relieved that I haven't given up on physics, just as she hasn't given up on me.

So from my childhood bedroom, I access data coming from the farthest reaches of the universe, collected at the bottom of the world. I sift for the ghost particle's ghost. The work is similar to what I was doing before, but my new analysis requires a shift in perspective—to consider those who spin in opposing directions, allowing them to transform in ways unexpected.

13

My father is more crotchety lately, perhaps jealous of his son's success. I'll discuss with Chris, who'll soon be home. Before calling Dad to dinner, I add finishing touches to my Cajun-Korean bouillabaisse.

But an hour later, the stew is lukewarm, and only my father sits at the table, watching Korean TV on his iPad. "Your mother would've given up by now and let others eat first. She always complained she starved because of me, waiting all the time," he says with laughing eyes, clear and bright, "but she was always chubby. Looked good on her."

Chris calls, apologizing for missing dinner because he needs to meet his lawyer friend. When I ask why, he replies he'll explain later. I tell my dad it'll only be the two of us tonight.

"Good," he says, picking up a crab leg. He cracks it with his teeth, then sucks out the flesh. "I told your brother to do this, talk to his lawyer friend about a will." He dips a spoonful of rice in the viscous red broth. A tiny octopus floats in his soup. I worry it's too tough to chew, so I dismember it for him, dropping the tentacles back into his bowl.

"Something you want to tell me?" I ask.

Miraculously, he dabs his chin with a napkin. "When you offered to stay in exchange for the garages, I thought Chris was pushing you. But even after my eyes healed, you stuck around. Then somehow, the boy's actually turning a profit. That's why I didn't put up a fight when you asked me to move into the house. Figured I was safer around you. Can't trust him. He's cunning—like a fox girl."

I sigh and push away. He grabs my wrist. "Listen, I only told him to discuss the process with his friend to distract and fool him. I have my own contact who'll help me write an official will. Everything will go to you. Everything."

I shake him off, but he won't let me go. "You're a good daughter, you'd make a good wife. Your brother though—don't sign anything he gives you. He told me when you first arrived, you'd stay as long as I couldn't see."

Wrenching myself free, I tell him I already knew he was messing with his eyes. But it's a lie. I didn't know, not for certain. Why aren't I more upset? I've been medicating myself for six months—first as ritual theater, then reckless experiment, which soon became habit. I don't recognize myself anymore. Don't recognize my family either. No more hallucinations, but I'm living with shape-shifters.

"He's just like his mother," he says, "only admitting what they want people to see. Makes them impossible to love. Easy to mistrust."

"What about you?" I dump our bowls into the sink—bones, shells, claws.

"I've got nothing to hide, say everything on my mind. You're like me." He scrapes his chair over the linoleum. "Or are you keeping something from me too? What are you doing all day in your room? Muttering and scribbling and tapping on your computer. I thought you were doing your physics work again, but sometimes you speak Korean. Why do you have your mother's old wood-chest in there? Why's it locked?"

I scrub the plate and the back of my hand until both are scraped raw. At first, I'd only dragged the wood-chest into my childhood bedroom to use as a nightstand, drink cart, and sometimes as a writing desk for when I was inspired but couldn't get out of bed. But how could I tell my father that when taking a break from ghost particles, I also play dress-up with my mother's hanboks, wondering how much I look like her? I certainly couldn't tell him I sometimes wanted to stuff my body into the emptied chest.

But lately, while wearing these silk gowns, I've also been reading my mother's letters out loud, haltingly, concentrating on my pronunciation, to shape my mouth and tongue like hers.

I can't explain this though. Even if I could, I'd remain inexplicable. So I offer the simplest truth. "I don't really remember her, but I still ache for her. Sometimes I put on her hanboks that I found in her chest, though I don't recall ever seeing her wear them. Go ahead, laugh at me."

He's dead silent. I turn from the sink, dripping soapy water all over my feet. He pulls himself up from the chair with trembling arms. "Please," he begs hoarsely, "please show me."

With my father beside me, I unlock my mother's wood-chest.

He wails, dropping to his knees, and reaches for a burgundy skirt. Running his hands down its shimmering length, he says, "I gave this to your mother when she was pregnant with your brother." He reaches his woodcutter hands into the cave to remove the nymph's turquoise gown. "This was in honor of you."

"I don't remember her ever wearing these."

"She never did. I bought her a new one each time she got pregnant. I always wondered if she'd tossed them, destroyed them somehow." He removes the moss-green skirt. "This one—have you found your sister yet?"

I yank it from him, hugging the silk to my chest.

"So it's true?" he asks. "Where is she?"

I gather the hanboks and back away. I treasured these, believing them symbolic of her wished-for life that I could also know. But they were just part of her petty, vengeful scheme to wound him. I don't know if I should be pleased or smug. I only feel sad. Still, my instinct is to protect them, especially the one meant for my sister—who was now made more real by my father's words.

"I never asked why she never wore them," he says, "if she still had them. Pride, I suppose. But you knew?" In trying to reach me, my father stumbles into the wood-chest. He curses, kicks it over with the sole of his foot, and I think of my mother who'd scream in anticipation. I wanted to believe it was her fighting back, a battle cry though she didn't move from the floor.

But when I see the chest overturned, I notice something for the first time. Before my father can glimpse it too, I toss the hanboks into the air—all the billowing skirts—so that they float and fall, smothering the wood in their silken embrace, hiding another of my mother's secrets.

"Please get out," I say quietly.

"I'm sorry. I didn't mean to." The first time I've heard him apologize to anyone.

I usher him out and lock the door.

Kneeling, I push aside my mother's skirts. The chest's nubby legs stick up in the air. I run my hands over the surface that's been face-down to the ground all this time. Words are carved out of it—traditional Hanja characters as well as Hangul alphabet letters. Phrases appear in clusters, and scattered among them are smooth patches, a breath here and there. The letters push themselves out of the wood, straining to be seen. A fine line forms a cross, dividing the wood into four segments. So much dust and grime in the cracks. I dig it out with my nails, then push down the center with both hands. The interlocked tablets come loose. I lay these woodblocks on my bed and brush my fingertips over the words.

How did Mom carve these in relief, and on top of that—in reverse? These are the mirror-stories waiting to reveal their legible counterparts. I press my hands against the wood, but can't decipher their indented fates on my palms, the lines of my flesh and my mother's stories crisscrossing and overlapping.

From the back of the wood-chest, I remove the typed sheet I'd found in the genealogy book that night Chris and I smoked on the rooftop. Though I haven't asked him, I'm pretty sure he created this assemblage of scattered phrases. "Two sisters," "a drowning in a lake," and "many murders committed by a vengeful ghost." But none of these details are found in the folktales I've gathered.

My recreation of Mom's quarter-folded sheet of wood-carved fates includes "Shim Cheong," "Emmileh Bell," "Woodcutter and the Nymph." So my guess is that Chris's typed fragments belong to the fourth woodblock tale—a story still missing from my mother's originals.

But this is a start.

Dear Elsa,

I'm so happy to hear from you. Please let me know how you're doing. I do care about you as well as your mysterious investigations. And though it's easy for me to elaborate on

Scandinavian and Korean artifacts, I hope you can read in between the lines of all this historical arcana—I'm showing off, trying to impress you, in hopes you'll find me indispensable.

Now on to my indispensability: Runestones were typically memorials for the dead, while Koreans used woodblocks for texts. E.g., the thirteenth-century *Tripitaka Koreana:* Buddhist scriptures carved on over 81,000 woodblocks, composed with over 52 million characters. Each block measuring about 25 x 70 cm. Also interesting: wood preparation. Birchwood soaked in seawater for three years. Blocks cut and boiled in salted water, then laid to dry in the wind for another three years. Only then ready to be carved with characters in relief—more difficult than engraving.

I don't have much experience with Korean woodblocks, but I've seen their printings. Easier to read than Viking runestones because Hanja characters and Hangul letters are still used today, unlike runes, which are a hybridized form, diverging into variants over region and time, all stemming from Old Germanic. Any woodblock with Hangul would only date back to mid-fifteenth century, but the oldest Hanja printings date back to ~700 AD. Runes were mostly replaced with the Latin alphabet around that time, though lived on a few more centuries in Scandinavia. Still, their original meanings and intentions are not easy to pin down.

As D. M. Wilson states in his First Law of Runodynamics: For every runic inscription, there shall be as many interpretations as there are scholars studying it. His Second Law is also choice: If you don't understand it, it must be magic.

In Dalarna, runic inscriptions were still used as recently as the early twentieth century, mostly carved in wood. Some traditions don't die off easily; some are revived, reclaimed...

E—

It's early dawn. Hint of light at the horizon. Sun's coming back soon. We're all giddy, some of us on the verge of tears. I knew the sun would return, but sometimes it feels like a dream I'm not sure will come true. Other times, I feel my skin tingling, and my body turns toward the point where darkness is melting away. Looking forward to the most beautiful sunrise of my life.

I admire you for forging ahead with sterile neutrinos—never took you as a pioneer, though of course, you are in many ways. I'll put you in touch with some physicists I know at MiniBooNE who might be doing something with antineutrinos soon.

Regarding the guy—don't be embarrassed you asked him to wait for you. I'm proud of you. What's more powerful than a woman who knows what she wants and goes after it? I used to think that us wintering over would give our relationship a real shot, but no. I never felt chosen by you, not like how I feel with Kate. You were always up-front about it though. No hard feelings.

Next time around, like when you go back for the guy, I hope you'll feel more comfortable in Sweden. This might help: no Swede feels comfortable in their skin, not in social situations. So don't assimilate too much. Besides, being around you is like a holiday from Swedish-ness. Tact is overrated. Your presence is more bracing.

Good luck with everything. Don't worry about the country. It's only geography. People like us shouldn't be limited by borders, not when it comes to love and physics.

—J

Oskar,

It occurred to me, by your description of woodblock preparation, that a decent source could be wood harvested from a shipwreck on shore. Also, I'd like to show you something in person—soon.

—Me

14

In the darkened loft, Chris sits in our father's armchair. An old boxing match plays on ESPN Classic. In ghostly black-and-white with muted sound, the fighters duke it out, the outcome already recorded elsewhere. The old furniture has been removed, but the cubicle walls are up again.

"Why's Dad in the office?" I ask while incandescent boxers pummel each other.

"Handing over the reins. I'm too intellectual for this, should be more than just some rent-collector."

"You were doing really well though." I sit on his armrest. He doesn't look at me.

"You're leaving anyway," he says with a shrug.

"Dad's better now," I say. "You can do whatever–"

"Thought I'd be happy for once. Don't even want the shop. Just thought it was owed to me, reparations for all the shit I went through. Then I got so hung up on it, as if this was the only thing that could–whatever–we'll just be, the old man and me. Hell is other people."

"You can still leave, Chris, even without the money."

"It was so much easier just wanting it, along with being denied, so I could be even angrier. That rage was pure and simple, justified, made everything clear about who I was, what this world kept from me. My anger fueled me, especially in my twenties—who am I kidding, most of my thirties too. Like fuck the world, fuck Dad, fuck Mom, and fuck you too, Elsa. But I didn't notice how it was aging me, making me physically sick—all this rage against the kind of Korean son she wanted me to be. Then I finally get what I want and it doesn't change how I see myself. So what's the point—at least I'll never be homeless. I'm outta fight anyhow—fuck, I'm no Duk Koo Kim, that's for sure."

"Who's that?"

"Seriously?" Chris finally turns to face me. "Have I taught you nothing? Duk Koo Kim took thirty-nine straight punches from Ray 'Boom Boom' Mancini."

"So he lost?"

"Not the fucking point," says Chris. "Night before the fight, this guy scrawled 'Live or Die' in Korean on his hotel lampshade. Everyone heard the little dude screaming in the locker room, punching metal. He psyched them all out from the start." Chris jumps up, bouncing on the balls of his feet. "Mancini's pounding away, but Kim shakes it off, pumps his arms, like 'Yeah boy, gimme more!' Even in the thirteenth, the crazy little gook won't go down! He's up against the ropes, then out of nowhere, tears into Mancini. Commentators go nuts, including Sugar Ray."

Wearing his boxers with a green blanket like a sarong, Chris dances around the carpet, swiping and feinting. I watch him as I've always done—mystified, disturbed, very much in awe.

"Mancini finally knocks him down in the fourteenth. Ref counts to ten, but Kim gets up! Ref pushes him back against the ropes, but the Korean keeps fighting till the end." Chris drops his arms. "After the match though, Kim falls into a coma, brain-dead. His mom flies in from Korea. Tells the doctors to unhook him from life support, signs over his organs so her boy can live on. Someone takes the kidneys, but no one wants the heart—heart of a lion. Three months later, his mom kills herself with pesticide. The ref kills himself with a gun."

"They changed the rules after," says Chris, stretching his neck muscles side to side. "Fewer rounds, shorter count. Dad and I watched it on TV—little Korean dude in a Vegas match. We Asian guys held our heads higher after that. He showed them all what we're willing to do. So yeah, wish I were more like him, like Dad, like all those immigrant mofos. You know Mr. Song who owns the batting cages in South Central? Some guy's making trouble, and Mr. Song grips a ball and punches the guy out. Mrs. Paik got shot in the leg, and the mad bitch drags it through her liquor store, chasing down her muggers. Even Dad—did you know he got pistol-whipped a few years ago?"

"What? Why didn't you tell me?"

"You were in Antarctica—what was the point? Anyway, he was getting ready to go to dinner with friends, some Korean couple hanging out with him. This big guy busts in with a gun, demanding Dad to open his safe. How did he even know Dad had one in his office? Anyway, Dad refuses, stares him down. Then the guy gets nervous, so he pistol-whips Dad in the head and takes off. Dad didn't even go to the hospital. He insisted they all go out to eat like planned. He probably bullied the other couple or it wasn't anything new for them either. If it doesn't kill you—then move on and fill your belly. He later told me it wasn't the first time he had a gun to his head. I realized I still don't know jack shit about everything he went through in the war."

It was true for me too, as I only knew the polished anecdotes he brought out for parties, for the swapping of war stories while gambling with Go-Stop cards with friends. Camel cigarettes and Budweiser cans were littered around them, props harkening back to the GI rations they bartered for or outright stole. As for Mom, I knew even less. The only war story she told in these social settings was how a white soldier had singled her out among the crowd of children, handing her a Hershey bar. The first time she tasted chocolate.

Chris raises his fists, curls his fingers in and out. "Koreans be crazy. I got the crazy, but whatever makes them so goddamn ferocious—I don't got." He plops into the chair. Duk Koo Kim's ghost is no longer in the room, along with whatever wild hope and ambition has been driving him these past months.

"So you're leaving today," he says. "It's okay, it's expected. The natural order of things. You know, with the body shop, I think some part of me needed to prove to *you*—more than to myself or even Dad—prove that I could make something, do something. But I finally realized that I don't got nothing to prove to you—*especially you.*"

I shake my head, mumbling, "No, no—not this, not now."

He cuts me off. "Pitting myself against you, making you into my adversary—that's all on me. You're not like that. I know you don't see me as the family hero anymore—you did once though. But you're not like her—you think I'm OK. I'm probably still the coolest guy you know despite all this. So you go on to your nice life, Elsa. I'll hold down the fort with Dad."

His surprising generosity makes me hope he'll understand what I need to do. "I'm not just going back for work or that guy—I'm going to find our sister. I need you to be OK with this."

Chris groans with his entire body. "Oh Elsa, don't go chasing that old story."

"I know who my ancestors are. I need to find our sister, so she can know them too."

He moves toward the bookshelf. Gently, he says, "You've been away for so long, all on your own." He withdraws a black hardbound book and hands it to me.

"I don't need rolling papers. Don't need these either." I place his pill bottles on the table.

"Take your genealogy book," he insists. "We've got two copies."

"I'm not in it."

"Then write your name all over it! These are your true ancestors, not myths. The real women are between the lines. From this history of sixty-some generations, you are the revised version, the latest update. No need to chase imaginary family—you've got plenty right here."

Chris flips to the last pages, showing me two photos of ancient painted portraits. "Mom ever tell you about her? She's our ancestress on Dad's side, princess from northern India. This Korean king here, Kim Suro, dreamt he'd find his queen at sea. She had the same dream, sailed out to meet him, and married him on condition that her seventh son would take her name, which is *your* last name. She's the head of our clan, and you're her descendant."

"Is it true?"

"Why is this any goddamn less believable than what Mom told you? Look it up on the internet! Our family wasn't always blue collar. Colonization and immigration bumps you down a few classes. Like you, she's an immigrant. Pioneer, expat princess following her dreams."

I take the book, thanking him. I even want to forgive him for burning Mom's stories to ash. But for that, he'll have to forgive her too. I have the scans of the originals on my laptop anyway, and stories know how to shape-shift to survive, whether through adaptation or translation, just as Oskar wrote in his letters. These folktales also began and lived long as oral tradition, passed over generations—stolen notebooks and burning paper can't kill these women.

Chris draws the blanket over his head like a hood, holding the edges under his chin. His chubby cheeks protrude like a baby's, his eyes glow bloodshot. "Hope you find whatever you're looking for, Elsa. I'm gonna stay right here 'cause I'm all out of fight. Wasted it in the early rounds. S'okay, in my own little world, I make up the rules." He heads for his cubicle, then stops. With his back to me, he says, "For a while, when business was good and I finally felt like a success, like a real man, I thought being God's other son was dumb. So who knows what I'll believe tomorrow." He curls onto his mattress.

I turn off the TV, laying the eternal sparring of these spectral boxers to rest. I knock on the cubicle wall. "Hey, Chris. It's Sunday. Why aren't you in church?"

"It's your last day. I don't know."

Chris is wrapped in his comforter, but the soles of his feet stick out—a part of him I rarely see, that I rarely see of anyone. His heels are cracked, only the arches clean. They're inelegant, with stubby toes, vaguely duck-like in their width and shape. But their similarity to mine—the unmistakable sign of kinship—is this what mothers feel when holding their babies' feet in their hands? Tenderness, recognition, one heart claiming another.

"I'd like to see your church," I say. "My flight's not until tonight."

"Service is over by now."

"I want to see the space so I can picture you in it. Whenever you mention church, I imagine Mom's old one, and I get bad vibes. But that's not where you are anymore."

We sit in an empty chapel with white walls and a honey hardwood floor. A podium up front. Behind this, a wooden cross, lit from behind, glowing in halo outline. On either side, whiteboards scribbled with scripture. And jutting from the ceiling, a projection screen tucked inside its metal husk. This could be a college lecture hall, except for the illuminated cross and the piano. Instead of pews, several rows of folding chairs. But what makes this holy is Chris sitting beside me while the skylight above beams a shaft of afternoon sunlight at our feet.

"I ever tell you about my other dreams?" he asks.

"Go ahead."

"I dreamt that Judgment Day would come in Dad's lifetime."

I sigh. "Yeah, you told me that one."

"Also dreamt of my wedding. Couldn't see my bride's face, but you were there, watching and smiling. Mom too. Not Dad though."

"Right. 'Cause this wedding is after Judgment Day."

Chris chuckles. "Somehow I knew we'd live in a good school district. 'Cause that's what I've always wanted—for you too."

"I know."

"You wouldn't have gone off to boarding school, and you'd come back more often if we'd lived in a nicer neighborhood, a nicer house."

"That last dream—it's not impossible, Chris, but you can't just wait for it."

He releases a deep breath, staring into space. "Doors closing left and right, that's what getting old feels like. In my twenties, it was physical, knowing all I'd never be—never a judo Olympian or running my own B-boy crew. In my thirties—never be a filmmaker, never publish a novel. Now it's physical again. Never have kids, never visit Antarctica." He glances at me with a smirking side-eye. "As for what I thought I wanted—the body shop—that was distraction. Would've been better if Dad kept it out of my reach forever."

"But now you can figure out what you really want and go for it."

He laughs. "Oh Elsa, you've never been religious like me and Mom, but you're the most hopeful one, the one who actually operates on faith. That's what keeps you going. Why else would you try so fucking hard at everything, never give up?"

Turning his entire body toward me, he uses both hands to cover mine and bows his head. He doesn't say anything, but I know he's praying—for me and us. I feel my brother's sadness and yearning—he'd break if he had to say the words out loud—but it's OK, I can feel his intentions, his tremendous love and wishes for good things for us both.

After he's done, I sweep aside the hair over his eyes. Dandruff flakes, drifting like snow in an afternoon shaft of sunlight.

I don't need to disprove that he's a son of God. I don't need to say I believe him either. I just need Chris to tell me what he feels, dreams, and wants. I need him to keep talking to me. I want him to know I'll be here with him now and other times in his life. I can't say this in a prayer though. So I'll find some other way.

In my father's reclaimed office, the overhead lights are off. Sitting behind his desk, he slides a bank pouch towards me. Inside, more cash than anticipated for his usual send-off. "It's not all for you," he says in Korean. "For your sister too."

How much did he know of my mission—how long has he known?

But before I can ask or think of my best strategic response, he pushes an envelope toward me too. I withdraw a paper slip, once crumpled, now soft and smooth. In my mother's handwriting: "Astrid Lilja, Fårö, Sweden."

What strikes me is the unusual lettering. My mother acquired her English cursive in university and ESL classes. Foreign shapes carefully copied and drawn—perfect, impersonal. But this name, island, and country was written with a bold-stroke urgency I recognized. As with her folktales, she was writing before time ran out.

"I visited your mother one night," he says in Korean. "She didn't talk to me but fixed me with her stare and gave me this. I returned to the shop, then the accident happened—burned my eyes. Your brother took me to the hospital. Soon after, we learned your mother had died."

On the slip of paper, the letters crawl and skitter like spindly legged insects. I beg them to come into focus and command my body not to collapse.

"She kept this from me until the very end," he says. "I kept it from you for only a little while. When she first told me she didn't want any more children, no more daughters, I was furious. But then she got pregnant, and I was so relieved that when she asked to visit Korea, I let her go. The doctor said it would be good for her to see family. But she stayed too long. She returned, saying the baby had been born early, born dead. My sisters heard she'd given the baby to a foreigner. People gossiped, said I couldn't support my family or that your mother had strayed. When she got pregnant again, I locked up her passport. I saved you, Elsa. You lived because of me. Lived with us at home."

I force myself to take a few deep breaths to quell the rage, pity, and frustration. I can't waste this energy on him. "Did Mom know I was living in Sweden?"

"That woman always had a thing for Swedes, maybe because they set up that hospital—not that they could save your grandmother. But those yellow-heads were different from the missionaries who'd come before, different from the Yankees who came later. I didn't even know when she'd insisted on naming you Elsa that it wasn't a proper American name. But I never really believed she could send my child there."

"Fårö is an island in the Swedish archipelago," I say. But I can't imagine a Korean woman, or really anyone, living there. Ingmar Bergman had lived there as a recluse, along with cows, octogenarian farmers, and fishermen. Perhaps my sister has a summer house. I can't picture her though in any setting because she's not entirely real, even with her name in my hands. *Astrid.*

Hannah Kang in New Jersey had been easier to believe. A sister like Hannah could exist in a rational world where an abused wife fools herself into thinking she's saving a child from a dangerous home.

But with these latest clues—I hesitate, frightened but also intrigued, and maybe even thrilled—a sister like Astrid means I live in my mother's folklorn world, of an imaginary friend as spirit guide, a quest with puzzle woodblocks, a ghost mother pulling strings from beyond the grave. But it also means I'm trapped in a scripted life in which I'm only a player, not the author—fated to dance only until midnight, to fall asleep for a hundred years in the castle, to lose my mother again and again at the beginning of every tale.

"Use the money to find your sister," says my father. "Let me see her face before I die."

"Why?"

"What if your brother takes everything—I need to give her something of mine before I go."

"Why?"

"A father passes on his wealth to his children so that—"

"What did your father leave you?" I ask.

He picks up a sheaf of papers and evens the borders. He places this pile at the corner of his desk and follows with a stack of envelopes. All edges in perfect alignment. I recognize this quirk as my own and loathe this one of many proofs that I am his daughter. My father had no choice in which trait he passed on. I have no choice either—can only suppress, maybe sublimate. Who was the girl I struck repeatedly in the mirror? All this time, I'd been fooling myself, only fearing the madness from my mother.

"When you first moved to Sweden," he says, "I thought you'd found her—someone once told me that many Korean babies had been adopted there. I thought that was why you stopped coming home."

For this name, island, and country—my mother paid Mrs. Kang of New Jersey fifty thousand dollars. What compelled me to apply for the Stockholm postdoc—had my mother's naming me Elsa planted a seed of curiosity? At age twelve, Chris filled out his parents' paperwork to legally change his name from the original Korean because the Anglicized "Chiang" sounded like a racist slur, even when not intended. He'd kept a few of the letters, but chose "Chris," anointing himself a Christ-child even back then.

"Why give this to me now?" I ask.

"If I gave this to you earlier, you would've left sooner. I give you this now, so you'll come back. Your sister wants to meet me. A child always wants to know where she comes from."

I leave the bank pouch and pocket the slip. "When I find her, she'll decide."

"When we'd sit together upstairs, you asking me strange questions and writing things down—were you writing bad things about me? To show your sister?"

I shake my head, but this feels like a lie.

"Do you talk to your cousins in New York?" he asks.

"We email, over the holidays."

"What about your cousin in Washington—when's the last time you talked to her?"

"We text sometimes. We're all busy, Dad."

He scoffs, contemptuous. My anger flares again, as these cousins are the children of his siblings whom he's disowned. But then I see behind him, all the family photos he's framed and enlarged and surrounded himself with, mostly of me. The latest addition—my mother's funeral portrait, draped in black silk ribbon, on the door of the supply closet.

My dad's own cousin used his fortune to build a factory in China along the North Korean border, hoping to find his siblings who'd been left behind during the war. He wished to see their faces one last time before dying. My father managed to bring his own siblings down South before the borders closed. Now, one was dead to cancer, another estranged, his brother somewhere in between.

I touch his shoulder. "Dad, call up your brother and sister. Tell them you're sorry. Offer forgiveness. You're all so old—maybe you'll find some peace at last." In the doorway, I add, "Take care of yourself and Chris. You two need each other." In the rectangle of sunlight framed by the opened door—my shadow self grows longer, stretching toward him.

"I had a dream recently," he says, not looking at me. "A girl who looks a lot like you told me you'd understand me someday. I hope to have that dream again."

Sister Ancestress

A Historical Account

My father and mother, the King and Queen of Ayodhya, dreamt of a kingdom across the sea in need of a queen. They told me I would meet my future husband when our ships met on the ocean waves. But in my dreams, I only tasted sand and salt as I lay among the sea-battered bodies of the holy men on the shore of a foreign land. I resisted the journey, knowing that my vision was the truthful one.

The twenty-two monks who set sail with me bound my body to my throne, which was then lashed to the red-sailed ship that would carry me to a land I'd never seen. Luckily for me, most of what the holy men had knotted to my chair were the loose folds of my dress. When the waves crashed over our heads and the ocean splintered our ship, the saltwater stiffened the silk, and I slipped out of my shell. I swam through the wreckage as banners of saffron and gold unfurled all around me, the monks twirling out of their robes.

The man who found me, the ruler of the Kaya kingdom,

had sought his own vision of a sixteen-year-old girl among the shipwrecked survivors. I never asked him whether he had dreamt me dead or alive. Several sailors and monks survived, but no one could tell who was who among the naked men, praying with bowed heads. The stone pagoda, brought onboard to calm the sea, had made it to shore as well, though broken into six pieces. Even my little brother had not drowned. We saw him floating in the water, his arms hugging the wooden box he'd carried onto the ship. Inside the box were keepsakes from our homeland that doubled as presents for a new kingdom—the hardiest of survivors, a single tea plant and the seeds of an orange.

I married the man who dragged a half-drowned girl from off the shore and into his bed. Perhaps because he'd been late to set sail and meet me on the seas as my parents had dreamt for me, he allowed his shipwrecked queen to pass her surname on to two of ten sons.

I am beloved by my new people. My descendants branded with my foreigner's name now number into the millions. My story was written down in the historical annals in the thirteenth century, more than a thousand years after my arrival, and is still remembered into the next millennium.

But what use is all that when my daughter left me for yet another unknown land, this time south across the water, taking with her as gift and keepsake—the faith and words of all my drowned monks?

Part III

A Sea Unfrozen:
A Family Ghost Story

1

Oskar meets me at Stockholm's airport. I walk into his arms, laying my head on his chest. "Long flight?" he asks.

"I'm shedding feathers. You've been shedding too." I brush my fingers against his smooth, beardless jaw.

"Comes and goes. But if you're the magpie, who's the princess?" For a moment, I wonder if I told him about my mother's folklorn claim. But no, he's only read her stories and noticed the same patterns I have.

"Doesn't matter who's who anymore," I say, "because I've got a real name in my hands."

"You're not Elsa Park anymore?"

"I'll explain later."

Last week, I emailed Oskar asking if I could crash with him for a bit. Haven't told Linnea or any of my colleagues I'm back yet. I'm in the early stages of planning a sterile neutrino analysis through antineutrino oscillation, communicating with other physicists at other detectors. But before I meet Linnea to discuss next steps—I have family duty to fulfill.

So for now, my only plans are to be with Oskar, get his help in translating the woodblocks, and drum up the courage to meet my sister. According to the online national directory, Astrid Lilja still lives on Fårö, but no phone number is listed. I'll have to sail to her island and knock on her door. After that, it's up to her—if she wants me to take her to our brother and father, or fuck off with my folktales. Whatever she wants, my will would be hers.

But first, let me have this short time with Oskar—just us—without the specter of another.

With his jeans, no beard, and his hair tied back, he looks younger than usual. As soon as we're inside his place, before he can turn on the lights, I slide my hand up the side of his neck and into his hair, tugging his mouth down toward mine. Shrugging my coat to the floor, I lead him to his sofa. He glances toward his bedroom, but I keep him here next to the runestone, wanting to rewrite that first night with him long ago, when I straddled him here on this couch, before I learned that my mother died and my sister was here on an island.

I lie back, wanting his weight on top to pin me down, but Oskar holds himself over me, tantalizing and annoying. I sense a question forming on his lips. So I pull off his shirt, and he laughs at my impatience. I remove my sweater, leaving only a silk camisole between our chests. But though I'm unbuckling his belt, he still keeps himself too far from me, propping himself up with one elbow. His thumb brushes my lips while I try to kiss and bite it in place. His palm slides down my neck to the side of my breast. Cupping it, he circles his thumb lightly and slowly over my nipple while wedging his thigh between mine—obliging like a gentleman, but still teasing. My bared arms shiver from the coolness in the room and the distance between us. The parts of me where he allows us to meet shiver for different reasons. The rest of me aches and arches to be closer, so that the heat where there is contact can spread and suffuse.

So this is how he makes me pay for the months of not replying to email.

I've come to fulfill the promise I whispered into his palm, to show him it was a promise I made to myself. Hooking my leg over his hip, I dip my hand behind the waistband of his jeans to scratch my own runic message along his hip bone. Then I finally bring the rest of him down.

Afterward, we lie together in his bed, the sheets twisted around our naked bodies, our long hair and limbs entangled. It's the middle of the night here, but my belly, on LA time, hungers for dinner. I stay awake anyway till dawn, holding Oskar. I want to savor every moment when it's just the two of us.

It's been a week since I stopped taking Chris's pills. I'm sure it was placebo effect, nothing to do with neurochemistry, because I want to believe it's my will that banished my friend and my will that can bring her back. Because I need her—the part of me I drowned in serotonin. I want her, even if she's the part that wonders if my mother was telling the truth, if she indeed created a new reality with her words.

I sleep during the day and stay up nights to revise my folktale translations, wanting only my mother's voice to come through for Astrid. I claim I'm still jet-lagged, but truth is, I'd rather see my friend when not alone. When she returns, I want someone nearby I can wrap my legs around and feel my skin against, to remind myself that I'm the one who's real.

Oskar's apologetic about being busy during the day. I reassure him I need the alone time after living with family. He doesn't press, not even when I show him the woodblocks. I tell him my mother carved these for me. He doesn't ask why I need them translated as soon as possible or why I'm revising. I can't tell him yet until I know for certain which reality I want to live in.

On my third night, after I sneak out of his bed, I work again on my revisions.

Something slithers across my toes. Moments later, a cool smoothness strokes my arm. I whip around and see her, not behind me, but in the far corner of the living room, huddled under drooping palm leaves. Her head is bowed, salt-encrusted. She rocks and moans while hugging her knees. Seaweed winds around her arms and legs, then melts into her skin.

I walk across the dim-lit room and crouch before her. "You're back," I whisper.

She flings her head back and glares with eyes veined in green, the pupils swimming in so much anger. "You're the only one who can see me, speak to me, and you left me all alone!" She looks around in panic, unsure how she got here. She regards me again, and the green recedes from her eyes. She's no longer frantic or struggling for air, but her ribbons sway behind her head like red snakes hungry to strike.

"I didn't mean to hurt you," I say. "I just couldn't anymore—getting rid of you though, that's what really made me sick. But now we're together, and I can be whole."

"Oh, it's always about you! Well, I always come back, Elsa, not because I have a choice. But this time, you didn't notice. I've been alone, while you've been with him." She looks at Oskar, sleeping in his room with door ajar. I study her gaze for malice, danger, but there's only sadness and longing.

"I didn't hear or see anything—you have to believe me. And Oskar's been helping me translate the woodblocks. He's already finished two."

"I was so scared."

"But you walked into the ocean without looking back."

"This time feels different. You're different." She walks arounds the room, her fingers skimming Oskar's things. Then she stops in the kitchen and points to the genealogy book on the table. "You don't usually bring this. Why now?"

I shrug, flipping through the book. "My brother gave it to me as a present before I left." But Chris gave me the copy with his cigarette holes and razor-blade cutouts. Thus, older names from previous pages appear alongside younger generations. Souls migrate through the centuries, mingling with descendants. Sometimes I think I must've inherited what will help me survive. Other times I think—am I really the best that sixty-something generations can produce?

"What's that?" she asks, coming closer.

Peeking through one cutout—my mother's handwriting. Turning the page, I find three scraps tucked like bookmarks. On the paper strips, written in Korean: "brother skinned a rat," "brother hid the rat in sister's bed," and "brother pushed sister into the lake, killing her." These handwritten scraps—all that survived from my brother's mutilation and his flames. The only mention he found of himself in her stories—excised and preserved in his gift of family to me.

My friend peers closer at the words. She seems more intrigued than me, but also confused, even disturbed.

From my folder, I withdraw the typed sheet and arrange these handwritten words into the blank spaces of the page. There's still a lot of white space, but I'm filling in the gaps. Without knowing the story but being familiar with the general structure of these tales, I sequence as best I can. I'm standing on the edge of something, but can't see past my nose. I ask my friend, "You say I never remember you, all these times. How far back do *you* remember?"

"From the beginning—"

"—of the story, right. So which one are you—which girl?"

"Sometimes I think I know. Sometimes I'm so sure. But then—" She shakes her head.

"Who do you think you are, sometimes?"

Her eyes widen in terror. "I'm not even sure anymore.

Lately, I think I'm only a dream or memory—yours—which means I'm nobody."

I glance away, considering what to say. When I turn back, she's gone. I swivel around the room and feel like I'm swerving, falling, hurtling through space—a common side effect of withdrawal. At least the headaches are milder, with less electric tingling in my brain.

My fourth day, I'm googling Astrid Lilja again. An old-fashioned name, popular once more after a generation. So all I find besides her address in the national directory are social media profiles of teen beauties, mostly blondes and a few who look Persian, Syrian, Somali, or Eritrean. There are also middle-aged women of all hair colors. No one living on the island though. No online mentions of adopted children or Korean connections. No one who looks like me.

I've only searched online a few times, always with pounding heart, shutting the laptop after just a few minutes. I haven't even dared to ask Oskar if he knew the name, but I feel the clock nearing midnight, so for the first time, while the lamb stew's simmering and Oskar's on his way home, I google "Lilja and Fårö" and find an obituary.

Gustav Lilja of Fårö was a doctor and humanitarian who'd helped to establish the Scandinavian hospital in Korea. He returned in the mid-1960s and served the rest of his career in Göteborg. Nothing more, but it's enough. I book a ferry ticket for the next morning.

When Oskar returns, I beg him to finish the last two woodblocks. He responds, "Let's pretend we're in uni, order takeaway, and pull an all-nighter." I throw my arms around him.

The two woodblocks Oskar's already completed tell the first-person stories of "Woodcutter and the Nymph" and "Shim

Cheong" in their barest bones. After a bottle of wine, Oskar works on the third, which seems to be the "Emmileh Bell." He jokes that they all belong to the same tale type because similar plot points echo across—a girl stolen or sacrificed, traveling between worlds or dimensions, transfiguring in appearance but remaining true at heart.

By process of elimination, the unknown fourth tale—featuring a skinned rat and two sisters, a drowning caused by a brother, and a vengeful ghost—must belong to this last woodblock. None of it is legible to me, however, because of the classical Hanja and the archaic Hangul—but this last one is most elusive. My eyes can't focus on the carved surface or the printings I've made, as if this tale isn't ready to be understood by me. Or it's another side effect of withdrawal—selective blurriness and instability of text.

So while Oskar works on the woodblocks, I organize my presentation for Astrid. Beside me on the sofa are my mother's original stories and my revised translations. Also, my mom's photos, which I found while rummaging through the house and the shop. I deliberated on which images to bring—which mother, at which age, would my sister want to see?

In the end, I chose the pictures that were most iconic of my mother in my childhood memories—in which she is beautiful and mysterious, from another world and time long before me, in which her youth reflects a graceful placidity, not yet exhausted or bitter. Blank and open, easy to project onto. Let my sister decide who this woman was and who she could've been.

In one photo, Mom poses with a parasol, Jackie Kennedy hair, and floral skirt suit in front of a giant Buddha carved out of a mountainside. In another, she's lounging on a beach shore in a hair scarf, capri pants, and a man's dress shirt tied at the waist. The sand is smooth except for a circle of bare footprints around her.

I hesitated because these are from her honeymoon. Once, I found an album with her wedding photos in the body shop loft. When I showed my mother, she cursed that day as disgusting, while simultaneously marveling at her own youthful beauty. Still, I chose the honeymoon shots because only these featured her alone—not grouped with friends, other moms, or children.

In my mother's tale type, according to her, the plot points that determined her life are: deaths of mother and sister during the war, and her marriage. One time, she confessed to me in a Marshall's parking lot that she'd grade her life a C. Her marriage was a definite F, but her kids brought up the average. The hidden compliment that I was finally an "A-plus" daughter, despite my "B-minus" skills with household chores, wasn't enough to make this moment less sad—because C for an Asian kid was a death knell of absolute irredeemable failure.

My father's pictures are from a different honeymoon. When he first arrived in the US, he came ahead of his family to secure a job and set up a home. He was in America for a full year before Mom and Chris joined him. But for the first month he took in all the sights, enjoying a cross-country road trip while coordinating with friends, fellow immigrants, on where to meet up—mostly national parks and patriotic sites. His solo portraits feature a man with a cigarette dangling from his smirk, while he's dressed in a skinny suit and cat-eye sunglasses, posing in front of the Washington Monument and Rushmore.

Did he first hear of these American Wonders from the GIs he worked for and stole from while he hustled to provide for his mother and siblings, while Grandfather was "shacked up with his concubine and her brats"? Did he plan his itinerary while an English language major at his university, almost failing all his classes because he was busy watching American movies at the cinemas and finessing his quickstep and foxtrot at the nightclubs?

In another photo, one of the more puzzling, he sits alone in the upper tiers of an open-air theater. I can't see the performance below, and the rest of the audience, all white, are crowded closer to the stage. But my suited-up father leans back in his empty row, legs jauntily crossed and arms outstretched, wearing an enormous sombrero on his head.

At the last moment, while compiling my portfolio of visual aids, I tossed in some family pictures into the mix to show Mom and Dad in their later years, including a few of Chris and me as kids from our respective decades. Sometimes, considering how alike we are, how we so easily push each other's buttons, it surprises me that we have no pictures of us together as children.

Needing a scotch break, I cup my hands around my tumbler and kneel before the glass case of his Kensington Runestone. A fake of a fake, but still mesmerizing. So much devotion and care went into its creation. Even if a hoax, reverence is evident in its craftsmanship. And those who believed it to be real—how transformative their faith, turning this rock into something more. As for the real runestones—were they carved for the dead or for those who'd come after?

"I just realized," I say, "how our methodologies are similar."

"How so?" Oskar mumbles from the kitchen, not looking up from his book.

I address my reflection. "For runestones, you piece together an understanding from the remains of a dead language. Neutrinos are undetectable, but when they collide with another particle, which only happens rarely, a blue light is emitted. We use this blue to reconstruct the path and origin of the neutrino. So for both your rocks and my ghost particles, we reconstruct the past with whatever rare glimpse we're granted now. And maybe, if I solve this riddle with these stories and woodblocks, I'll be able to reconstruct my mom and finally understand her." I finish my scotch. "But time travel would be easier. My mom is unsolvable."

Oskar's reflection appears next to mine like an apparition. He's also brought his glass and the bottle of Islay single malt. "Go on, Elsa. I'm listening."

"Here I'm talking about my mom," I say, "making you read and translate her, and now these wacky woodblocks. I'm sorry."

"Elsa!" He laughs. "Just because I don't know who my birth mother is doesn't mean you should never talk about yours!" He pours for us. "I've told you about all my many mothers anyhow. You were about to tell me about yours."

"You've read her—she's more myth than woman. She fell asleep before I could get to know her as an adult. My childhood memories are all mixed up, mistranslated."

He tugs on his jaw, his phantom beard. "Language is a trickster. Of my earliest memories, only a few cry out in Korean, but as I lost my first tongue, many of these became doubtful. Losing more of myself. Not being able to trust my own mind. When I learned Korean again, those early memories resurfaced, while some others remained narrated in English. Removed and rationalized, projected upon the past—though I suppose all memories are."

I nod, slipping my fingers in his. I rarely speak Korean, only with my father, yet in my deepest sorrow, fury, or terror, it erupts unbidden, like some primal force from my unconscious. My inner Korean martyr perhaps. Does she also wear a braid ribboned in red?

He brushes my hair off my face. I do the same for him, and he laughs. "It's different now," he adds. "Less pressure to choose one identity and language and forsake the others. Less need to fragment the mind. Easier perhaps, as some have revised what it means to be Swedish, or at least their regard for it. You may have heard things or people described as svensk or osvensk?"

"Swedish and not-Swedish."

"Depending on the context and speaker, it can be positive or not. Usually, an old-fashioned type may approve of behavior or a face that's very Swedish. Typically, the younger person, maybe a Söder hipster, will praise a brash soccer player for playing in a way that's very osvensk." He whispers in my ear: "Or envy an American colleague with 'no fucks to give'—is that how you say it? I hear it's even trendy to be ethnic these days, in certain circles."

"My brother noticed that when it was my turn to be a teenager."

"I do envy these younger adoptees. They're politically aware at a younger age. They have a larger network for support, not just here in Scandinavia, but elsewhere." He swirls the scotch in his glass, then sighs. "I'd like to think that despite my unethical journalistic forays, I helped in some way to make it easier it for them now, to feel less alone."

"Are you on better terms with your friends whose stories you—you've apologized, right?"

"To most, yes." He shrinks from me and finishes his drink. "Most have forgiven me, but some replied to pointedly deny me their forgiveness, as is their right. In penance, I've become less involved, certainly less vocal. The Swedish media have found more congenial spokespersons to put on TV. And many of my former friends now work mostly in Seoul anyhow—too far a distance between us in many ways."

"They moved back? They chose Korea over—?"

"Not repatriation. They're activists against transnational

adoption. They crusade for domestic adoption in Korea, state support for single mothers, sex ed in schools, that sort of thing. They advocate for very Swedish policies in Korea, the policies that Sweden has always been at the forefront of." Smiling ruefully, he sets his emptied tumbler on the table.

"I was an ass for much of my twenties," I tell him. "Most of this past year too, actually. I'm sure your friends would be more understanding now—after all this time."

He pours into his glass more than a couple fingers of scotch, some splashing onto the table, which he uncharacteristically doesn't bother to wipe away.

I had considered asking him for contacts into adoption agencies in Seoul, or anyone who might help me get info from official Korean registrars. But I don't think he's ready. Neither am I.

Instead, I ask, "Would you want to live in Korea? You *are* fluent and a man. Two huge advantages. I always feel too big-boned and unkempt over there. Same here too though. I've been told I laugh like an American and I'm loud like an American. But in Korea, it's my posture, my walk, even the way I look at someone is totally wrong."

"I *have* lived in Seoul, as a research fellow. Only the Hongdae art students had beards and topknots, however. But even with my fluency, I showed my foreignness. Easier as an Asian man, of course, even if Westernized, which comes with its own advantages anyway. But not for the Western Asian woman. The feminine ideal persists for them too, I'm sure you've noticed. But no, Sverige is my home." He kisses me, then adds in whisper, "You're not as loud as some other Americans I know. Just loud enough for my old-man ears. No need to change."

"Weirdo." I shove my shoulder into him, a bit too hard, nearly pushing him over.

"Not everything is about culture. Many things about you are simply you, Elsa. Your propensity for aggression to counteract tenderness, for instance."

Sighing, I lie on the tufted rug with my head in his lap. He strokes my hair. From this vantage, I don't see the runestone, only the beveled edges of the glass coffin. Close to him, but shielded from the lamplight and his gaze, I'm emboldened to ask: "In your letter, you mentioned your foster mother—I didn't read anything cruel in your editorials—yes, I googled."

"You're wondering why I seem more ashamed of hurting *her* over how I appropriated my friends' life stories? Why fuss over the lone white woman, not my many brothers and sisters?"

"I'm trying to figure out the guilt thing—does it come from them or us?"

He's silent, sipping and thinking, finishing then refilling. But he keeps stroking my hair and hasn't shifted or tensed his thigh, so I wait patiently.

"Many Swedes," he begins after a while, "think of racism in terms of the overt, violent and visible. They abhorred apartheid, good on them. Olof Palme condemned the Jim Crow South and excoriated the US on Vietnam, comparing the attacks to Guernica and Treblinka. But the insidious subtleties of othering and being othered in everyday life—how that distorts one's self-perception, consciousness, even one's reality—*that* is harder to grasp. Mental health is seldom acknowledged here too. For Swedes, like Koreans, therapy is hampered by stoicism, fear of losing face and airing dirty laundry. And the counseling offered by national health isn't always—well, a couple of my Swedish friends prefer to pay a private therapist, an American expat. They like to add that he's Jewish and a native New Yorker. Take that as you will. They conduct therapy in English, actually. Perhaps also why I speak so freely with you."

"I don't charge by the hour. You're giving me shelter anyhow."

"Happily," he says. "Anyway, on top of all this, Swedes would rather not talk about race at all. Some adoptive parents take the stance of: 'I don't see your race, you are simply my child so that other part of you needn't be acknowledged in this reality I've inserted you into. Never mind those around us.' You can imagine then how anxiety and depression would be more destructive, even fatal, for those more isolated in such a culture."

I nod, keeping to myself my own research in peer-reviewed journals of the high rates of depression and suicide among Asian American women.

"I wanted to cut through the statistics," he says, "which, though alarming, do not evoke or haunt as much as a childhood anecdote or words spoken by a parent. So I utilized confessions from friends to show how we are harmed, even if the scars are not visible. I justified that I needed to appear objective, journalistic. I claimed this was best to interrogate colonialist psycho-dynamics and imperialist economics, paternalistic oppression and so on and so forth. Utter fucking bullshit. I was a coward. Couldn't confront my own pain, much less put it in words under a byline. I didn't disclose names, but they recognized themselves and others did as well."

"Why didn't you ask first?"

"I knew they'd say no. But they'd done the work of examining, whereas I had not, so I needed their stories. What surprised me, however, was the aftermath. Korean adoptees weren't asked to respond or provide interviews. Instead, my foster mother and a few others, including white adoptive parents, were hounded by journalists for their reaction, their defense. I hadn't even named her. I didn't want to individuate those who oversaw transactions and escorted babies and matched them with families because they'd already had the opportunity to speak and pitch, to sell and justify. Yet despite my discussion of wider societal and historical issues, a few individuals felt personally attacked. Actually"—he chuckles—"reminds me of my postcolonial lit seminars—how even while we're discussing works by African and Arab writers, a few young white men feel personally judged, as if they are still and always the center of attention.

"But whereas I can laugh at them, my foster mother's response—not a rebuttal in the paper, but a handwritten letter full of wounded feelings—enraged me more than expected. How could she still not see or hear me? Then again, how could she, when I hid behind so many others and spoke on high as if an authority? It wasn't until I was much older that I could admit how hurt I'd been by her response. However, I regret now not trying harder to help her understand, to be more patient. If we cannot do so for those we love, what hope is there? Pride, stubbornness, heartbreak kept me from reaching out. She'd also reacted with pride, stubbornness, and heartbreak in how she read me. I let time pass, and then it was too late.

"With my adoptive mother, over successive holidays, decades—rapprochement came about eventually. But with the woman who brought me here—it's easy to keep her in a certain role, preserved in memory with language I craft and impose. Peculiar thing was, we spoke Korean together—she was my last link to the life and world I had before. Thus, so many of my memories with her seem unreal, dreamlike or illusion, confusing yet beautiful. It's easier to simply leave it all there, in that place, with her." He sighs again with finality.

I sit up to cradle his face in my hands. His eyes are bloodshot, unfocused. His stubble past five o'clock, nearing midnight. I move closer for a kiss, but he only allows a peck before pulling away. We sit in silence.

Then gradually, I tell him about how I've shifted my research proposal yet again. "At this initial stage, while I'm refining my analysis, I'm only working with a small percentageof the data. Do you know why physicists use a blinded analysis?"

Oskar shakes his head no, visibly relieved about the change in topic.

"Human nature intrudes otherwise. If we form our inferences while looking at *all* the data, we cherry-pick or misinterpret based on our ego, desperation, and biases, both conscious or unconscious. So in the initial stage, we only look at a fragment. We work to deepen our understanding first. This stage can take years before an analysis is approved by higher-ups, and the physicist is allowed to 'unblind' the data or 'open the box,' as they say in my field."

"Prudent," he says when I pause. He's polite, but I'm not reaching him yet.

"Oskar, in your letters, you wrote that *now* might not be the time for me to understand my mother's folktales, but that I'd meet her through them again and again in the future. While I've been working with my limited antineutrino data, I've been thinking—I wish I'd worked harder to understand my mom first, but anyway—I do read her stories differently now. Maybe you should also consider how you and the people in your past—the data was so limited back then. You understand more now—you can try again—maybe access more, see each other more fully?"

"Not to be pedantic, Elsa, though it is my most salient characteristic—you had all the stories from the start—all the data. I don't see how this blinded analysis parallels you and your stories or me and my—"

"Yeah, not a perfect analogy or metaphor or whatever, but that's *your* specialization. There's a connection, I sense it—you figure it out. Anyhow, you're also wrong because the stories were the fragments. More data has come to light recently."

"The woodblocks?" he asks.

"And other things," I reply.

"That you're not ready to share with me—including how they all fit together and what it all means to you."

"I want to. I will—just not yet."

"I've not yet earned full access?" he asks with a teasing smile. "My analysis needs to be approved first before I can open your box?"

"Oh honey, you've already opened my box many times—and very well, I should add."

"Excuse me?"

"My point is, knowing I've got only fragments or scraps keeps me humble, makes me work harder. Even when we're unblinded, there's always more to discover. The parallels aren't perfect but—you've been refining your own analysis of yourself, and maybe those you've hurt long ago can see that now and be willing to forgive you? Maybe your foster mother is also hoping for another chance? Even if she hasn't done the work, seems like you'd be able to forgive yourself more if you made the effort. Fuck, maybe I *should* charge by the hour."

"I can't make that first step, Elsa, though I've long wanted to. It's partly selfish because I think talking to her would help me lay claim to my early memories. I thought I was happy at times, but how can that be? Have I simplified my own narrative in such a way that—I don't even know if she's still alive. Why harass an old woman about the past?"

I used to view my own childhood and family memories rather monochromatically, which made them easier to dismiss and move on from. But being home again, despite everything, has broadened the palette considerably. "Maybe, if you had a pushy American give you a gentle shove—you could take it the rest of the way?" I hope he'll smile again, but he gives me his polite, distant version instead.

"I'm sorry, Elsa. I can't stay up any longer. Had too much to drink. Can we postpone the fourth woodblock till tomorrow?"

I'm reminded of how I'd retreat when Jesper got too close. Sometimes, I wanted him to persist, egg me on a little more. Oskar has the same tendency to hold back, and at the beginning, it made him into a challenge I couldn't resist. But now's not the time. I have my own reckoning to grapple with. "You go on to bed," I say. "I'd like to keep working."

Bleary-eyed, he takes the near-empty bottle with him, slipping into his bedroom. For the first time while I've been here, he shuts the door.

I cancel my ferry ticket. I'm not ready to meet Astrid. If she stays on her island and I never find her, then she is both existing and non-existing, both alive and dead, both happy and unhappy. If she remains theoretical, I'll never know if she blamed my mother, if she was the "Oriental Princess" of her family, or the one who discovered she wasn't really Swedish when she moved to the big city and met Real Swedes who kept asking where she was from originally and how did she speak such excellent Swedish, while she wonders why her adoptive parents didn't prepare her, why she has to readily explain her existence to everyone. I don't want to know if she hated me for not finding her earlier. I'd rather her bitterness remain a possibility, not a certainty.

I fill the kettle with water, place it on the stove.

"You fear reaching the end, but you needn't be," says my friend.

I raise the flames high.

"You'll find the truth and share it with those you love. You'll have fulfilled the story and join those who've been broken by it thus far."

When the kettle whistles, I picture the bird that crashed into the taxi. A single magpie waking from its long slumber. Her neck would've healed by now, her skull, no longer crushed. I imagine the bird getting up on two small feet, using her wings to steady herself. When she sings, her voice awakens the thousand other broken birds that foolishly chased after the wrong girl.

Reverse migration, a fluke in the genetic programming of long-distance migratory birds, is becoming more common these days, mostly in Siberian species that normally winter-over in Southeast Asia, but end up in Northwest Europe instead. A neat 180-degree turn away from the correct destination—the same distance, but wrong direction. All this verified by a Danish ornithologist to explain the "large number of Asian vagrants appearing where they don't belong."

Most of the birds die anyhow. A few adapt. But some manage to correct their migratory pattern for the following winter. I can see them now, a black swarm rising off the ground to seek another person worthier of crossing their backs, who actually needs a bridge of birds.

I ask my friend, "Why did I obsess so much over the words of dead women? I'm going to write my own story. That's what makes me human."

"No, it's what makes you American."

I shut off the stove and pour the boiling water into a glass pot, scalding the tea leaves. I carry my ruined tea to the kitchen table, loaded with books, journals, and papers.

Stacked on the table corner are three woodblock printings. I brush them aside, and they fall like leaves, floating onto the black-and-white tiles. I fight the urge to order them, but the compulsion overpowers me. I stack the sheets again, perfectly aligned within a white square. The impulse might've originated from my father, but it's all me now. I claim myself. I can never forgive you, Dad, for how you succumbed to your weakness, but I will never deny you. I will always be your daughter and resolve to use what you've given me for some better purpose.

I pour myself burnt tea, pausing when it's full to the brim, rounded with surface tension, then keep pouring to break it. The tea flows onto the table, over its edge, onto the printings below. Sheets soak up liquid. Most of the layered curse is illegible. Soon, it will all turn to pulp.

"What have you done?" my friend cries. Her red ribbons spill from her braid, splashing off the black-and-white floor. Crimson silk unspools all around, smothering everything.

I step onto a chair and shout, "None of this is real!" The silk billows as though winds are caught in its weave. The flowing red grows more delicate now, like gossamer, but is spun with dizzying speed. My friend is submerged to her waist. I climb up on the table and extend my hand. "Forget Astrid! Let's run away together, just you and me!"

A door cracks open. The red silk contracts into a whirlpool around my friend, sucking her and everything else down a drain.

"Please, come back!" I kneel on the table, weeping as I beg. "I don't want to be alone. Why'd you leave me? Why'd you leave me all alone?"

Arms lift me off the table. It's only Oskar. "She's gone, Elsa." He carries me, stumbling out the kitchen, toward his bedroom. "Your mother is gone, but you're not alone." I look over his shoulder—woodblock printings on the floor, soaking in tea that continues to steam.

He lays me on the bed, but I grab onto him with my entire body, not letting go. So he sits and holds me while I sob. Exhausted, I roll away and burrow under the covers. He curls around me. We're both blind drunk, our limbs heavy, our faces wet with tears.

A few hours later at dawn, I pack my bags while Oskar sleeps. On the fridge, I leave the story reconstructed with fragments from Chris and my mother. The layered woodblock printings on the floor are still damp, and I can't separate the wrinkled pages. So I hang the stuck-together leaves in the kitchen window, using binder clips to affix their corners to either curtain. After writing Oskar a note of thanks, I take a cab for the seaport.

I hope for many things out loud with head bent over clasped hands. The driver lowers the radio music so that my prayers will be heard.

Sister Shadow

(A Reconstruction from Family Scraps)

We were two in the womb, but only she survived the birth. Like a shadow I clung, holding on to her heel as she was lifted out of our dead mother's sliced belly. My flesh was buried alongside Mother's, but my spirit cleaved to my sister. She was the only one who could see and hear me, who loved me. Because of her, I knew I existed.

Then Stepmother came into our house and slept in Father's bed. She bore him two sons. All the while, my sister and I slept on a pallet on the floor, guarding each other. When our brothers grew bigger and stronger, we kept Mother's eun-jang-do unsheathed between us. Worn every day at her breast, its silver scabbard had marked Mother as nobility. The blade had preserved her fidelity—to be used against would-be defilers or against herself, if need be. We hid the dagger even from Father. Sister sharpened the blade with stone.

One winter day, while hiding in the barn shadows, I saw Younger Brother catch a rat and Elder Brother skin it with a kitchen knife. Later, in the middle of the night, Stepmother woke everyone by shouting about a dream she'd had. "Her shame has ruined us all!"

Stepmother appeared in shadow behind our bedroom's sliding doors, paneled with rice paper. Her silhouette darkened and sharpened before she whipped the doors aside and pointed a finger at my sister. Father stood behind her, his tilted candle dripping wax on the floor. Our brothers rushed in and tore off our blanket. My sister's nightgown was stained red between her thighs. She scrambled off the pallet and huddled in the corner. On the bed, where my sister had lain, was a creature with tiny eyes and narrow jaw. Its short-limbed body, curled in and blood-slick, gleamed in the candlelight. The dead skinned rat lay like an insult, stripped of its fur.

No one knew what to make of this defiled animal until Stepmother cried, telling everybody what to see: "This half-formed fetus is proof of carnal sin. The slut has dishonored our family!" Her words transfigured flesh and face, from animal to human to horrific shame. Father said nothing while the servants whispered and stared.

My sister ran out of the house and into the snowy woods. I chased after her and our brother chased after us. I tripped over skeleton bushes and fell facedown on leaves, crisp with frost. Belly to ground, I watched my sister run to the edge of the frozen lake. Elder Brother shoved her onto the ice. She slid further out. The lake top shattered, and she dropped from sight.

Elder Brother walked past me. I waited for my sister to reappear. Then I waited to disappear. But nothing happened. For the first time, I was alone and free. So I stayed where I'd fallen in the snow, not knowing if I even existed anymore.

Months later, when the snow melted and the ground thawed, when the frozen lake became water once more, my sister returned to me, saying, "We've got work to do."

No longer alone, I echoed her rage and mirrored her violence. With our mother's eun-jang-do, we killed a magistrate, then another, for these men of justice had failed to protect our innocence. The third one finally asked—when we lingered at the foot of his bed—"What is it you truly need?" We took him to where the dead rat was buried. He dug and showed Father the truth—not a half-formed babe, but a lie planted in my sister's bed. Father grieved, tore out his hair. The Magistrate executed Stepmother and her sons.

We returned to the lake. My sister buried my feet near the shore, piling dirt over my toes, slathering my heels in mud. "You can't come with me," she said, our mother's blade at her breast. "I returned a ghost, but now I'll become nothing. But you, dear sister, were never one of the living. Whatever you'll become—memory's shadow or a story's echo—will always remain."

2

From a port south of Stockholm, I board a three-hour ferry to Gotland. My pulse quickens when I walk through the glass walk-way connecting the waiting lounge to the boat's interior, but this passage is stable, not at all like the plank of a pirate's ship. There'll be no need for a virgin tossed overboard for this smooth ride.

I booked a private interior cabin without portholes. My only visitor is a woman with a beverage cart. She takes one look and offers seasickness medication, but I order gin and tonics. My third cocktail forces me to venture to the bathroom, where I see three unsettling faces in the mirrors above the sinks. I whip around and crash through a stall door. Immediately after I lock the door, a woman asks, "Är allt okej?"

I manage to say, "Jag är okej. Tack tack."

My accent gives me away. She replies, "You sure there isn't anything I can do for you?"

"Please leave me alone, thank you."

A tiny, imperious voice demands, "Why are you talking to her, Mum?"

"The lady's sick, dear. Come wash your hands now."

When the voices are gone, I emerge from hiding. The three faces in the mirror must've included the woman's and her daughter's. One looked Asian, the other mixed. My story sisters have come for me, as my mother promised. But my own reflection was the one most unlike me—skin blotchy, eyes puffy with sorrow and salt. Was this how I haunted Oskar's apartment, expecting him to translate more than words but also touches, glances, and whispers in the night?

When we finally dock, I follow the backs of shoes through the boat's corridors, over the connecting walkway, and down the steps. Not until my feet touch a dusting of snow do I look up to see where I've arrived.

Past the waiting taxis and seaside hotels and restaurants, I look above their rooftops to the hill, where the old stone wall stretches across. Sections have crumbled. Brush sprouts from the cracks. But the towers remain, having survived storms, marauders, and time.

The taxi driver takes me past the main town, past the coastal rental cottages. He eyes me in his rearview mirror. Beyond the pebbled coastline, grey islands float in the distance like whales sunning themselves on the water. As we continue on unpaved roads past fields of stone and grass, the sun dips past the horizon, and the island mutes itself in twilight colors. Rising before us—church and castle bones, the magnificent ruins—proof of Gotland's wealthy past. But it's not until we reach the northern village that I gasp.

In the gloaming, a full set of giant, jagged teeth jut from the earth. An oval formation of hulking stones. The pale rocks reflect the nascent moonlight. Behind, the dark woods deepen in shadows. The driver slows the car. "The oldest stone ship in all Scandinavia," he says. "Or maybe number three oldest. You want to see?" He parks, leaving the headlights on, steps out with a flashlight. I follow him through the tall waving grass. "For the dead," he says, "so they may sail on in next life."

The stones, wedged into the ground, tower over me. I walk

around them, the pattern tracing the long stretch of a Viking ship, with the front and back narrowing to a point, marked by the tallest rocks. I slip inside. A ghost ship made of burial stones, a vessel for the dead on their ultimate journey. The wind blows and I shiver. The tall grass sways around my knees. The ship is steady, but the flashlight flickers and goes out. "Oy oy oy," says the driver, shaking his head. He walks away, leaving me to sail on by myself.

I walk to the other end of the ship where instead of grass, there's a patch of snow with tiny footprints weaving in and out, looping around the stones. I peer into the forest beyond, looking for the small creature leaving these traces behind. But I'm all alone.

Then from the shadowy woods, something unfolds in the night—silver wings catching the moonlight as they beat the air once, then twice—stretching wider, feathers lengthening. The bird glides toward me, then lands atop the tallest stone. Tucking in its wings, its head swivels to regard me with orange unblinking eyes. A long-eared owl. Tufts of brown feathers, yellow-tipped, adorn his head like Viking horns.

I hold my breath and wait, not moving as the owl judges me. Then a crystalline laugh echoes deep within the woods, twinkling from tree to tree. The owl pumps its wings and sails toward the sound, disappearing into the forest. Something touches my shoulder. I whip around and face the driver. Smiling, he waves his flashlight like a magic wand. He mimes shivering arms, and I nod. For the rest of our silent drive, I lean my forehead against the cool window, hearing the echo of laughter in the distance.

The innkeeper Ulrika greets me in the doorway of a large stone house with green window shutters. With candy-red-dyed hair, she's a tarted-up Mrs. Claus. She welcomes me and calls for Anders. A tall, iron-bearded man wearing a blue sailing cap appears. Ulrika directs him to take my bag but I hold on to it, shaking my head. She waves him off. Anders slips away. Ulrika's chattiness is refreshingly osvensk, but I'm not in the mood for coffee and buns in the parlor. She leads me to my room upstairs, asking if I'd like a proper meal.

"Thank you. I'll eat anything. You can leave it outside my room."

After a hot shower, I sit in an armchair. Did my mother ever hear my sister cry? If she had, my mother would think the softer the voice, the farther away, the safer the girl would be.

But my father wasn't a monster. His powers are few. He never transformed a girl into a lotus, but he did reconfigure his pain into fury, his fear into dominance. Gentleness couldn't keep anybody, any family, any country together. So he cast his love into power, kept those remaining under eye and hand. I'll explain this to my sister so she won't be afraid any longer.

The next morning over breakfast, Ulrika says, "I hope it was not too loud."

Could she also hear the bell's song, seeping from my dreams into hers?

"The foghorn from the lighthouse," she says, pointing out the window. I can't see anything through the mist. "Would you like another saffron bun?" She presents me with her basket. I take the golden curlicue pastry and bite off the raisin-dimpled end. She lays out more cheese and cold cuts on the table, though I'm the only guest. I warm my hands on my coffee cup.

"Are there any tourists on Fårö these days?" I ask. "It's very close, isn't it?"

"Right now, no tourists, only old people who want to be alone." Ulrika sits across from me and makes herself an open-faced sandwich. "My brother and I, we were born there, but our family moved to the big island when we were young." She lays three identical cucumber slices on her bread. "Not much happens on Fårö—very old-fashioned. They still speak the old dialect, one of the oldest languages in Sweden. Usch, so boring. Nothing but cows and pensioners."

"Has it always been like that?"

"In the past, it was wealthy, like Gotland. Trade from all over the world. All of Gotland was very international a long time ago. Our sailors traveled far, and we were very central in the Hanseatic League. Many foreigners come to our shore. More exciting then, I am certain. But now it is mostly for people who refuse to become modern. They are like a museum, popular for some tourists. You are from China? Japan?"

I nod to both. "When was it so international?"

"Five hundred years ago. Or more." She refills my coffee. "That is why we have so many old buildings and churches—the ruins." She moves toward the window, looking out again.

"They're beautiful."

"Ah!" she cries, twirling so that her apron whips around a second later. "There used to be a military base when I was a girl. So many handsome soldiers in pretty uniforms. But actually, it was sometimes very boring then too, so many rules. No foreigners were permitted then on Fårö, or even on Norra Gotland. So many signs in different languages to forbid them. But do not worry, now foreigners are very welcome. Maybe you would like to see the raukar? Do you know the raukar?" She says, pointing out the window at the mist.

"Limestone formations or monoliths carved from erosion over millennia," I answer confidently. "From the last several ice ages." I read about them in the inn brochures. She smiles and smooths the pleats of her apron. "No, I don't know," I say. "Please, tell me."

"Oh, they are quite strange and a little frightening," she

whispers. "They look like stone sculptures, but are all natural. They have been on the beach since ancient times. Some look like animals, some like people." Her fluttering hands carve and shape the air between us. "You can also see the sunset colors on the raukar. If you like, my brother Anders can take you in his boat."

"Is it safe to go in this weather?"

She laughs. "The storm has passed. And soon the fog will clear too."

In my cardigan pocket is the slip of paper. I want to ask Ulrika if she knew the Lilja family, the famous doctor and whoever Astrid is, but of course she must know them. Instead, I say, "Yes, I would like to visit the raukar. Are you sure your brother won't mind?"

"It would be his pleasure. In fact, he often goes to look at them by himself. Some nights, he even sleeps in his boat, quite close to them. I think he is in love with one of the raukar. That is my joke. Maybe one of them turns into a beautiful mermaid at night. Wouldn't that be romantic?"

Anders wears the same blue sailing cap from the night before. Wordless again, he helps me into his boat. I've no fear—I've already done this, and will do so again. He drapes a wool blanket around my shoulders. I bow my head in thanks and stand at the prow. We move through dense fog. It's the smallest boat I've ever been in, but the waters are eerily calm. After minutes or maybe hours, Anders cuts the engine. Water laps against the boat and the foghorn moans. The mist subsides, revealing a vision on the other shore.

Craggy formations rise from the water, stretching into arches and towers, the ruins of some cathedral once submerged undersea. I should marvel at how these were produced naturally and randomly over successive ice ages, but I can't think in those terms, wondrous as they are. For among the disfigured pillars, obelisks, and bones of ancient sea creatures hulking along a bone-white beach—a lone woman stands, a shawl draped over her head and clutched around her body. She is motionless, except for her long, black hair, escaping her cloak to whip in the wind.

I face her, tempted to let my own blanket slip from my shoulders and sail over the water toward her, wondering if her shawl will also take flight to merge with mine in mirror image. Losing my balance, I drop back into the boat. The woman on the beach disappears.

Anders pours me coffee from his thermos and holds out a tin of his sister's saffron buns. We fika together, looking out at the raukar. The black tar of the coffee burns my tongue. I dip my hand into the ocean. Touching finger to mouth, I taste the salt of memories. Focusing on the rauk tower closest to us, I count the horizontal sedimentary layers, but I can't remember that far back. The stratification in stone, ticking off millions of years, blurred into a smooth, continuous face. I see the outline of the whole, silhouetted against the sinking sun.

Bizarre and beautiful shapes built from the rhythmic interplay of time, sea, and wind. I used to take comfort in being infinitesimal and avoided entanglements. The chance neutrino collision is treasured for its rarity, hunted for its secrets, but the continual interactions before me are also miraculous. They create steadily over time, without assurance that what is built will last.

The fog closes in on us. Anders starts the engine and guides the boat back to where we came from. I ask him if he knows the name on my piece of paper.

"Astrid Lilja," he reads. "Ja, she is living on Fårö." He steers the boat toward the dock.

"How long has she lived there?" I almost add: *Does she look like me?*

"Most of her life. It is her grandmother's house. A fine house, but too giant-size for one."

"Was she born—did she grow up in that house?"

"She was born on that island. She grow up there."

I feel the ocean's movement under us, making me queasy. It's difficult to breathe.

Anders says, "Astrid is from the island, but for a long time, she live in another country. When she come back, she live with many children. But now her house for children is finish."

"Is she there now, do you know?" I wrap the blanket tight around me.

Anders looks over his shoulder toward the small island as though he can peer through the fog into the front window of her home. He says, "Ja, Astrid Lilja leave many time in her life, but she always coming back." He stops the engine. In the quiet, we float closer. He secures the boat with rope and helps me step onto the wooden jetty.

"Your blanket," I say, turning to Anders, but he's already maneuvering back out to sea.

I remain, the blanket wrapped around my shoulders. I'm as still as the rauk woman on the other shore. I knew that Astrid might not be my sister. This isn't a setback.

I pull out my phone. A few missed calls from Oskar, texts and voicemails.

"I'm calling you from the middle of the sea," I say. "Between two islands. Technically, I'm on a jetty, but it extends pretty far over the water."

"Where are you, Elsa? Why did you—"

"Can you hear the water? I'm not terrified anymore because I've seen my story sisters."

"What sisters—please, tell me exactly where you are."

"I took a ferry all by myself to get here. And I found the

woman of the island. But she's not my sister. Her name is Astrid Lilja. But she'll help me find my sister, I know it."

No reply on the other end, but I can hear Oskar breathing. So I continue talking, facing the sea. The waves lap at my feet, sending their rhythmic, continual force through my toes up my body. I'm tingling all over. My tongue is light and loose.

"My mother wrote down Astrid's name, along with her island. We always thought her other daughter was imaginary, but she's real. My dad hated my mom for giving her away, punished her for it. Mom paid some woman in New Jersey for this info. Mrs. Kang is scared of the Blue Lady, which I guess is my mom's ghost. Maybe she feels guilty for getting so much money for so little. But it's in my hands now—the last thing my mother wrote. That's why I had to leave so suddenly. I'll meet my sister soon. The woodblocks! They're so heavy and I didn't think they mattered—same stories, right? But now that I found her—would you mind bringing them here? I'd be so grateful. I don't even need the last one translated."

After a long pause, Oskar says, "You're on Fårö."

"How did you know? Well, I'm on Gotland actually, on the northern tip, but I'll be going to Fårö tomorrow. Anders will take me. He's the innkeeper's brother. Grönkulla Inn."

"I'll take the next ferry," says Oskar. "Wait at the inn for me."

"Really? You're coming today?"

"As soon as I can. And yes, I'll bring you the woodblocks and printings, and maybe together, we'll find the missing pieces of our story."

3

While I sleep, waves rock through my body, mist on skin. It's not the seaside chill that knocks me out though, but something like certainty. My mother was also calm just before...

Oskar knocks and I invite him in. He pulls an armchair close to my bed. "You scared me, disappearing like that."

"I left a note."

"As well as an art installation in my kitchen."

"On the phone—I only told you about my sister, right? The one my brother said wasn't real?"

"You said your mother wrote a name down on paper, that your father gave it to you."

"Yeah, there's a whole lot of other drama involved." Leaving out the ancestral curse and my emissary friend from the world of lore, I give him the gist. He takes it all in stride, saying that he'd wondered if there were hidden reasons for me asking about adoption, especially when I mentioned the woman who'd returned to Korea to give away her daughter.

"You mentioned Astrid Lilja too," he says. "That she might know something about your sister." Oskar looks troubled. I feel guilty making him worry so much about me. "What do you know about Astrid?" he asks, his voice catching.

"I'm getting used to the idea she's not my sister. I was so convinced. She keeps morphing back and forth in my mind, from a Korean woman my age to an old white lady. But Anders said she'd lived in another country and brought back children with her—so maybe—"

He's distracted, thinking about something else.

"Sorry I've been such a mess," I say. "After we find Astrid, I promise to be better."

He's still not looking at me, but smiles absently, fingering the edge of my blanket.

"What's that you got there?" I ask, trying to engage him, pull him back to me.

"Yes, of course," he says, reaching for his portfolio. "I finished the last woodblock. Worked on it all morning, but couldn't identify the folktale, not until I saw the cut-and-paste story you left on the fridge. The stories are the same—is that why you left it for me?"

"No, just some things I found and put together—"

"Well, both the fragmented tale and the fourth woodblock evoke a ghost story I'd heard long ago—about two girls from different worlds, an evil stepmother and trickster sons. The girl is chased into a lake, returns as a ghost, and seeks vengeance alongside her sister, only gaining peace when the secret of her death is revealed to all."

"Sounds Korean to me," I say. "How were the girls from different worlds?"

"Could be different social classes, kingdoms, or even dimensions. The fragmented story describes the two girls as sisters. But this is what's most fascinating—what you left in the window." From his portfolio, he removes the wrinkled sheaf of woodblock printings. The sheets have dried stuck together, tea-stained. They look like a single antique parchment. Most of the characters are blotted and illegible, but some are visible in the blank spaces, peeking underneath.

Clearly excited, he says, "There's an old art technique used in East Asia in which a woodblock print was produced by stamping different woodblocks, coated in various colors, onto the same sheet. The overlaid patterns and textures produced a multi-colored image. So these sheets matted together made me wonder. I even ran out to the art store to get some paints to pour into pans, then did my best to produce this."

He lays another sheet on my lap. Clear solitary words in red, blue, or green—arising from the surrounding muddied letters. "The stories are similar," he says, "but when the bones of the four are overlaid—another is revealed." Oskar explains how the common elements of the four stories are "banishment or exile of a daughter," "separation from family then reunion," with "trials and transformation" in between.

"Elements from each," he says, "merge to present an older legend, that of Princess Bari. But Bari is no mere folktale figure—she is a goddess, the patron goddess of Korean shamans, because she was the first to travel to the Underworld and return. She did so to retrieve medicine water for her father, the king who'd tried to drown her at birth for being a girl."

I can't even react with my eyebrows, so unsurprising this is.

"So Princess Bari," Oskar continues, "is invoked by mudang even today, but only by the most powerful. Together they travel between the living and the dead, guiding lost souls between worlds. They fight off demons and free tortured souls. Her story is similar to others in her tale type in the beginning—but she has no true ending because she ripples into eternity."

"So Bari is trapped in her story, trapped in hell like an eternal tour guide until some Korean woman hollers for help? How do the mudang come to be anyway? Do they heed the shamanic call? Or are they born with it?"

"Sometimes hereditary, sometimes not. Either way, the would-be mudang first succumbs to sinbyeong, a 'spirit sickness.' This causes physical weakness, fever dreams, and hallucinations. They may converse with ghosts and gods. The symptoms can last months, years, even decades—sometimes the would-be mudang is driven into madness, so that she wanders the fields or mountains far from home."

"Huh," is my elegant reply. "And how does one recover from this sinbyeong?"

"Once she accepts her role and its powers—becomes one with the spirits, so to speak—she recovers through a ritual that also serves as her initiation."

I nod along, trying to appear casually intrigued. "And how do the mudang call on Bari—how do they travel to hell and back?"

"There are regional and historical variations, but generally, the trance possession involves drums, maybe a gong or cymbals, singing and dancing in which the mudang uses knives in both hands to slash through the gates of hell. Symbolically, that is."

"But I'm not so good with knives," I say. "Symbolically or not."

"Another method I know involves long rolls of cloth laid out on the ground. These are the bridges to the underworld. A great deal of money is thrown on the fabric. One mudang, whom I saw on a BBC documentary, would gather the banners as she danced, wrapping their length around her head during her trance. This was her signature move in freeing a trapped soul."

"How did my mom carve this—even think of it—like your runestone, but..."

"Perhaps what matters most is how it feels to you. The Kensington Runestone has its own myth and history, independent of its creator's intention. But for what it's worth, I believe your mother wanted you to see that Bari only emerges when all the stories come together." Oskar takes my hands in his. "I hope you find your sister, and I'll do everything to help. I'm also grateful you've led me here. Tomorrow, Elsa, we shall cross over—together."

Sister Bari

I was the seventh daughter of my father the emperor. He'd wanted a son, but I was born a girl, just like the previous six. At least, I was the only one sealed in a stone box and dropped into a lake. Even my name Bari conveys that I was "thrown away," as if to brand me, as if I could ever forget. The gods pitied me, however, and sent a dragon king to spirit me to heaven.

But when my father became ill, my mother begged the gods for help. Overhearing her prayers, I volunteered to travel to the Western Sky of the Outer Worlds for medicine water. I journeyed there, married the gatekeeper, bore him seven sons, and worked nine years to complete my payment. When I returned home to my parents with the cure—both were already dead. The water revived them. But my father trembled before my newfound power.

Even now, no matter how many times he ends his life, I can still wrench him out of death. When I resurrect him, I ask each time, "How could you do that to me, your last-born daughter?" I am never satisfied with his answers.

Now I travel between the living and the dead. The gods even gave me a flower that could transform the vast sea into an icy land, so that I may cross it anytime I wish, in between worlds.

I allow some of the mudang to accompany me in my journeys. These women mostly travel to Hell in order to ease the suffering of those in torment or aid them in escape—for a reasonable sum, of course.

Like me—the mudang, most of them women, are also considered of lesser value. They rank among the whores, butchers, performers, and sorcerers—a notch above the slaves and untouchables. However, although the mudang are shunned in polite society, the desperate pay for their services—their abilities to summon deities, to speak for the dead. The mudang wear the clothes of both male and female, inviting possession by gods and goddesses. They are liminal, they are both, they are all-encompassing and beyond.

Sometimes, the mudang relay this message from the dead to their family: "My sins are too great and require more coin for redemption, more gold to grant me release from Hell." Often, the living are satisfied with this, only wanting to be certain that their dead are where they belong.

I admire these cunning outcast women, for they risk their own souls becoming lost and trapped in the Underworld in order to feed their bellies and go on living. I only did so out of duty and obligation, which I mistook for love.

When I come looking for him, my father hides himself in the shadows of Hell, but I always take him back with me. Once, he asked why I couldn't just leave him and cast him out in the same manner he did me. I said he was still my father. While he had six other children, I only had him to call my own.

4

"Good morning!" Ulrika pulls a tray of buns from the oven. "Your gentleman friend went for a walk. Very handsome—and such lovely Swedish! A very fine accent indeed."

"He grew up here," I snap.

"No," she says slowly, "he's not a Gotlander. His accent is pure Lidingö, very posh. Cannot be learned, only inherited."

Ulrika presents her saffron buns. I stuff my mouth in lieu of biting my tongue.

"But it was surprising," she continues, "how he used dialect with me. He must have come here before or known an islander. Do you know?"

I shake my head, not knowing Oskar's relation to this island because I never asked.

"We are very popular to mainlanders in the summer. Right now, not so many tourists. But perhaps you two will see the Northern Lights? On this shore, it will be glorious."

"Here? But we're too far south. It's not even winter yet."

"But you must have heard the news? A great storm on the sun has sent its winds to Earth. Tonight will be best for viewing, and we have no city lights. I thought that was why you and your friend have come here."

I trace the bun's S-shape with my finger. Almost a figure

eight. Eternity, with a raisin tucked in each loop. I turn the topic toward—"Anders told me about Astrid Lilja—"

Ulrika drops into a chair and scoots close. "Oh my, are you, the two of you—hers?"

"What do you mean—'hers'?"

"One of her children, the children she brought from Korea. She brought many to her father's house. Such a lovely house. Perhaps you saw it when you visited the raukar?"

"You mean she adopted many children from Korea?" *Could one of them be my sister?*

"No, Astrid was a nurse. She and her doctor father, they went to Korea with many mainlander doctors and nurses to work at the Swedish Red Cross hospital. This was during the war in that country. Yes, I was a little girl, and it was so sad because we often go hear Astrid play piano. She promised to teach me, but then she followed her father to that country. Many of our doctors and nurses worked there, but the Lilja family stayed longest, even after the war. They helped build the Scandinavian hospital. When she returned years later, I was already married. I always wished to learn how to play piano, but never did. One of many regrets in my life."

"What about the children?"

"When she came back, she brought children with her! Then she went to that country again and came back with more and more. This continued for many years."

"She ran an orphanage?"

"Not an orphanage," says Ulrika. "Can you imagine all the work? More difficult than an inn. No, Astrid was an agent for adoption. Because she lived and worked in Korea, she traveled with them on the airplane. She was like the Mother Goose in the English storybooks, riding the great goose with babies in her basket. A funny picture, don't you think?"

"But why bring them here? I thought the adoptive parents met the babies at the airport?"

I wish Oskar was here to help me make sense of all this. Then I finally realize—how incredibly self-centered of me. Oskar had told me about living on an island with a Swedish woman. Astrid must be his foster mother. What else has he revealed while I've been so selfishly oblivious?

Ulrika disentangles a curlicue bun. She nibbles thoughtfully. "Maybe Astrid wanted to spend more time with the children. Some, she might have known from the hospital. Or because of—we say in Swedish—papperskvarn. Like a mill that makes paper."

"Paperwork? She brought them here because of paperwork?"

"*Precis.* Because of buråkrati—how you say, red tape? This was more difficult then because of our military base. Foreigners were not allowed for some time on Fårö, but the Lilja family is very wealthy with much influence, so the children were not considered foreigners. They were not Swedish, but they were in the care of Astrid Lilja, so she was their temporary mother. She take care of the children and wait for the document to be finished and wait for the new mammas to come to her island and take the children away. A very lovely place to wait, I believe. Can you imagine all the Oriental children running around the raukar and swimming in the ocean? It must look so mysterious and exotiska, yes? But I never saw them. I was here on Gotland, and I only heard about them from others."

"She ran a halfway house." I need to let Oskar know I'm here for him too, for his own journey into the past—but maybe he isn't ready for me to know.

"Yes, it was like halfway, as you say, in between Korea and Sweden. That is what we used to say about Astrid's house."

"How long did she do this?"

"Let me think—I married quite young and moved to Malmö. When my husband died, I came back to the island in

1989, and Astrid was no longer in her house. So there must not have been any children then. She moved to Stockholm then lived in London, I believe, for some time, and moved back to Fårö only a few years ago. We islanders all come back home, eventually."

"What happened to the children?"

"I do not know." Ulrika massages her temples with her fingers. She turns to me with a smile. "Actually, I cannot recall ever seeing them. I can only imagine—Oriental children running around the same forest I played in as a child. I only heard about them—how they were brought in on boats, then taken away again. Like fairy children. Very magical, don't you think?"

"This must be quite different," says Oskar, "from your California beaches."

The shoreline is paved with sun-bleached pebbles. Gnarled trees bow against the incoming tide. I picture children being moved through air and over sea, contained in a jet body, then a vessel manned with soldiers, to be stationed on an island, one of ten thousand in the Swedish archipelago. I hope Oskar sliced his temple on that journey because it would be easier to understand how the cut had been accidental during the confusion of shuttling so many from one side of the world to another. Easier to accept than a rock, blade, or shard, inflicted by either mishap or cruelty, either in the country he was born in or the one he was brought to.

"I prefer this beach," I say. "I look better in sweaters. By the way, Ulrika mentioned knowing Astrid Lilja from way back when—the children—the island—"

He takes my hand but doesn't look at me. "I can't wrap my head around it, how you've brought me here. But first, *you* have questions for her, Elsa. You have her name on a piece of paper given by your father. I wouldn't even know where to begin with her—so let's leave me out of it for now, please. I doubt she'd recognize me anyway, and Anders is here with the boat."

We climb aboard. With me are my photos, my mother's stories and her originals. But the woodblocks, the palimpsest of past and future and its layered destinies—we leave behind. I've also brought back Anders's blanket, but he only smiles, gesturing I should keep it because my cardigan is insufficient. I wear it like a shawl, grateful for this woolen mantle, this armor against the ocean chill and whatever else is coming.

Anders guides his boat past the raukar to the far side of Fårö. He touches his cap and nods to us both. Not until we dock does he finally speak. "Astrid's house is there." He points to a chimney growing in the distance. "Better to walk this path from beach and go into little forest."

Oskar thanks him in English.

"Tell Astrid," says Anders, "that Ulrika and Anders say hello. I do not know if she remember us, but tell her. Also," he says, looking away and adjusting his hat, "if she take you through the wall, can you look and remember and tell me what you see?"

"Through the wall?" I ask.

"I can remember little, but I wish to remember more."

"Yes, of course. We shall do as you ask," says Oskar.

Oskar and I wait at the door of this stately, old-fashioned house, pale blue with white shutters, looming on a hilltop and surrounded by woods. Neither of us speaks. We wait for a spell before ringing the doorbell. When steps approach, I hold my bag in front like a shield. Oskar removes his hat, and his long hair falls forward, obscuring his face. The door is opened by a tall woman, hair cut into a steel bob. Hanging from a silver chain around her neck, her glasses rest on her formidable chest. We must look like Asian tourists looking for a B&B. I study Oskar for any recognition of this woman, but he's not meeting her eyes, not speaking Swedish either. So I ask in a whisper: "Astrid Lilja?"

"Det är jag. Kan jag hjälpa er?" *That is I. Can I help you?*

"Ulrika Henriksson called you this morning on our behalf," I say. "We would like to speak to you, if possible."

"The house is not for sale." Her English is British-accented, more so than Oskar's.

"It's about my family," I say. "I believe my mother knew you."

She studies me with her grey eyes, then glances behind her. She withdraws a key from the wall, then steps onto the porch. "Let us speak in the solarium."

Astrid leads us around the house to a glass-paned room, a greenhouse parlor. Inside, she directs us toward wicker furniture enclosed in a jungle of green. The air is moist, warm. We sit on a sofa. Across the coffee table, Astrid settles herself in an armchair. I shrug off my blanket shawl, but Oskar keeps on his coat.

Astrid, fingering the silver chain from which her glasses hang, punctures the silence with: "Who is your mother and how do I know her?"

"I'm not sure," I begin, forgetting everything I'd rehearsed.

"What have you come for—are you two journalists? Filmmakers? Is this another attempt to tarnish my family name, to shame us and befoul our memories? We were not, most certainly not, in the business of importing 'pets' or selling 'souvenirs.' That is a terrible, ugly thing to say. We were not accepting 'tribute' from a lesser country. It was not 'noblesse oblige' or 'white man's burden.' It was compassion, that is all."

I can't speak. Oskar is silent as well—beside me, but far removed. Taking his hand in mine, I whisper, "We've brought each other here, but only one of us knows her. If we're going to get anywhere with her, she needs to know who you are. I can wait."

"You sound American," Astrid says. "Is this for a dissertation perhaps? Or maybe you are a novelist? I've met some of those, and I don't care for either—scholars or scribblers. I've nothing more to say to your kind. Plenty has been mistranslated about me already."

Oskar lifts his gaze to meet Astrid's and says, "It was not a mistranslation, not a willful one. But I devised my own interpretation of how and why things happened, one that supported my anger and pain, and I arrogantly ascribed it to others. It was wrong of me to speak for more than myself and hide behind the suffering of my friends. It was wrong of me to ascribe intentions to those who—how could I blame you for lacking foresight, when this was new terrain for us all? I was young when I wrote those things. Not at home in the world, not with myself."

Astrid rises shakily from her chair.

"And you were young as well," says Oskar, "when you brought us here."

She moves toward him.

"It was never an attack on you," he says. "I only wanted to challenge your naïveté, your willful idealism, to make you aware of your—"

"Blindness," says Astrid. With lips barely parted, she releases the softest cry of surprise and relief and mourning. She mouths Oskar's name in question, and he nods. She raises a trembling hand to his cheek and traces his scar. "Oh my Oskar, you've come back to me."

"I'm sorry for hurting you," he says.

"They really did that to you?"

"Doesn't matter anymore."

Astrid struggles with her breath. She grabs the silver chain around her neck and coils it tight around her wrist. Her hand turns white. "I didn't know. I should have known."

"How could you have?" Oskar unwinds the chain, freeing her wrist, and holds her hands in his. "I'm not here to blame you, not anymore. I thought I had to be angry to be heard. I shouldn't have spoken for all of you and all of us."

"We thought we'd rescued you all—we were, I admit, proud of this. Yes, I see that now."

"Astrid, not everyone is as kind and—we are not all alike either, in our needs, our loss and hungers—shelter isn't enough, family not so easy to make, love not so easy to find."

"We thought you'd all have better lives—compared to—"

"Better isn't so simple to define."

"All we wanted for you—I only wanted good things for you."

Oskar says something in Swedish. Still holding her hands, he brings them to his chest. He continues to speak as her head dips lower. He ends with words I understand: "Förlåt mig." Astrid's forehead rests over their clasped hands. "Och jag förlåter dig," he adds.

I knew the phrase because I'd used it for "sorry" and "excuse me" on the subway or sidewalk. Jesper explained that this was much too strong for these instances. "Förlåt mig," which translated to "forgive me," was only spoken in the most profound, most necessary of situations. Jag förlåter dig—I forgive you—was rarer still.

Astrid echoes Oskar. "Förlåt mig." He kisses her head in reply.

I realize what my mother had meant to say when she wrote a name for my father. What he wanted to say when giving this name to me. And underlying this, there was another secret, buried even to the speaker maybe. An admission of love.

Astrid holds on to him, weeping. I look away, feeling intrusive. But Oskar notices my shrinking and tells Astrid that he didn't come for himself only. "My friend Elsa came to seek you first. I've been helping her, not knowing she'd end up bringing me here. She needs your help in finding her sister."

Astrid blinks away tears, staring at me in confusion. "How would I—I don't understand."

After being privy to all this, I'm surprised for attention to be directed at me. I feel emboldened though, believing my sister to also be one of her children. Everything's been leading me here. I show Astrid the slip of paper with her name on it, my proof I'm also meant for this island, where I'll find my own reunion and revelation, to be seen and embraced.

"My mother, who recently passed, was named Hae Rim Park, maiden name Song. She wrote down stories for me to translate and give to my sister, who was born in 1976. She was given up for adoption in Seoul. I don't know her name or where she is. All I have is your name and your island. And these—" I show her the handwritten stories and photos of my mother.

Astrid glances at the pictures, puts on her glasses, and studies them again. She reads my mother's writing, looks at the photos, murmuring something like "Miss Blue." Regarding me carefully, she says, "Please, wait here. I'll return shortly." She hurries to the door connecting the solarium with the main house, pausing to look at Oskar in wonder before disappearing.

My friend sometimes called me "Miss Blue." Mrs. Kang of New Jersey claimed to be haunted by the Blue Lady. I must've noted the coincidence, but made nothing of it because what could it possibly mean anyhow? I'm too overwhelmed to puzzle it out. Then taking me by the hand, Oskar says, "I want to show you something."

"Astrid told us to stay right here."

"I promise you won't get into trouble." He leads me to a fountain hidden by vines. Oskar dips his hand into the algae-coated water and pulls out a brick from the fountain's inner border. He removes something, then opens his hand to reveal a toy ship, coated in muck but still colorful with red and white sails. He cradles the boat in his hands.

Who'll dislodge the stone ships buried across the lands? To where will they sail? And did Astrid really say "Miss Blue"?

Steps approach. Oskar hides his toy behind his back. Astrid smiles knowingly, glancing at the fountain. "Come Elsa, this belongs to you," she says, carrying a box in her arms. My first thought—how can my sister fit in that small thing?

Leading us back to the wicker sofa, she says, "These are not the only letters I've received from Koreans. My father was one of the first European doctors to arrive during the war." She places the box between us on the table and passes my mother's stories back to me.

"We lived there for many years," she says. "After the war, my father helped to establish the National Medical Center in Seoul, and so we received messages from political figures and the like. Then I started to work for an adoption agency. In the years that followed, more letters arrived. Newspaper articles were written about us. Many Koreans knew who we were. Sometimes, I received letters from children who'd lived with me. Their first in Swedish."

Astrid opens the box, revealing all kinds of loose paper. From the top, I pick up a few. Some lined, some not. Notebook paper mixed with floral stationery and typewriter sheets.

"But these are the only words I received from a mother writing to her child," she says.

There are a few birthday cards, and I realize that the blank cards I'd found in her bedroom drawers that I'd assumed were purchased in bulk were not all for me. But most of her letters are handwritten stories, not entirely in Korean. The topmost are half in English, with some words even copied in Swedish. The highlighting, arrows, and parentheticals make the pages resemble my more inspired and desperate calculations, when I felt my mind was on fire either with brilliance or hopelessness. Beneath these, the letters feature fewer Swedish words and the English is limited to phrases. In the middle of the pile, the English diminishes. I dig deeper—the pages yellow and warp as I reach into the past. The text transmutes into a more uniform Korean, no longer labored and annotated, for there are no foreign shapes to be carefully copied, only a mother's native longing for her child.

"They came every year or so," says Astrid. "Those at the bottom were the first to arrive. More followed. Sometimes just a single page, sometimes a bundle. This one on top was the last, more than fifteen years ago."

Oskar asks, "No sender's name or address?"

"No, and I could not read them right away. I had to find a translator. My Korean is simple. Mostly spoken and informal, appropriate for children." She and Oskar glance at each other.

I dive for the very first letter. "What did you discover? What did she write?"

"An apology. To her daughter."

"When did you receive it?" I ask.

"I remember it well because my father had just died, and I was so confused to receive it among the condolences," she says. "January 1986."

I was in kindergarten then. I have vague memories of her writing on blue airmail stationery—delicate sheets that tuck into themselves—ready to be sealed, stamped, and sent par avion. Could they have flown here on their whisper-thin wings?

I unfold this first letter. My mother's handwriting makes my heart ache with recognition. She introduces herself, explaining whom this letter is for. I know she addresses a girl because in describing Chris she used oh-bbah, the gendered Korean word that a female would use for her older brother. She also writes, "You are an uhn-ni to Elsa."

I point to my name. "My mom wrote about me to my big sister, my uhn-ni."

"But dear," says Astrid. "That's the puzzling thing. You said your sister was born in '76? I did not bring any more children to the island after '72. Oskar was one of my last. And I was living in Seoul in between those years, only coming back to the island in '78."

"Maybe I got the year wrong."

"Also, I did not bring any girls to the island. They are easier to place with foreign families, so the larger agencies took care of them. My children were boys, a little older. My family—we had influence and the right contacts among the wealthier families."

"Why did you keep these then, if you didn't have my sister with you? That doesn't make any sense at all."

"I could not stop them from coming. Couldn't discard them either. Part of me believed they were meant for this island, that someone would come to claim them, if I kept them safe."

"Did you read them?"

"I couldn't, once I realized—" She fingers the chain that drapes over her collarbone. "The stories are written with much love and struggle, but they are the same, near identical words written endlessly in different languages. An unjustified act, committed over the years, repeated faithfully as though expecting a different result, a different response."

"The definition of insanity," I murmur. "People claim Einstein said that, but it's actually part of the Narcotics Anonymous text. And refining a translation isn't a repeated mistake. She was fine-tuning her experiment, testing languages, recalibrating for the reader." I hold up a few letters to the light and pretend to see something that everyone else has missed. "She was methodical and stubborn—but she wasn't delusional." Once uttered aloud, my words don't sound very convincing. But I push this aside along with Hannah Kang's claim that her mother sold mine a little bit of hope for a whole lot of money.

"There is something else." Astrid slows her cadence. "It was many years ago, and I'm not entirely certain but—your mother's photo reminded me of someone. When I lived in Seoul, I spent a lot of time in the hospital, especially the foreign women's ward, keeping the patients company and helping to serve as cultural interpreter. Mostly wives of diplomats, UN workers, and missionaries, but there was one Korean woman who was a US citizen, and she wanted to be called Miss Blue. This is what the nurses told me. Her baby had been stillborn, but she refused to accept it, and demanded her baby be returned to her. She was about to be moved to the psychiatric ward. It was heartbreaking. She truly believed her baby had been stolen from her."

Astrid continues, "I tried speaking to her a few times, but she was beyond consolation. One time, Miss Blue saw my daughter and me passing through and she called me to her. Crying, she reached for my girl, only two at the time. I held her back, but Marina wasn't fearful. She patted the woman's head and asked why she was so sad—or in her Marina parlance—'Why you "sadding"? That's what my child used to say, most often to me. Miss Blue stared at Marina then told me in Korean, 'You may take my daughter with you. Take her to your world. Keep her safe for me.' The nurses escorted us out. I never saw her again, but how could I ever forget her?"

I nod and keep nodding, trying to jog my mind into motion and make the gears turn. My heart, however, comes to a standstill. "Yes, that makes sense," I say. "Rewriting reality—all that trauma and loss and grief—coping mechanism—makes perfect sense." Unable to hold myself up any longer, I sit and stare at my mother's handwriting.

Oskar puts his arm around me. "Elsa—"

"It's OK, Oskar. I'm OK. This is what I always thought anyhow. What my brother told me." I shrug his arm off me. "I'm OK. I'll be OK."

After some silence, the three of us sitting together, not looking at each other, Oskar whispers, "I didn't know you had a daughter."

"I had her in Seoul. But I was an unwed foreign woman with a mixed-race daughter. Marina was the last child I brought to this island, but in many ways, she was the one bringing me home. I'd love for you to meet her, Oskar. Marina and my granddaughter Karin are here visiting from London. Arrived a couple days ago on the ferry to see the Northern—"

I cut her off. "Maybe my mother was wrong, and the baby was a boy. A hospital mix-up. It was a boy my mother was writing to, and she knew he was with you." I flip the box over on the table, spreading the letters out. On my knees, I move the pages around. "There's a secret code, like the woodblocks. Oskar, help me solve this. Look for a pattern or sequence."

Kneeling beside me, Oskar's hand hovers over mine but dares not touch.

"How old is your girl?" I demand from Astrid.

"I'm so very sorry, Elsa." She speaks with so much compassion that I will myself into stone. "My daughter is not your sister," she says. My mother's writing dissolves. Sentences trickle off the table's edges. Words melt into inky puddles at my feet.

"I'm sorry I cannot help you any further, my dear," Astrid continues. "But please, take these letters. They belong to you. They've been waiting for you. I hope you find something in them that—" She shakes her head, then takes my hand gently in hers. "Both of you, please, stay for dinner? Marina will be back soon. I would love for her to meet you. If you like, you can meet my granddaughter now. She's in the library."

I gather the papers in the box and thank Astrid. I've stolen enough of their time together. Theirs is the true family reunion.

All I really want to do is sink into the earth and not think or feel anything except for Oskar's arms around me while we hide in the dark. But Oskar's already given me so much, so I beg him with my false brave smile to pretend with me that I can be strong for him. My heartbreak can come later, it's already in process, doesn't need another participant or observer. I reassure Oskar I'm OK, reassure him I want to stay for dinner and meet Astrid's daughter and granddaughter. Let's go to the library and meet this little girl who actually exists. I kiss Oskar to let him know I'm still here with him, for him. My eyes tell him I'll fall apart if he keeps looking at me like that—there's plenty he can do for me later—for now, just let me keep moving and breathing while carrying my dead mother's letters to her imaginary daughter.

How morbid to hug a box of fiction that's more like remains, like carrying a coffin made for a lost child never laid to rest, forced to live on in her mother's fantasies in order to inadequately console herself and torture her husband. How much pain did my mother nurture by imagining this daughter? Or was it bittersweet instead, writing to someone who lived free from everything, including reality, bound only by waters from which to set sail in every direction?

Astrid leads Oskar by the hand. It's comforting, at least, that my mother's dream conjured this other reconciliation between parent and child. Her letters brought forgiveness to those willing to receive messages from afar. A flicker of brightness, enough to keep me following.

5

Astrid leads us into the library. It's piled with rugs, and moss velvet armchairs cozy up to the fireplace. But its elegance seems unnatural. The built-in bookcases are stuffed with leather-bound tomes that seem too perfectly arranged, as if for display. I peer under tables for the missing child, but Oskar points to a bookcase. It's a painting, a convincing trompe l'oeil with meticulous details. There's an outline around it. A knob juts between painted books.

"Oskar, go with her. I need to get something," says Astrid.

I twist the knob and open a door. We pass through the wall to the other side.

The space on this side is larger than the outer library and twice as high, with three pillars sculpted like trees in the center. Coming closer, I realize the pillars are tree houses with hollowed trunks and ladders visible through their entrances. The platforms are barely visible through the curtains of weeping willow leaves. Fairy lights are strung up between the trees. Circle windows close to the ceiling are tinted in yellow, orange, pink, and purple—like moons or planets. And surrounding us, a continuous forest mural on all four walls.

The trees are painted in ghostly greys and birch whites. Between them, far into the deep—a darkness so tempting I don't dare step in. Unlike the sculptured trunks growing from the moss-colored floorboards, the mural trees sprout only a few branches each, naked except for small birds of blue, perched on the highest branches. Behind these, the forest ground swells into rolling mounds. Shimmering in this gloomy beauty are ethereal girls, kneeling at the edge of the dark river that flows around the room. The illusion is completed by wraith-like figures in the water—the diluted reflections of the phantom children painted in moonglow.

Kkum-namu—I came across a poem once, describing adoptees as dream trees, planted in one spot of the earth to sprout in another. What would it be like to be in a dream forest, roots elsewhere, but leaves mingling overhead, a canopy of woven crowns?

"John Bauer," says Oskar. "Swedish fairy-tale painter. This is his style."

"What about those big-nosed trolls?" Earth-colored with black ringlets and small round eyes, they must've sidled from behind the trees. They look down at the children at the river's edge, but they don't look hungry, only bemused.

The door swings open. Astrid steps through waving a red-and-white checkered tablecloth behind her. She calls out to the trees in Swedish. "I need to catch the girl before she leaves cinnamon crumbs everywhere."

That's when I hear the giggling—the laugh that zooms from corner to corner then floats and dissolves, just like it had in the forest next to the stone ship. Oskar and I point at different trees. Astrid picks the middle one and pokes her head through the trunk. Something squeals inside the leaves. Satisfied, Astrid stands a few steps away, bundles the tablecloth, and counts to three, whereupon she throws up the red-and-white checkered net. Just as it catches air and balloons, a small hand darts between the branches and pulls it into the tree's crown.

Astrid says, "Karin, could you come down, please. My friends would like to meet you."

"Just a few minutes, please. I'm almost done with my book," says a crisp, imperious voice I've heard recently. On the ferry? I hadn't noticed the accent before. What was it about a certain kind of British accent in a child's voice that somehow hinted at the fantastical and otherworldly?

"Yes, Your Highness," says Astrid. "Is that all right with you two? Miss Karin would like to finish her book first. She's a very quick reader."

I want to climb the tree to join her, simply to read alongside and lose myself in the dream-grown trees. "It's an amazing playroom," I say.

"It's not a playroom," says Oskar with mock-huffiness. "It's the library." He leads me to the circle of large boulders. Shelves are carved into them, with storybooks stacked low enough for a child's reach. Around us, plump red toadstools, spotted with white, wide enough to sit on. I want to rest my head on its pillow-cap and sleep. It matters a tiny bit less that I've journeyed this far to find my sister long gone, for here it seems that everything is false anyway, with some illusions more comforting than others. "Astrid," says Oskar, "something looks different."

"The walls have been repainted. My granddaughter insisted. I helped her, though she did most of it herself. She doesn't like the yellow hair that Bauer favored for his princesses, so she painted their heads auburn to match her own. That one is painted sable to match her mother's. My silver can be found on the troll queen, of course. The one with the very wide hips."

Astrid leads us to a far corner. Next to the draped organza waterfall is a cluster of thick trees, protruding from the wall and hollowed with shelves. "Oskar, kom," she says. She withdraws a book from the trunk—Oskar's collection of folktales. "I loved these stories. I read them to Karin. But why Engelska? Korean or Swedish, I'd understand, but English?"

"Broader readership," he says in a joking tone. Then seriously, "It's neither here nor there."

Astrid nods with a sad smile. She turns to me. "As for stories, your mother is quite powerful. I failed to give her stories to her child, so she sent her other daughter to retrieve them and deliver the letters to the rightful reader. How amazing she is to move you like this, even in death. And how kind, to lead Oskar to me as well." Her eyes well with tears. "I must get started on our dinner. I'll leave you, Oskar, to host Elsa for now."

A little girl peeks out from the parted curtain of willow branches. "I can't read some of these words," she says. "I need someone to help. Who are you two?"

"My name is Oskar, and this is my friend Elsa."

"Elsa, can you read English?" asks the girl.

"Yes," I reply.

"Then you may come up."

Astrid nudges me on. I duck into the hole in the trunk. When I stand, the tight space and darkness give me a moment's reprieve. I can confront the truth in private—that my sister is long dead—with no one to watch or pity me.

"Are you coming up or not?" asks the little voice.

I look up. The trunk stretches higher, the walls close in. The circle of light shrinks to a pinprick flare. I'm at the bottom of the ocean. Or sealed in a stone box or melted into a bell. I can't remember who I was and what I'm supposed to do, but I put my hands out and find ladder rungs. Someone is waiting for me. So I climb, grateful for an action I can do reasonably well. I move my arms and legs and keep my focus on the light above.

As I climb, I remember how my mother would whisk me to an art museum or a botanical garden and direct my gaze, sometimes forcefully—"look closer, fill your eyes"—as though I could soak up enough beauty to counteract the violence I'd seen just hours before at home. She'd take me on these trips by herself, buying me a souvenir, even though I didn't want to keep the memories because I couldn't bear any more of her sadness. Her rigid profile with its unblinking stare, lit by the red brake lights in front of us as we waited in a line of exiting cars after a symphony concert, was more vivid than the music, because she was trying so hard to be a good mother while I was biding my time until I could get away. She couldn't grant me my wish for escape, but she'd granted it to her other daughter, who never lived in our world, but was never forgotten. Our mother was a good mother to her as well.

Mom is gone, but I'm still here. If I had the chance, I could be a good sister. Then I remember—my friend has called me Miss Blue a few times, in a voice weighted with longing. I realize that while my mother's letters were never answered, I can communicate with my sister because I've inherited all the stories before me, even the ones I asked for but never got to hear.

"Uhm-ma, what was her name—my sister who died when she was a baby?"

"Don't fill your mind with such sad things."

"You told me, but I forgot."

"I'll tell you the other name I have for her, for her other life. Her secret name is . . ."

"What kind of name is that?" It didn't sound Korean, didn't sound like anything I'd heard on TV or at preschool. "Say it again for me?"

"If you say her name too many times, she'll disappear. So I'll write it down for you." In the greyish margin of her newspaper, she wrote some letters.

"But I can't read yet."

She tore off the strip and balled it in her hand, then blew into her fist and showed me her empty palm. "If you want her to stay with us, you must keep her secret. Now that you've heard her name and seen it, she will always be a part of you and you won't ever need to ask me again."

When I reach the top, I see my sister. She's sitting beside the little girl. The story isn't about me after all. My sister is Shim Cheong, the lotus, seeded with other people's memories, cast from one dimension to another, while only hoping to be seen.

"Hello Elsa, you've found me again," she says.

"I'm sorry I'm late." We can't embrace, but I wrap my arms around her anyway.

"I shouldn't have doubted you. You always find me."

"She's been waiting for you," says Karin.

"What? How can she see you?" I ask my sister. "What is she?"

"I'm Karin. And your sister is one of my raukar friends. Not many can know about the raukar. I suppose you are an expection."

"You mean exception."

"I'm only seven," she says.

"I don't understand," I say, turning to my sister. "How can she—is she like us?"

"I don't understand either," my sister replies. "She saw me while I stood on the shore and invited me here. But who cares? Let's just be together for now. Maybe we are the expections."

My sister and I laugh together, setting the leaves of our tree aflutter.

6

Our first night on Fårö, all of us, including my sister, venture outside to look at the Aurora Borealis. As Ulrika promised, a global forecast has announced a geomagnetic storm watch with the potential for supercharged auroras, owing to strong solar flares unleashed toward Earth. The lights will be visible in places as far south as Wales and Pennsylvania.

Fårö has so few people, especially on this northern tip, that we are alone on the beach. Marina points out the constellations that she grew up with to her daughter. Astrid leans onto Oskar's arm. In the starry sky, near the horizon, celestial green whispers above the dark sea.

"Is that it?" asks Karin. "I can barely see it."

"Yes, dear," says Marina, "just wait for it to grow."

"It's getting brighter. Still, I only see squiggly lines. Don't know what all the fuss is—looks like your cursive, Mum. And Dad says no one can read your writing."

"Funny. I was thinking it looks like the art you leave behind everywhere. Just the other day, while hoovering, I found your lovely graffiti in purple marker behind my headboard. And yellow handprints under the sofa, on the newly polished hardwood."

"I'm leaving behind secret messages for future architects."

"Archaeologists, dear. Not architects."

Karin hops up and down, flapping her arms like wings. "Mummy! Look, look!" Marina crouches beside her so they are eye-level, looking up at the sky from the same angle. Karin turns around and to Astrid says, "Mormor! Ser du?"

Astrid crouches beside her on the other side. "Ja, Karin. Jag ser—fantastiskt." *I do see*, says Astrid, and *how wonderful*, as she keeps her gaze on Karin's face, watching the Northern Lights reflect their beauty in her granddaughter's eyes.

Oskar sidles up next to me and slips his hand in mine. On my other side is my sister, who seems more luminous lately. Or maybe she's always been, but I never noticed before.

I know that the auroras are solar-charged particles interacting with nitrogen and oxygen in the atmosphere, but I ask Oskar what people in the past believed them to be. I ask for their stories, how they understood their world and how they wanted to explain it to their children.

"The Old Norse sagas mention them a few times," he whispers while the lights dance, "but without an accompanying story. Curiously, although there's no corroboration in the old texts, *Bulfinch's Mythology* claims that in Norse myth, the lights are the flashing reflections of the Valkyries' shields and armor as they race on their horses toward Valhalla."

"Really?" asks Karin.

"Yes, and in more recent folklore of northern Sweden, the lights were believed to be reflections cast in the sky from huge schools of herring, swimming close to the surface."

"Of course." I stifle laughter. "Herring. This country." Oskar shoots me a playful warning look.

"For many myths," he continues, "the teller tries to understand the inexplicable with what's familiar or most important in her everyday life. For many in the north, there was nothing more beautiful, more life-affirming and sustaining than a giant school of herring."

Astrid turns to me and nods. "I agree it lacks poetry, Elsa. The Finns believed the lights to be warring angels, bearing torches, I believe. And the Danes saw a bevy of swans, flying north, trapped in the ice and flapping their great wings to break free."

"Oh, so it's poetry you all want. Well, I only have a PhD." Oskar kneels beside Karin. "The Sami call the aurora the *guovsahasat*, meaning 'the light that can be heard.' They believe that the lights are the souls of their ancestors. So when the lights are bright, people should be quiet and still, and girls must keep their heads covered, lest the forces get tangled in their hair."

Karin squeals. Her little hands fly to the top of her head.

"I won't let any forces near you, love," says Marina.

"But most wondrous of all," says Oskar, "some of the Sami believe they can make the heavenly lights change their pattern. They say that certain lights signal the end of a warm spell or promise a coming chill, so they call up to the skies, 'Northern Lights—Flutter! Flutter!' And if the people's spirits are strong enough to carry their voices, the lights will indeed move, making room for whatever it is their hearts desire." Oskar glances at me, and I smile.

Then my sister steps forward ahead of us all. She stands on the shore, raises her hands then waves them across the sky, rippling her graceful fingers. Karin runs forward to stand beside her and shadow her gestures, then jumps up and down, shouting, "Flutter! Flutter! Flutter!"

Suddenly, the sheer green ribbon across the horizon sails upward, quivering more frantically across the sky—its double, mirrored in the sea below. The ribbon slows its dance, then exhales a smoky green arc like an echo, then another and another. These merge into a billowing curtain, its hem flaring in fuchsia. Everything unfurls toward the shore—sky and sea united.

We all see this, but only I can hear the light. Not a ringing or whistling, but dizzying cymbals and syncopated drums. Faster, more rhythmic, pulse-quickening, then nothing. Nobody else reacts, not even my sister. But I'm not afraid. It's music to my ears.

Before we gathered on the shore, I sifted through my mother's words and found a letter, more recent than the others, about her revision for "The Tale of Two Sisters."

She wrote in Korean, with difficult phrases annotated in English—parenthetical and asterisked definitions, copied out from a dictionary, just as she used to write for me in cards and letters when I was in junior high. Compared to the other letters my mom sent to the island during this period, the extensive use of Korean is notable—as if she had to write down her thoughts, regardless of the reader's fluency. The gist of it was:

"I used to overhear your little sister speaking to you in the bathtub, under her bed, in the closet. Somehow, she could see and hear you. I don't hear Elsa talking to you anymore—perhaps because of me—but she is learning many new things, far beyond me. I wonder if she will surpass us all and figure out how to trick fate—yours and hers. I certainly hope she appreciates how I drive her around to all her extra lessons and classes, wheedling your father for the money to pay for them. Though I admit, it's also fun to use her as an excuse to a take a more roundabout way—sneak off to swim laps at the gym or browse at the mall or get my hair done. Never expected to have such a clever daughter. Let's see how far she can take it—though I do hope she develops some common sense along the way.

"So I've changed this 'Tale of Two Sisters' from before. Maybe in traveling to such far-flung places—maybe with

Elsa studying the death and rebirth of stars and whatever else she dreams about—you two will be able to rewrite your destinies. So never mind the old versions. In this new one, though you'll never be in the same world, you'll always be together."

More than once in her life, my mother believed she could make the heavens transfigure their design and pattern, reorder the words and redirect the pages. But her greater faith lay in me. She dreamt up an origin myth, trying to understand how her life came to be and how it couldn't change, how she was connected to her mother and sister and daughters. She wrote with faith, that where she was biased and wrong, her daughters would forgive and correct; where she failed to understand herself, her daughters would read between the lines and know her anyway, know her intentions.

I'm more like her than I realized. Faith in future generations underlies all we do, just like Linnea wrote. I picture the shipping containers full of subatomic astronomical data leaving the shores of Antarctica, two copies sent to two separate places on Earth, to be preserved for future scientists who'll know more than we do, who'll build on what we leave behind, and understand what we cannot. And even though I might've initially run toward science for the explanations, I'm sticking around for the unknown.

I look at all of us on shore. A universe of mystery in each person. It doesn't frighten me; it leaves me in awe. How sad it would be anyway, if all was solved and understood—what point would there be to look up at the stars? Or look at the face beside us?

The Northern Lights can't hear my mother's voice anymore, but they can damn well hear mine.

Dear Chris,

I'm writing this on an island both our parents knew about but never reached. Something was waiting for me here. Before I reveal it, I want to thank you for the genealogy book and share with you an interesting factoid I recently learned from my friend Oskar.

As you know, the character "soo" in our names is shared by our cousins in Korea and elsewhere, everyone in our generation. Dad and his siblings and cousins share a different character. For the following generation, another will be assigned. I thought this character sequence was determined by a bureaucratic office or clan secretary or some linguistic pattern. Actually, it's designated by a poem composed by family elders at the founding of a clan. In the sixty-two generations recorded in our book, we've completed an entire cycle—we're the last breath of a poem composed almost two thousand years ago.

You're right, there's no reason to fear our inheritance. It's not a curse that runs through our family, but a poem, which can be interpreted in multiple ways. Even a single word can mean different things. But you knew that already.

Did Dad ever tell you what you, as the only son, were supposed to name your child? Because our generation is the last character of the poem, your son and his peers are supposed to begin the next cycle—the first character of the exact same poem, repeated all over again. But Oskar says that when a family enters a new socioeconomic class or resettles far away from its previous home—across the ocean certainly suffices—the elders can compose a new poem to unite the descendants of a revised clan. What will you write for your children?

So I'm sending back the genealogy book, along with some other things that may help you compose a new poem for those who'll follow us, by blood or whatever else. Those essays you wrote for your students—you don't need their ambitions or their parents' money to write. They're your excuse. Write for yourself instead, for your theoretical children or mine, or for whomever. Assure your readers they're not alone, that they can influence and shape whatever trait is inherited or shared among them. Maybe you'll think of something cunning, so that no one will feel limited by the character or variable they're given.

What's more difficult to explain are letters that Mom sent to this Swedish island for many years. Most are folktales that she wrote and rewrote for her daughter who died long ago but grew up in spirit on this island. Mom told me these were cautionary tales, but she could've used a bullet point list: never go skinny-dipping in lakes, never trust pirates or monks, beware of sea turtles. Instead, she wrote them in many variations, in multiple languages. I finally realize how much she loved these stories for their story-ness—just like you.

Scattered among these are confessions. Mom hoped that her lost girl would grow hair like her brother's, black waves that couldn't be tamed. She hoped that this daughter would be as brave but more prudent when playing heroics. Mom also feared that she'd put too much pressure on you to make up for all that she found wanting in her husband. Your boldness and originality, evident even when you were a child, fooled her into thinking you could be more than a little boy, make her sadness disappear, give her a better life someday. She admitted that she didn't know how to raise a good Korean man, didn't want Dad's influence on you, but didn't know better herself. So eventually, she just let you go, hoping you'd find your own way.

Most important, she prayed the other girl would learn the traits she wished she could've passed on to us: humility, adaptability, a love of this world for what it is on the surface and for what it could be if you tilt your head and...

As for the other sister—you'll see her emerge in these letters. I wish you could see her elsewhere. Maybe someday.

As for me, I'm staying longer in Sweden—one reason is my new analysis and the other is Oskar. For both, I must be patient in order to learn more, be willing to stretch beyond my usual capabilities. Still, I've got a good feeling about both endeavors.

What I can't explain—although I believe Oskar and I could be a real thing together, I'm more confident that my work will lead to something huge, even revolutionary. Might be years before my analysis is approved and the rest of the data unveiled, but until then—I'll keep my focus on the shape-shifting antineutrino. I will reveal how she transforms in ways that most of us doubted, but a few dreamt possible, thus requiring all to revise our current foundation of physics. Then we shall rebuild our understanding of the universe and of everyone in it. How's that for ambition? Or maybe it's closer to faith.

Astrid has invited us to stay for the weekend. We have meals all together, and while she has long talks with Marina and Oskar, Karin shows me and my sister all her favorite haunts.

On Sunday, after dinner, I retreat to the guest room. On the writing desk is the letter for my brother. Beside it, a sealed box of my mother's letters. Draped over the chair is Anders's blanket that I use when going for walks along the beach with my sister. I slip the letter into my pocket and tell Oskar I'm getting some air.

With the blanket around my shoulders, I run out of the house and through the shortcut in the woods that Karin showed me. When I emerge from the forest, I scramble down the rocky cliffs to reach the shore, scattering pebbles. My sister is standing among the raukar, at the edge of the water, facing the ocean. At this hour and latitude, the clear night sky is ultramarine; the pale sands, lavender. The moonlight reflects a wavering path along the dark glassy sea from shore to horizon. I run toward my sister, keeping my eye on the red ribbon, but it only hangs down her back, motionless, though the winds whip my hair in my face.

When I'm beside her, I catch my breath so I can tell her, "Oskar says he must go back, but I know he wants to stay longer, and Astrid really wants him to. He can cancel his classes this week. We can have more time together." My sister shakes her head.

"We can give the letter to my brother in person," I say. "We can go back together."

"I rather we end it the usual way. I like to know what's going to happen. Don't want to fade out on a plane or while arguing about what exactly to tell our father. So tomorrow morning, I'll watch Anders take you back across the water. You'll mail the letter, and I'll return to the story's beginning and guide you here once more. Let's just enjoy the little time we have left."

"It always ends like this? But you said I veered off course this time."

"There are variations, but they all add up to the same thing."

"But the woodblocks—you said that was the biggest difference. How I didn't bring them myself, but Oskar did. You were worried when I left them behind, that I wouldn't find you, realize who you were."

"Well yes, this time you found our story fragments left by Chris, that *is* a bit different. Our story only appears whole in the woodblock, however, and only Oskar figures this out. When you left him before he could translate, I disappeared, terrified, not knowing what would happen. But then he came to show you 'The Tale of Two Sisters.' So now we must end as we always do."

A wave lurches over my feet, glittering sand across my shoes. The freezing water jolts through me. I slip off my flats and step forward. The wet sand rises against the arches of my feet, my heels sinking into the earth. I am rooted and strong. I know who I am.

"Even without the fragments or woodblocks or Oskar, I would've realized eventually, that you—my lifelong friend—were my true sister. I must believe this—that even if I didn't know I was Princess Bari, I'd see across the stories, across death, and see you. I'm sorry it's taken me this long, but maybe my coming without Oskar means something—I stepped aboard without fear to find you. Instead of evidence, all I had was hope—that has to mean something, doesn't it?"

"Who is Princess Bari?" She's genuinely confused.

"The first shaman. The four overlaid woodblocks reveal Bari's story. Is that new to you?"

She nods, trembling all over.

A shaman calls on Bari and becomes possessed by her spirit.

I drop my blanket on the shore.

With Bari's power, the shaman can slash through the gates of hell and free a trapped soul.

I walk around my sister and my footprints bind her in a circle.

Sometimes the bridge to the underworld is just a roll of cloth to dance upon.

I grab the end of her red ribbon, winding it around my wrist.

Or simply rags to tie around one's head in a trance.

I yank the red silk and it comes away easily.

My sister's braid unravels. I feel no breeze, but her hair is caught in multiple winds, twisting and flying in every direction. She takes me in her arms, and for the first time, I can feel my sister as she holds me close. "Goodbye, Elsa," she whispers. "And thank you."

I hug her tighter, clutching her. I will my bones to melt around hers and bury my face in the curve of her neck. But her body grows cold and rigid. Her flesh becomes stone, scratching against my collarbone. I hear rocks scattering down the cliffside. I let my sister go.

Oskar approaches, calling my name. I slip my sandy feet back into my shoes. I pick up Anders's blanket that I dropped in the water and drape it over the head of the rauk woman who's taken my sister's place. I wrap the soaking wool around her body, and the blanket clings to her lovely shape. In my hand is a red string, frayed at the ends. I tie it around my wrist and press a finger against the knot at my pulse.

"What are you doing out here all alone?" he asks.

"Remembering," I say. Taking his hand, I lead Oskar away from the shore. Instead of following the path we used to get here, we wander into the woods in search of everything waiting to be discovered.

Acknowledgments

I am forever grateful to my agent and champion, Sarah Bedingfield, for her editorial wisdom, ferocious loyalty, and endless support. This is *our* book.

My editor, Sarah Guan, is beyond brilliant. Her guidance and faith pushed me to my best. Our conversations unlocked what was hidden; her questions summoned the missing pages waiting to be written. What we have together—editorial alchemy.

Marty Cahill is the kindest advocate and savviest marketing/publicity consigliere, and a fantastic writer to boot. Courtney Paganelli's enthusiastic support in the final laps is tremendous.

Thank you, Liz Gorinsky, publisher and founder of Erewhon, for envisioning this wonderful home for books and authors, and for making all our dreams come true. You've assembled a mighty team, and I treasure everyone including: Jillian Feinberg, Cassandra Farrin, Rachel Kowal, Michelle Li, Leah Marsh, and Kayla Burson.

Thanks to my friend Dr. Eun Soo Kwak-Peacock for allowing me to steal her book on Korean shamanistic folk paintings. Dr. Angela Bourke's class on oral literature and Irish folklore was another gift of inspiration. Dr. Heinz Insu Fenkl's work on Korean folklore and shamanism was vital to my research. Also crucial was Dr. Tobias Hübinette's writing on Korean adoptees in Sweden. Janet Hong's friendship, feedback, and translations were influential, especially her translation of Seo Hajin's "The Woodcutter and the Nymph," to which I allude with the passport detail.

For all matters on physics and Swedish, I owe infinite gratitude to my husband, Dr. Henrik Johansson, and his Antarctic research and dissertation: *Searching for an Ultra High-Energy Diffuse Flux of Extraterrestrial Neutrinos with IceCube 40.* Thanks also to Stockholm University's Department of Astroparticle and Elementary Particle Physics and the Stockholm International Peace Research Institute for the unauthorized use of their printers.

My novel and I grew together over the last decade, nurtured by amazing teachers and mentors. Michelle Richmond and Laura Chasen taught me how to focus and clarify. Kelly Link revealed the love and ghosts in *Folklorn*, and her transformative feedback and support saved it from being trunked. Peter Ho Davies, Mat Johnson, Alexander Chee, and Matthew Salesses inspired me with their work, insight, and teaching. Thanks to the life-changing Tin House Workshop and Napa Valley Writers' Conference, to David Naimon's *Between the Covers*, and The Ruby. Valerie Sayers, forever. Thanks to a secret fairy godparent scout, Rafi, and Chelsea, for their early passion.

I'm so lucky to have generous friends in Chia-Chia Lin and Celeste Ng. I am indebted to the following who are brilliant in their critiques, forgiving and supportive as friends: Myung Joh Wesner, Emily Breunig, Dr. Kate Rees, Margaret Lee, Kimberly Kane, Pam Squyres, Wes Shih, Janet McNally, Barrington Williams, Ryan Flament, Kaitlin Solimine, and Michael Simonetti, who read some of the earliest pages and told me to keep going. I also cherish Aram Kim, Michael Estes, Dr. Joohee Lee, and Lisa Gonzales.

Thanks to my brothers, Min and Charles, for teaching me about storytelling, the tragicomic, and the absurd. For music and film and for giving me countless opportunities to learn, grow, and dream.

아빠, you never gave up on me. I wish you could've seen this. Sometimes I think your ghost bullied all these folks into supporting my novel.

엄마, the first writer in the family, you taught me how writing can enrich our lives with beauty and meaning.

When I was at my most doubtful, when I thought this book was a lost cause, years before it found an agent and publisher, I drafted my acknowledgments to remind myself of all those who believed in me, all those I wanted to make proud and didn't want to let down. These names inspired me to work harder. They include Inger and Roine Johansson. Tack så mycket.

Henrik, this book and who I am now would not exist if not for your love. Olivia and Axel, this is also for you, a different kind of genealogy book, with more myth and magic.